this
is
where
we
live

Michael McGee

Short Stories by 25 Contemporary North Carolina Writers

Edited by Michael McFee

The University of North Carolina Press

Chapel Hill and London

this
is
where
we
live

© 2000
The University of North Carolina Press
All rights reserved
Designed by Richard Hendel
Set in Quadraat and Eagle types
by Tseng Information Systems
Manufactured in the United States of America
The paper in this book meets the guidelines for
permanence and durability of the Committee on
Production Guidelines for Book Longevity of the
Council on Library Resources.
Library of Congress Cataloging-in-Publication Data
This is where we live : short stories by 25 contemporary
North Carolina writers / edited by Michael McFee.
p.   cm.
ISBN 0-8078-2583-2 (cloth : alk. paper)—
ISBN 0-8078-4895-6 (pbk. : alk. paper)
1. Short stories, American—North Carolina.
2. North Carolina—Social life and customs—
Fiction.   I. McFee, Michael.
PS558.N8 T48   2000
813'.01089756'09049—dc21   00-029929

04   03   02   01   00   5   4   3   2   1

For my

students, teachers, colleagues,

and many friends at UNC–Chapel Hill

over the past quarter-century

CONTENTS

ACKNOWLEDGMENTS

Thanks to all who helped this book come into being:
my creative writing comrades at UNC–Chapel Hill,
especially Doris Betts, who provided encouragement and
information all along;
my student assistants—Jessie Tucker, for cheerful help in the
early stages of research; Elizabeth Byrd, for aid just before and after
the manuscript deadline; and particularly Tara Powell, for exemplary
bibliographical, biographical, and xerographic efforts during the
summer of 1999;
the Center for the Study of the American South at UNC–Chapel Hill,
whose generous summer stipend underwrote a graduate research
assistant and other project expenses;
the University Research Council at UNC–Chapel Hill, for faculty
research publication grants that greatly assisted with permissions fees;
the Humanities Reference Desk and Interlibrary Borrowing at
Davis Library, UNC–Chapel Hill, whose staffs were so helpful with
queries and requests for so long;
David Perry at the UNC Press, for supporting this and other
anthologies of contemporary North Carolina literature;
my wife Belinda, the resident fiction expert for several decades,
whose diligent reading habits are a constant inspiration;
and the North Carolina literary community,
especially our prolific fiction-writers, without whose
terrific work such a book would
obviously be impossible.

INTRODUCTION

For a dozen or so lean but happy years — from 1980 into the early 1990s — I was a regular book reviewer. I could try to fancy that title up, and call myself a book editor (which I was, for the *Spectator* in Raleigh) or book critic (which I guess I was, for WUNC-FM in Chapel Hill); but, in fact, I was just a reviewer, reading and writing about books on a pretty-much weekly basis, which seemed like a wonderful fate for a former English major. Early on, though, I had the panicky realization that I couldn't keep up with all the new books I wanted to: I had to be selective, to focus my reviewing attention somehow. And that's when the literary gods smiled on me, because I was lucky enough to be living in a place — North Carolina in general, the writer-rich Triangle in particular — that was beginning to explode with first-rate literature, fiction and poetry that needed somebody local to pay some attention to it. As a native Tar Heel and young writer myself, I was delighted to do so.

Once I thought I had discovered my specialty as a reviewer, I had my second uneasy insight: this new wave of North Carolina writers was so prolific, there was no way I could keep up with all the books they were producing. It was like trying to jot notes during an avalanche or tsunami, or (in Tar Heel weather terms) a hurricane or tornado, a truly overwhelming outpouring of novels and short stories and poems and nonfiction. I've heard this period described as "North Carolina's literary renaissance," but really that term seems too mildly Latinate for such a cloudburst, such a flash flood, such a landscape-altering surge of contemporary writing.

The fiction-writers led the way, of course. From Thomas Wolfe and O. Henry on, North Carolina's best-known authors have written novels and short stories, and that tradition continued in the 1980s, with well-established authors like Reynolds Price and Doris Betts and Fred Chappell as well as newcomers like Clyde Edgerton, Kaye Gibbons, and Jill McCorkle — the latter three all published by Algonquin Books of Chapel Hill, a significant force in the outburst. Many of those writers were anthologized in

The Rough Road Home: Stories by North Carolina Writers (University of North Carolina Press, 1992), a volume which confirmed that something very substantial indeed was going on in our literary state. But valuable as that book was, the Tar Heel fiction scene was so vigorous that editor Robert Gingher couldn't possibly cover it all, even with 22 stories: due to space restraints and other factors, he had to exclude a number of fine authors. And North Carolina short story writers continued to flourish during the rest of the 1990s, so much so that—already—another anthology is called for.

However, *This Is Where We Live: Short Stories by 25 Contemporary North Carolina Writers* is not a sequel to *The Rough Road Home*: among other things, it presents its contents in a completely different manner from the previous volume. Even so, given that both are published by the same press, and that both focus on recent North Carolina writers, I chose not to include works by any authors from the previous book in *This Is Where We Live*, so that I could present an even more inclusive range of our state's contemporary short fiction. It's a testimony to the scope and scale of the ongoing North Carolina literary eruption that I could exclude a dozen or more well-known *Rough Road* authors—like Lee Smith, Allan Gurganus, Robert Morgan, and Randall Kenan, who have continued to write and publish short stories in recent years—and still gather so many excellent story-writers into this new anthology.

The book's descriptive subtitle reflects further attempts to narrow the fictional field and to clarify the guidelines under which work was considered for this volume:

"Short Stories." The story must be a short story, deliberately written in that distinctive literary form. No novel excerpts or other fictionesque varieties of prose, however interesting or entertaining, were considered: there was simply no need for such genre compromising, given the wide range of good new short stories out there.

"Contemporary." The story must have been published, in a book or magazine or journal, during the past fifteen years—a particularly rich time for short stories, as suggested by the success of Shannon Ravenel's annual *New Stories from the South*, first published by Algonquin in 1986. This anthology contains no unpublished stories, and nothing published before 1985. During the past fifteen years, each of these authors must have published at least one book of fiction, whether a novel or a collection of short stories.

"North Carolina Writers." Each of these authors is a North Carolina writer, by which I mean someone who has spent a lifetime here, someone who was born and raised here before leaving, or someone who has moved here and stayed for a significant time. I call these "North Carolina short stories" because their authors are North Carolinians, not because the stories are fictional interpretations of "characteristics and features of life in North Carolina," which was Richard Walser's approach in his ground-breaking anthologies *North Carolina in the Short Story* (1948) and *Short Stories from the Old North State* (1959). However, a number of the stories are specifically set in our state, and most of the others are set in a very North Carolina–like place.

Within these three guidelines, I considered everything, reading hundreds of published short stories by dozens of living writers from the past decade and a half. The 25 stories presented in this volume were, to me, the best of the batch, the liveliest and most representative sampling I could make. In the end, my basic concerns were: which of an author's stories seemed the strongest? which had the most memorably distinctive characters, or storyline, or style? which had the power to grab me upon first reading, and again, and again, and not let me go? which had the sizzle, the charge, the surprising energy of originality? which made me laugh, or nod in agreement, or shiver at its sheer rightness? which, finally, satisfied me most?

Having picked these favorites, I arranged them in an order that was partly intuitive, partly deliberate. I hoped to juxtapose stories that had some sort of link in setting or situation, in tone or theme or other characteristic. I tried to make larger groupings or sequences of stories that brought out their mutual strengths, so that each story could become part of a longer, larger story called *This Is Where We Live*. I realize that I might have adopted a different arrangement (alphabetical? chronological? geographical?), but this is the one that seemed most pleasing to me. I wish I could have included a number of other recent North Carolina fiction-writers, some of whom had published only novels, some of whom had published novel excerpts but not short stories, some of whom had actually published short stories that I just couldn't fit into this book: to all of them, my sincere apologies. I hope the variety of stories in this anthology—some rather long, some very short; some set well in the past, some utterly contemporary; some patient as novels, some quick and intense as poems; some hilarious, some disturbing, some both—gives as much pleasure in the reading as it gave in the choosing.

The main title of this book, *This Is Where We Live*, is adapted from a sentence early in Tony Earley's "The Prophet from Jupiter," where the troubled narrator—a mountain damkeeper—suddenly says: "This is where I live and this is what I think: a dam is an unnatural thing, like a diaphragm." That sentence has haunted me since I first read it, and (with the pronoun pluralized) it seems to suit this anthology as a title, for a number of different "we"s. Obviously, for the characters in these stories, this is where they live, in the written words on the page. The same could also be said for the authors: this is where they live, where they are most alive as creators, in the stories they have painstakingly made and then shared with us. In general, the same could be said for the readers of these stories: this is where they live, imaginatively speaking, in this fiction that quickens them in the reading and makes them part of the unfolding story. And finally, in particular, the same could be said for any Tar Heel reading these North Carolina stories: this is where we live, in these stories populated with characters like us or like others we know, doing familiar things in familiar places. And yet these writers have taken the raw material of North Carolina life around or within us and converted it into art, shaping it into stories that embody a sort of truth about our complicated past and unsettled present and uncertain future. Where we live now, in turn-of-the-century and turn-of-the-millennium North Carolina, is not where we lived before, as citizens or writers: it's a profoundly changed and profoundly changing world. This fiction is where we really live, in a world of words that articulates—perhaps better than we ourselves ever can—what we think, and what we feel, and what we really are.

this
is
where
we
live

Commit to Memory

Occasionally, during those nights when the ring would cut through the late night quiet, one of my brothers or sisters would beat me downstairs to the table in the hall where the phone sat in the dark, but more often than not, I'd be the first to reach it. I'd pick up the receiver quickly to silence it, whisper my slow, hoarse hello. Sometimes they didn't even wait for me to speak before they started in with their pleas, and when I think about it, those years seem permeated with voices — with the whiskey-slurred words of the penitent, the frightened, the defiant and the adamantly innocent. There were times when I couldn't understand the first word, especially during produce season when the Mexican and Haitian migrants, midway through their grueling northward sweep, were locked up for knife fights, drunk and disorderly, misdemeanor B and E. But it really didn't matter what they said: they all wanted the same thing, wanted my father down there pronto to go their bail, and I understood everything from the tone, which was always the same: the tone of someone with only one phone call.

My father has been dead for ten years now, and the thing that I remember most clearly about him is how heavy a sleeper he was. For a long time this fact was less memory than fleeting image: his bulk beneath a quilt, curled and turned toward the bedroom wall, would appear briefly then fade before things became detailed and emotional. Not until one night a few weeks ago was I able to connect this image with our life together.

Because of my father's work as a bail bondsman, I grew up used to the phone ringing in the middle of the night. That sudden postmidnight ring that seems to so many a signal of certain tragedy was commonplace in our house. And because of my father's ability to sleep through sonic booms and thunderstorms I came to hear, almost nightly, the voices of those he called his people: people who would night-blind deer with foglights that bug-eyed from truck bumpers; people who would crouch beside cars with garden hose snaking from mouths into gas tanks. Utterers, forgers, passers of bad checks—his people, who acted as if every day was the end of daylight savings time and every odometer in every last-leg Buick on the lot was a clock begging to be turned back.

I suppose he was good at his work, if gaining the respect of hundreds of dubious characters is any measure. Financial success was a different matter. My father's people, if they paid at all, were not the most punctual of debt-settlers, a characteristic which drove the only other bondsman in our county to declare, before he closed up shop for good, that all the honest crooks had either died or moved away. My father hung in there, encouraged by the diminished competition. He nickled and dimed his creditors, nickled and dimed my mother with promises and charm.

From her he withstood a great deal of pressure. One winter we were so poor that we couldn't afford to retrieve our wool clothes from the laundry where they'd been put in storage during moth season. My mother would take my little sister and me down every other Friday to try and haggle another sweater out of hock. The laundry clerk was a girl my mother once taught in her refresher Civics class out at the high school—a Tindall from way out in Tindalltown who had it in for us because my mother had once reported her for necking on campus with her soldier boyfriend.

"I'd like to get the red pullover and the children's car coats today if I may," my mother said one afternoon at the laundry. She pushed a five across the counter, anchoring it with two fingertips so that the breeze from the huge floor fans would not blow it away. The Tindall girl, who adopted the blank, bored manner of a student in a postlunch study hall whenever she waited on my mother, looked down at the fluttering bill and erupted into a spiteful spray of laughter.

"You got to be kidding coming in here with just five dollars," she said. "I can rip one of y'all's vests in two for five. Maybe cut a foot or two off one of them scarves."

When my mother complained my father said only: "At least we have the woolens to store. Something to look forward to is how I see it. If we got them out all at once, think of the void it would create."

My father had not set out to become a bondsman. As he was fond of saying, it was not something one went to school for. What he'd always been passionate about was geography. He seemed to have been born with an unfathomable curiosity about the names of places, mostly places he knew he'd never lay eyes on. Maps, charts and globes were like icons to him. There wasn't a corner of this earth that you could point to without him ticking off a squall of place names.

Like most children of obsessed people, we sometimes suffered. Instead of more passive endurances, like being carted off to Civil War battlefields during summer vacation or spending the occasional weekend at an antique car show, we lived with one who insisted we share his passion. Each of us had to learn by age eight the fifty states and their capitals — commit to memory were the words he used. On the Fourth of July following our tenth birthdays a ritual quiz tested our knowledge of the hundred counties of North Carolina as well as their county seats. The entire family gathered in a circle of saggy lawn chairs in the backyard while whoever was in the hot seat spouted off the names of obscure coastal plain counties — Currituck, Pasquotank, Perquimans — followed by a feast of field peas, corn, cold ham. After each correct answer we were awarded small prizes — a handful of Tidewater salted-in-the-shells, a sip of icy Falstaff — and we were awarded larger prizes when we completed the quiz. I got an old bitters bottle that one of my father's people had unearthed in the woods behind the dog pound while digging for worms; the bottle was the color of cobalt, shaped like a fish. After their county quizzes my sisters both got chokers. One of my brothers received a biography of Woodrow Wilson, who had once lived just down the road from us in Wilmington, and the other got a leatherbound copy of A History of the Johnstown Flood, which I spotted on his bookshelf just a few years back.

The field of geography, as my father often explained, constitutes much more than the memorization of place names. It is a complex and multileveled discipline, and if what led him to it was his curiosity for names, what kept him intrigued, after he'd memorized all the maps, were the other emphases: demographics, population control, statistical studies. Geography, my father soon decided, was really about helping people live on this earth.

He had little trouble distinguishing himself in the Geography department up at the state university. The only student in his class to finish with honors, he was accepted at several of the top graduate programs in the country, but the summer after graduation his father died, leaving him with debts and a dependent, my grandmother, who was too old to work. He came on home to the house he grew up in, the one I grew up in as well. Six months later he got engaged to my mother, who was just through her first year of teaching Latin and Civics. At home, married, he set about finding something to do.

I don't know how he first got the idea of being a bondsman. I have a feeling it was something as simple as walking through the bottom end of downtown and seeing Charles Hatch's neon BAILBONDS sign blinking through the haze of dusk. Whatever it was, it happened suddenly: one day he was in the management trainee program at Dusselbach's Furniture; the next day when my mother and I came in from school he was sitting at the kitchen table, filling out forms for the state bailbondsman license.

My mother was aghast.

"Aren't bailbondsmen usually sort of, well . . ."

"Sort of what?" he said without looking up from his paperwork.

"Riffraffy."

"I'm not so sure that's even a word," he said. "But if you mean are they usually married to teachers of Latin, the answer is no. But what the hell, why not? Let's us deviate from the norm."

"I thought bailbonding was something of a sideline," my mother told him, "something one runs out of the back room of a pawnshop."

"I don't happen to have a pawnshop to run a business out the back of," my father said. "Hatch is getting old and tired I hear. In a few years, when he retires, I can have his clientele."

"But think about what you're saying when you use the word clientele," said my mother. "Thieves and drunks and felons and who all knows what. You'll have to deal with them every day of your life."

"This is the closest thing I've found to what I want to do with my life," he said. "This is the closest thing to geography available to me around here."

My mother said: "I don't mind telling you that I completely fail to see the connection."

"Of course you do. Most folks would fail. Most will. If I can't help people doing what I was trained to do, I'll help them some other way. You might not understand that, since you're getting to do what you want."

"Right," she said. "Teaching a dead language to comatose students. One out of every fifty might go on to use Latin, and then only in the Sunday crossword."

He capped his ballpoint and smiled. "You don't need to be pessimistic on my account. Not only are you doing what you want, you're good at it to boot."

"So by bringing the do-goodness of geography to selling bail bonds you're going to change lives?"

"I doubt it," he said. "But if I have to be here I might as well be doing something I think is worthwhile. I figure if I'd gotten to pursue the geography, I'd be off in some tiny African nation or traipsing through a South American rain forest. I'd be seeing things I wouldn't normally see, spending time with folks who are different from the run of the mill around here. Same with this career."

He hung out his shingle. For a few weeks he sat idle in his office, killing time by poring over his maps and atlases. Then he had his first client, and news of his willingness to extend credit, as well as his lenient repayment plan, brought in more. I don't think he changed lives — don't think he even tried — but he did develop a sense of worth I doubt he would have gained selling couches at Dusselbach's. He felt, somehow, as if he was making it easier for people — his people — to live on this earth, and he quickly became as dependent on his clientele as they were on him. Since so many were unemployed, or worked only when the sun went down, his office was always filled, and he kept up with everyone; he always knew who had a meeting with a probation officer or who was due down at the jailhouse to wash the deputies' cars as part of a parole. "Call me if you need me," he would say as the office emptied and invariably he'd be taken up on it, usually when the house had gone as quiet as the town outside, when he was too deeply asleep to hear the phone ring.

My father was thought of as odd, but his choice of employment didn't really ostracize him any further in the community. Most folks seemed pleased by the fact that my father, who'd been quiet and aloof all the way through school, had had his notions of becoming a globe-trotting geographer debunked and was now working out of a shabby storefront across the alley from the auto parts store.

I never paid much attention to what he did for a living when I was young. I got as used to criminals calling in the middle of the night as the children of the newspaperman must have been to old ladies interrupting supper with complaints about the wild pitch of the paper boy, or the doctor's kids to the harried calls of a first-time father-to-be. There were lean times but we got by, mostly on my mother's salary and the bizarre but often useful barters my father's people exchanged for bail: stovepipe, a new roof, a septic field, a series of root canals for my brother from our dentist, who had a bad habit of driving everywhere with a quart of beer between his knees.

My father kept my mother at bay during those lean months by cutting a deal with the Tindall girl, whose boyfriend had gone AWOL and gotten himself arrested for trespassing. She agreed not to pitch our woolens in exchange for free bond.

"You should have bargained to get everything out at once," my mother said when he told her of the deal, but it wasn't his way to push, and as a result two winters passed before he could save enough money to rescue that natty tweed overcoat he had affected while an honors student in Geography. He weathered the February winds with a flimsy parka, and it became apparent that unless something miraculous happened my father would have to abandon his bailbond business.

Eventually something occurred that bolstered my father's business considerably: a family with too many kids to count moved to town and my father suddenly had enough new customers to draw every last woolen out of hock. The boom in bond writing was traced to the repeat offenses of four teenaged boys who were seen regularly going in and coming out of the new family's house, across the street from the post office. Our chief of police described them publicly as "accomplished criminals," yet despite their experience they seemed to get caught at everything they did. They continuously underestimated the local law enforcement from the day they moved to town, when a sheriff's deputy had caught the two youngest inching a paper stand down a back alley, armed with hacksaws they hadn't even bothered to conceal.

They weren't at all smooth, but they paid their bills. Every time one was arrested their father would show up within minutes, and he always paid in cash. He never seemed surprised at being summoned to my father's office: he bailed his boys out of jail with a curious mix of alacrity and concern, as if he were simply picking them up sick from school.

The presence of this family—they were called the Pasteluccias—was felt immediately. The way the younger kids played right out in the street made our paltry two-block business district seem suddenly very urban and deprived. People who saw them playing hide-and-go-seek in alleys previously used only for deliveries and trash removal would think, someday somebody's going to get hurt back there, or, isn't it awful those kids don't have a yard to play in. This town certainly has grown, people would think when they'd spot those kids kicking deflated balls across empty parking lots on a still life Sunday afternoon.

The strangest thing about these Pasteluccias was how you'd suddenly see one of them you'd never seen before. Anna showed up at school one day, walking down the hall with a lit cigarette in hand. Classes were changing, and I was drifting toward my locker when I saw her. The way she held her Marlboro so heedlessly—the ember nearing her knuckle, her jean jacket sleeve an eighth inch from ignition, stopped me.

Later that week, Anna showed up in the Rec Room. The only other female we'd seen there was Star, a dancer from Fayetteville who wandered over sometimes when the Fort Bragg maneuvers were underway. Star was pretty tough but she still played pool like a girl. Anna was the first female pool player any of us had ever seen who didn't use a bridge for the awkward shots. When the shot called for it, she'd hike herself across the table with an irresistible agility, one leg cocked perpendicular like the automatic arm at a railroad crossing. Her black hair would graze the fabric of the table top, making it look like a field that you want to stop and lie right down in.

The Pasteluccias had been in town awhile when word started around that attempted to explain their presence. I'm not sure who it was that spilled the story first—some say the Thornton boy the sheriff had specially deputized during a brushfire, who got drunk down at Williams Lake and couldn't keep it in any longer. But soon everyone in town knew that the Pasteluccias were wards of the Federal Witness Protection Program, that Mr. Pasteluccia had either seen something he shouldn't have or knew something he had no business knowing. The fact that the specifics of this case were so vague had little bearing on the many versions offered, all of which had Mr. Pasteluccia acting with a valor unknown among apathetic urban types. The unpronounceable name and the number of offspring made the leap of logic easy for most folks. Those who couldn't pronounce mafioso simply whispered "mob."

Mr. Pasteluccia immediately gained respect. Whatever he had done, it had been bold enough to warrant a new identity, which struck us as unreal, like something off "Sixty Minutes." How odd it must have been to wake up and be someone else, having a strange town, a strange climate and strange ways to contend with. The general consensus was that they came for him in the middle of the night, that his car was still parked by a curb somewhere, parking tickets thick under the windshield, battery and hubcaps long gone. People wondered why he wasn't given a local name like Tindall or Strickland, but someone pointed out that he didn't really look like a Tindall or a Strickland. The more his situation was discussed, the more the man was pitied. Plunged into unknown territory, not allowed to work, and he always, always had to look over his shoulder.

But Pasteluccia didn't seem to mind his new situation. He worked out a pretty good schedule for himself. Mornings he sat around on his front porch, waiting for the call from my father's office to come through. Soon he grew restless and took to strolling down the hill after lunch to hang out all afternoon, lounging in the corner on the bus-seat sofa. He and my father became close. One night I overheard my father tell my mother that Mr. Pasteluccia was sensitive to the fact that some of the more narrow-minded folks in town put him and his family in the same category as welfare recipients. Down at my father's office there was no such prejudice. Mr. Pasteluccia's reputation among my father's people—and the fact that his sons were basically keeping the business afloat—led my father to extend him full credit, the generous terms of which allowed for a quarterly, as opposed to the usual monthly, tab.

One day at school, Anna Pasteluccia appeared behind me in the hallway and laid a warm hand on my shoulder. She pressed down a little with her palm. Smoke rose from between her third and fourth fingers.

"Translate," she said, her fingers half-curled around my collarbone. "You look like the type."

"I barely know English," I said.

"This isn't English I want to know, it's local. What do those boys mean when they come up to me and say: 'Whattayasay?' "

"Oh that. It's a greeting. Like hello."

"But why do they say that when I haven't said anything?"

"It's a rhetorical question," I said. "One that does not require an answer. Like 'How are you?' "

"I've been telling them, 'I didn't say anything.' I even asked one was he deaf."

"What'd he say?"

"All my questions must be rhetorical. I haven't gotten a straight answer from anyone but you since I've been down here."

Anna Pasteluccia leaned in close. "In study hall," she said, "I look at you out the very corner of my eye."

I stared hard at the very corner of her eye.

A few weeks later Anna said to me, "Don't ever come by my house after supper. Don't you even call. We drink wine with our meals and after supper I get real sentimental. In a big way, you know? All of us go sappy, even the little ones; we don't even answer the phone for fear of being so soft on wine we'll say yes yes yes to anything."

MICHAEL PARKER

I had tried to call her at night before but there was never any answer. No one saw her past seven o'clock, nor did any of the other Pasteluccias, even those four wild brothers, ever turn up after dark.

It bothered me that I couldn't see or talk to Anna at night. I hardly ever saw her at school and that left only late afternoon for us. She usually wanted to shoot pool, and it was hard to talk in the middle of that dark space, with the swampy jukebox ballads echoing off the divider blocking poolroom from plate glass and passersby, with Jay Jay Drawhorn drooling in the corner, propped up on a broom. I'd walk her home at dusk and this is when we'd talk.

Our conversations were careful, restrained. She never alluded to her previous identity, and I certainly never asked. The only part of her past that was admissible was the six weeks she'd been in town; the future seemed equally forbidden, filled with the threat of retribution from whatever dangerous parties her father had so gallantly exposed. When I'd try later to reconstruct our conversations they were filled with gaps, like censored wartime correspondence.

I slowed, then, to the moment, strolling with Anna through the settled, suppertime downtown until we reached her house. Her brothers and sisters would be swarming in the alleyway, engrossed in some enigmatic city game played with found equipment like sticks and trash can lids. They made that last hour of light look grey, gritty, industrial. The sight of Anna at the door calling them all inside for supper turned my town into someplace else. Everything seemed burgeoning then: my chances with Anna, my father's business, even the town I'd long since begun to tire of. I waited all day for those moments.

It occurred to me one night that Anna might have been using a little psychology in begging me not to call or come by after dark. Maybe this was just her way of encouraging me. I tried her number and when I got no answer I walked on over.

No answer at the front door either, although all the lights were on. I went around back: two vans were pulled up to the porch, both with out-of-state tags. I didn't mean to look in the window—I'm sure this is probably the hackneyed defense of all Peeping Toms, but it's true, people should put up curtains. Most of the kids were there, and in the bright kitchen light I noticed something odd, something I'd never noticed before: none of those kids really looked much like each other. They were all busy moving things around—stereos, televisions, boxes—and while I stood there in the shadows, the back door kept opening, kids kept coming in and out, some carrying boxes, others empty-handed. I saw Anna. She was walking around the kitchen opening boxes, writing things down on a yellow legal pad; as she passed by the window she looked right toward me, and I ducked.

The next evening in front of the Post Office we sat down on the wall and I said: "So what do y'all do with all those TVs and tape players?"

She looked at me and smiled. I think she was pleased. It meant she had a past now, and a future, although these were things I'd never hear about.

"Opening a Radio Shack franchise. Do you think it'll go over better downtown or should we move out to the mall?"

"Maybe try another town," I said. "We already got Parson's Electronics. He sells that same crap except it's new, not used."

"We thank your father for our lovely stay here." She stood then and kissed me on the forehead. "We never would have been able to manage without his generous assistance."

She crossed the street, calling to all those kids who looked nothing like her, and disappeared inside the big house that was vacant by morning.

For as long as I could after Anna left I kept my mouth shut and avoided my father. The late night calls began to bother me so much that I secretly unplugged the phone when I went to bed and replugged it in the morning. The little bit of pleasure I got from this sabotage soured immediately when my father would sit down to his morning coffee and say with surprise: "My, what a quiet night."

The way he sat in his armchair after supper, bent over his dog-eared Rand McNally, brought out such resentment that I was forced to leave the house. The fact that he was a bondsman—a common bondsman—I suddenly found intolerable. The Pasteluccia incident raised questions I'd never let myself confront: what type of man does it take to equate the study of geography with writing bonds for street scum and hoodlums? And what kind of reason is it that purports to be "helping" people by bailing them out of jail?

My father never commented on the sudden departure until after Mitchell Thornton came forward with his story about how Mr. Pasteluccia had approached him at Williams Lake and offered him five hundred dollars to spread the rumor that he was a part of the Federal Witness Protection Program. By that time the local law enforcement, the same stalwart outfit we all thought the Pasteluccia boys had underestimated, linked the recent rash of burglaries to the culprits, a month or two late of course. Rumor held that none of the Pasteluccias were kin or even Italian.

MICHAEL PARKER

Because he and Mr. Pasteluccia had been so tight toward the end, and because he had represented the financial interests of the family in their dealings with the state, my father was questioned by the sheriff, but nothing ever came of it. Privately my father expressed doubts about the sheriff's theory, which held that Pasteluccia had instructed his boys to blunder their petty daytime crimes so as to cover up for the more lucrative moonlight larcenies. According to the sheriff, Pasteluccia suspected that no one would believe his boys were into anything big if they were picked up constantly for so many amateurish offenses. My father called the sheriff's reasoning "malarkey." We argued about it every night at the table, until one night when I said something which allowed us never to speak of it again.

"Why do you think the sheriff would come out with a theory that casts his department in a bad light if he didn't absolutely have to?" I asked him that night. "He's admitted they were duped. We all were."

"Nonsense," my father replied. "I know my people."

"You don't have a clue, Dad," I said. "You know your geography, and that's about it."

He looked at me for a long time without speaking. My mother came out from the kitchen, watched the two of us stare at each other, then disappeared again. I didn't regret saying it. I didn't think then that it came close to saying all I wanted to say. I was ashamed of the way he'd allowed himself to be used and I could not forgive him for turning Anna into one of his people: someone with only one phone call, another disembodied voice of the night.

Of course Pasteluccia, or whatever his name was, left without settling his tab, and my father had to make good on the bonds. Soon after the sheriff cleared him of any wrongdoing, my father declared bankruptcy. He hung around the house for a week and a half before taking a job selling insurance.

As totally happy as he was studying geography, as totally satisfied as he'd been as a bondsman, he was that unfulfilled selling insurance.

"Selling insurance reminds me of those dances they do with poles down in the Caribbean," I heard him say once. "It's one big limbo, this business. I get lower and lower each year. By the time I retire I'll be a snake in the weeds."

Because I still held him responsible for what happened with Anna Pasteluccia, I didn't allow myself much sympathy for his whining; selling insurance seemed the sensible thing to do. For years when I was visited by those flashes of him I forced myself to think that his life in the end was decent, that he was lucky not to die destitute, in the middle of the afternoon, attended only by someone accused of transporting a minor across state lines. For years when I thought of my father at all it was as a quilted mound snoring through another night of desperate calls, dreaming no doubt of a tilted, spinning globe.

And I continued to think of him this way until recently. Late one night the phone rang, and although I had been asleep for hours I found myself racing to answer it, just as I had done when I was a kid. Hurrying down the stairs I saw my father, sleeping soundly in a room as dark as the one I'd just left. It never occurred to me that the call might be bad news, nor did I think that it might be—and at that time of night the odds are higher that it will be—a wrong number, a mistake. As I moved toward the ringing in the dark and curled my hand finally around the cool receiver, I was too busy wondering if I was doing what I wanted, and if so, if I was doing it at all well.

HEATHER ROSS MILLER

Monette's Fingers

Every afternoon Bev got off the school bus and asked Gage, "Is my mother happy or mad?"

It was the first thing Bev asked. And it made the worst kind of a difference. The events of Gage's day led up to Bev's one question. He put her on the bus in the morning as a thin white mist lifted out of the brush to shroud the Carolina pines. Then he followed his state park routine, answering mail, answering telephones, answering radios. And he met the bus bringing Bev home with the same question:

"Is my mother happy or mad?"

Gage wouldn't answer the question. But he waited for and dreaded it every afternoon, watching David chase the dumb friendly dog and throw sticks at the big park mailbox. The sun going down across the highway blushed Gage's face, turned the world bronze.

He dreaded Bev's question. He was ashamed.

Gage felt something slipping away from both him and Bev. It slipped away with a softness, like bare feet padding across a polished floor. It turned a corner, got gone quick. Truly gone.

The whole thing made Gage homesick and dopey. There was nothing he could do. The clumsy school bus chugged toward him and David. Its red signals flashed, the STOP sign swung out, and the bus reminded Gage of the old plow mules on his father's farm. He thought if he yelled "Gee, ha!" "Whoa!," the old bus would obey.

Bev jumped down, her eyes solemn, dragging a plaid book satchel. She didn't smile or wave back at the kids screaming through the bus windows. She ran across the highway to Gage, catching her breath. "Is my mother happy or mad?"

He drowned her question with questions of his own, busy chattering: "Hey, sweetheart. Did you have a good day? What'd you get for lunch? Pizza?"

Gage met the solemn expression in Bev's eyes briefly, then blinked away. She knew what was going on. He took her plaid satchel and looked inside, calling, "Hey David! Look what Bev did at school."

David came grinning, his face and hands grubby, ready to admire the crayon drawings, the flimsy pitched-roof houses with smoke spirals, birds like V's swooping off the page, goofy stick kids chasing goofy stick dogs.

"Daddy." Bev showed Gage a wrinkled page of numbers. "I didn't do no good. I got a bad check."

The 3's were turned backward so they resembled E's.

Gage folded the page. "It's okay."

Look, he wanted to soothe, the first grade's hard, Bev. You have to ride a bus. You have to stand in line. You eat pizza slices in a noisy cafeteria.

He blinked at her. The first grade is too goddamned hard for anybody. Making your 3's backward.

"It's okay," he said again. "Now, race you to the house!"

Gage clapped his hands and Bev and David broke into a wild run through the pines. "Can't catch me! Can't catch nothing!"

When he caught up to them, they were both sitting on the door steps with the panting dog, their faces red and proud. "We beat you, Daddy."

The children watched Ena all the time. She cried, raged, threw stuff. They watched. They waited for her to calm down. She had all the power in the family. No wonder Bev asked him, "Is my mother happy or mad?" Bev didn't want to be around Ena unless she was forewarned. And forewarned, Gage shrugged, was forearmed. Like the old cliché.

But, Gage tried to convince himself everyday, you don't have to explain this to a kid. Goddammit, he couldn't even explain it to himself.

Ena opened her arms and loved them one day, then shut herself up cold and hateful and silent the next. She was moody as hell. Unpredictable. Aggravating. He gritted his teeth. Just once, I'd like to show her what she's like. Just once make her see it.

Gage wouldn't bring himself to question Ena about what was going on between them, between her and the kids. That would be recognizing the dreadful problem. Giving it a name, maybe. Encouraging it to live out in the open. That would mean he had to do something.

He had no problem. He just shut up and hoped it would go away, whatever it was. Then things would go back like they were when he had brought them to the state park: Bev three, Ena pregnant with David, and Gage, proud of himself for getting out of the navy and Korea in one piece, picking back up his civilian life so easily it almost bothered him.

It did bother him. But Gage shoved it off. Rejoiced in all that he had. David born, they were a full American family. Nothing could spoil this.

David grew. Bev went to school. But in the splendor and isolation of the North Carolina state park, Ena changed. She said terrible things, threw plates, then withdrew into long awkward silences, coming out of them only to rage and throw more plates. *I hate you. I hope you die.*

Then after dreadful tears of penitence, sitting in the middle of the floor, kissing first Bev, then David, saying, "I didn't mean that. I'm sorry," Ena would swing back to overwhelming them with love, doing favors for everybody, picnics, stories, batches of cookies.

Then, days, weeks, months, maybe, later, in a split second, no forewarning, no forearming, she was back to her rages and her long silences, the bitter contempt.

And Bev was back to asking when he met the school bus, "Is my mother happy or mad?"

Gage was afraid if he answered Bev, the things that they all still shared, such as Ena on her good days, would dissolve like old-fashioned picture proofs in the hot sun. He couldn't risk the loss.

Supper was peaceful. Ena sat across the table from him and passed plates and laughed and listened. She charmed the two children and they turned their faces like bright lanterns, blinking, delighted.

Your mother is happy, Bev, he wanted to point out. To actually point at Ena and say, Look, Bev, she's happy. Keep this picture of her, Bev. Save it in your mind. Go back to it later.

In the night he touched Ena's shoulder. She turned from him, and just the stiffening of her back was enough to kill.

The puzzlement, the old dread and resentment reared like a stone wall. It won't last long, Bev. Save it in your mind. Go back to it later.

The next morning was cold and white. "This is the first frost," said Gage as they hurried out to meet the school bus.

"Oh, Daddy, I want it to snow!" declared Bev. "I want it to snow up to the roof!"

"I want it to snow, too!" mimicked David. "I want it to snow *over* the roof!"

The dog barked in circles, his breath clouding.

"It's not cold enough to snow," said Gage. "It has to be *cold*." He exaggerated, wrapping his arms around himself and shivering. "It has to be *cold* as Christmas."

"*Cold* as Christmas!" Bev swung the book satchel, grinning. "Brrr!" She shivered like Gage.

"*Cold* as Christmas!" David grabbed at her satchel.

The bus pulled up by the big mailbox and Bev ran to get aboard. "Bye! Be good! See you!" David and Gage waved her off.

Gage watched the bus until it rounded a curve in the road, then was gone. *Truly gone.* He shook his head, herded David back to the house. It was a good brisk fall morning. Ena would see how fine it was. Gage gritted his teeth, he would *make* her see. And he was surprised at himself.

But, he quickened his step, he would make Ena see, *too*, how things slipped away from you, rounding the curves in the road like Bev's school bus until they were gone forever.

Ena sat in the wing chair with a coffee mug. The scent of lemon-lilac softened the room. She was calm, smiling, the sunlight curling around her face and hair. It made Gage hesitate.

He was afraid of Ena.

He hated himself for that. Hated her.

He went ahead anyhow, chancing. "It's perfect for a hike," he said. "Down to the lake, what do you say? You and David and me?"

Ena gazed at Gage a moment and her eyes, big and green, so resoundingly green that they startled him, Ena's eyes were warm.

She lifted the mug. "I don't know."

David scattered a bag of plastic soldiers across the floor and began setting them up in battle formations. "Kpow! Kpow!" he shot them down.

Gage watched Ena curl a strand of hair over a finger, a habit she had. Curl it up tight, then slip the finger free.

"Look," he coaxed, "just try it. Come on."

The finger slipped from the tight curl. "Okay," she agreed.

It's okay, he marveled. I thought it was going to be bad. But it's okay.

Gage, Ena, and David, the dog frisking and scouting in the brush, walked spiritedly under the brisk blue sky. Leaves drifted through long chilly shafts of air between trees, hardwoods, and taller pines. As they walked, Gage indulged his favorite fantasy.

"This is all mine," he said, stretching out both arms. "Look, Ena, all these woods and the lake, everything, it's all mine. Four thousand acres of the best North Carolina parkland. And you know what?"

HEATHER ROSS MILLER

He dropped his arms. Ena grinned, snapped her fingers at David. "Daddy's bragging."

"You know what?" Gage repeated. "I'm giving it all to you, if you want it, sweetheart. All four thousand acres."

"This is all mine," mimicked David. He ran ahead, his arms like an airplane, the dog barking. "All mine!"

Ena rubbed her nose. "God, I'm freezing. Aren't you cold?" She blew on her hands. "I didn't bring my gloves."

Gage folded her hands in his, jammed them in his pocket. "Come on, let's walk faster to warm up. David!"

He motioned the child to hurry. David laughed, jammed his hands in his pockets, too, and skipped on. The dog barked at squirrels in the pines.

"Daddy, I can't run none with my hands in my pockets." David returned to them, stuck out his cold fists.

"We'll warm you up," said Gage and he took one fist and Ena took the other and they both rubbed David until he giggled.

Ena glanced overhead. "Look at all the grapevines up there. Look how high up they are."

"Who eats grapes way up there?" asked David. He tipped his head back so far, he collapsed, giggling more.

"Nobody," said Ena, tipping her head back, too.

Gage stopped rubbing David's fist. "That better?"

David nodded and ran on to the clearing he and Bev called The Secret Place. There a spillway from the lake fell in a glassy rush over a rock dam and filled the creek to its banks. Threads of bright water spangled the undergrowth. And as the dog nosed through thorn bushes, Gage noticed with a slight thrill thousands of drops clinging to the black sharp thorns, each one lit up by the sun. The unexpected beauty stung.

Four people were already in The Secret Place. A pregnant woman, a man with fishing gear, and two children like his and Ena's, an older girl and a younger boy.

"Oh, hell," said Ena. She resented park patrons.

"Calm down," said Gage.

The dog halted, raised a paw, and growled. The pregnant woman whistled, slapped her thigh, and he bounded over, wagging his tail, sniffing her shoes and fingers.

"Look at that damn dog," scoffed Ena. "A lot of good he'd be if they pulled a gun on us. They could kill us and he'd just wag his tail."

"Nothing would be any good if they pulled a gun on us," said Gage. "Calm down. They're just fishing."

The two children stared briefly at David, then went on with their play. They jabbed big sticks in the water and threw rocks as far as they could over the lake.

The man eyed Gage's uniform. "Is it legal to wet a hook here, mister?"

"Got a state license?"

"Yeah."

"I need to see it."

The man grinned and wiped the end of his nose with a sleeve. "Well, I ain't got it on me. Can't I just cast a little?"

His ingratiating giggle got on Gage's nerves. "Where're you from?" he asked. "What kind of bait are you using?"

The man hesitated. Gage said, "Look, if you're from Stanly County and if you're using natural bait, okay. You can fish in this lake without a license. That's all I'm asking."

The man giggled again. "We from over at Porters. You know where that is? Other side of Albemarle. I got shrimp. I use shrimp."

"Okay," Gage agreed. "But it's too cold to catch anything. Nothing's going to bite."

The man sobered, took on a proud look. "I bet you, mister, I can get a bite. I bet you, mister, if they's a fish in that water, I'll catch it."

He thumped his chest and bent to search his tackle, then stood up irritably.

"Ain't we got no more shrimp? Why ain't you told me the shrimp is gone?" he snapped at the woman.

"You know I can't fish without no shrimp. Now I ain't got no damn bait." He kicked the tackle.

The pregnant woman's pale hair, pulled back from a smooth forehead, dangled to her waist. She fixed her dark button eyes on Ena, scanned her up and down. Then, still patting the dog, said out of her pink mouth, tight as a bud, not even looking at the man, but straight at Gage as if to measure the effect on him alone:

"Use one of Monette's fingers."

The little girl stopped playing and stared at her mother, then her father, then Gage, Ena, and David. Her button eyes were as dark as her mother's, her forehead as smooth, and her long hair as pale. But her pink lips were not tight. Monette's pink lips poked out full, then parted over her small hard teeth.

HEATHER ROSS MILLER

"Whaaat?" she drawled.

The woman scratched the dog's ears. "I said 'use one of Monette's fingers.' " Without the slightest hint of a joke. No giggle. Just a straight cold-blooded fact.

Use one of Monette's fingers.

Gage blinked when he heard that. He knew the child heard it right the first time. Monette's face wavered a moment between terror and surprise, then hardened to definite defiance.

"You just try," she said and fisted both hands.

Gage stepped back to grab the cold hands of both David and Ena. He stood between them, squeezing their hands, jamming their hands into the pockets on either side of his jacket.

The pregnant woman snickered.

In a quick sickening vision, Gage saw the finger barbed on the hook, the hook flashing over the water, sinking, the finger darkening under water, then struck, bitten, swallowed by a fish.

He started to say something, almost believing his fantasy, when the woman jumped up, scolding, "Clifford! Clifford!"

The little boy was crawling out on the rock dam, slapping at the hard rushing water with his stick.

"Clifford," continued the woman, "that water looks mighty cold. Get back from there, Clifford. That man don't want to have to pull you out."

The dog rolled at her feet. She put a navy blue Ked tenderly on his belly, pressed until he groaned with delight, and still scolded the boy on the dam.

"I don't want to have to make that man pull you out, Clifford," she repeated. She looked hard at Gage, then at Ena, and finally at David. She looked as if she expected them all three to strip and plunge into the cold water immediately.

Ena dropped Gage's hand, took a step. "I hate you," she said to the pregnant woman. "I hope you die."

The woman took her foot off the dog, gazed a moment at Ena. Gage felt paralyzed by the cold, sickened by the invasion of these vulgar people in his four thousand acres of parkland, what his children called The Secret Place.

And now Ena challenged this woman who just got through offering her husband one of Monette's fingers to catch fish with. Ena, he realized with a mixture of pride and fear, Ena was as solemn and formidable as Bev when she got off the school bus.

Is my mother happy or mad?

It was too dangerous. Everything wound up too tight. Gage wouldn't take the risk. He had to get them all out of there.

"Ena," he said quietly out of the side of his mouth, "shut up."

"No," Ena blazed back. "I hate her. I hope she dies."

The pregnant woman snickered again. "Who do you think you are, lady," she asked, "telling people you hope they die?"

"Who do you think you are," said Ena, "talking about using a little kid's fingers for bait?"

"That's just a joke," said the man who had been sulking and watching the whole development. "And that ain't none of your business, lady."

Monette, joined by Clifford, stared at Ena. "You shut up," Monette said. She balled her fists now at Ena. And Clifford did the same. "Shut up."

"See?" jeered the pregnant woman. "It's just a joke. And it ain't none of your business."

"Come on." Gage steered Ena and David around, never glancing back, hurrying back down the park road. Twenty feet away, he turned, whistled for the dog. The pregnant woman was standing and stretching both arms over her head, the man casting hook after hook into the glittering water. The two children chased each other.

How did he let this ugly thing happen? These four people behaving almost as caricatures of Gage's own family. He hated them. Ena was right. *I hope you die.*

Back inside their own warm safe house, Ena sat again in the wing chair, curling a strand of her hair over a finger. She studied it a moment, pink as a curled-up shrimp.

"What if they really meant it, Gage?" she asked, pulling her finger free. "What if they really used one of that kid's fingers?"

She mimicked the pregnant woman, rounding her green eyes like hard green buttons, tightening her mouth. "Use one of Monette's fingers."

Gage gazed at Ena's curling finger and considered everything he had to lose in his answer. The brisk sky over four thousand acres of North Carolina parkland. David, setting up the plastic soldiers on the floor again, warm and healthy and unafraid. Bev, struggling with backward 3's at school, all her fingers intact. Bev, returning home in a few hours to ask, "Is my mother happy or mad?"

Ena, the source of their happiness or their grief, sat winding the hair over her finger again, waiting for his answer.

Ena, he understood, like the pregnant woman at The Secret Place, could kill or let live. Women like that loved and killed each other in their own way. And then closed ranks. Made you feel it was your fault.

That's a joke, lady. And it ain't none of your business.

Gage smiled. "They didn't mean it, sweetheart."

She studied him a minute. Then, "I hope you're right, Gage," she shrugged him off and closed her eyes.

Just that, and nothing he could do about it.

TONY EARLEY

The Prophet from Jupiter

My house, the damkeeper's house, sits above the lake on Pierce-Arrow Point. The dam juts out of the end of the point and curves away across the cove into the ridge on the other side of the channel. On this side is the water, 115 feet deep at the base of the dam, and on the other side is air: the gorge, the river starting up again, rocks far down below, a vista. Seen from my windows, the dam looks like a bridge. There are houses on hundred-foot lots all the way around the lake, and too many real estate brokers. They all have jangling pockets full of keys, and four-wheel-drive station wagons with coffee cups sitting on the dashboards. The coffee cups are bigger at the bottom than they are at the top. Sometimes, at night, the real estate brokers pull up each other's signs and sling them into the lake.

A family on Tryon Bay has a Labrador retriever that swims in circles for hours, chasing ducks. Tourists stop on the bridge that crosses the bay and take the dog's picture. You can buy postcards in town with the dog on the front, swimming, swimming, the ducks always just out of reach. There is a red and white sign on the Tryon Bay Bridge that says NO JUMPING OR DIVING FROM BRIDGE, but teenage boys taunting each other and drunk on beer climb onto the rail and fling themselves off. I could drop the water level down a foot and a half any summer Saturday and paralyze all I wanted. Sometimes rednecks whoop and yell *Nigger!* and throw beer bottles at Junie Wilson, who walks up and down Highway 20 with a coat hanger around his neck. Junie drops a dollar bill into the water every time he crosses the bridge.

The Prophet from Jupiter brings his five young sons to the bridge to watch the Lab swim. The six of them stand in a line at the guardrail and clap and wave their arms and shout encouragement to the dog. The Prophet drives an ancient blue Lincoln that is big as a yacht. He says he drove it in another life, meaning Florida. Down in the water, the ducks let the dog get almost to them before they fly away. They fly maybe thirty, forty yards, that's all, and splash back down. The townies call the dog Shithead. You may not believe me, but I swear I have heard ducks laugh. Shithead, as he paddles around the bay, puffs like he is dying. This is where I live and this is what I think: a dam is an unnatural thing, like a diaphragm.

The most important part of my job is to maintain a constant pond level. But the lake rises all night, every night; the river never stops. This will worry you after a while. When I drive below town, coming back toward home, I'm afraid I'll meet the lake coming down through the gorge. When Lake Glen was built, it covered the old town of Uree with eighty-five feet of water. As the dam was raised higher and higher across the river, workmen cut the steeple off the Uree Baptist Church so it would not stick up through the water, but they did not tear down the houses. Fish swim in and out of the doors. Old Man Bill Burdette, who lived beside the church, left his 1916 chain-drive Reo truck parked beside his house when he moved away.

The diver who inspected the dam in 1961 told the Mayor that he saw a catfish as big as a man swimming by the floodgates. It is a local legend, the size of the catfish the diver saw. At night I fish for it, from the catwalk connecting the floodgates, using deep-sea tackle and cow guts for bait. It hangs in the water facing the dam, just above the lake's muddy bottom. Its tail moves slowly, and it listens to the faint sound of the river glittering on the other side of the concrete. The Prophet from Jupiter says, *When you pull your giant fish out of the water, it will speak true words.* When they tell history, people will remember me because of the fish, even if I don't catch it.

The Prophet from Jupiter's real name is Archie Simpson. He sold real estate, and made a fortune, in Jupiter, Florida, until nine years ago, when God told him—just as he closed a $4 million condominium deal in Port St. Lucie—that he was the one true prophet who would lead the Christians in the last days before the Rapture. The Prophet says his first words after God finished talking were, *Jesus Christ, you gotta be kidding.* He is not shy about telling the story, and does not seem crazy. He has a young wife who wears beaded Indian headbands and does not shave under her arms.

Old Man Bill Burdette's four sons hired divers and dragged their father's Reo truck out of the lake fifty years to the day after the water rose. It was almost buried in mud, and hadn't rusted at all. The Burdette boys spent six thousand dollars restoring the old Reo and then said to anyone who would listen, *I don't know why Daddy left it. It was just like new.* Bill Junior, the eldest son, drives it in the town parade every Fourth of July, the back loaded with waving grandchildren. The oldest ones look embarrassed.

Before I start fishing, I pour ripe blood from the bottom of my bait bucket into the water. I use treble hooks sharp as razors. A reel like a winch. Randy, the assistant damkeeper, is an orderly at the hospital in Hendersonville, and fishes with me after he gets off work. He does not believe the story about the fish as big as a man. I fish all night. Sometimes small catfish, ripping intestines from the treble hooks (they shake their heads like dogs, pulling), impale themselves and make a small noise like crying when I pull them out of the water. I hold them by the tail and hit their heads against the rail of the catwalk and toss them backward over the edge of the dam.

At dawn I open the small gate that lets water into the turbine house, throw the generator switches — there are four — and go to bed. The Town of Lake Glen makes a million dollars a year selling electricity. Everybody who works for the Town of Lake Glen has a town truck to drive. The trucks are traded for new ones every two years, and Lake Glen town employees use them like whores, driving at high speed through all the potholes they possibly can, because the trucks do not have to last. The Prophet from Jupiter makes miniature ladderbacked chairs that he sells wholesale to the gift shops on the highway. His young wife braids long bands of cowhide into bullwhips and attaches them to clean pine handles. With a hot tool she burns a small cross and the words LAKE GLEN, NORTH CAROLINA on the sides of the handles. She once said to me, *I know that what my husband says about God is true because every time we make love he fills me with the most incredible light.* The bullwhips she makes hang, moving in the draft from the cars on the highway, in front of the gift shops, and tourists stop and buy them by the dozen. It is inexplicable. In town, in front of the Rogue Mountain Restaurant, there is a plywood cutout of a cross-eyed bear wearing patched overalls. The bear holds up a red and white sign that says EAT. Once, during lunch in the Rogue Mountain Restaurant, the Prophet from Jupiter looked down into his bowl of vegetable soup and said, *You know, in the last days Christians won't be able to get corn.* LAKE GLEN, NORTH CAROLINA. The high-voltage wires leading away from the turbine house, you can actually hear them hum.

Sometime during the afternoon — cartoons are on television, the turbines have spun all day, in the Town Hall they are counting money, the skiers are sunburned in their shining boats, and the fishermen are drunk — the water level drops back down to full pond and the alarm goes off. I get out of bed and go down the narrow stairs to the turbine house and close the gate. The lake leans out over me. I feel better when I get back to the top of the stairs. All around Lake Glen it is brilliant summer: the town policemen park beside the beach and look out from under the brims of their Smokey the Bear hats at the college girls glistening in the sun. The night of the Fourth of July, the main channel of the lake fills up with boats, and seen from the dam, the running lights on the dark water glitter like stars. The fireworks draw lines on the sky like the ghosts of the veins in your eyes after you have stared into the sun.

People who should know better play jokes on Junie Wilson. If they tell him that hair spray will scare away ghosts, he carries a can with him everywhere he goes, like Mace, until the joke gets around and somebody tells him differently. If they tell him that ghosts live in ski-boat gas tanks, he will not walk by the marina for days or get within two hundred yards of a fast boat. The Prophet from Jupiter says that Junie has the gift of true sight. The Mayor gives Junie rides to keep him out of trouble.

This is what it's like to live on Lake Glen: in the spring, before the water is warm enough for the skiers to get on the lake, the sun shines all the way through you and you twist down inside yourself, like a seed, and think about growing. There are red and white signs on the water side of the dam that say DANGER MAINTAIN A DISTANCE OF 200 YARDS, but you can't read them from that far away. In April, the wind blows down out of the mountains and across the cove toward my house, and the sun and the water smell like my wife's hair. I don't know any other way to tell you about it. Along the western shore, in the campgrounds beside the highway, gas lanterns glow like ghosts against the mountain. Boys and girls who will never see one another again, and somehow know it, make desperate promises and rub against each other in the laurel; they wade in their underwear in the cold river. In the summer night bullwhips pop like rifles.

Lake Glen was built between the mountains—Rogue Mountain and Rumbling Caesar—in 1927 by the Lake Glen Development Company. They built the dam, the municipal building, and a hotel with two hundred rooms before the stock market crashed. My wife's name is Elisabeth. She lives, until I leave Lake Glen, with her mother in Monte Sano, Alabama, and has nothing to say to me. Twice a day the town gives guided pontoonboat tours of the lake. The boat stops two hundred yards from the dam, and I can hear the guide over the tinny loudspeaker explain how it would be dangerous to get any closer. Two summers ago the town made a deal with the family on Tryon Bay to keep Shithead penned until the tour boat came to the bay at ten and two. The ducks, however, proved to be undependable. Shithead in his pen became despondent. Tourists pay two dollars a pop to take the tour. The problem was that the ducks swim on Tryon Bay every day, you just never know when. Elisabeth says that for years I had nothing to say to her, and that I shouldn't expect her to have much to say to me. I am ashamed to admit that this is true. There are hurricane-fence gates at each end of the dam, and only Randy and the Mayor and I have keys. When fishermen approach it in boats, I stand in the kitchen and ring the alarm bell until they leave. They shout at me perched on top of a cliff of water. This is something they do not consider.

The old people say that when Aunt Plutina Williams left her house for the last time before the lake was flooded, she closed her windows and shut and locked the doors. The Lake Glen Development Company planned, before Black Friday, to build four more two-hundred-room hotels and five eighteen-hole golf courses. Some of the streets in the town of Lake Glen still have the old development company names: Air Strip Road, Yacht Club Drive, H. L. Mencken Circle.

Elisabeth, before she left, taught the church preschool class every other Sunday, and when she got home from church repeated for me, word for word, everything the kids said. One Easter she brought her class here for an Easter-egg hunt, and when she unlatched the gate on the front porch, they tumbled in their new clothes down the grassy slope toward the lake. Elisabeth followed me down to the turbine house once, and over the roar of the generators screamed into my ear, *Why won't you talk to me? What are you holding back?* The new police chief asked for a key to the hurricane-fence gates, but the Mayor refused to give him one.

The Lake Glen Hotel is sold and renovated about every five years, and banners are hung across the front of it on the days it reopens. A crowd gathers and drinks free Cokes. Old men sit and watch from the shade under the arches of the municipal building. A Florida Yankee makes a speech about the coming renaissance in Lake Glen. The Mayor cuts the ribbon and everybody claps. Most of the old streets are dead ends. The town of Lake Glen doesn't have an air strip or a yacht club: the hotel never stays open longer than a season. Most of the time, the signs of every real estate broker in town are lined up in front of it like stiff flags.

Elisabeth stood in the lake that Easter in a new yellow dress; the water was up over her calves. With one hand, she pulled her skirt up slightly from the waist. She held a glass jar in the other hand and looked into the water.

TONY EARLEY

The children squealed on the bank. Maybe then, watching Elisabeth, I believed for a minute in the risen Christ. This is what has happened: my wife, Elisabeth, is pregnant with the new police chief's child. Randy never mentions my misfortune, unless I mention it first. I am grooming him to be the new damkeeper. From the catwalk at night we see in the distance across the channel the lights of the town. There is no reason to come here and stay in a hotel with two hundred rooms. There is no reason to stay here at all.

Randy fishes for crappie with an ultralight rod that is limber as a switch, and will some nights pull seventy-five, a hundred, out of the dark water, glittering, like nickels. He comes to the dam straight from work and fishes in his white orderly clothes. He smells disinfected and doesn't stay all night. This is what I have done: I took the passenger-side shoulder harness out of my Town of Lake Glen truck and bolted it with long screw anchors to the side of the dam, behind the catwalk. I buckle up when I fish. I don't want to be pulled into the water.

Randy is twenty years old and already has two children. He is not married. His girlfriend is tall and skinny and mean-looking. Randy says she fucks like a cat. The old people say that the morning of the day the water came up, they loaded Aunt Plutina Williams into the bed of Old Man Bill Burdette's new truck. Somebody asked Aunt Plutina why she closed her windows and locked her doors, and she said, *Why you never know, sometime I just might want to come back.* Junie Wilson has seen her. I am afraid that someday I will see her, too. Maintain a constant pond level. The last time I slept with Elisabeth, two hearts beat inside her.

Randy will go far in this town. He knows how to live here without making anyone mad, which is a considerable gift. Sometimes I can see Elisabeth bending her back into the new police chief. Randy says don't think about it. He is an ex-redneck who learned the value of cutting his hair and being nice to Floridians. He someday might be mayor. He brought his girlfriend to the town employee barbecue and swim party at the Mayor's glass house, and her nipples were stiff, like buttons. My shoulder harness is a good thing: sometimes late at night I doze, leaning forward against it, and dream of something huge, suspended in the water beneath me, its eyes yellow and open. At the party I saw Randy whisper something into his girlfriend's ear. She looked down at the front of her shirt and said out loud, *Well Jesus Christ, Randy. What Do You Want Me To Do About It?*

During the summers in the thirties the Lake Glen Hotel was a refuge for people who could not afford to summer in the Berkshires or the Catskills anymore. Down the road from the hotel, where the Community Center is now, there was a dance pavilion built on wooden pilings out over the bay. Elisabeth stood in the lake in a new yellow dress, holding a jar. The kids from the Sunday school squatted at the edge of the water and helped her look for tadpoles. The Mayor was diagnosed with testicular cancer in the spring, and waits to see if he had his operation in time. He owns a mile and a half of undeveloped shoreline. Real estate brokers lick their lips.

From my dam I have caught catfish that weighed eighteen, twenty-four, and thirty-one pounds: just babies. Randy said the thirty-one-pounder was big enough. He thinks I should stop. I think I scare him. I got my picture in the paper in Hendersonville, holding up the fish. My beard is long and significant; the catfish looks wise. I mailed a copy to Elisabeth in Monte Sano. The new police chief drives up to the hurricane-fence gate after Randy goes home and shines his spotlight on me. I don't even unbuckle my harness anymore. The Mayor is not running for reelection. I will stay until inauguration day. I learned this from the old men in the hardware store: the new police chief will live with Elisabeth and their child in the damkeeper's house; Randy's girlfriend is pregnant again, and the house isn't big enough for three kids. The Town of Lake Glen police cars are four-wheel-drive station wagons with blue lights on the dashboards. It is hard to tell the cops here from the real estate brokers.

The dance-pavilion orchestra was made up of college boys from Chapel Hill, and black musicians who had lost their summer hotel jobs up north. The college boys and the black men played nightly for tips, in their shirtsleeves on the covered bandstand, tunes that had been popular during the twenties, and on the open wooden floor out over the water the refugees danced under paper lanterns and blazing mosquito torches. Bootleggers dressed in overalls and wide-brimmed hats drove their Model T's down out of the laurel and sold moonshine in the parking lot.

The new police chief came here from New York State and is greatly admired by the Florida Yankees for his courtesy and creased trousers. I try to hate him, but it is too much like hating myself for what I have done, for what I have left undone. I am the man who didn't miss his water. Florida Yankees have too much money and nothing to do. They bitch about the municipal government and run against each other for city council. They drive to Hendersonville wearing sweat suits and walk around and around the mall. Randy will not express a preference for city council candidates, not even to me. He will go far. His girlfriend will be the first lady of the town of Lake Glen.

TONY EARLEY

The Mayor came here on summer break from Chapel Hill in 1931 and never went back. He played second trumpet in the Lake Glen orchestra. He took his trust fund and bought land all the way around the lake for eighteen cents on the dollar. He is the only rich man I can stand to be around. At the end of the night, the Mayor says — three, four o'clock in the morning — after the band had packed up their instruments and walked back to the hotel, the last of the dancers stood at the pavilion rail and looked out at the lake. Fog grew up out of the water. Frogs screeched in the cattails near the river channel, and there were cold places in the air. I can hear the new police chief's radio as he sits in his Jeep, outside the gates of the dam. The Mayor says that the last dancers would peel off their clothes and dive white and naked into the foggy lake. He says that when they laughed, he could hear it from the road as he walked away, or from his boat as it drifted between the mountains on the black lake, just before first light.

I hear laughter sometimes, when I am on the catwalk at night, or faint music, coming over the water, and it makes me think about ghosts, about those ruined dancers, looking out across the lake. Some nights I think that if I drove over to the Community Center and turned off my lights, I could see them dancing on the fog. Junie Wilson has taught me to believe in ghosts. The music I hear comes from a distance: I can never make out the tune. I remember that Elisabeth used to put her heels against the bed and raise herself up — she used to push her breasts together with her hands. *Ghosts is with us everywhere,* Junie Wilson says. Whenever I drop the lake down at the end of the season, the old, sawed-off pilings from the dance pavilion stick up out of the mud like the ribs of a sunken boat.

The old people say that the town of Uree held a square dance on the bank of the river the night before the water came up. They say that Jim Skipper, drunk on moonshine, shit in the middle of his kitchen floor and set his house on fire. The week before, the Lake Glen Development Company dug up the dead in the Uree Baptist Church graveyard and reburied them beside the new brick church on the ridge overlooking Buffalo Shoals. They even provided new coffins for the two Confederate soldiers who had been buried wrapped in canvas. The work crews stole their brass buttons. This is something that happened: Elisabeth and I tried to have a baby for seven years before we went to see a fertility specialist in Asheville.

The old people say that the whole town whooped and danced in circles in front of Jim Skipper's burning house, and that boys and girls desperate for each other sneaked off and humped urgently in the deserted buildings, that last night before the town began to sink. All the trees around the town of Uree had been cut. They lay tangled where they fell. The dead twisted and turned in their new holes, away from the sound of the river.

During the Second World War the government ran the Lake Glen Hotel as a retreat for Army Air Corps officers on leave from Europe. The Mayor says that the pilots—the ones who were not joined at the hotel by their wives—lay in still rows on the beach all day, sweating moonshine, and at night went either to the dance pavilion—where they tried to screw summer girls, and girls who walked in homemade dresses down out of the laurel— or to the whorehouse on the second floor of the Glen Haven Restaurant, a mile outside the city limits, where the whores were from Charleston, some of them exotic and Gullah, and the jukebox thumped with swing. The Mayor says that the Glen Haven during the war was like Havana before the revolution. The house specialty was fried catfish, and hush puppies made with beer. The Prophet from Jupiter and his young wife live with their five sons in the Glen Haven building because the rent is so cheap. There are ten rooms upstairs, five on each side of a narrow hall. One room, the Prophet says, always smells like catfish, even though they have scrubbed it. One Sunday morning in the early spring, the Prophet's son Zeke told Elisabeth that he dreamed Jesus came to his house and pulled a big bucket of water out of a well and everybody drank from it.

The fertility specialist, Dr. Suzanne Childress, said that I had lethargic sperm. *I knew it wasn't me*, Elisabeth said. *I knew it wasn't me.*

Dr. Suzanne Childress said, *Your sperm count is normal. They just do not swim well enough to reach and fertilize Elisabeth's ova.*

They say that Jim Skipper camped out under his wagon for three weeks beside the rising lake. He borrowed a boat from the Lake Glen Development Company and paddled around the sinking houses. He looked in the windows until they disappeared, and he banged on the tin roofs with his paddle. He collected all the trash that floated to the surface—bottles and porch planks and blue mason jars—and put it in his wagon and studied it at night by a fire. He said he did not know how to live anywhere else. They say that before Jim Skipper shot himself, he stood in his borrowed boat and pissed down Old Man Bill Burdette's chimney.

Elisabeth said, *You always thought it was me, didn't you?*

Dr. Suzanne Childress said, *I think that perhaps we can correct your problem with dietary supplements. Vitamins. Do you exercise?*

Elisabeth said, *I'm ovulating right now. I can tell.*

Dr. Suzanne Childress said, *I know.*

They closed the dance pavilion for good in 1944 when a moonshiner

TONY EARLEY

named Rudy Thomas, in a fight over a Glen Haven whore, stabbed a B-27 pilot from New York eleven times and pushed him into the lake. Rudy Thomas died of tuberculosis in Central Prison in Raleigh in 1951. They say that Jim Skipper was a good man but one crazy son of a bitch.

Several nights a week during his second summer in town, the Mayor leaned a chambermaid named Lavonia over the windscreen of his 1928 Chris-Craft and screwed her until his legs got so weak that he almost fell out of the boat. Junie Wilson says that the boxes on the sides of telephone poles — if the ghosts have turned them on — make him so drunk that he is afraid he is going to fall into the lake. The coat hanger around Junie's neck protects him from evil spirits.

Sweet Lavonia, the Mayor says, *had the kind of body that a young man would paint on the side of his airplane before he flew off to fight in a war.*

The young Mayor took his clothes off as he drove his boat fast across the dark lake. Lavonia waited between two boulders on the shore near Uree Shoals. The Mayor cut the engine and drifted into the cove. Lavonia stepped out from between the rocks, pulled her skirt up around her waist, and waded out to the boat. The white Mayor glowed in the darkness and played gospel songs on his trumpet while she walked through the water. There wasn't a house or a light in sight. Lavonia told him every night while he squeezed her breasts, *You're putting the devil inside of me.* The boat turned in the water, and the Mayor owned everything he could see.

Randy in his orderly clothes, jigging for crappie, tells me there is nothing wrong with me, that to make a woman pregnant you have to fuck her in a certain way, that's all. You have to put your seed where it will take.

Junie Wilson woke me up one morning yelling, *Open the gate, open the gate.* One of the town cops had told him that ghosts wouldn't walk across a dam, that walking across a dam while it made electricity was the way for a man to get rid of his ghosts once and for all. Junie sees three ghosts in his dreams: he sees a man standing in a boat, he sees a woman looking out the window of a house underwater, and he sees his mama wading out into the lake. This dream torments Junie most, because he doesn't know how to swim. He stands on the bank and yells for her to come back. We walked across the dam, the water up close beside Junie, the air falling away beside me. Junie said, *She better get out of that water if she knows what's good for her.* What my wife said is true: I never thought it was me. Elisabeth after we made love kept her legs squeezed tight together, even after she went to sleep. *Ghosts is keeping me awake,* Junie said. *I got to get rid of these ghosts so I can get me some sleep. Ghosts is crucifying me.* Out in the bay the new police chief watched from his boat. The siren whooped once.

Something's wrong with me, Elisabeth whispered. *I can't have a baby.*

I said, *I still love you. Shhh.*

Before we went to see Dr. Suzanne Childress, I liked to sit astride Elisabeth, hard and slick between her breasts. Lavonia tried to kill the baby inside her by drinking two quarts of moonshine that she bought in the pavilion parking lot from a bootlegger named Big Julie Cooper. Junie didn't speak until he was four. Ghosts began to chase him when he was twelve. The first time Lavonia saw Junie touching himself, she whipped him with a belt and told him that if he ever did that again, a white man would come with a big knife and cut it off. Elisabeth, when I was finished, wiped her chest and neck off with a towel.

Bugs fly like angels into the white light of the gas lantern and then spin and fall into the water. Randy jabs the air with his index finger: *It's special pussy, man, way back in the back. It burns like fire.* The Mayor gave Lavonia a little money every month until she died, three years ago. He does not give money to Junie because Junie drops dollar bills off the Tryon Bay Bridge. He does it so that the ghosts won't turn on their machines when he walks by telephone poles. The Mayor says, *Jesus Christ, if I gave that boy a million dollars, he'd throw every bit of it off that damn bridge.*

Randy says, *Man, women go crazy when you start hitting that baby spot. They'll scratch the hell out of you. You gotta time it right, that's all. You gotta let it go when you hit it.* He slaps the back of one hand into the other. *Bang. You gotta get the pussy they don't want you to have.*

Junie Wilson and I walked back and forth across the dam until the alarm went off and I had to close the gate and shut down the generators. I didn't tell Junie about the machines in the turbine house. The new police chief still watched from the bay. Elisabeth said over the phone from Monte Sano, *I know you won't believe it now, but all I ever wanted was for you to pay attention to me.* In a sterile men's room in the doctor's office, I put my hands against the wall and Elisabeth jerked me off into a glass bottle. The Mayor eats bananas to keep his weight up. Junie Wilson said that he did not feel any better, and I said that walking across the dam does not always work.

In August the air over the lake is so thick you can see it, and distances through the haze look impossible to cross. The mountains disappear before lunch, and even the skiers in their fast boats get discouraged. The water is smooth and gray, and the town of Lake Glen shimmers across the channel like the place it tried to be. At the beach, policemen sit in their station wagons with the air conditioners running. The college girls are tanned the color of good baseball gloves. Randy's girlfriend is starting to gain weight, and Randy fishes less; the crappie have all but stopped biting. When it is this hot, I have trouble sleeping, even during the day, and eat white ice cream straight out of the box with a fat spoon. The Prophet from Jupiter winks and says that in hot weather his wife smells like good earth, and that God has blessed him in more ways than one. The Prophet and his wife have made love in every room at the Glen Haven. In the hot summer, the ghosts keep their machines turned on all the time, and Junie Wilson staggers through town like a drunk. If there is one true thing I know to tell you, it is this: in North Carolina, even in the mountains, it takes more than a month of your life to live through August.

September is no cooler, but the sky begins to brighten, like a promise. Gradually it changes from white back to blue, and the town begins to pack itself up for leaving. The college girls go first, their tans already fading, and motor homes with bicycles strapped to their backs groan up out of the campgrounds to the shimmering highway. Boys and girls damp with sweat sneak away to say good-bye in the laurel and make promises one last time. Around the lake, family by family, summer people close up their houses and go back to where they came from in June. The Florida Yankees have mercifully decided among themselves who the new mayor will be—he is from Fort Lauderdale and is running unopposed—but the council candidates drive around town at night and tear down each other's campaign posters. My beard is down to the middle of my chest. Junie Wilson walks through town with his hands held up beside his face like blinders, to keep from seeing the bright faces stapled to the telephone poles. At night, the frogs hum one long, deep note, and one afternoon I slept in front of a fan and dreamed it was spring: Elisabeth waded in the lake and I sat on the porch and held a baby whose hair smelled like the sun. When I wake up now, my bathroom makes me sad because the mirror is so big. I dialed a 1-900 number for a date and charged it to the Town of Lake Glen. A woman named Betty said she wanted me to come in her mouth. In the closed-up summer houses, burglar alarms squeal in frequencies that only bats can hear, and the lights burn all night, turned on and off by automatic timers, but the rooms are empty and still.

In the fall, the wild ducks fly away after the summer people in great, glittering vees. Maples catch fire on the sides of the mountains around the lake, and weekend tourists drive up from Charlotte and Greenville to point at the leaves and buy pumpkins. The ducks skim low over the channel in front of my house, their wings whistling like blood, and then cross the dam, suddenly very high in the air. The Floridians burn leaves in their yards and inhale the smoke like Mentholatum. Randy said, *Man, I hope there ain't going to be any hard feelings*, and stopped coming to fish. Early one morning my line stiffened and moved through the water for twenty yards. When I set the hook, the stiff rod bent double against a great weight. And then it was gone. And that was it. The next night the new police chief sat outside the gate in his Jeep and played an easy-listening radio station over his loudspeaker. In the town of Uree, Aunt Plutina Williams sits and looks out the window of her house. The sun is never brighter than a distant lantern. Jim Skipper wanders in and out of the houses. A giant fish moves through the air like a zeppelin. The new police chief said over the loudspeaker, *Look, chief, I just want*, and then stopped talking and backed up and drove away.

In November 1928 the Lake Glen dam almost washed away. A flash flood, shot brown with mud, boiled down out of the mountains after a week of rain, and the damkeeper, new at the job, did not open the floodgates in time. The water rose and filled the lake bed like a bowl before it spilled over the top of the dam. Old Man Bill Burdette, who lived five miles away, drove down the mountain in his new truck to warn people downstream: the lake had turned itself back into a river and was cutting a channel through the earth around the side of the dam.

They say that the men of the Lake Glen Development Company construction crews hauled six heavy freight wagons of red roofing slate from the hotel site and threw it over the side of the gorge. Local men, when they heard, came down out of the laurel and worked in the rain filling sandbags and tossing them into the hole. But still the water ran muddy around the side of the dam and over the tops of the sandbags and the roofing. The workers, without waiting for orders, rolled the six empty wagons in on top of the pile. They say that they carried all of the furniture and both stoves out of the damkeeper's house and threw them in. They pushed three Model T Fords belonging to the company, as well as the superintendent's personal Pierce-Arrow, into the channel the river had cut around the side of the dam. But the water still snaked its way through the wreckage, downhill toward the riverbed.

This October, Town of Lake Glen workmen hung huge red and yellow banners shaped like leaves from wires stretched between the telephone poles. They built cider stands and arts and crafts booths and a small plywood stage in the parking lot in front of the Lake Glen Hotel. The Chamber

TONY EARLEY

of Commerce hired a small carnival for the third Saturday in the month, called the whole thing ColorFest!, and promoted it on the Asheville TV station. Hundreds of tourists showed up, wearing bright sweaters even though it was warm. I saw townies look at me when they thought I wasn't looking, and their eyes said I wonder what he's going to do. My beard is a torrent of hair. A high school clogging team from Hendersonville stomped on the wooden stage. Old men sat and watched from underneath the arches of the municipal building. Little boys stood at the edge of the stage and looked up through the swirling white petticoats of the girl dancers. Shithead's owners walked him through the crowd on a leash. The Prophet from Jupiter and his wife sold miniature ladder-backed chairs and bullwhips from a booth, and gave away spiritual tracts about the coming Rapture. An old Cherokee, wearing a Sioux war bonnet, for two dollars a pop posed for pictures with tourist kids. Junie Wilson, crying for somebody to help him before the white man came to get him, showed his erection to three of Old Man Bill Burdette's great-granddaughters, who were sitting in the back of the 1916 Reo truck.

In 1928 the workers at the collapsing dam looked at each other in the rain. Everything seemed lost. The superintendent of the Lake Glen Development Company produced a Colt revolver and a box of cartridges. Big Julie Cooper took the superintendent's gun when nobody else would and one at a time shot twenty-four development company mules right between the eyes. The workers threw the dead and dying mules in on top of the cars and the wagons and the red roofing slate and the furniture and the stoves, before the rain slacked and the water retreated back to the lake side of the dam. Then the superintendent threw his hat into the gorge and danced a jig and said, *Boys, you don't miss your water until your dam starts to go.* When the roads dried out, the development company brought in a steam shovel to cover the debris and the mules with dirt and rock blasted from the sides of the mountains, but not before the weather cleared and warmed and the mules swelled and rotted in the late-autumn sun. They say that you could smell the mules for miles — some of them even exploded — and that workmen putting the roof on the hotel, at the other end of the channel, wore kerchiefs dipped in camphor tied around their faces. They say that a black funnel cloud of buzzards and crows spun in the air over the gorge, and that you could see it from a long way away. At night bears came down off of Rumbling Caesar and ate the rotting mules. It is all covered by a thick growth of kudzu now, and every winter, after the vines die, I think of digging into the still-visible spine in the gorge beside the dam to see what I can find. Big Julie Cooper says, *By God, now let me tell you something, that son of a bitch liked to of went.*

When Old Man Bill Burdette's three great-granddaughters screamed, the new police chief twisted Junie Wilson's arm behind his back. Junie screamed, *Jesus, Jesus, Oh God, Please Don't Cut Me,* and tried to get away. The whole ColorFest! crowd, including the Indian chief, ran up close and silently watched while Junie and the new police chief spun around and around. *I'm not going to hurt you, Junie,* the new police chief said. Two other town cops showed up and held Junie down while the new police chief very efficiently handcuffed him and tied his legs together with three bullwhips that the Mayor brought from the Prophet from Jupiter's booth. The new police chief covered Junie's erection with a red ColorFest! banner shaped like a leaf. Junie's coat hanger was bent and twisted around his face. The new police chief pulled it off and handed it to the Mayor. Junie screamed for his mother over and over until his eyes rolled back in his head and his body began to jerk. Shithead howled. The high school clogging team from Hendersonville the whole time stomped and spun, wildeyed, on the flimsy plywood stage.

The first Monday after Thanksgiving, I raised one of the floodgates halfway and lowered the lake eight feet. Randy will fill the lake back up the first Monday in February. It will be his job to maintain a constant pond level, to hold the water in the air, to try to imagine what the weather will be four days or two weeks from now. Every day I try to piss off the river side of the dam in a stream that will reach from me to the bottom of the gorge, but it is impossible to do. The water comes apart in the air. When the lake level is down, the exposed pilings of the boathouses are spindly like the legs of old men. Randy's girlfriend has started to show, and her breasts are heavy. The new police chief spends three days in Monte Sano with my wife every other week. The hotel is dark and for sale and locked up tight.

When the water is down and the mud between the shore and the water dries out, the people who live here year-round rake the leaves and trash from the lake bottom in front of their houses, and replace the rotten boards on their docks and the rotten rungs on their uncovered ladders. All around the lake, circular saws squeal. The water over the town of Uree seems darker somehow than the rest of the lake, and I've always wanted to drop the lake down far enough to see what is down there. At the end of that last night, when Jim Skipper's house had burned down to a glowing pile of ashes, the people of the town of Uree sang, "Shall We Gather at the River Where

TONY EARLEY

Bright Angel Feet Have Trod," and then stood around, just looking at their houses and barns and sheds, wishing they had done more, until the sun came over the dam at the head of the gorge.

The Mayor stays mostly in his house now. His successor has been elected. Randy wore a tie and met with the mayor-elect to discuss ways to generate electricity more efficiently. The Mayor keeps his thermostat set at eighty-five and still cannot get warm. The word from the state hospital in Morganton is that Junie Wilson has no idea where he is or what has happened and screams every time he sees a white doctor.

The lake began to freeze during a cold snap the week before Christmas. There were circles of whiter ice over the deeper water where part of the lake thawed in the sun and then refroze again at night. The temperature dropped fast all day Christmas Eve, and the ice closed in and trapped a tame duck on Tryon Bay. Shithead, going out after the duck, broke through a soft spot in the ice and could not get back out.

Within fifteen minutes, most of the people who live in the town of Lake Glen were on the Tryon Bay Bridge, screaming, *Come On, Shithead, Come On, Boy, You Can Do It.* Nobody could remember who had a canoe, or think of how to rescue the dog. The Prophet from Jupiter, before anyone could stop him, ran across the frozen mud and slid headfirst like a baseball player out onto the ice. The duck frozen to the lake in the middle of the bay flailed its wings. I stood beside the new police chief on the bank and screamed to the Prophet, *Lie Still, Lie Still,* that we would find a way to save him.

The Prophet from Jupiter moved his lips and began to inch his way forward across the ice. It groaned under his weight. Cracks in the ice shot away from his body like frozen lightning. The Prophet kept going, an inch at a time, none of us breathing until he reached forward into the hole and grabbed Shithead by the collar and pulled him up onto the ice. It held. The dog quivered for a second and then skittered back toward shore, his belly low to the frozen lake.

We opened our mouths to cheer, but there was a crack like a gunshot, and the Prophet from Jupiter disappeared. He came up, once — he looked surprised more than anything else, his face deathly white, his mouth a black O — and then disappeared again and did not come back up. On the bridge the Prophet's five sons ran in place and screamed and held their arms toward the water. Randy's girlfriend kept her arms wrapped tight around the Prophet's wife, who shouted, *Oh Jesus, Oh Jesus,* and tried to jump off of the bridge. By the time we got boats onto the lake, and broke the ice with sledgehammers, and pulled grappling hooks on the ends of ropes through the dark water and hooked the Prophet and dragged him up, there was nothing even God could do. The duck frozen to the lake had beaten itself to death against the ice. The new police chief sat down on the bank and cried like a baby.

Elisabeth's water broke that night. The new police chief called the Mayor and left for Monte Sano, and the Mayor called me. I walked back and forth and back and forth across the dam until all the ghosts of Lake Glen buzzed in my ears like electricity: I saw the Prophet from Jupiter riding with Old Man Bill Burdette, down the streets of Uree in a 1916 Reo truck, toward the light in Aunt Plutina Williams's window; I saw catfish as big as men, with whiskers like bullwhips, lie down at the feet of the Prophet and speak in a thousand strange tongues; I saw dancers moving against each other in the air to music I had never heard; I saw Lavonia, naked and beautiful, bathing and healing Junie in a moonlit cove; I saw Elisabeth standing in the edge of the lake in the spring, nursing a child who smelled like the sun; I saw the new police chief in a boat watching over his family; I saw the Mayor on his knees praying in Gullah with Charleston whores; I saw Jim Skipper and Rudy Thomas and Big Julie Cooper driving a bleeding pilot beside the river in a wagon pulled by twenty-four mules; I saw the Prophet from Jupiter and his five young sons shoot out of the lake like Fourth of July rockets and shout with incredible light and tongues of fire, Rise, Children of the Water, Rise, and Be Whole in the Kingdom of God.

TONY EARLEY

LUKE WHISNANT

Across from the Motoheads

They're at it again. From Gran's screened-in porch we can see straight into their front yard, where amongst corroded junk and clumps of weeds a Harley hangs, chained ten feet up to an old oak branch. Rust-pitted, skeletal, like some strange carcass swinging dry in the wind, it's their banner, their heraldic arms: here live the Motoheads. They stand outside in full view, large and hairy, troglodyte, popping beers and burning red meat over an open-pit fire — a brick-lined hole dug with much cursing in the early afternoon. Their chests are bare under sleeveless jeans jackets. They roar at each other not to park their bikes on the lawn. They park their bikes on the lawn.

Gran says she's not afraid of dopers and that she's seen them worse. We believe her. Like everywhere else, the neighborhood has gone downhill. Even the cops lock their car doors. "They ain't gonna do a thing to me but maybe burn my house down with me inside it," Gran says. She won't move, though. She's lived here for twenty-two years, ever since she got back from Manila. "I wish you could have seen the yards there — pretty as a golf course. And every blade in place. You can't get help like that here, I hope to tell you. Those Filipinos. They cut the grass with a scissors, one piece at a time, down on their knees."

My uncle Bubba laughs because he's heard all this so many times before and because Gran's been after him for two days now to mow the lawn. But Pop's old push mower's too dull to cut, he says; it just smashes the grass flat.

Gran snorts. "Looks like my own son could do some yard work once in a while instead of me paying good money to those little black boys," she says. "What do you think, Jake?"

"Pretty damn slack," I say, winking at Bubba.

We've been looking at TV. Most nights Gran does up the supper dishes, I put the food away while Bubba sits; then we watch the news. It's still too hot to stay inside, though, and so we move out to the porch as soon as we can. Bubba and my mother bought Gran an air conditioner last summer, but she doesn't like to run it much; "Gives me the arthritis," she says. Tonight Newsroom Nine from Charlotte showed a segment about a handgun crackdown, and that reminded Gran of something: she herself had once bought a gun, without a license.

It's been a while since I heard her tell it, so I ask. And Bubba shakes his head, laughing.

"You can laugh now," Gran says. "I don't remember as you laughed then."

He hadn't been in Korea a week, she says, speaking directly to me and ignoring him, before a letter came: Dear Mom, sell anything you got, get me a .38 and send it airmail. All the guys say if your rifle jams, and the gooks are charging . . . Gran shivered just to think of it, she says. "I went out that afternoon and sold our radio—and it was brand new, a new Philco, I think—and where I sold it they showed me two little guns, I don't remember what kind now, and so I got one, the biggest one, and with bullets too, because who could say if Bubba could of got the kind he needed there in Korea? And it burnt a hole in my bag all the way back on the streetcar; the conductor was looking at me funny, asked me was I okay, and all the people were looking at me like they could see through my clothes. All those men . . . When I got that gun home I closed all the drapes and put it dead center of the kitchen table and then I set down and just looked at it. I was shaking like a pudding."

"Where was Pop?" Bubba says.

"He wasn't here."

She bought a big fruitcake. She hollowed it out and set the gun inside and wrapped the whole thing in wax paper and then in newspaper, in the *Weekly Gazette* social page with a photo of one of Bubba's prom dates announcing her engagement—

"Which I never even noticed and never heard you say something about till now," says Bubba,

"—and yet it was, don't contradict me, Ellen Louise that married what's-his-name, you know the one I mean, divorced just a few years ago and never did have a single child."

"Maybe I ought to look her up," Bubba says. Gran tells him he's broken enough poor girls' hearts in this town, and Bubba just blows her a kiss off the ends of his fingers. I forgot to mention that he separated from his second wife two weeks ago and has been up here from north Florida eating Gran's home cooking ever since and lying around in his T-shirt and army fatigues full of holes like they'd been hit with buckshot or like he'd spilled battery acid on them.

Across the street the Motoheads are dancing weird sixties dances and laughing at themselves. Their arms make swimming motions in the air, their torsos bend and jerk, their heavy feet hardly move. Two shaggy Moto women dance with each other. They toss their heads like dirty horses.

"What happened to the gun?" I ask.

"You know what happened to it," Bubba says.

She sent it to Korea. She stood in line at the post office and hefted it in her hands and wondered how to stop her voice from shaking. And she told the counter clerk it was a fruitcake.

"I was sick for months about that thing. I thought that I had bought something for my only boy to help him kill somebody and it like to made me crazy. I couldn't stop thinking about it, nights, couldn't sleep, couldn't eat, 'cause here was Bubba off in that God-awful faraway place and maybe he was shooting at people with a gun I had bought. I don't know why the army don't give enough guns to its soldiers, you'd think they would, wouldn't you? But he just had to have it, and so I went out and broke every law in America for that gun, and it got so I couldn't pass a police on the corner without ducking my head. Every night I prayed. And for a solid year I hid whenever the mailman come to the door."

And Bubba laughs and laughs and says, "She was afraid they were gonna return to sender, and she'd have to find something to do with it, find some way to get rid of the damn thing."

"I worried about it every blessed minute till Bubba come home from that awful place. And he didn't have a single gun on him. Not his rifle or even a bayo-net or the pistol or anything. Just his uniform, khakis, they called them. And do you know what he had the nerve to tell me about that pistol," Gran says, "that I had broken every law in America for and could go to jail for and maybe even the electric chair?"

"No," I lie.

"Lost it in a poker game," Bubba says.

Gran says he had to go to Korea to stay out of trouble. And Bubba, gray-haired, grinning, laughs.

"You laugh," he tells me, "can't nothing touch you. That's all I learnt over there."

It's early still. The sidewalk puddles are still pink from holding the sun all day. A kid at the stop sign burns rubber, the Motoheads cheer derisively, and I know that the story I've heard ten thousand times, as regular as moonrise, is coming up again:

"Most everybody'd pulled back," Bubba says, "running like bejesus—"

But he was cut off. He knew to run south, since they were fighting the North Koreans, but somehow he'd gotten turned around in a snowstorm. Hugging the ground, circling back through a scree-clotted valley, he'd lost his wits and his rifle and he almost ran smack into a tank. He stood there, muzzle to muzzle, you might say, and the turret swung and stopped and lowered itself and drew a bead on his heart, two feet away, and Bubba laughed. He could smell the barrel—powder, oil, and heat rising off it in waves—and he could have reached out and touched it—that's how close he was. Fish or cut bait, you slant-eyed sons of bitches, Bubba says he said, and then he sat down in the snow and laughed.

Probably inside the tank the Chinese were laughing too, since there wasn't anything else they could do. Something about my uncle appealed to them, I guess, sitting cross-legged there, scratching himself and grinning, or maybe they just couldn't see such a waste of heavy ordnance, overkill, blowing a hole the size of a football into a man at such close range, blood and tissue flying everywhere. Maybe somebody made a joke about how it would ruin the shine on their brand-new nice clean tank, and then they got tickled and couldn't machine-gun him.

He walked away. Inside of half a minute the blizzard had covered him from view and he came to his senses and began to run. For the rest of the war he tried not to shoot anyone unless he had to. "I even gave Gran's gun away," he says, "lost it in that poker game."

What I say is what I always say: "That's a good story, Bubba."

The phone rings and Gran comes back a minute later to tell Bubba that his mother-in-law wants to talk with him. "There sure is no love lost between the two of you," Bubba says, rolling out of the hammock and heading indoors.

"Well, she's been calling every blessed night," Gran tells me. "Set your clock by it. I don't know what's wrong with that boy, Jake, that he'd leave Bonnie. She's just as sweet to him as she can be."

"Maybe he's just restless."

"Huh. Just no account, you mean."

I ask if Bubba really used to be wild.

"Lord, yes. Hot rodding up and down the street, running with a fast crowd, drinking. I don't guess they had all those drugs back then, but he'd of done 'em if they had. Pop had to bail him out of jail one time too many, and finally the judge said Bubba could join the army or else get sent up to the penitentiary."

When Bubba comes back out, his face is set like maybe he's decided something. He takes his time reloading himself into the hammock. Gran won't look at him. "Well?" I ask finally.

"Same as yesterday. Had I called Bonnie? Had Bonnie called me? Could she give Bonnie a message from me? I wish you two would kiss and make up, I'm so upset, I just don't understand it. Etcetera, etcetera."

"What did you tell her?"

"I told her I was tired."

Gran makes a disgusted little sound under her breath.

Across the street a Motohead pisses into the fire. Two Motoheads crawl on all fours, barking like dogs. A cop car pulls up, blue light flashing, and then two more. "Look at that," I say.

The cops are all out of their cars and most of them start walking up through the yard, slow and real steady. One Motohead raises his empty hands above his tangled hair. All the other Motoheads raise their hands, grinning. "Hello, officers," they chant. The cops leave their guns sheathed. The 'heads ask them in.

"Looks like a powwow," Bubba says. "Gran, why don't you go in the kitchen and get this boy and me a Co-Cola?"

"I'm not your Gran," she says.

MELISSA MALOUF
From You Know Who

That sneaky old Lilly had been reading the letters for near up to three months before she got the nerve to tell me about them. As if I would ever confiscate them for no reason! You can bet I told her that her not sharing them right off was a shameful thing. Here we've been under this same roof over seventy years, but she acts sometimes like she doesn't know who I am. So I gave her a rough piece of my mind about it, even though I know she got that fear about her private things being confiscated from our father. He once even confiscated our schoolbooks, we never did know why. It got to where Lilly and me were digging holes out back near the cherry orchard in order to save things.

Richard hid things too, only nowheres near the orchard. Lilly said she found the letters in a cave too small for a person my size to crawl into, over on the hill some folks call Rock Ridge but we personally (meaning me and Lilly and Richard) always called Heath's Cliff after that book of Emily Brontë's that our mother read to us more than once when we were small.

The letters were all tied up in neat bundles, stored in old coffee cans, and just left there in the cave. Lilly showed me how she was still keeping them in the cans, all lined up on a shelf in her room like encyclopedias. But I made her throw those rusty old cans away and keep the letters in the special box that we used for the good silverware until we sold it all. The box is lined inside with purple velvet that I like to run my fingers over whenever I take the letters out or put them back.

Richard was born after Lilly and me. She was first, then me two years later, then Richard five years after that. Our mother, her name was Daphne —that's a name I like—she died when Richard was four or so, they didn't know from what. Father said we weren't to speak of it. Before she died she said to me, "Edith, you and Lilly take good care of your brother." So we threw ourselves hog-wild into pampering him. He was the prettiest and the sweetest-natured boy you'd ever want to meet. We keep a picture of him over there on top of the piano from when he was seventeen or thereabouts, not too long before he went over to that war and got killed by some people we'd never heard of. I forget now what they were called. But it doesn't matter, I guess, since somebody told us that country doesn't exist anymore anyway.

From the letters we got the idea that this girl of his had a picture of him too. Probably like the one we have, it's such a handsome rendering of Richard's smile. Like a cat holding a live dragonfly in its mouth, about to let it go. Surely he gave her some picture just like it. I would have, if it'd been me. Folks around here figured that secret look in his brown eyes meant he'd grow into a poet or some such type of person. That's what they said, though to my personal knowledge Richard never did write a stitch of anything his whole life.

That girl of his is another story. When Lilly first let me in on the letters, I told her the girl wrote enough to keep a whole roomful of lovers good and busy for weeks. Keep them all out of trouble, I told her. I was teasing, of course, but Lilly wouldn't have any of it, as usual. She got on me right away, all long-windedly. Called me Edith May Martin, my whole name, to let me know she was good and mad. Said I had the dirtiest mind she ever met or ever thought to meet in an old woman. A woman twice as old as those scraggily old apple trees we can see from the front porch. She said I was scragglier. Worse than that was her saying she had a mind not to let me see any more of those letters. Finders are keepers in this world, she told me.

I could see right then and there by the uppity way she talked that Lilly and me were likely to have some indecorous dealings over those letters. It plain wasn't right the way she claimed to be the boss over them. But back then I thought I'd best be circumspectful and kindly around her as much as I could. There looked to be near five hundred letters to read. It wasn't until later that I found out there's exactly six hundred and twelve, but I knew after I'd had a taste of the first few of them that I needed to read the rest. Had to. 'Course I didn't breathe a word of my having-to to Lilly. I just knew that I needed to read those letters the way some folks I've heard of need to slip any old object into their pocket every time they drop over to the five-and-dime. Can't help it.

This girl wrote to Richard sometimes up to three letters a day. Each one's the same. She always squeezed her longings onto a piece of plain white paper, five-inch by seven-inch, according to my measuring. At the top she'd put Monday Morning or Monday Evening, but never any dates. Never signed her name. Lilly said it didn't matter about the dates because Richard would have kept them all in order, week by week. I myself wasn't so ready to see him as being all that tidy a man. So we'd disagree now and again, me and Lilly, about what goes where. But that wasn't near as bad as when we got to arguing about what they meant. Lord. I'll show you what I mean. Here's one we never did see eye-to-eye on. I don't believe we ever could.

Tuesday Afternoon

Richard darling—

I still have the smell of your hair and your skin trapped here in my hands. So I opened up my fist just a tiny bit to let the pen in. I need more than ever to write to you after we've been so close that way. I do love you so. The times between the times when we're together go so slowly they would surely come in last against a snail. The way you touched the bottom of my foot, do you remember? I keep on feeling the broad smooth tips of your fingers on me. I love that it's getting to be that we talk more now. I have to know all there is to know about you, inside and out, and I know you want the same. We are one in body and spirit and always will be forever.

from You Know Who

You can see for yourself what a ninny Lilly was about this letter. To my mind, it's plain as soup that Richard and this You Know Who girl were full lovers, that's what I'd call them. When she says here "so close that way" I know enough to know which way she means. It's as close as a woman can get with a man. I tried to get Lilly to see how the girl makes no bones about saying that they'd been doing a whole lot of something that's not talking. Then I said how I liked that part about the foot, but the part about the pen was all silliness, seems to me.

Lilly was all the while turning purple as a turnip left too long in the ground. She said there was nothing specified about them being full lovers. That's what a ninny she is, like I told you. As far as she's concerned, it's all in my mind, which is a dungheap. She tried to show me how it was all spiritual. That when the girl writes about them being one in body it's only a manner of speaking. Same as when they talk about us eating the body of Christ and don't mean that at all. Lilly acted as if the case was closed when

MELISSA MALOUF

she said, "and besides, this letter was written on Tuesday *afternoon.*" To her this meant that the two of them would have been doing their whatnot in the morning. And that's an idea Lilly can't think of and never will.

But I'll tell you, it makes sense to me. There were some mornings out there on our hill — it's been years and years since I was up there. On some of those mornings there'd be a perfectly middling breeze, the kind that sways right there between cool and warm, and now and again presses your skirt against your legs. New sunlight would seem about to lick the petals clean off the stems of the violets. It would have been on such a morning. I can't see the wrongness of it. Depends on how you look at a thing. After all, I said to Lilly, when it's morning in Vermont, it's nighttime in China far as I know. But Lilly just shook her head. Then she packed up the letters and wouldn't let me see any again for a week. Not a one.

I calculated the whole thing between Richard and that girl lasted about eight months altogether, right up to his going off in the winter sometime. Father had already gone off, I remember, and left us to ourselves. I won't say abandoned. He'd come around every so often, we didn't know from where. Besides, me and Lilly were over twenty by then. The last time we saw him was after we'd gotten word about our brother, how he'd been killed over there. They never did tell us what killed him or why they couldn't send the body back. We thought maybe Father knew, but we didn't ask him. Father had got some money somehow, more than he ever thought he'd have, in connection with the war. He gave us enough so we could pay off the farm and go on living here. He didn't want our thanks, he said. We never could figure him out. He confiscated even on that last day. Went on into our rooms and took up the little bit of jewelry our mother left with us. He said unmarried women didn't need any jewelry. And no one would want to marry us anyhow. I guess he was right.

According to that girl of Richard's, marrying wasn't all that needful for a woman. She told him as much. Must have been he was feeling on edge about them not being married. It would be just like him to worry about not offending, doing what others wanted. He once told Lilly and me, a long time ago, after dinner one night, I think — yes, it was after dinner, and we'd eaten some pheasant he'd brought home that same afternoon, and Lilly cooked up the best stuffing we ever ate. It was nobody's birthday, but it seemed like it that night. Anyway, Richard said it was positively proper we weren't married because no man in our whole neck of the woods was worthy of either one of our hands in matrimony. Told us we were both princesses in a land of dullards and brutes. That's how he talked. So high-minded and poetical. I can't help but wish I'd seen his face when his girl wrote and told him she wasn't fretting over marriage. Wouldn't do it if she could, I suspect. I'll show you what I mean. Look here.

Thursday Evening

Dearest Richard—

Let us dream exactly the same dream tonight, and it won't resemble the dreams of any others. We're not like them at all, so we won't dream about fancy clothes or churches or new luggage that would make diminished stories of our vows. I know you know this is true, even though I could almost taste the concern that settled in around your eyes this afternoon when we spoke of it. And it was like the taste of aniseed. When I am with you tomorrow I will lick whatever's left away, then kiss your eyes while you unbraid my hair. We are one and I am with you always.

from You Know Who

This girl flies in the face of everything a body could suppose a girl to want. But I didn't say so to Lilly. She'd find some way to turn Miss You Know Who's gumption into something ordinary as oatmeal. It was getting to where I hadn't the stomach anymore for my sister's watered-down versions of things. So I kept the not-marrying business to myself. Let Lilly twist it into whatever she wanted.

But I couldn't keep mum about everything. It was when we'd gotten up to the two hundred and fourteenth letter that I decided to bring out into the light of day how curious it was that Richard was able to see so much of this girl, he needing to be here for chores most of the time and all. Lilly gave me one of those narrow looks of hers and asked me what I was insinuating. That's the exact word she used. Insinuating. But I was careful not to get worked up over it. For all I know, if I said the wrong thing, Lilly would take those letters, lock herself up with them, and throw the key into some crack in the wall. So I said, "I was only speculating, that's all," in about as sugary a voice as I could. "It seems that girl must have had a place close by," I told her. "Maybe she fixed herself up some sort of quarters out at the far silo. Maybe so, don't you think, Lilly?" But she wouldn't answer. Just stared at me hard as nails. Like she always does when she thinks I'm lying about something or other.

We'd been reading seven letters a day every day except Sunday. That's how Lilly determined we'd read them. She kept the key to the mahogany box on a dang-blasted chain that had to be unclasped each time since it wouldn't slip over her head. After breakfast she would stroll over to the

MELISSA MALOUF

box—it sits all by itself there on the buffet. Then she would unlock it. Then she would take out exactly seven letters, which she said followed the ones we'd read the day before. She wouldn't change this procedure one iota. And she always got to hold the letters in her lap. Said I wasn't to be trusted with more than one at a time. I never have been able to figure out what she thought I'd make happen if I held two of those letters at once. But there was no reasoning with her. She allowed that we could read the seven over again as many times as we wanted during the day, long as chores got done. But the reading had to stop at suppertime. No looking at them in the evening. No reading by candlelight. Lilly eats that way too, in tiny bites, always saving something up, the best parts, for later, for tomorrow or some other day.

She's spoken hardly a word to me since I took over the management of the letters. The box, the key, the schedule, the whole kit-and-caboodle. And I'll tell you, I haven't tried more than what's reasonable to make up with her. For all I know, she kept the letters all to herself those first three months so she could read every darn one of them privately, anytime she chose. Out of spite or I don't know what kind of meanness she put us on that seven-a-day system in order to torture me. Pay me back. So I didn't even tell her that I got part of the idea of how to get some say-so about the letters from Miss You Know Who herself. I've got them all right here. Yessir. Here's the one I borrowed some of her gall from.

Saturday Evening

Richard my love—

Late this afternoon after you walked away with a golden sliver of straw wrapped up in your brown curls I found the key to Miller's storage shed. It's so full of things to eat it's hard to choose. He discovered me there but he knows I know his secrets so he'll do nothing, there's nothing he can do but let me go there now and then. So in the morning when the first light begins to press itself against my door I want to open it and find you standing there. And I'll have a surprise—a breakfast of four fresh eggs, a hunk of deep orange cheese, two apples, almost purple. We are we forever.

from You Know Who

When I was sure I'd burn up and disappear into a puff of smoke if I had to sit with those measly seven letters one more time, I one morning just up and snatched the key away, chain and all, as Lilly was about to open the box. I remember trembling something awful, like a wet dog, from the grabbing and then hearing my sister scream some words at me that I didn't even know she knew. It turned out her palm was cut pretty deep from trying to hold onto the chain. But I was afraid to help her tend it, knowing she might try to get the best of me. I figured I better do first things first. Put the plan I got from that letter into effect. Quiet and serious as a judge I said to Lilly, "You've had your turn. Now it's mine. And if you try to do anything to upset this new arrangement we've made, I'll tell everyone some secrets about you that you don't want known." All she said back was that I was an incestuous monster. She went out of the room and I didn't see her again until the next day. Which was fine with me. When I opened that box for the first time all by myself I kept thinking about what that girl wrote about its being so full of things to eat it's hard to choose.

It could be you're thinking that me and Lilly are always unkind to each other. Sometimes we might have done things we aren't proud of. I'm not one to pull the wool over it. We've been mainly civil though, all these years. Mainly civil, but not what you'd think of as close friends. Mine for the longest time was Sandra Lynn Hopper, until she got married when she was twenty-eight to a gentleman-farmer named Sorenson Lee. They weren't married for too long, I heard, before he shot her in the stomach and went off to St. Louis. But Lilly and me have always been together, right here, day in and day out. Went to the same school and all. But didn't talk all that much about things. Seems as if early on we knew we were different as could be. She doesn't know this, mind you, but if I had to keep my promise and send out word about her secrets, I'd be put to shame. I was only guessing that after all this time on earth she'd have at least one thing she doesn't want the world to hear about. I have a secret or two myself, of course, but chances are they're not worth telling.

After Lilly stormed out of the room that morning, first I fixed the broken chain so I could wear the key around my own neck. Then I read letter after letter. All day. And stayed up all night to finish them. Then I started over again from the beginning. Around lunchtime the next day Lilly came out. She was wearing our mother's blue robe. She said, "What's your hurry?" That's all. You can bet I didn't see any reason to answer such a ragged-ended question as that. Besides, my mind was feeling pretty disorganized from all that reading.

It still strikes me as curious how I get so flustered up reading the letters. Richard's girl, even when she's writing about his going off to war, stays peaceful as that loaf of bread cooling off by the sink. Don't know how she does it. I'll give you a for instance from one of these last letters. Here she

MELISSA MALOUF

talks some about Richard's hair—I wonder he never got tired of her doting on his hair. Then she goes on calm as could be about this fellow named Avery who'd been killed in some other war, seems like.

> Avery took a lucky charm with him when he rode off to the war on his high-stepping chestnut mare. It was the greenest clover leaf caught forever inside a teardrop of sap, near the size of a rosebud, that had hardened after a while and was like glass. He used to hold it in his palm and rub it with his thumb and fingers over and over, and we'd beg for a turn, and he'd say children don't need such luck, especially girls. But his charm didn't save him after all, the way my love will save you and bring you back whole, breathing that same sweet breath you tickle my skin with. . . .

I got this idea she might be related somehow or other to one of the Averys. There's plenty of them around here, used to be, at least. Maybe she got her calmness from them. I said so to Lilly while she was making herself a cup of tea. But she pretended not to hear me. I went ahead anyway and spoke what was on my mind. Which was that Richard's girl might still be alive, close by, grieving her heart into dust. And that we ought to look her up, locate her, I told Lilly, through one of those Averys. "Maybe she'd like to know us," I said, "us being the sisters of Richard and all. Even though it's been more than fifty years. I know sure as I live that our girl would never have taken up with someone else. It's too deep." Lilly just drank her tea. Didn't offer me any. So I went on. "Since you and me aren't fit for traipsing around the countryside, why don't I ring up MaryJane, over to the post office, and see if she'll give us a hand? Help us find the whereabouts of this girl?" It was like I was talking clean out loud to no one, doing all the planning by myself. Lilly just sat there like an old statue, except for those measly tears of hers that came out of one eye, then the other, and landed in her lap.

RON RASH
Last Rite

As he had done almost every night for months, this Saturday night Sarah's dead son Elijah was calling her. It was a child's voice she heard in the laurel slick. She stumbled again and again, the laurel welting her face and arms and legs as she thrashed deeper into the slick, her legs growing wearier with each blind step, the voice that called her never closer or farther away.

Sarah woke with the quilt thrown off the bed, her brow damp as if fevered. She lay there in the dark and waited for first light. When dawn came she would dress, then walk the six miles to Boone to hire the surveyor.

When the sheriff had stepped onto her porch that afternoon eight months earlier, he'd carried his hat in his hands, so she knew Elijah was dead. The sheriff told her how the drovers had found her son's body beside a spring just off the trail between Boone and Mountain City, a bullet hole in the back of his head, his pockets turned inside out. The sheriff told her of the charred piece of fatback in the skillet, the warm ashes underneath, the empty haversack with the name ELIJAH HAMPTON burned on it. The drovers had nailed the skillet in a big beech tree as a marker. They'd buried him off the trail a few yards from the tree.

"Murdered," Sarah said, speaking the word the sheriff had avoided. "For a few pieces of silver in his pocket."

It wasn't a question but the sheriff answered as if it were. "That's what I reckon."

"And you don't know who done it."

"No, ma'am," the sheriff said. "And I'll not lie to you. We'll likely never know." The sheriff held the haversack out to her. "Your daughter-in-law didn't want this. She said she couldn't bear the sight of his blood on it. You may not want it either."

Sarah took the haversack and lay it inside the doorway. "So you've already been to see Laura," she said.

"Yes, ma'am. I thought it best to see her first, her being the wife." The sheriff reached into his shirt pocket. "Here's the death certificate. I thought you might want to see it."

"Just a minute," Sarah said. She stepped into the front room and took the Bible and pen from the mantle. She sat in her porch chair, the Bible open on her lap, the piece of paper in her hand. "It don't say where he died," she said.

"No, ma'am. That gap where they found him, it's the back of beyond. Nobody lives down there, ever has as far as I know." The sheriff looked down at her, his pale-blue eyes shadowed by the hat he now wore. "Mrs. Hampton," he had said, "they don't even know what state that place is in, much less what county."

Sarah closed the Bible, the last line unfilled.

The dew darkened the hem of her gingham dress as Sarah walked out of the yard, the cool slickness of grass brushing her bare feet and ankles. She passed her nephew's farmhouse, pausing to sip from the spring, then followed Aho Creek down the mountain to where it entered the middle fork of the New River. She stepped onto the wagon road and followed the river north toward Boone, the sun rising over her right shoulder. Soon the river's white rush plunged away from the road. Her shoulder began to ache, and she shifted the haversack to the other side.

Sarah stopped at a creek on the outskirts of town and unwrapped the sandwich she'd carried in her dress pocket. The first mouthful stuck in her throat like sawdust. She coughed and her throat thickened with the coppery taste of blood. She scattered the rest of the sandwich for the birds. Her gingham dress was soaked with sweat. She knew she looked a sight but could do nothing about it except take the lye soap and facecloth from the haversack and wash the sweat from her face and neck, the dust from her feet and ankles. She took out her shoes as well and walked on into Boone, the main street crowded with farmers and their families come to spend Saturday in town. Her eyes searched the storefronts until she found the sign that said BENEDICT ASH, SURVEYOR.

His age surprised her, the smooth brow, the full set of teeth. Like the unweathered sign outside his door, the surveyor's youth made Sarah wonder how experienced he was. He must have realized clients would wish him older, for he wore a mangy red beard and a pair of wire-rimmed glasses he did not put on until she appeared at his door. Sarah told him what she wanted and he listened, first with incredulity and then resignation. She knew he had been in Boone less than a month. He needed any client he could get.

When she had finished, the surveyor spread a map across his desk. He took off the glasses and studied the map intently before he spoke. "My fee will be six dollars. It'll be a full day to get there, do the surveying, and get back. I don't work Sundays, so I'll go first thing Monday morning."

She took a leather purse from the haversack, unsnapped it, and removed two silver dollars and four quarters. "Here," Sarah said, handing him the coins. "I'll pay you the rest when you're done." She poured the silver into his hand. "What time do we leave on Monday, Mr. Ash?"

"We?" he asked.

"I'm going, too," Sarah said.

Sunday night Sarah could not sleep. She listened to the crickets and tree frogs, the occasional whinny of the stabled horse Laura had brought that afternoon.

She had seen Laura at church that morning, wearing a blue cotton dress, her widow's weeds packed away for three months now.

"You'd think she'd have worn them a year," Anna Miller had whispered as they watched Laura enter the church with Clay Triplett.

"She has to get on with her life," Sarah replied without conviction as Laura leaned against Clay Triplett to share a hymnal. As Sarah listened to the others sing she tried to be charitable toward her daughter-in-law, reminding herself that Laura was barely eighteen, that she had been married to Elijah less than a year. The young could believe bad times would be balanced out by good. They could believe the past was something you could box up and forget.

After the service Sarah asked Laura if she wanted to make the journey with her and the surveyor, unsure if it pleased or disappointed when Laura said yes. Sarah asked to borrow one of the horses, offering to pay for its use.

"You know I wouldn't charge you, Mrs. Hampton," Laura said. "I'll bring the horse over this afternoon on my way to Boone. I'll spend the night with my aunt in town so I won't have to get up so early." Then Laura had walked over to where Clay Triplett waited for her in the shade of a live oak tree. He ground out his cigarette and helped her into his wagon to take her home.

It had been almost suppertime when she'd brought the horse. "I reckoned you'd want Sapphire," Laura said. "Elijah always said she was your favorite." Laura opened her grip and removed a photograph of Elijah taken when he was twelve years old. Laura handed the photograph to her. "I think it best if you keep this now. Something else to remember him by."

"Why are you giving me this?" Sarah asked.

Laura blushed. "Me and Clay," Laura stammered. "We're going to get married."

"I figured as much," she said, her voice colder than she intended.

"I'd hoped you'd understand, Mrs. Hampton," Laura said.

She looked at the photograph, Elijah dressed in his Sunday church clothes though it had been a Saturday morning in a photographer's studio in Boone. Elijah stared at her grim faced from a decade away, his eyes dark and serious. "You keep it," Sarah finally said, handing the photograph back. "I won't forget what he looked like. You probably will."

"I loved Elijah," Laura said.

"I still do," Sarah replied.

Sapphire whinnied out in the barn, the same barn the horse had been foaled in seven springs ago. Will had died the previous winter, so it had been she and Elijah who delivered the colt. Sarah wondered if Sapphire remembered the barn, remembered she had been born there.

In the darkness Sarah thought of the dream that had come almost every night for eight months. Then she remembered what was not dream but memory. It had been August and Elijah was five. She and Will had been hoeing the cornfield down at the creek. She'd left Elijah at the end of a row, the whirligig Will had carved him clasped in his hand. When she'd reached the end of the row, Elijah was gone.

They had searched all afternoon, working their way back to the farmhouse and then above the pasture where the woods thickened, the same woods where they had heard a panther that spring. She'd shouted his name until her throat was raw, her voice a harsh whisper. As the night came on, Will had taken the horse to get more help. Sarah had lit the lantern and followed the creek, calling his name with what little voice she had left.

A half-mile downstream he had answered, his trembling voice rising out of a laurel slick that bordered the creek. She had pushed and tripped through the laurel, making wrong guesses, losing her sense of direction in the tangle of leaves and branches. She'd found him lying on a matting of laurel leaves, the whirligig still clutched in his hand. That had been just like him, Sarah thought. Even as a child he'd been careful not to lose things.

Careful in other ways too, so that even at eight or nine he could be trusted with an axe or rifle.

Sarah and Laura met the surveyor Monday morning in front of his office. He had not bothered to wear the glasses, but an owl's head pistol bulged from the holster on his hip. "That three dollars," he said to Sarah. "I can take it now and lock it in my office."

"I'd just as lief wait till you earned it," Sarah said.

They rode west out of Boone, she on Sapphire, Laura on the gray stallion Will had named Traveler a decade ago, the surveyor on his roan. The land soon became steeper, rockier. Sarvis and beardtongue bloomed on the road's edge. Dogwoods brightened the woods like white fire. The horses breathed harder as the air thinned. Sarah felt lightheaded, but it was more than the altitude. She had been unable to eat any supper or breakfast.

They passed through Oak Grove and Villas, then turned north, passing through Silverstone. Sarah wondered what the people they passed thought of this strange procession, of the armed young man wearing jeans and a long-sleeved cotton shirt, the clanking surveying equipment that covered the roan's flanks like armor, the nineteen-year-old girl dressed in widow's weeds behind him, and she last, also dressed in black, holding the reins and a family Bible, a woman of forty-two years but already an old woman. For that was what Sarah had realized that morning as she'd ridden to Boone. When she'd looked down at her hands that balanced the Bible on the saddle, she'd seen they were coarse and wrinkled, the purple veins stretched across the back of her hands like worms that had burrowed under her skin.

Outside of Silverstone the wagon road narrowed until it was no longer a road but a trail. The Stone Mountains loomed in the distance like thunderheads. The surveyor's blue eyes scanned the woods that pressed close to the trail, the stone outcrops they passed under. Sarah could feel Sapphire strain as the grade steepened and the air grew thin. A rattlesnake slithered across the path and she patted the horses's flank and spoke gently until the animal calmed. Sapphire remembered her, though the horse had been gone from the farm for nineteen months.

She had given Elijah Sapphire and the other two horses that last morning he had waked under her roof. Sarah had fixed him breakfast but he was too excited to do anything but push the eggs and grits around his plate. He talked about the house he was building at the foot of Dismal Mountain, the house where he and Laura would spend their first night together under its unshingled roof. She called the horses a wedding gift though, to her way of thinking, they were already more his than hers. Elijah had been the one who had looked after them after Will died. Elijah had been only fourteen, but there had not been a morning or evening he forgot to feed or groom the horses. He had treated the animals with care, like everything else in his life, which was why he had not ridden Sapphire to Mountain City. He had been afraid the mare might break a leg on the rocky back slope of the mountain. Always careful, Sarah thought, but somehow not careful enough with what was most precious of all.

They traveled another hour before entering the gap, the mountains and woods closing around them, sunlight mere glances in the treetops. No birds sang and no deer or rabbit bolted into the undergrowth at their approach. The trees leaned over the trail as if listening. The awfulness of the place fell over Sarah like a pall.

"I didn't know it to be this far," the surveyor grumbled. "To be honest, Mrs. Hampton, I don't believe six dollars is enough."

"My son lost his life for less money," Sarah said.

They came to the spring first, the bare, packed ground of a campsite beside it. They unmounted and let the horses drink. The skillet rusted on the big beech a few yards down the trail and in the woods behind it they found the swell in the ground. Like it's pregnant, Sarah thought. The drovers had done as much as could be expected. A flat creek rock no bigger than her Bible leaned at the head of the grave. There were no markings on it. A few broom sedge sprigs poked through the brown leaves that covered the grave. Another winter and she knew the rock would fall, the grave settle, and no one would know a man was buried here.

She wondered if she'd be alive by then. Her stomach had troubled her for months. Ginseng and yellowroot, the draught the doctor had given her, they did not help. She had no appetite, and last week she had coughed up a bright gout of blood.

The surveyor spoke first. "I'm going to get my equipment and go a ways up that ridge there." He pointed west where a granite-faced mountain cut the sky in half. "It's too steep for the horses. You all stay here. It shouldn't take more than a hour," he said, turning and walking back to the spring.

Laura kneeled beside the grave and cleared the leaves from the mound. She took a handkerchief from her dress pocket and unknotted it. "I brung some wildflower seeds to put on his grave," she said, looking up at her. "You want to help plant them, Mrs. Hampton?"

Sarah looked down and saw why Elijah had been so smitten with her, for her eyes were dark as July blackberries, her hair yellow as corn silk. But pretty didn't last long in these mountains. Too soon, Sarah knew Laura would stand before a looking glass and find an old woman staring back at her.

"Yes," Sarah said, and kneeled beside her daughter-in-law.

"I'll be at the spring with the horses," Sarah said when they'd finished.

She was tired from the journey, the night without sleep. She took the blanket off Sapphire and spread it on the ground where her son had died. She lay down and closed her eyes, the Bible laid beside her.

"Name it quick," she had heard Granny Watson say that night when Will had asked if the child was all right. Sarah had been on the bed, Will and the midwife on the other side of the room with the baby. She'd been so tired by then, the mattress soaked with sweat and blood, the hours trying to push her child into the world.

"Boy or girl?" Will asked, his face drawn and pale.

"Boy," Granny Watson said.

"Get the Bible," Sarah said, raising her head, the rest of her body paralyzed with fatigue.

They had not known she was awake.

"What?" Will asked, bending over her.

"Get the Bible and pen," Sarah had told him. "Elijah, call him Elijah." She lay her head down when she saw Will begin writing.

"I hope he lives," Granny Watson said to Will. "Her insides are all tore up. You'll not have another."

Those had been the last words Sarah had heard before the room had tilted and collapsed into blackness.

She had thought for years that the old crone had been heartless to say such a thing at that moment, but she knew now that the midwife's words had not been cruel, not even harsh or bitter. They were the words of a woman who had seen enough disaster to grow comfortable in its presence. Laura was the opposite of Granny Watson. She was too young to see disaster was inevitable. And Sarah, Sarah was between them, too old to believe she could outlast grief, not old enough yet to grow inured to it.

She slept and soon Elijah called her again. It was dark and she could see nothing, but he was close this time, just a few yards deeper into the laurel slick. Branches slashed at her face but she kept stumbling forward. She was close now, close enough to reach out her hand and touch his face.

"Mrs. Hampton." The surveyor stood above her, the equipment burdening his shoulder, his face scratched and sweaty, one of his shirt sleeves torn. "Where's Laura?" he asked.

"At the grave," Sarah said. Her right arm stretched out before her, open palm pressed to the rocky dirt. She raised that hand to shield her eyes, for it was now midday and sunlight fell through the trees straight as a waterfall.

"North Carolina, Watauga County," the surveyor said as he took a handkerchief from his pocket and wiped his brow. "Granite, yellow jackets, snakes, and briars, that's all that mountain is," he said. He stuffed the handkerchief back in his pocket. "I really think it only fair that you pay me two dollars extra," the surveyor said. "Why just look at my shirt, Mrs. Hampton."

Sarah did not look up. She took the pen and the bottle of ink from the haversack. Then she opened the Bible. She found the name, date, and place of birth, all written in her dead husband's hand, beneath these words the date of death in her own. Sarah clutched the pen and wrote each letter in slow, even strokes, her hand casting a shadow over the drying ink.

A Girl in Summer

Alice hid in the long trail of leaves from the scuppernong arbor and watched Rilla eat dirt. Rilla's slender hands were birdlike, picking at the thin mouldy cover of the ground. Their very quickness seemed to have nothing to do with her quiet form. Only her hands and lips moved, the long mobile lips that fascinated Alice. I could tell, she thought. Her pocket was full of grapes, and she pressed one against her teeth as she peered through the vines. Alice sucked on the grape, spitting the globe of pulp and empty sack on the sand. Around her was a confetti of drying skins.

Rilla stood up and collected the chipped chamberpot and slop pot. She had come out to throw the slops over the fence. She wasn't supposed to work there anymore, but she came anyway. They paid her in food and in stock from the store that failed. Alice was sure she couldn't stay away. The dirt pulled her. All the cleaning was so she could get back to the dirt. Rilla's hand moved in her pocket. Alice smiled and reached in her own. Now Rilla was picking grapes. There must be grapes and crumbs of dirt together in that pocket, Alice thought. When Rilla started to walk toward her hiding place, the child couldn't wait and jumped out.

I saw you, she shouted, I saw you. But Rilla did not seem the least surprised and stood still while Alice butted against her. With her free hand she touched the little girl's hot blond hair.

Child, said Rilla, your papa.

Alice stared up at her. Rilla's eyes were looking off, although her mouth worked slightly and let Alice know she was here and now. Look at me, Alice insisted. She pressed against Rilla and could smell her sharp spiciness, a good smell of skin mixed with cooking and the piercing odor of slop pots. Look, said Alice.

I see you, said Rilla, I see you.

Alice followed Rilla up the sand yard. Sprouts of grass everywhere, and she thought about getting out the big hoe to chop them down. Every afternoon until his illness, her father had come home from work, taken off his collar, and neatly hatched off any stray sprigs of grass. It had been a year now since he lost the store and land to the government, and months since he had come out of the back bedroom. He lay in the high bed with his swollen leg propped on a feather pillow. Alice looked at the dirt, which before he had raked into elaborate patterns in the afternoons. She would follow him, careful not to disturb the ground where the rake had passed. Sometimes they ended up in the corner of the yard, away from the house. He would wink and say, Looks like I painted myself into a corner this time. Now she scuffed behind Rilla. Rilla clanked the pots down on the back porch and spit onto the bricks in the shallow drainage ditch below. Everyone spit there, tobacco and grainy mouthfuls of baking soda. Once real toothpaste, so that it looked to Alice as if a crowd of birds had hovered near the porch.

Rilla turned, and finally looked at her. Don't get out of the yard, don't get near the smokehouse, she said.

Why not the smokehouse? said Alice.

There's another man locked up in there, said Rilla. You stay away. Don't go messing with trouble.

I remember the last time there was a man, said Alice. I remember it and the sheriff had a star on and locked him up in there. Rilla gazed down the yard to the slop pile. One hand reached into her pocket. Alice watched. A grape, or a piece of dirt? Rilla spat something like a glob of mucous on the ground. Grape, thought Alice.

No, said Rilla, not even looking at her. You don't remember, you weren't even born. This she said with the finality of an oracle. In her soft men's slippers she crossed the porch and vanished into the darkness of the kitchen.

I did see him, I did, said Alice, but softly.

There was nothing to do. Sweat dribbled along her shoulder blades and, gathering speed, plunged down her back. It's hot, she said aloud. No one to play with. Can't go out of the yard, can't go by the smokehouse. Maybe she would swing on the front porch. But her mother said the squeaking would bother Papa. Alice knew he wouldn't mind. He'd like her to be out there in the swing, pretending it was a boat. Outward bound, mate? he would say, and she would answer aye, sir. She wandered around to the front of the house. The yard was silent, though once she heard the soft pluff sound of a rotten persimmon falling onto the dust. She walked to the edge and put her toes out into the pink dirt road. If she could only run to the end of the street she would be at the highway. She liked that. The tar came up in reddish bubbles on the road, and you could pop them with a stick. Sometimes she stuck ants on them. She would pretend the ants were dinosaurs that had slipped into tar pits, and watch them sink slowly toward the pocket of water inside each bubble. Afterwards she might tuck them in with more tar.

She sighed. She would feed the chickens. She hadn't done that yet. Over by the crib, Rilla was throwing chickens off their nests. Alice raced towards her.

You gonna get heat stroke, predicted Rilla. You gonna be sorry. With one hand she reached under Alice's hair and felt the damp curled hair underneath and the hot neck. Child, you are hot, she said. Alice looked into Rilla's apron pocket. There were five eggs in there already, white against a dark seam of dirt.

I thought you weren't gonna feed Mr. Cock Comb, said Rilla. And Confederate Army is like to have a fit trying to eat my feet.

They're *always* hungry, said Alice, reaching into the bin. She was glad Rilla was there. Lately she had to get the hard dark corn out of the crib herself. It was always alive with rustles, and she was afraid of seeing a thousand beady eyes, alight and staring. She hammered a cob against a brick until a few grains flew off. The pockets left by the kernels were hard and sharp. Her thumbs worked busily, popping seeds from the cob. It was hard to shell corn. It was good to have somebody by to help get it started. The chickens gathered around, their heads bobbing. Jeremiah's Girl, Acts of the Apostles, First Dalmations, Slop Pot, Confederate Army, she murmured. Rilla had named them all. Sometimes when she felt cross, Alice threw handfuls of corn at the chickens. The corn would rattle around them like shot, and send them dashing fitfully after the kernels, clucking with a gargling sound.

Did you feed that man? she asked.

Hmm, said Rilla. Feed him slop pot.

You did?

I ain't feeding no locked-up man, said Rilla, adding an egg to her pocket. You stay away from there, mind. She unlatched the wicket.

Don't go. Rilla, don't go. Alice jumped up and down.

This Rilla has got to go, she said. But you feed them chickens, she added, tucking a wad of something in her mouth.

Dirt. Hmm, said Alice.

As soon as Rilla rounded the woodshed Alice threw down the corn. I'm going to get me some figs, she decided. The trees in the back lot were ancient, scabbed with lichen. The figs were all picked over, only a few pulled away easily. She lifted the broad leaves. It was strange how they could flower out of the tree's dry bundle. Adam and Eve and Pinch-Me-Tight, she sang, looking under the leaves. The biggest tree was out by the pump and weathered cleaning table, where the family split watermelons and ate boiled green peanuts. Alice made a pyramid of figs on the table. When she bit into one the juice glazed her thumb. Eugenia said they looked like tiny hot air balloons in pictures at high school, but inside they were rosy and golden, tumbled bits of softness. The juice sweetened her arm.

Hey, little girl, came a voice. Alice looked around, and at a loss, stared straight up at the sky. Over here, called the voice, in the smokehouse. A delicious coolness settled over Alice. She had forgotten about the man. She turned around and stared at the little structure. It was the only brick building in the town, and it had a slatted iron door, which you could shut and lock if you had a padlock and key. She sucked on a fig.

Bring me one of them figs, willya? It's real hot in here, real hot. How about it, little girl? Say what's your name, anyway? Alice considered and rocked on her heels. She couldn't see into the smokehouse, but she knew its dense darkness and hanging mummy shapes, some as large as a child. Underneath them were dark drip stains and pools of black. Sometimes to frighten herself she would stare through the metal slats. After a while she could see. But in the bright sun she could not see into the room. His voice, though, didn't sound very scary. And she had never really seen a prisoner.

Pretty please? said the voice. Hey, pretty please with a cherry on top. No, thought Alice, it's not such a nice voice after all. It sounded whining and strange. Still, this might be her only chance.

See little girl, continued the voice, you push some of those figs through these bars. I'll back up, OK?

Gathering up a pile of figs, she edged toward the smokehouse. She stopped and stared a few feet away. She could see him dimly. Then she ran forward and pushed the figs through the grating, but thinking he had started toward her, she jumped and spilled some of them into the sand. She ran back to the table and turned.

Thank you little girl, even though I don't know your name, came the voice. Alice could feel her pulse beating in her neck and chest. She tightened her lips. She wouldn't tell her name. After a minute she saw one of his fingers come wiggling out of the bars and feel around in the soft dust for the rest of the figs. It looked like a white, pasty worm hunting for its food. It was so white, thought Alice, maybe something was wrong with him. Maybe he was an albino! She had heard of them, girls with pink eyes, men who lived in circuses. Her hands were cold.

Are you an albino? she said.

What? No, I ain't no—Hey sis, you wanna see an albino? Come over here and I'll show you one. His voice was coaxing. She crept closer to the door and stopped. He was sitting in a chair. In the darkness his head was a white O, marred by the blots of eyes and mouth. In his lap she could see something moving. Was it his hands? Suddenly the creepiness of the prisoner seemed to wriggle deep into her bones and she flung herself away and sprinted for the back porch.

There were Rilla and Eugenia, wringing out clothes.

Rilla, Eugenia, I saw the man and he had a big white fish in his lap!

Rilla spat. Come up here and let me spank you, she said. Folks that looks deserves to see what they see.

Told you stay away, Rilla continued, half to herself. Knew you'd go anyway.

Eugenia put her arms around Alice and hugged her. Where you been all day, baby? she said, tickling her side. Alice sniffed. Her sister smelled of powder.

Last baby, muttered Rilla. Eugenia you better watch out, girl, she said. Get that baby gate open, hard to get it close again.

Where's Kate, asked Alice. Eugenia laughed: She's off pooterscotting to Claxton.

Well, how can she, said Alice. When we don't have any money.

Some boy, said Eugenia. Rilla made a noise.

Alice watched while they squeezed the lengths of clothes. She glanced in the tin tub. There were her old diapers floating in the water, which was tinted red. Yuck, she thought. She knew what those were for. It wasn't so nice being a girl, even if it was natural. Even if they were lucky. Grown girls at school had to use rags.

I don't want to grow up, she told Eugenia. I guess you don't have to worry about it anytime soon, her sister said. Alice hopped on one foot up and down the steps by the drainage ditch, now washed clean. Eugenia and Rilla were talking in low voices. There's nothing to do, Alice thought, sitting on the bottom step.

In a minute she bounced up and stood under the pear tree. With its heavy golden fruit and small leaves, the tree blocked most of the sun. Showers of lighted points shifted in the air. The child danced under the tree.

Look at that wild thing, said Rilla, flapping a towel toward her.

Alice stopped, one foot cocked in the air. There's a snake in the tree, she called.

Eugenia ran down the steps, her arms still wet. The two girls stood under the tree, looking up. There above them was the dark festoon of a snake.

There really is a snake, said Eugenia, backing away in case it felt inclined to fly.

Where? Rilla demanded. A snake in my pear tree? She slapped down the long rope of a sheet and rubbed her hands together.

The three stood under the pear tree, necks craned and mouths partly opened.

There's a snake all right, said Rilla. Snake, get behind me. Snake head belongs under woman's heel, yessir.

How was Rilla going to put it there? thought Alice, dancing behind as Rilla marched off to the toolshed.

Eugenia, watch that snake, Rilla threw over her shoulder.

In a moment she was back under the tree with a hoe. Snake get his mouth on pears, said Rilla, and he suck and suck till there ain't nothing left but skin. I've seen it. Eating up my good pear sauce. Alice's neck hurt. She thought she could see the snake's mouth, stretched open like a hinge.

Get him while he can't think anything but pear, said Rilla. The long hoe wobbled about in the tree, between the loaded branches.

You girls hush and stay back, she said. Alice was excited. It was her snake, she had found him. Still, she wanted to see what Rilla would do. The blade pulled at the snake. For a long time it seemed to Alice that the snake hung its twisting lasso in the air, then with a thud suddenly beat a curve into the dust while Rilla leapt backwards. Then peck, peck, peck like a chicken and its head was fastened by a shred. The hoe bobbed up and down. The snake looked like the wooden jointed snakes at the dime store now, but it kept lashing its body around. Like it was trying to say something, thought Alice. Soon it stirred only faintly. Rilla picked it up by the hoe. The disjointed head swung from one end, the long pendulum of the body from the other.

Take him out to the trash barrel, said Rilla, that's what.

Alice's mother appeared at a window. What's happening, she called. Alice, come here, you should be in bed right now.

Mama, cried Alice, jumping beside Eugenia. There was a snake, Mama, and I found it. She looked at Rilla, who was bearing the snake away, then back to her mother.

Come in, called her mother. Leave Rilla alone and come eat and have a bath.

Eugenia pushed her, and Alice ran in to the sweet-smelling dark of the kitchen.

In her bedroom upstairs she lay on top of the sheets, clean after a cat-bath in the tin tub, and full. The sun looked in the western windows and lit the room, which billowed with long gauze curtains. Even though the evening wind had begun to lift, there were already points of perspiration over Alice's lip, and across her forehead.

Tell me a story, she said sleepily. All around her she could feel her mother's smell of lavender.

A hand passed over her brow. All right, her mother said. I'll tell you the story of how the west wind floated Mama Saussure and her cats and four poster bed all the way to the Gulf, and how on the beach she met the most handsome man she had ever seen and came home married —

Alice's eyelids trembled. She could hear her mother's footsteps going out of the room and ringing one by one on the stairs. Wait, she wanted to say, but couldn't open her mouth. She was poised over the porcelain walls of the well on the porch, poised and then falling, pinwheeling slowly down. When she finally forced open her mouth to cry out, she broke through the blue surface and her throat was filled with water and she remembered nothing.

She woke soaked with perspiration. The room was drenched in twilight, and she could hear a faint buzz, which resolved into far-off words. She sat for a moment, dizzy, with her legs dangling from the high bed, then slipped downstairs. She opened the front screen slowly, careful to avoid its cricket squeak, and ran onto the front porch, trailing its curve around the house.

There in the dark had to be the sheriff and one of his deputies, along with Rilla and the prisoner. The man's face hung pale and moony in the blue dark. Alice rubbed her eyes. She could see the silver bracelets on his wrists, and thought she could even see the star, settled on the sheriff's chest. She slapped as the needle of a mosquito penetrated her gown.

One of the faces swung in her direction. Hey little girl, called a voice. Fish, said Alice under her breath.

Get back in that house, called Rilla, right now.

Alice didn't move, except to slap her arm. Fireflies were beginning to rise from the ground, pulsing irregularly as they lifted higher and higher. They lit the blackness of the pine tree, shining even brighter in its night, then were released above it. Alice looked at the tree, then to where the fireflies hit the spangled stars. And up there was Orion, wheeling through crowds of stars. She crept down the steps and felt the soft sand of the yard with a bare foot. Still hot. The air in the yard was a deepening blue, and in a few minutes the group of men rounded the corner of the toolshed and disappeared into night.

Rilla shook her apron. For an instant she stared at Alice, then turned and strode off toward the back porch. Alice waited, then ran to the edge of the street. No one in sight. They must have cut up the alley, she thought. She remained there for a minute, hopeful, then walked back toward the house. On the back porch she stood in the big pane of light cast through the screen door. Inside Rilla was shelling peas that made a tingling sound against her metal bowl. Her hands worked quickly, stripping the hulls, dropping them in a paper sack.

If he want a drink, give him a drink, Rilla was saying. Bad enough without him laying there all hot and thirsty. I can't see no harm in it.

Alice could hear Eugenia murmuring. Then her shadow crossed back and forth over the window by the pantry.

I don't care what Dr. Loomis say, said Rilla. Give the man a drink. Maybe he need a drink, wash the poison out that leg.

Alice sat on the bottom step. They were talking about her father again. After a while she could hear Eugenia crying, and then Rilla's voice, gone low again. She thought about how hot it was, and about the twilight-colored chunks of ice sugared with sawdust that the iceman brought. Her stomach hurt, thinking about her father sweating in the back bedroom. I bet he'd like ice tea, she thought, with mint in it.

A firefly wavered up beside her knee. She snatched it, and watched the yellow light trundle about in the jail of her hands. Then she pinched off the beetle's light and carefully attached it to her gown. She sniffed her fingers. Bugstink, she said aloud. Within half an hour the front of her nightgown was covered with glowing rhinestones, each fastened by its own juice. In the yard by the side porch, she stood with a firefly in her hands, then let it go.

Noiselessly she climbed the steps, and peered into the back bedroom. It was shadowy. She could see her mother, bent over and asleep in a straight chair. Then her own face, a blur above a constellation of lights, reflected in the pier glass. Her eyes lit there, then moved on. Lying propped on pillows in the brass bed was her father. She tiptoed in, closing the screen slowly. He looked crooked and uncomfortable, and his right leg was sticking out from under the sheets. She had seen it before, looking tense and hot, as red as the deep red roses her mother clipped and watered. Her stomach hurt again. A strange smell was in the room, and she wanted to wake him up.

Papa, she said softly, wake up Papa.

She was relieved when he opened his eyes and gazed at her. He looked her up and down, then laughed with a dry, cracked sound.

What, he whispered, little firefly.

I brought you a magic drink, she said. To make you feel better now. So we can go play together. Alice could feel the ache behind her eyes, pushing on them. She held up her hand, and pretended to pour ice tea into her father's mouth.

That's, he whispered again, the best drink in a long time. His smile lingered after his eyes shut again.

Papa, she said, are you awake? Papa?

His breathing became deeper. Asleep. Everyone was asleep, everyone but herself. It was a bad dream, she thought. She moved away from the bed, sniffing the lavender smell as she passed her mother. I am just a little girl, she thought.

She leaned on the dry sink and looked into the mirror. It was out of place here, too tall for the back bedroom. Her eyes stared dark and unblinking back, and behind them the white flow of sheets where her father slept and the crumpled shape of her mother. The only lights were the fireflies and moonlight that sifted in the screen door. She reached out a hand toward her glowing image, and the mirror turned back her hand.

Missing Women

Three women have vanished—a mother, her teenage daughter, and the daughter's friend—purses and cars left behind, TV on, door unlocked. The daughter had plans to spend the day at the lake with friends and never showed. The phone has rung and rung all morning, unanswered. Puzzled friends walk through the interrupted house, sweep up broken glass from a porch light before calling the police. Broom bristles, shoe soles, finger pads smearing, tamping down, obscuring possibilities. Neighbors come forward, vague. It was late, they say. A green van, a white truck, seen in the area, trolling. A man with longish brown hair, army jacket, slight to medium build. Down by the train tracks, panties. A single canvas sneaker.

Details are not clues. What happened? Police conjecture an intruder or intruders intended only to deal with the mother, to rob or to rape. The girls' arrival was unexpected. Panicking, the perpetrator or perpetrators abducted all three. Haste should have made the abductor or abductors sloppy, dribbling evidence all the way to some lair. But little is found: a single drop of blood in the foyer, but it belongs to a friend—she nicked her finger sweeping up broken glass. We're aghast at all the friends who tidied up. No alarm in broken glass? Those purses; women don't leave their purses.

There is truth and there is rumor. The missing daughter, Vicki, has not been particularly close to the missing friend, Adelle, since junior high. They went in different directions—the stocky, glossy Vicki somewhat of a party girl, her hair bleached yellow-white against iodine skin; Adelle the more academic and wholesomely cheerleaderish one, willowy and fine-boned. Graduation-party nostalgia brought them back together that night, when they let bygones be bygones, forgiving the small betrayals. Adelle called home to say she'd be spending the night at Vicki's house, the first time in almost four years. Her shiny compact car blocks the driveway to show she made it as far as that.

In her abandoned purse is medicine Adelle must take every day. Early on, this is what worries her parents most. They circle the town doggedly, their station wagon filled with flyers, her face emblazoned on their sweatshirts. *Please. If you know anything, anything at all.* In a video they lend to the TV stations, she is modeling gauzy, diaphanous wedding gowns for a local dressmaker. With her skirts and hair swirling, her perfect pearly teeth, we feel that she is innocent and doomed.

Of the missing mother, Kay, and daughter, Vicki, we are not so sure. Their estranged husband/father cannot immediately be located. Vicki's exboyfriend once had a restraining order against him and is taken in for questioning. He is at first sullen and uncooperative with investigators. With grim confidence we await his confession, but he foils us: a punched time card and a security video corroborate his third-shift presence in the chicken-parts processing plant that night. The husband/father likewise disappoints. He is not on the lam but simply lives out of state. Someone calls him and he comes, and the son/brother too. They are briefly suspicioned, then cleared. But there is another shady matter. Kay ran a beauty parlor with increasingly disreputable ties. Some say she laundered money for drug dealers and got greedy, funneling too large a share for herself. The police deny all this, but we note her expensive tastes, the leather in her daughter's wardrobe, and conclude the worst.

Still, each of the three might have had her own reasons for wanting to disappear. Kay had maxed out her credit cards and was falling behind in her mortgage payments. Was Vicki pregnant? Some say police found an unopened urine test kit in her bureau. Adelle, the consummate perfectionist, was failing precalculus. Running off might have been easier to contemplate as a group: the girls plotting new looks in better towns; mother Kay mulling over the practical details of bus tickets and low-profile jobs. We cannot rule out anything, but the strongest current is foul play, not the gentle fantasy of escape that we all have entertained.

Seventy-two hours pass without a trace, and the search kicks into high gear. Divers slick in neoprene suits bob the shallow lake as if for apples, rake the algaed muck along the bottom. City workers sonar the reservoir. The waters yield nothing, but the surrounding woods still swarm promisingly with hunters and hounds. We admire these hunters who have volunteered to don their orange caps and peer through binoculars, their dogs fanning out ahead and weaving through trees, loyal noses snuffling the ground. We admire the highway patrolmen in their thin summer khakis, poised in the roadside gravel, dogged but polite at the roadblocks, checking licenses. The churchwomen bring pies and fried chicken and cold cans of soda to everyone tired and hungry from searching, and we admire them too.

All of us admirable, the way we rally together. We say "we." We say "our community," "our women," basking in the evidence of so many heroes lured out by tragedy: storefronts papered by high school kids with flyers provided free by local printshops, reward donations quietly accruing, information streaming through the phone lines, the cards and letters of commiseration. Surely this abundance of goodwill, mercy, and blatant, selfless volunteerism will prevail over the darker elements that abide here. For there are certain haggard people on the street, there are certain small pockets of immigrants who will not master our grammar, whose children are insolent and fearless. There are certain people who look and sound uncannily like the rest of us, but if you shine a light in their crawl spaces you might find the difference. Any might have stared with longing and hatred into the bright windows of pretty blondes.

There are leads. A reporter gets an anonymous call about a box hidden in the park, containing information about the missing women. The caller will not disclose the nature of this information, will not linger on the line. Police are dispatched to the park, locate said box nestled amid gazebo shrubbery, examine it for explosives, dust it for prints, pry it open to find: a map, hastily sketched, of a floor plan. A park official recognizes the U shape of the building, the tiny hexagonal kitchen and bathroom appendages flanking individual units. Police converge on the apartment building. Excited tenants cluster in the halls as rooms are searched. Nothing. *Wild Goose Chase,* go the headlines. *Police Vexed by Fruitless Search.* Again Adelle's parents appear on television. Their anguish chastens other would-be pranksters, but was it just a prankster? Someone who could snatch three women away without a trace might then goad the searchers. No person of authority will come right out and say so, but there it is. We feel it, huddled indoors or venturing out in twos and threes.

A Waffle Hut waitress comes forward. She is fairly certain she served the three women omelets, French toast, and coffee around two A.M. on the morning of the disappearance. They seemed quietly anxious, not like the raucous post-bar crowd she usually waits on around that time. The cheerleader type asked for boysenberry syrup, and when told there was none, sank into a sullen lassitude.

A SuperDairy QuikMart clerk comes forward. Around two A.M. on the morning of the disappearance, a woman resembling the missing mother burst into the store abruptly, asked if he had seen two teenager girls, and stormed out when he said he hadn't. She sometimes bought cigarettes there, and milk in single-serving containers.

The graduation party attendees are questioned further. The two girls were spotted leaving the party together variously at one A.M., two A.M. and three A.M. The hostess thought she heard them arguing in the bathroom, something about a borrowed necklace. The hostess's parents said both girls were polite and charming but seemed troubled. The hostess's boyfriend saw them hugging on the lawn. Others said the lawn embrace was a brawl; Vicki had Adelle in a choke hold. Or Adelle held Vicki while she vomited malt liquor onto the zinnias. Unless it wasn't those two at all. The salutatorian has his doubts. At around one-thirty A.M., he says, he was sitting alone on the back patio. He had turned down a joint, only to have the smoke blown into his ear, leaving him giddy and fretful and confused. He is going to Yale in the fall, and the prospect was then lying heavily on his mind. Now he feels relief and a delightful anticipation of leaving, but that night he brooded while the full moon silhouetted two figures dancing together on the lawn. The salutatorian watched in darkness two moving bodies he could identify as female only by their shapes, the pitch of their laughter. It's possible they kissed or merely whispered. He is pale and stammering in recall. Police seize his journals but return them the very next day, almost dejected. His nervous intelligence seemed so promising—a budding sociopath?—but his journals hold only the sex-obsessed ramblings of run-of-the-mill adolescence: "May 5—Would absolutely rut Bethany R. given half a chance. Tits like grapefruit and she smells like bubble-gum-flavored suntan lotion and sex."

The time is ripe for confessions, so people start to confess, as if in fits of misguided volunteerism. Some march right into the police station or the newspaper editor's office. Some hold press conferences. A man calling himself a freelance private eye and soldier of fortune says he helped the women conceal their identities and relocate, to where he is forbidden to disclose, but rest assured they are alive and well, enjoying lucrative careers in finance. A youth generally regarded as troubled leads police and reporters to an empty culvert, a deserted rail car, and on a hike through acres of abandoned field. Someone claiming actually to be one of the missing women comes forward but will not specify which one she is—she resembles none—and is vague about the other two, saying only that they ditched her. Her parents convince her to recant. A group calling itself The Urban Tide says they have taken the women hostage in belated protest of the U.S. invasion of Grenada. They are revealed to be performance artists living off college fellowships. They say their intention was to "tweak the media and thereby tweak collective perceptions." There is talk of dismantling the university's theater arts program altogether, which is hotly debated until the diversion of Vicki's ex-boyfriend's appearance in a television interview.

He reaffirms his innocence and describes their first date: They had agreed to meet at the football game. She had not permitted him to kiss her that night. The first thing he admired about her was how she blew smoke rings, "like she was forty years old or something." They dated for two years and got preengaged. She loved red hots and for him to knead her shoulders after a long day of school and sweeping up at her mother's shop. The restraining order grew out of a misunderstanding, he explains. He was a jealous guy, he admits. She could be sort of a flirt, but no more than that, he is careful to emphasize. No speaking ill of the missing. He has grown up a lot since then, he swears, and in a pretaped clip, his former guidance counselor agrees. What's next for this wrongly accused young fellow who has stolen all our hearts? He's studying for his General Equivalency Diploma and plans to enter technical school. Weekends he fishes with his dad and brothers.

Lovely Adelle had (has? We must be careful with what tenses imply) no boyfriend. She seemed unapproachable, schoolmates say. Boys were intimidated by her height and her perfect smile. She carried herself as if maybe she thought she was a little better than everyone else. We detect the trace of a smugly superior smirk in her wedding dress video. Her parents start to seem a little too perfect in their televised worry, forever circling the town, meeting with the police chief, presiding over candlelight vigils. We can't help but wonder. Don't they have to work? The friendly wood panels on their station wagon begin to come across as less than sincere. When Adelle's face appears alone on a billboard and a separate award fund is established from her college savings, we say they are elitist. Someone rents a billboard featuring only the faces of the other two, and passers-through unfamiliar with the case think they are unrelated disappearances.

The paper still presents them as a united front, the Missing Women, and prints their photos side by side in equal rectangles. The rectangles have shrunk in size, though, and are delegated to the B pages except on Sundays, when a summary appears on the front page, featuring the best of the tip cards and the psychic du jour. In the absence of verifiable fact, reporters track the psychics' emanations and contribute wispy, artful meditations on the nature of truth itself. One reporter suggests that the women never really existed at all except as modern local archetypes: Kay the divorced mom, Vicki the short-skirted slattern, Adelle the model child from a better neighborhood. Cruise any strip mall in town, he muses, and you will see several of their ilk. Subscriptions to the paper take a nosedive until the reporter resigns and a larger-format, full-color TV schedule is introduced.

How we are holding up: summer presses on, August flares. As the ringing phones wane, crime line volunteers drop off reluctantly, like rose petals. Friends and relatives of the missing women who have flocked to town must return to their respective homes, more immediate families, jobs. There is no such thing as indefinite leave unless you are the missing women. Flyers in windows start to flap at the edges, tape losing its tack. Still, church attendance remains up. Moonlight strolls are kept to a minimum. Locksmiths can't install deadbolts quickly enough. Neighborhoods stay illuminated by floodlights and seethe with attack dogs. Psychologists from the university advise us, in these prolonged times of stress, to be absolutely forthright with one another and to get plenty of rest and light-to-moderate exercise. Sixty-four percent of residents polled believe there will be more disappearances. Seventy-nine percent say the missing women are dead. Eleven percent believe that the supernatural was involved. Two percent suggest they know something about the disappearance that the rest of us don't, and they aren't telling. The poll has a two percent margin of error.

Our police chief is often spotted raking his hand though thin, whitening hair, loosening his collar. He has gained thirty pounds. We worry that the ordeal will force him into early retirement. Mostly we appreciate what he has done for the town, keeping both the leftist fringe and the religious zealots at bay to preserve our moderate sensibilities. Whereas our mayor is perceived to be an ineffectual weasel, the apprehended drunk drivers, college rowdies, neo-Nazis, drug dealers, and other assorted riffraff can attest that our police chief has kept the peace. But even he cannot collar this invisible threat to our women, this thief who whisks them away into the night, leaving only their plaintive flat faces pressed against yellowing planes of paper, asking everyone: Have you seen us?

August simmering down, the newspaper finally succumbs to investigative inertia. No news is no news; they've been carrying the missing women for weeks now, without a single new development. Journalism must prevail; the women's photos are stricken from the B pages. Without the newspaper's resolve, we let the county fair distract us, then a strike at the chicken-parts processing plant, then the college students coming back to town. There's talk of rebuilding the stadium. We have our hands full.

The mayor orates, finally. This tragedy has torn at the heart of our community, he says. We are shocked, saddened, and bewildered, he says. Grappling for clues. Desperate for answers. Neighbor pitted against neighbor in suspicion and fear. We are momentarily tensed by the drama of his speech, but he is voicing sentiments of weeks ago. A belated coda. We've gotten on with it. That's his problem: no finger on the pulse. He's slow to evaluate, even slower to act. We resent his jowly, bow-tied demeanor. He proposes a monument in the square, a small gas torch that will stay lit, eternally vigilant, until the women return. Donations trickle in, guiltily.

From this, the newspaper enjoys a brief second wind of missing-women coverage. After the press conference, there are additional quotes to be gleaned from the mayor, the locally available friends and family of the missing, and the major contributors to the gas torch. There is even a statement from the fire marshal, attesting to the relative safety of the proposed monument. The newspaper's cartoonist, known for her acid social commentary, calls attention to the downtown homeless by drawing bums and bag ladies toasting skewered rats over the torch's open flame. It is generally derided as tasteless, and the editor prints what amounts to an apology under Corrections, saying "We regret the error." The cartoonist resigns under pressure and files suit. She donates part of her settlement to the torch fund, part to the soup kitchen. There will be other, occasional flare-ups. Adelle's parents will reemerge woefully from time to time, but in retrospect we will see that it was here the story's last traces turned to ash.

And what of the missing women? They do turn up, but only in dreams. We're at a party, and though the dream seems intended to air private anxieties (we find ourselves naked in a room full of people), there are the three of them, lingering over the bean dip. Or we walk into an alcove filled with light, to see Adelle in her wedding dress, spinning, spinning, her face aging with each rotation, the smile lined and straining, g-forces undulating her cheeks. Or from the reception area of her beauty shop, we watch Kay cutting hair that drops in soft heaps, the yellow-blond hair of her daughter, black at the root. Or the girls are wearing graduation caps and robes and clutching scrolls. The scrolls are not diplomas but maps of their whereabouts. They offer us a peek, but when we lean in to look, they pull away, snickering with teenage disdain, and vanish. Or in the one we don't speak of, we are running down a familiar forest path, hunted, and we sense them beneath the pads of our feet, planted deep in the dark green woods, bones cooling, and we wake, knowing they've been here all along.

JENNIFFER OFFILL
The Deer

Three dogs chase a deer down the street. They are Labs, black and sleek as otters, owned by people in the neighborhood. These dogs have collars and yards of their own. They are not wild. Children come to pet them when the dogs wander across campus. Only the weakest children are afraid of the Labs, the same pale-skinned children who are afraid of low flying birds and of escalators. These children are easily shaken. The stronger ones tie them to posts by the strings of their hooded jackets. When the drawstring is pulled tight, the hood covers the entire face.

A father holds his daughter up to the window. The deer is almost to the woods. Run, the girl says, but it comes out like a breath. Run. The Labs fly like dark arrows through the snow. They are not wild. One is named Bobo and wears a red collar. He picks up his dish with his mouth when it is time for dinner. Bobo, the dish says. Bobo belongs to the girl's next-door neighbors, the Tates. The Tates belong to each other because they have no children. They are childless, but trying. Everyone waits for Jessica Tate to grow big. The Tates have a large house, one that many other teachers covet. Someone should fill that house with children, the other faculty wives say, but only when they are not themselves.

The deer reaches the woods. The dogs reach the deer. The girl knows this will happen before it does. Every Sunday, she watches *Wild Kingdom* at her grandfather's house. Although she is only six, she has seen many zebras and antelopes die. Her grandfather roots for the lions every time. "Atta boy!" he says, holding her tight on his lap. Her grandfather is a fierce man. She has seen him spit out a tooth in the sink and wash it down the drain. Still, he has promised many times to save her from disaster. In airports, he carries her so that her feet don't touch the escalator. His legs are thin as broomsticks. She worries that they will break as he stamps up the silver steps with her, softly humming.

The girl can no longer tell Bobo apart from the other dogs. In truth, the dogs all look alike now, standing over the deer, their ears sleek against their heads. The girl's father puts on his boots and goes outside. Other neighborhood men are on their porches too. They are all boarding-school teachers like her father. They live in houses filled with books and papers. None of them hunts or has ever bloodied his face in a fight. As if by some signal, the men head toward the woods. Silently, the girl says, Run, run, but her father and the other men walk deliberately through the snow, like children leaving tracks.

The Labs break away from the deer one by one as the men approach. They wait, wagging their tails, to be led home. The girl sees her father kneel in the snow. Bobo barks and runs toward him. Her father pulls the dog by its collar, leaving the other men to tend to the deer. Slowly, he struggles through the snow to the Tates' house where thin, pretty Jessica frets on the porch. "He has blood on his mouth," she says. "Do you think they'll shoot him?" She cradles the heavy, happy dog in her arms. The father shakes his head. No one owns the deer, he tells her. No one will seek justice.

All this time, the deer is dying but not dead. The men touch her hooves and heart like careful doctors. They move cautiously across the red snow. Something must be done, they say to one another. We can't let her go on suffering. The doe's legs twitch as if she is being shocked. Her eyes glisten with fear as the men circle her slowly, touching head and flank. None of the men owns a gun, though they live in a town surrounded by hunters. In the fall, the hunters are everywhere, moving through the trees in their bright vests. At twilight, they ride through town with deer tied to their trucks, honking their horns at each other as they pass. When the season is over, the children return to the woods to find their forts, now strange with snow.

The deer pumps her legs like an animal running in a dream, like a dog asleep and dreaming of a hunt. The men wish for books; they wish for guidance. Something must be done. Everyone is agreed.

The history teacher's house is closest to the woods. He runs to the house and fetches aspirin and a sharp knife. He is a nervous man, bitter from years of small-town gossip. He lives alone, has never married. His closeness to his students is sometimes misconstrued. At parties, determined faculty wives dare him with their eyes. Their tongues move intricately within their mouths, tying cherry stems into knots.

The history teacher runs with the knife through the snow. He is out of

JENNIFER OFFILL

breath when he reaches the deer. Kneeling, he puts aspirin beneath the doe's tongue and waits, stroking her twitching legs. It is a long wait. The doe's eyes flicker wildly from face to face. There is blood on her fur and too much brightness in her eyes. Finally, the panic that rings her eyes recedes a little. He takes out his knife and slits her throat with great care, as if he were opening a letter. Afterward, he shuts the doe's eyes and sops up her blood with his scarf. Together, the men lift the deer and carry her into the bare woods. There in the woods they bury the deer near the abandoned forts of their children.

That night, the philosophy teacher returns from the city. He is later than he intended and drives quickly through the snow-filled streets. He imagines his wife in the doorway, her hands pressed flat against her stomach, saying, Are you in love with another? Outside, the snow is filled with boys. They dart and feint across the white lawn in the dark before dinner. When he pulls into the driveway, his wife lets out the dog to greet him. "Down boy," he says, struggling up the icy walk. "Easy." The dog runs circles of joy around him. His black fur is covered with ice. "I'm glad you're home," his wife says. Snow falls on his face. He lets the dog inside, then kisses her cheek.

At school, the children talk of the deer that their dogs killed. The dogs have become like puppies again, endlessly interesting to the children. The night after the deer, they examine their pets' teeth. They offer them gerbils to bite, but the dogs are tired and well-fed. One fat, dreamy girl claims that her dog brought home the deer's ear and hid it in his doghouse. The other children grow agitated and excited by this claim. They divide into teams to play deer and dog. Only the child who is afraid of escalators refuses to play.

The men too talk of the deer and of their dogs. The history teacher admits that he has had troubling dreams. He speaks a little quickly, moving his pale hands through the air. His lips are wet when he finishes speaking.

The other men glance at each other and then away. They speak of their restless dogs and nervous wives who keep the children in now after school. The English teacher listens, but is silent. He thinks of his father-in-law at Thanksgiving, fiercely carving the turkey. "Jack," he said to him. "If we were all in a burning house and I couldn't save everyone, you'd be the one I left behind." He passed plates of food around the table as he spoke. The English teacher spread his napkin in his lap and waited. "Blood comes first," his father-in-law said. "It's nothing personal."

His priorities during a disaster are a theme his father-in-law returns to often. On previous holidays, he had made it clear that he wouldn't save his son-in-law from a sinking boat or nuclear war either. The English teacher thinks of his own daughter, barely six. Last summer, she collected fireflies in a jar. He can imagine himself running toward her through rooms of flame.

The teachers laugh a little over lunch as if to say, It wasn't so much, I barely remember. The lunchroom is filled with the yells of teenage boys, clamoring for air, for space to hurl their bodies through. The philosophy teacher remembers his wife baring her pale neck to him the night before. He imagines telling a child, You were conceived on the night Bobo killed a deer. The dog might be old by then, half-blind, afraid of snow. The afternoon bell rings. The teachers wait patiently for the room to empty, their books beside them like heavy weights.

Later, when the deer had become another story to tell, people began to talk of the flower that had grown over its grave, a blood-red flower, a weeping willow tree. The littlest children were told that the deer had escaped, that she had turned into a tree just as the dogs fell upon her. One of the wives organized a nature walk and took the children to the spot, long hidden, where the doe was buried. On the grave was the promised flower. It looked faded and crooked in the afternoon light.

When the children stole back to dig up the grave, they found that the flower had no roots. Hand over hand, they dug through the dirt until they reached the bones of the deer. There was much fighting among them as they divided up the dirty bones. All the children wanted a leg bone, but there weren't enough to go around. One small girl was given the rib cage instead and started to cry. Exhausted, the children retreated to their forts and polished the doe's bones until they gleamed like ivory. After a time, the leg bones were freely passed around and became clubs and swords, canes and batons, that the children crouched and leapt through the woods with until the last of their shine was gone.

The Woods at the Back of Our Houses

All our domesticity has a perimeter of wildness, and when I was fourteen, mine was the woods which began where our neighborhood ended. This was the summer man walked on the moon and my mother walked out. I couldn't stand the empty feeling of a house my mother had quit, or the sound of my father forever hammering on the damaged sportsfisher he had bought when this latest piece of misfortune entered our lives. My father, convinced that my mother would regain her senses and leave her dentist boyfriend, spent his spare time patching up the big boat for her homecoming.

"This baby is destined to round Cape Hatteras," he said certain afternoons when bourbon had assured him things would get better. He claimed he and my mother and I would dock the boat at a cottage—the kind high on stilts—that he would buy in Manteo, where the first English attempt to found a colony in the New World had failed. My father wasn't bothered that his choice of spots to start over was probably jinxed.

"We'll get these rascals floating." He motioned around our crowded backyard. "Then we'll leave this neighborhood of landlubbers and head for the coast, where it's hello good times."

We were the only people in our North Carolina neighborhood who owned three wrecked boats—one for each time something had gone astray in my parents' marriage. We had a skiff celebrating my mother's miscarriage and subsequent nervous breakdown, a ski boat honoring the time my father tried to quit drinking, and the sportsfisher. The sportsfisher squatted at that point in the back of small yards where our neighbors plotted vegetable gardens or chained German shepherds. Past that, all our properties gave way to woods whose trees were the huge, fairy tale kind — mostly ancient sycamores and a few great oaks wrapped thickly with kudzu. Any number of old paths led to certain points of interest: a hole excavated (and abandoned) successive summers in search of lost Confederate gold; a pen where a man named Mr. Hans cursed in Dutch as he pitched together roosters to teach them to fight; and a tumbled structure said to have been a slave quarters or a cathouse, depending upon who told the story. On the east the woods were cut short by the Haw River, where some of the backwaters had been dammed to make Jake's All Nite Carp Pond. Here men waiting to hop a freight train to distant places loitered alongside the out-of-work. A few old men fished eternally for a carp with a tag on its tail which would win a grand prize. Women were rumored to have disappeared around the pond, and once, after we had carved hearts and our names in the tops of the tallest trees, I watched with the other boys as the men with grappling hooks unsuccessfully dragged the muddy water for a missing person. All this and the fact that Jake sold cigarettes and bootleg whiskey to minors made the place irresistible.

My best friend that summer was an orphaned boy named William who had three testicles. We were our neighborhood's paperboys and Peeping Toms. Evenings we slipped into the woods and joined other boys out to see the same sights. We watched people pass from window to window as they acted out their evening lives. One boy — a stutterer we called Ba Ba Bobby — fell from a tree and broke his arm as we watched the Turner girls bathe and compare breasts, and the feel of that unmoored summer will always be for me the panicked sensation of holding my breath on dry land to avert catastrophe as he fell past a window where bathers compared secrets. That boy falling, and the queasy feeling of witnessing pieces of people's lives I wished I hadn't: Doyle Scroggins knocking his wife into the cabinets then mounting her on the kitchen table as she moaned in a language as foreign as other people's dreams; Jewel Rainy singing to her retarded daughter as she untangled the girl's hair and wove it into one long braid; and the hard way old man Walker cuddled his dog after he had gotten drunk and beaten it. We were voyeurs reluctant to recognize any part of ourselves in such desperate rooms.

"I swear, Richard, she knows we're watching," William said to me. We had gotten rid of the other boys and were at Mrs. Hans's house. The Hans were our customers, and we considered Mrs. Hans our secret possession. We watched Mrs. Hans waltz naked around her living room and stop to ex-

DALE RAY PHILLIPS

amine her beauty in the mantel mirror. I had never seen a naked woman with a tattoo before; once, when I collected for the paper, she had flung open her robe, and I had stared in disbelief at the anchor on her breast. Mr. Hans had shoved her away from the door and explained drunkenly in his accented English that she was a woman who would lay with colored and children for a drink.

"That floozy is putting on a *show* for us, Richard." William handed me the whiskey stolen from my father. Mrs. Hans moved to a music we couldn't hear. Mr. Hans's feet were propped on the couch—he habitually passed out there—and every few moments she would spin his way and dance before him. I had always thought of Holland as an Old World country chock-full of people who doted over tulips and made wooden shoes, where the women wore pointed white caps which made them resemble kind nuns, but Mrs. Hans wasn't like that. Each of her dances ended with her pouring something from the kitchen—usually flour—on her sleeping husband and laughing wildly.

She cut short her dance by pulling down the shade. We waited for her to step onto the back porch and call in the cat. She sang the cat's name and swooped it up and talked to it the way lonesome people do. We were close enough to my home to hear my father hammering at his sadness as she conversed with the cat, first in English, then in Dutch. The ease with which she switched languages made me understand how far she had traveled to inhabit an old sorrow. She had adapted to the customs of a people who were easily duped by love.

My mother was an extremely nervous and dangerously beautiful woman who had little luck with love. A few times each week she called to question me about our life without her and to complain that Michael Michaels—the dentist she left my father for—wanted her for only one thing. I supposed she meant sex and changed the subject. I rambled about the paper route I shared with William, the sportsfisher, the maid we hired (a lie) to keep the house spotless, and the peanut boiling party my father gave annually at summer's end.

"We're getting along fine," I said. The kitchen was littered with empty sardine tins and half-eaten cans of beans and franks. "We eat out a lot—steaks and shrimp and stuff. We make sure we get in all of the basic food groups."

"Of all the nerve," my mother said. "You throw a party to celebrate something, *not* when your wife leaves you."

"When are you coming back?" I asked. She had had other boyfriends, but she usually tired of them in a few months. And, she had *never* left home for one of them.

"Oh, Richard, I'm so confused." When she started to cry I hung up.

Once a week I rode my bike some five miles to the far side of the woods where Michael Michaels's subdivision began. I always stopped to sneak a cigarette at the hill on Tucker Street where our neighborhood ended. The power company had cut a four-mile swath through the woods and erected steel steeples to carry electricity to distant places. I climbed past the DANGER, HIGH VOLTAGE sign and sat on a girder and practiced my smoking. Some of the houses in Michael Michaels's neighborhood had slate roofs, and I wondered what type of noise rain made on them. I got a sense of detachment from looking down on the tops of things. At such a height, the piedmont along the fall line resembled an old, medieval tapestry on which everything people did—eat and drink and sport—was bordered by woods.

I smoked and thought about the time my mother had insisted we play the game she called electricity. I had been eight and she had just gotten back from an institution. She had instructed me to hold her hand in paper doll fashion while I grabbed the hot wire which protected her flower garden from woodchucks. I had stood there being a conductor, feeling nothing while my mother got the shocks. I was full of the discrepancy of being separate from her pain yet connected. My father had come home and caught us at the game, flinging his briefcase full of x-rays taken by the machines he sold. They scattered though the yard like strange seeds which saw through the flesh of things and threatened to take root and expose. He screamed she was a drunk who was trying to make a nut of me too, and then he had grabbed her hand and a metal stake to ground us. We held hands so tightly that my palms perspired, and I understood that here was sweaty proof of how we were connected—safe from shock as long as we stood like that.

This was the woman I was reluctant to visit, and at Michael Michaels's she was sunbathing—something she never did at home. There was a pool, and she tested the temperature before diving in. I was ashamed at not knowing that she could swim.

She asked me was my father drinking too much, did he have a girlfriend yet, was the house in shambles? Once, when she had been gone over a month, I visited when Michael Michaels came home early from work. He walked toward my mother with two tall, sweating glasses. He gave her one and bent to kiss her and pinched her neck.

"Snooks," she said. "That hurt."

"Does it, now?" he said. He turned and sized me up. "Richard," he said. "You don't have to be such a stranger around here." He stuck out his hand, so I gave him my best grip. What did my mother see in this old man who drank gin with her at one in the afternoon and who yanked teeth for a living and whom she called "snooks." He mumbled he had forgotten the limes and went back inside the house.

"Don't you miss me?" my mother asked. Instead of saying *yes, please come back*, I started saying my good-byes. I claimed that, as a paperboy, I had a huge responsibility to deliver the news on time. The big headlines that summer were all about the moon shot; I told her NASA counted on people like me to inform the public about their great effort to put a man on the moon. I explained that I was a small but vital link of a chain which connected every household with the world.

That afternoon William and I delivered newspapers as most of the fathers were driving home with their elbows angled out car windows. Even men who didn't know me waved at the part of themselves they recognized. Near the road which fed to the interstate, a traveler flagged me over to buy a paper and ask directions. The way he eased back onto unfamiliar streets made me imagine standing on the interstate with my thumb out. For an instant I fathomed the strength it would take to quit this place. A few customers on the end of the route were eating at their picnic tables to escape the kitchen's heat, and I fought the crazy urge to introduce myself as someone who had decided to join their family. In another yard, three children too young to know better ran naked through a sprinkler. The Warrens' old dog, Trixie, which had lost a hind leg to the garbage truck, was already worrying a trash can set out for the next day's collection. I understood that my mother, by staying with Michael Michaels and becoming a person who could swim and leave us, risked not getting back. I remembered a story my father had told me about John Glenn; my father claimed the man kept falling in the shower after he got back from outer space. Imagine it: a guy gets the water just right and thinks he's in for a good shower; then wham, out go the lights and he wakes up with a knot on his head and his wife leaning over him after she has called the doctor. My father claimed it was all those miles John Glenn traveled catching up with him which made John Glenn faint. What I wondered about, as I threw the last paper, was that instant before John Glenn's fainting spell hit. Did he feel a part of himself come up from behind and pass that man in the shower, did his heart skip a beat, or did he experience the sensation that all travelers feel when, the journey about to begin, you make peace with a part of yourself you have decided to leave behind? Then the empty paper bag parachuted behind me, and I rode hard against its seat-belted feeling.

"At least you got a mother to visit," said William. We had finished delivering papers and decided to spend the night fishing at Jake's. The carp were so often caught that their mouths were a nest of old sores. We fished alongside men who couldn't sleep at night and who mumbled to themselves. Everyone bank-fished with their rods secured in stands. A string of bare bulbs around the pond afforded at best a stark fisherman's light which swung with an evening breeze. The dirt road which encircled the pond allowed people to fish from the hoods of their cars. You bought a ticket to fish at a cinder-block building which doubled as an ill-equipped grocery store and pawnshop. When someone quit the crap game going on inside to bang out the back door and urinate with both hands against the building, the pinball machines inside dinged with the promise of free games. On busy nights Jake sent Marathon—a half-wit who ran in the manner of the retarded with outstretched hands—to collect dollars against a five-buck prize for the biggest fish of the night. Marathon rode an old bike with wire baskets and a bell which he rang like a cash register when someone paid him. He had some albino in him, and all around the pond people rubbed his head for luck.

To fish for anything as worthless as carp is an act of faith. You catch them with doughballs flung as far toward the pond's center as you can manage. Sometimes you land a catfish, potbellied from a diet of dough, and you fry it on the spot. The flesh tastes faintly of the pond's bottom and of unseen things. When a carp hits, the drag sings and the rod bends double. They are not of the class of fish which leap and somersault, but of an older order which hugs the bottom and subsists on detritus. In the water they resemble golden flashes, things come up from the deep to manifest themselves briefly. A scale or two usually gets damaged from the netting and falls off, smooth to the touch, a silver-dollar-sized and translucent coin of passage. If the fish is big enough, you yell for Marathon, who will weigh it. Fishermen come over to inspect your catch and huddle around it. Marathon cradles it like he'd cradle a baby because he hasn't mastered the art of paralyzing a carp with his thumb and medial finger in its eye sockets. You saw a paralyzed woman once, when your father took you to the hospital to visit your mother, and you think about that—a person unable to feel anything. Then you pinch your arm hard to feel yourself hurt. You wonder

DALE RAY PHILLIPS

why your father doesn't go over to Michael Michaels's and slug him and win your mother back.

"Picture?" asked Marathon. He always carried a camera for such occasions. William and I gave him a buck to take our picture. We each held a portion of the fish, and I was suddenly glad my parents were alive and I didn't live with an uncle who put belt marks on me, as William's did. I thought it might be nice to send the picture to my mother, a snapshot of me and my pal William who had, miraculously, three testicles and much trouble, holding a carp between us, not the carp with the tag on its tail, but at least a big carp. It was one of those moments of goodwill which, like the picture, never got delivered.

Every time that summer my father broke down and called my mother at Michael Michaels's house, we were working on the sportsfisher. The hole we would never adequately repair made the hull look cannon-shot. Two old Evinrudes sat powerfully beside each other on sawhorses with their props in big steel drums. Certain nights my father filled the drums with water and started the engines and smiled at their grumbling. Black oil bubbles surfaced and burst into colors, and he would stare at them as if he could divine them. Soon he'd amble inside and pick up the phone. The big boat had a canvas top we sometimes sat under when a quick rain caught us working late. We'd switch off the motors and the work light and listen to the rain on the canvas and the woods. You could feel people living around you more than you could see them, and most of the houses were dark except for bathroom lights or the paleness of a room where a husband lay sleeping in front of a television. Now and then someone came to the back door to study what they could see of the weather, and at the first mention of lightning our nearest neighbor would scream for her kids to get out of the bath. Rain on canvas made me feel shipwrecked, but it reminded my father of my mother.

"Excuse me, Richard," he'd say, and trudge to the house. He walked with his hands in his pockets and his head bent against the weather. I left him alone to call my mother, because I didn't want to hear him beg. He always came back pretending he'd gone inside for a cold beer, and the festive swish saddened me as he handed me an opened can. He explained I should watch out for the stuff—it could get the best of anyone, he said—and I never knew if he were talking about drinking or about what had transpired on the phone. When the rain quit, we'd work and talk.

"When your mother comes to her senses, Richard, you'll have to help her put this summer behind her. What we'll do is move to Manteo, like colonists, and start things over."

"Those guys got lost," I pointed out. "Why in the hell do you think they call it the Lost Colony? Besides, we're never going to move to Manteo." I had gotten tired of his crazy dreams.

"You've got to put this behind you, Richard." Then my father patted the sportsfisher's hull. "We've rounded the cape once before, and when we get this baby in shape, we'll do it again."

Rounding Cape Hatteras was my father's way of reminding me that we were hewn from tough stock. In better times, my father and I had once chartered a boat to troll for king mackerel past the shoals. The sea had been so rough that day that even the captain had taken a healthy swig of my father's whiskey. I listened to my father sand the sportsfisher's hull, remembering how we had safely crossed rough water. The diesel had rumbled solidly beneath the cypress decking as my father and I had found our sea legs and the mate had set out the lines. My father believed we could do it again—power through all those whitecaps and laugh at where we had been.

After several days of hard drinking, my father decided to throw his peanut-boiling party early to celebrate man landing on the moon. He felt connected with the space program because the x-ray manufacturer which employed him made a vacuum tube used by NASA. He bought fifty-pound burlap sacks full of peanuts and got out the big kettles. He strung his boats with colored Christmas lights and lettered a banner which proclaimed THE MOON IS OURS! William and I rolled invitations inside the newspapers and delivered them to the entire neighborhood. My father spent the day of the party running errands and buying things we couldn't afford. Some checks had been bouncing lately, and I mentioned this when he came home with a hundred-and-fifty-pound half hog.

"I'm running this show." My father claimed it was uncouth to eat boiled peanuts without barbeque. The hog would only fit in the bathtub, so that's where we put it, and my father rushed off to buy ice while I started digging the pit. While he was gone, my mother called.

"Richard," she said. "This bastard won't let me leave. He's holding me captive here." Her voice sounded drunk and crazy and strained. "Put your father on the phone. I need him."

"Lady." I tried to talk in a stranger's voice. "You've dialed the wrong number. The family who lived here moved." I hung up and took the phone off the hook.

William and I greeted the guests and showed them the backyard, where my father had positioned as many TV sets as his credit card could muster. From any point in our yard, you could see at least one set which would broadcast man walking on the moon. Of the hundred and fifty people invited, only fifteen came, and those were already drunk. I had been a Peeping Tom on several of them, and I felt odd inviting them into my own yard and my own calamity, especially Mrs. Hans. She came in an ill-fitted party dress designed for an Old World occasion. The thing had an apron. William complimented her on her attire. She had crooked lipstick, and she had forgotten we were her paperboys.

"I live on the next street," she said. "I have sore feet from these slippers and from walking here." She took off her shoes and handed them to me. "I am sorry I am late." She wobbled toward the drink table. Mr. Hans arrived huffing shortly afterward. He claimed they had been at a party in another neighborhood—he showed us a bottle of champagne they were *giving* away—where he had misplaced his wife.

"Here's her shoes." Then I pointed toward Mrs. Hans apologizing to a group of men, claiming she was sorry she was late. Mr. Hans stuck the fancy slippers in his pockets with the heels pointing out. He seemed about to say something—I guessed it might be about his wife—but he thought better of it, and he shrugged. He seemed suddenly both a foreigner and a kinsman. I wanted to ask Mr. Hans, who had been pulled here nearly four hundred years after the Lost Colonists and the first settlers, if he could remember his first glimpse of what was once called the New World? Did it take his breath, was it like rounding the cape and gauging where you were going by where you had been, did he hug his wife tightly and point toward the life he imagined somewhere past the circling seagulls? All that traveling, based on something as unfounded as a hunch that life would improve where there was space enough to start over, all that traveling to land here in this small backyard filled with wrecked boats and people who had not been invited to other parties or who had no place to go. Suddenly, my father's party seemed a sad celebration attended by people who had missed the holiday.

By midnight, the revelers had stormed the house and found the stereo and records my mother had left. They played Lady Day so loudly she filled the backyard. Mr. Hans was drunk and had lost his wife again. He looked for her under chairs and in the trailered boats; then he sat back in the dewy grass and passed out. I peeped in the kitchen window and watched a neighbor answer our phone and explain his presence. At the far end of the yard, my father was showing his boats to a man caressing the back of a woman who wasn't his wife. Walter Cronkite was excited because the guys had landed on the moon and would walk soon. He described the complicated suits the astronauts would wear to sustain life in a hostile realm. When my father started telling anyone who would listen of his navy days during the Korean conflict, when he had shot the big guns from the destroyer at the enemy, William and I decided to sneak to the carp pond with some commandeered whiskey. My father kept explaining that their target had been invisible below the horizon.

At the carp pond, we met up with Ba Ba Bobby who said that he'd swap some of the whiskey we waved for a treat we'd never forget.

"We don't feel like looking into people's houses tonight," I said.

"I'm not talking about *looking*." He scratched under the arm of his cast. "I got me a gold mine tonight," he claimed. "Come on, now."

We followed him through the woods along the old path which smelled damply of dew and forgotten places. William cursed at a spiderweb and threatened Ba Ba Bobby that this better be good. We circled back through the woody darkness of where we lived. The noise from my father's party came in waves as someone fiddled with the stereo's volume or as laughter from an old joke grew and subsided. The stolen whiskey made me slow to understand our whereabouts.

"Look." Ba Ba Bobby giggled. "She's drunk so much whiskey she don't know who she is." He hooked both thumbs in his belt loops. "I've already had her twice, with her begging for more of me and more whiskey."

Mrs. Hans had taken a sheet from her clothesline, and she sat cross-legged in its middle. She was naked. She asked Bobby had he brought what she had requested; I didn't know whether she meant us or the liquor. William rubbed his hands together at our great, good luck. We lounged beside her like three boys at a picnic who were not in the midst of a naked lady. We passed the bottle around like old chums. I worried about Mr. Hans, until William reminded me that he was passed out in my backyard. Between slugs of whiskey, Mrs. Hans allowed us to grope her and fondle her breasts. She gave us wet kisses and tickled my brain with her tongue in my ear. She said she had taught Bobby something special which he would now show us, and when he pulled his face away, I took my turn putting my face there too.

"We will now screw like dogs," Mrs. Hans said. She growled and barked and was very much out of control. I unzippered and massaged my erect awkwardness until my turn. Strangely, she wouldn't allow us to enter her until we murmured we loved her—as if that phrase magically righted our actions. By my turn she seemed hungry enough to devour me, but seconds later I didn't care; let her do what she would with me, as long as I could journey into that sensation again. I had never come with anyone before, and when I did, I felt jettisoned. We practiced grappling with love and other newfound feelings under a fat moon where men were walking. It's strange, the way you learn to wear the weight of such moments.

Back home, my mother's car sat in the driveway. I eased around the corner of the house like some stranger returning to peek in on his own past. My father was explaining to my mother what she had missed—over a hundred people at his moon-walking party! My mother said that Michael Michaels had taken advantage of her, that she'd just come back to get some things she'd forgotten, but that she was tired and needed a place to rest for the night. My father mixed her another big drink, and she laughed when he pointed at two drunks asleep in the grass. One was Mr. Hans, and I felt not guilt but relief. When "Strange Fruit" came on the stereo, my father asked her for one last dance. I wondered how many more drunken nights this could continue.

When my father saw me, he twirled my mother and said, "Look who's back." He gave me a look which said he knew it was only for a few nights, but that I should accept it. This unwillingness to let go was all we had left of one another. We seemed three Lost Colonists, waiting for a boat with provisions which would arrive too late. I thought about how those colonists had been forced to quit their bickering and to wander inland and lose themselves amidst a wilderness. More successful colonists would follow, towns would get built, towns with neighborhoods and lives like the ones we were quitting. What would one of those early colonists think if he were to wander from the woody dream of lost times and witness my parents dancing the way people dance when they know the night is over, but they are reluctant to allow it to end?

"Hey," my father said when the song had passed. "What we all need here are some freshly boiled peanuts." He promised there was nothing in the world boiled peanuts couldn't fix. The other guests had carted off whole joints of barbeque, and I suspected he was trying to hide the fact that he had little else to offer. "I stashed an untouched sack in the closet, so these hungry bums couldn't get at them."

My mother said for us both to stay put; she'd boil them on the stove in a jiffy as the fires had gone out. My father said that by God we'd christen the sportsfisher by eating them in it. My mother went inside, and my father and I shared a beer and the good feeling of one of the last suppers we would all ever eat together. When my mother returned with a platter of peanuts, we climbed into the boat, and I stared at the strong back of this strange man who could welcome disaster back into his life as if she were a goddess in disguise.

Is that what happens when your childhood quits on you and you are face-to-face with your luck as an adult, full of that queasy feeling which comes from too easily accepting the strange slipperiness of following where others have already traveled? I sat amazed at the type of person I was becoming—one who had taken advantage of a drunken woman but who didn't feel guilty enough to confess. How had events become too complicated to unravel from intentions? I sat there that night with my mother and father in the trailered sportsfisher, reluctant to go anywhere, hungry for a meal as simple as salted, boiled peanuts with these people who had already gone their separate ways. Out in the woods at the back of all our houses some cats were wrangling.

"Listen to them go at it," said my mother. Those cats caterwauling seemed the oldest noise in the world. The darkness became suddenly frightening as we sat listening for something friendly to save and to remember. We lumbered out of the sportsfisher only after my father remarked that it was already the next day and time for bed.

"I got an idea," said my father. "Let's walk like those guys on the moon." He had taken our hands, and together we imitated the movements of people who weren't afraid to test space. My father said we should walk more stiffly—after all, he said, we were in a place where gravity was lessened. It was like stumbling through a dark room whose furniture had been rearranged, and where each moment you dreaded the shock of striking something new.

Moon Pie over Miami

Because Ida had wanted to go to Florida to go swimming, and because her husband, Tommy, had decided they would not go, she was in a particularly bad mood.

Unaware of this, he came home from work and, as usual, put his shoes and socks in front of the recliner and pulled the lever to lean back. The footrest knocked his shoes into the center of the room, between him and the television.

"Move them things, will you?" he asked his wife.

Ida leaned in the kitchen doorway with her arms folded. She was thin, and sideways she seemed no thicker than the door itself.

"And when you move them, give me a kiss, too, how about it?"

She removed the cigarette from her lips and held it in front of her so that it looked like she was aiming it at her husband.

"Do what?"

"But get me a beer first," he added.

She opened the can and brought it and a single serving pack of Cheez Doodles to him. The Doodles were crisp, and they cracked like twigs as he ate them. Dusty orange crumbs soon covered his shirt and lips, which were not going to be kissed and which were as orange as a clown's.

"You got any more?" he asked.

He had knocked the remote control off the arm of the chair and he stretched out a bare foot and grasped it like a monkey between his toes. Ida sneered from behind his back.

"You don't need anymore," she said, "and pick up that bag and throw it in the trash can."

"Huh?"

"You heard me."

For the first time since he'd come home, he turned around and looked at her and studied her face, trying to figure out what brought all this on, and then he leaned over and got the wrapper, crumpled it and tossed it toward the can. It unfurled and caught the air and landed on the carpet, sprinkling more powdery bits around.

"Now clean that up, too."

"I will be damned if I will," he said and began to change the channels.

The way he changed them, so without regard to her or even what was on the program, felt like a slap in the face each time the screen flipped.

"Turn that thing off!" she said.

"You go to hell."

She flicked her cigarette into the kitchen sink and for a moment she looked like a soldier from World War II footage who had taken one last drag before going into battle and then casually tossed the butt away.

After that, she moved across the room so fast she had his hair and the back of his head before he had time to change the channel even once more. She pulled him backward over the top of the chair and jerked down. Had it not been for the force she was applying, and had it not been for his legs and feet flying up into the air, it might have looked like he was getting ready for a shampoo in a beauty parlor chair.

She had pulled him so hard she lifted herself off the floor and the chair tipped backward and teetered and would have crashed on her had she not let go. When she did, the recliner slammed back down.

"YOU WANT TO WATCH MORE TV?" she screamed.

She picked up the 27-inch set, which weighed almost as much as she did, and ran with it and shoved it into his lap. She let go of it and it almost fell over to one side, and Tommy, whose eyes were as wide as the tires of his riding lawn mower, held it, trying to save it and himself.

"AND YOU WANT ME TO CLEAN THIS UP?" she asked.

She took the Doodles wrapper and put it in the trash can and then dumped it all on his head.

"What in the heck did I do?"

"Like you don't know," she said and discovered the remote control and dropped it on the floor and jumped in the air and landed on it with both feet.

"Now I'm going to hurt you," he said. "I'm going to lay you out."

"Lay me out?"

He was trying to get out of the chair, but the footrest and the backrest were jammed in the reclining position and he couldn't do it.

"You haven't laid me nothing in so long you wouldn't know how!" she yelled.

She dove on top of him and they finally succeeded in flipping the chair onto its back.

When it landed, Tommy's head smacked the floor at the same time her forehead smacked into his. They hit hard, and made a noise like two hollow wooden blocks clapping together. Stunned, they lay still.

For the first time in a few very long minutes, there was no sound and no one was moving and the television was silent and the Doodles bag, which had started it all, lay half out from under the large set, which had fallen on it.

The way it stuck out, it appeared to have been killed by the set, the way a body would stick out from under a car that had run over it. The whole scene looked as if it had tumbled out of the screen from the "911" show, as if the television set had disgorged itself into their living room, as if the drama of so many actual years had finally merged with what was on the set.

The timer in the kitchen began to buzz. Ida heard it as if she were swimming, as if she were under water, and it continued to buzz while she swam around in circles, not at all like swimming off the coast of Miami, but swimming, nevertheless, side by side, with her husband.

MARIANNE GINGHER
Teen Angel

"If memory never failed us and if we were always willing to tell the truth, wouldn't we be able to anticipate our problems?" my friend Becky Reece asked. She picked an Opera Creme apart to lick the filling. "Who'd need psychoanalysis?" It was Saturday morning, early in the summer of 1962, and we were lolling around Becky's kitchen doing one of our philosophy gigs, watching her mother roll out piecrust.

"We'd have to get into the habit of thinking backwards," I said.

"*Yes!*" Becky agreed. "Spontaneously and with precision. Thinking backwards. I *like* it, Jennifer." She chewed her Opera Creme thoughtfully. "It's like this," she said. "All of today's problems have the equivalent of family trees, *ancestral* problems."

"Please," Mrs. Reece said, stirring something. "You girls are giving me a headache."

Becky said, "Mom, if we could think backwards, misery might reverse itself. Sort of like when the universe collapses, time will run backwards."

"If the universe collapses, who'll hang around to reset their watches?" Mrs. Reece said tiredly.

She said this at the exact moment her husband barreled into the kitchen and slammed her around. I remember because it broke her watch. Actually he didn't slam her—I was only fifteen and memory is prone to exaggerate—but he shoved her aside, brutishly, then he threw a sack of oysters at the sink, which missed, hit the drainboard, and broke several dishes.

"And in front of *you*," my mother said later when I told her. "*Company!*"

Well, I was hardly company. I came closer to being a piece of furniture with all the time I logged at the Reeces'. We lived at opposite ends of Dogwood Drive, and Becky and I had been friends since first grade. I was drawn to their house as if to great adventure. It was cluttered and squabbling; but Mrs. Reece understood me in a way my own mother didn't, and Becky had an older sister, Rita, who was heartily sexual and told us every detail of her exploits with a kind of flat-faced erudition while she gooed on her makeup. At the Reeces' I got to smoke cigarettes and eat crème de menthe parfaits and play strip poker unabashedly. You could lounge around on the living room furniture and put your feet on the coffee table. Best of all there was the thrilling unpredictability of Mr. Reece's fury to reckon with.

"Yikes!" Becky said, swooping a protective arm around her mother as her father blew past. "Should we feel like simpletons?"

I didn't know what she was talking about. I was too horrified to try to guess. I stooped to pick up all the Opera Cremes, which had somehow loosened and scattered themselves.

"Mom," Becky said patiently. "Think backwards."

Mrs. Reece gawked at her. "He's a maniac!" she shouted. "Think *backwards*? Okay, he was a maniac yesterday, the day before, last year. He was a maniac in 1942 when we got married. He was a maniac in high school. I knew every girl who dumped him and why. *Why?* Because he was a maniac. He was a maniac at birth—a breech. It almost killed his mother. Is that far enough back? I'll take him right back to the Garden of Eden, if you like. To his slimy perch in the Tree of Knowledge."

I had no idea what the fight between Mr. and Mrs. Reece was all about. I supposed it had something to do with the sack of oysters. I was straining to think backwards, even though I had the barest facts and observations. I'd seen some of their other fights, and none of them ever seemed to make sense. I always felt as if I'd entered the movie late, that the high drama had already happened offstage and the ragtag exchanges I'd come upon were an effort at patching up rather than dismantling their scarecrow marriage. Once I'd watched them fling shoes at each other. Once I'd seen Mrs. Reece dig what she called a grave in the backyard and bury her wedding album.

On the whole the Reeces seemed more quirky than violent, and I was going through a stage where I was infatuated with quirkiness. My own home was bland and regular. Everyone was soft-spoken and polite. If I wasn't well behaved I got sent to my room. My parents, although never openly passionate, were kind and deferential toward one another. If you want to know the truth, we all kind of treated each other like company. When I think back on my childhood, I see a tidy beige home filled with Coke bottles dressed in little terry cloth sweaters so as not to leave rings on the furniture. I recall a perpetual, calming sound of sloshing: clothes in the washer, dishes in the dishwasher, toilet brushes churning the water of our toilets, keeping us clean. The rhapsodic scent of Airwick sweetened every room.

The very air at the Reeces' house roiled overhead, sparky and volatile. Everybody smoked, including Rita and Becky, but that's not what I'm referring to. It felt like atmospheric conditions over there, emotions gusting up on you that, like severe weather, were always beyond your control. Everybody seemed to place high value on argument. Argument had as much shape and volume and independence as any member of the family. It came and went as easily as I did.

Later, on the afternoon of the thrown oyster sack, Mr. Reece appeared in the kitchen wearing the sort of docile-looking house slippers that have always made me think of hound dogs. Maybe it was their innocuous, shuffling sound that implied a doggy contriteness. He padded about the kitchen like nothing had happened, whistling and gathering utensils. He concocted a dip of horseradish, ketchup, and lemon, which he poured into a saucer. He pried open a dozen of the oysters and tried to cajole us into learning how to eat them raw. He ended up eating all twelve oysters himself in a gluttonous, show-offish way, smacking his lips and delighting in our chagrin. Addressing Mrs. Reece, his voice had a teasing quality, intending more to wheedle than insult. Once he kissed the nape of her neck. Becky and I discussed the kiss later, cringing. It seemed like a mating ritual.

Maybe that was the night we heard them making love or thought we did because Rita had told us that oysters were aphrodisiacs. I can't really believe we were fifteen and did what we did, because it seems that we would have felt too ashamed or fearful. But I vividly recall our snaking down the dark hallway toward their bedroom and lying on the threshold, flat on the floor, listening to the rush and tumble of their sheets.

"One, two, three, push," Mr. Reece said, and Mrs. Reece laughed her smoker's throaty laugh.

Were they really making love or simply, as Becky preferred to think, trying to fix a broken bed?

There was a vaguely comic side to whatever sorrow persisted between Mr. and Mrs. Reece, and although I couldn't explain this to my parents, who were forever questioning my devotion to such a family, I was bedazzled. I suppose, looking back, that I observed far more of their spectacle than their pain, and that they were really more private than I gave them credit for being. Becky and I, with our blithe philosophy, reduced her despair about her parents by always finding something to laugh about. That's what I remember most about our style of philosophy: we philosophized until something made us laugh. Once, in the wake of one of Mr. Reece's outbursts, Becky and I invented curse poems. We called them voodoo haiku and planted them like bad-luck fortune cookies in the innersoles of Mr. Reece's shoes.

Becky's sister, Rita, was a day student at a local college and madly in love with a senior named Howard Cox. We loved to pester her on weekend nights when she was getting ready to go out. We followed her from her vanity to the bathroom, back and forth, observing her ministrations, and I suspect that we learned everything there is to learn about grooming one's body for romance. Rita shaved her legs to the hipbones and daubed drops of Estée Lauder on the insides of her thighs and the plush well of her navel. She plucked her eyebrows into graceful, wispy arches and applied this miracle makeup you could only buy at McFall's Drugstore and which transformed even the most rocky complexion into peachy, placid terrain. It was called Liquimat and was manufactured in San Antonio, Texas, out of probably the same mud they used to build adobes. She ratted her short, bleached blond hair until it surrounded her head like a dandelion puff, then she patiently tamed it into a voluminous, smooth bubble and attached a velveteen ribbon to one side of her bangs.

She waited to dress last, parading around in her underwear, which was lacy and scant and unquestionably see-through. She had fabulous, perky breasts and she talked about what it felt like for Howard Cox to touch them. She showed us through her brassiere how she could make the nipples hard by touching them herself, but she said that Howard could make them harder. She relished showing us and loved to shock us. Once she parted her legs and showed us what she called her "love bud." She told us everything about Howard's anatomy, too, only she called him "How hard" in a breathy, lunging voice. She told us that once they'd done it in a phone booth while he was talking to his mother long-distance.

I don't mean to suggest that Rita was crude or that I ever came away from our gabfests feeling offended. I came away feeling informed and inspired. Her detached manner of delivery was almost scholarly. Her sexual discoveries filled her to the brim, and what we learned from her was like an overflow she couldn't contain. She talked with similar zest about the books she read in college. She loved reading. She loved finding things out. I've often thought that it was only her curiosity that was promiscuous. And I've never been certain of any clear difference between promiscuity and the sort of enthusiasm that is so wholehearted you simply abandon good judgment.

She was reading Ayn Rand the evening I witnessed Mr. Reece attack her. I can see the books even now, stacked together on her vanity, dog-eared paperbacks she obviously cherished. RITA LOVES HOW HARD was inscribed on the front cover of the topmost book. Years later I would read these books, I'm embarrassed to say, searching for the salacious passages that I'd always believed prompted Rita's reading selections.

Becky and I were sitting on one of the twin beds, watching Rita get ready for Howard and trying to listen to "Louie Louie" on the record player. Rita wanted us to hear the dirty lyrics and you had to slow the record down to 33 rpm's to hear them, she said. Becky and I weren't having much luck; the words still sounded garbled to us at the slower speed. But Rita, in tune with that vibrant netherworld that so enthralled and eluded us, laughed at the music and slapped her knee with bawdy apprehension.

She was wearing only her panties and brassiere when Mr. Reece blasted, unannounced, into the room. He had a lit cigarette in his mouth. In one stride he reached her vanity and with a ferocious swipe of one arm he scattered her makeup, hair curlers, and the two books across the room. He looked wall-eyed with rage. But as if he'd realized that he hadn't done enough damage yet, hadn't realized his revenge, he began to grasp and crush things indiscriminately: a pack of Rita's Newport cigarettes, a dried souvenir corsage. He snapped an emery board in two. He grabbed a pair of her nail scissors and surveyed the room until his eyes locked upon the chair where she'd laid out her garter belt and stockings. Swiftly he seized the stockings and cut them in two at the ankles. It was horrible; I tucked my feet up under my bottom. Finally he dug a little plastic case from his pocket, flipped it open and removed a white rubber disk. I recognized it as the diaphragm Rita had shown us. Mr. Reece regarded it bitterly. He held it away from himself with two fingers, wincing as if it were something dead. Then, quickly, he took the cigarette out of his mouth and burned a hole in the center.

I sat there quaking after he stomped out of the room. "Louie Louie" was stuck on a scratch, and Becky finally unfolded herself from our huddle on the bed and turned off the record player. She picked up the perforated diaphragm and handed it to Rita. Rita had often referred to it as her "joy toy." It had seemed a whimsical device. Now it just looked evil. It made me think of rape. Seeing it convinced me that Mr. Reece was a maniac and that the Reeces were all trying to fool themselves with philosophy and their easy-

MARIANNE GINGHER

come, easy-go theory of domestic unrest. Eventually somebody was going to get killed; I knew this in my heart.

I glanced sympathetically at Rita, but she wasn't even crying. There was a kind of radiance about her, a look of ultimate triumph. She picked herself off the floor and scooped up Mr. Reece's smoldering cigarette where it had rolled under her bed. "Just look at this mess," she said with a tone of dismay. She stepped over the rubble of makeup and spilled perfume to the record player. She removed "Louie Louie" and slipped the record into its jacket. She paused a moment, thinking, looking out the window into a far-reaching night, and then she put on "Teen Angel."

We all listened for a while. It was a chance to catch our breaths, maybe to think about a truer victim of disaster. "You know," Rita said finally, "the girl in this song is a real jerk. But somehow I really love her."

I just sat, still stunned, watching as Rita and Becky straightened up the room. Eventually they got to laughing about the diaphragm. "Have a donut!" they said, laughing, flipping the diaphragm back and forth. They took down one of Becky's old Barbie dolls and put the diaphragm on her like a hoopskirt. They said she had a heavy date with Ken.

I began to see what Mr. Reece's rage was all about: he simply didn't count. He was exiled. They had decided long ago and for reasons I couldn't determine that he was unnecessary to their happiness and utterly dismissable. He was fighting them for access.

One of the neat things about Mrs. Reece was that you could talk her into practically anything. She enjoyed Becky's and my company and, eager to be included, she'd offer to drive us anywhere we liked. On Friday and Saturday nights we liked to choose the Boar and Castle.

The Boar and Castle was a drive-in hamburger joint that specialized in deep-fried foods. There wasn't a menu, just the Boar and Castle's reputation for specialties like skillet bread and onion rings. They sold a soft drink called the Esther Williams. It was the aquamarine color of a swimming pool and turned your tongue blue. In our town blue tongues had become sort of a status symbol, proof that you'd been whooping it up at the good old B and C.

The most popular high school kids hung out at the Boar and Castle. They liked to try to outcool the carhops. The carhops were old, garrulous black men who wore white coats and hats. They'd worked there for years, a real fraternity of raconteurs. They'd seen just about everything there was to see at least twice and they liked to jaw with you about it. They'd cultivated raspy, obliging voices like Rochester's on "Jack Benny" and the sort of flattering banter that guaranteed them good tips. They'd do anything for a tip. Rita told us that once Howard Cox sent one of them across the street to the Bi-Lo service station to buy him a rubber.

Behind the Boar and Castle, under a lush grape arbor, there was a parking area known as the Passion Pit. It was an unspoken rule that you didn't park in the Passion Pit unless you were committed to getting passionate. If you parked there with your date, you made your reputation. Everybody treated the Passion Pit with respect. If you parked anywhere close by, you tried to be discreet. You'd signal the carhops by flashing your headlights rather than honking.

Becky and I were still young enough to squander our pride, and so we always talked Mrs. Reece into parking in the Passion Pit. She'd protest, assuming it was her duty as a mother to protest, but she'd end up doing it. She got a real kick out of our bossing her around, and she was a good sport. She'd dated at the B and C when she was a young girl, and she could still call most of the carhops by name. Something about the way the grape arbor smelled in the summertime turned her face sweet.

After we'd wolfed down our supper, the main business of the evening began. Becky and I would take out our compacts and position the mirrors at various angles so that we could spy on the inhabitants of nearby cars. Sometimes Mrs. Reece would take out her compact, too.

We rarely observed anything other than an arm or a leg unraveling from the dusky interior of a car. Occasionally a girl would rise up and start to cry. Once somebody threw a class ring out an open window and it shot into Mrs. Reece's car and bounced into my lap.

I don't really know what we were watching for. It seems unlikely that Mrs. Reece would have indulged such shameless perversion, even joined it, yet she did. And what a peculiar comfort to have her along, holding up her own compact and giggling alongside us. Whenever she lit a cigarette, the match illuminated her plump, girlish face. In the pinkish gold flare she looked fifteen herself: mischievous, sly. Her charm bracelet tinkled as she extended a hand to flip an ash. She seemed at deep peace with whatever disappointments she'd suffered. Even to the point of returning to the scene of what she often referred to as her original sin: falling in love with Mr. Reece right there in the Boar and Castle Passion Pit back in 1942. She could return with her daughter Becky, who was most likely on the verge of making similar mistakes, and she could flip open her compact and pretend to powder her nose as if nothing ruinous was happening all around her.

MARIANNE GINGHER

Once we'd screeched off to the Boar and Castle after one of her fights with Mr. Reece. It had something to do with the way she sorted and balled his socks. She'd been cooking supper, but after the fight she took a balled-up pair of socks, lathered them with mustard, and sandwiched them between two pieces of rye bread. She smacked the whole package on a plate with a garlic pickle. "Your dinner's ready!" she called to Mr. Reece, then hustled Becky and me out the back door and into her car. We zoomed in the direction of the Boar and Castle without our even suggesting it. When we arrived at the Passion Pit, she cut the ignition and slumped in her seat; her posture suggested relief. She breathed deeply, thrust her face out the car window into the lush, sleepy scent of grape leaves. Then she rummaged in her purse, not for a Kleenex, but to find and withdraw her compact.

"Mom," Becky said sympathetically.

"Shhh," Mrs. Reece cautioned, gazing steadily and tearlessly into the mirror. "I'm thinking backwards, dear."

I noted, then, an eerie lack of anger in her voice. Thinking backwards provided her neither solace nor insight. It seemed more a trick of erasure. Her eyes glazed with forgetting. When she lit a cigarette, the match illuminated a calm, remote girlishness. She thought backwards perhaps to imagine herself making different choices. She could have been anybody; it was a miracle to see her believing it.

That summer, between eighth and ninth grade, middle and upper school, Becky and I lived at the neighborhood swimming pool. We took a transistor radio and beach towels with beer logos, and we camped out all day. For lunch we bought hot dogs and Zero bars at the Snack Shack. We took a thermos of lemonade that we alternately drank and poured over our hair to lighten it. We rubbed our darkening skins with baby oil and Coppertone.

We'd been tomboys and bookworms together, and boys had never paid much attention to us, but that summer things started changing for Becky. Not that she was *looking* for a boy to like. When we weren't practicing our jackknives off the high dive, we were reading under the straw sombreros that we'd bought at the Family Dollar Store along with flipflops and Holly Golightly-style sunglasses with big black round lenses.

Becky loved horror stories and had checked out this real tome from the public library called *Supernatural Omnibus*. It had a skull and crossbones on the cover, and she looked formidable reading it.

I tended to engross myself with science magazines. Since I thought I wanted to study medicine and become a dermatologist like my father, I took his *New England Journal of Medicine* to the pool. I admit I was a bit of a show-off about it. It delighted me for Pansy McBride, the voluptuous high school girl who was lifeguarding that summer, to ask me what I was reading and for me to flash her a nauseating full-color shot of *Pemphigus vulgaris.*

As Becky's first romance developed, I often wondered that if I'd been reading *Supernatural Omnibus* with unself-conscious fervor whether I might have been the one he spoke to—the tall, pale boy with glasses Scotch-taped together at the nosepiece. Becky and I were practically twins in our hats and sunglasses and tank suits and brownish, lemonaded hair—except for our books.

I was first aware of his shadow, and then he squatted down beside Becky, so sudden and graceless that she jumped. "Have you read 'The Beckoning Fair One'?" he asked. " 'The Monkey's Paw'?" He shuddered dramatically. "Never read them alone late at night," he cautioned.

Becky, immediately intrigued, invited him to sit on her beach towel. As soon as I found out that he was a philosopher type as well, I knew Becky was a goner. His name was Randolph Lake. All afternoon he regaled us with his theory of objective expressionism.

As best as I can remember it was the theory that objects hate people. "You're getting out of your car with a heavy bag of groceries," Randolph said with ominous glee. "Inside the house, your phone starts to ring. On your rush to the back door, you trip over the garden hose. Your keys are all scrambled up and you have trouble making the right one fit. Inside the house, your phone rings a fourth, a fifth time. You're really starting to sweat. Finally you jam the proper key in the door and dash inside. On the way to the phone, you fall over the footstool. You reach the phone on the seventh ring and—" he paused, reared his head back and laughed a laugh resonant with jeerful recognition of human folly—"nobody's there!"

"Whose side are you on anyway?" Becky said.

"It was a conspiracy!" he whispered. "The phone rang all by itself to excite you. The garden hose positioned itself in your way. The keys tangled themselves deliberately. The footstool leaped into your path. Want to bet that the groceries in the grocery bag were laughing their labels off?"

Before the afternoon was over, Becky was rubbing Coppertone on his shoulders.

Most afternoons, after she'd gotten home from summer school and he'd been released from his summer job at the A&P, Rita and Howard Cox would show up at the pool for a dip. Rita wore a scandalous string bikini that she'd ordered through the mail and Howard a pair of white French-style

MARIANNE GINGHER

briefs that, once wet, might as well have been Saran Wrap. All the mothers at the pool cut their eyes at them. Pansy McBride put on a pair of dark sunglasses to better observe them undetected. Once they stayed underwater so long that Pansy blew her whistle and initiated lifesaving procedures. Out of *spite*, Rita said later. She'd gotten jealous, peering down from her lofty, prick-teasing tower. Rita said this in front of Randolph Lake, and he blushed.

I noticed a strange new brittleness in Rita. She seemed arrogant and impatient. I'd always thought of her as rambunctious, but now she seemed wild in a weary, hostile way. She wore a pouty, self-absorbed expression. She told us she was bored. She did cannonballs off the side of the pool that splashed our towels and got us all wet. She borrowed our Coppertone, wasted it, made fun of my medical journals, said our sombreros looked dumb. She'd try to pick fights with Howard, but he'd have none of it and dive into the pool.

"What's wrong with Rita?" I asked Becky.

But Becky was too preoccupied with Randolph and didn't seem to notice. She'd only shrug and say, "Maybe she's got her period. What do you mean?"

I didn't know what I meant. Just watching her made me feel restless, made me know that summer was ending and it was time for it to. By the first of August I was usually fed up with the wasteful, goofing-off feeling summertime gave me. I started anticipating my return to the rituals and habits of the school year weeks in advance. What excuses can I make? It was my upbringing: an irrepressible penchant for order, the beige tidiness of a classroom with a certified teacher in control. Deep down my parents had me, all my genes in their death grip.

In a week's time, Becky and Randolph Lake had become a real item. They enjoyed all the same things: Planetarium shows, listening to opera, playing Clue and Scrabble. They read H. P. Lovecraft stories to each other by moonlight. They invented this new theory called Layered Life.

"Imagine that you're driving down a highway with your parents," Randolph said to me cheerfully one afternoon at the pool.

"Do I have to?"

"Okay, then, with your boyfriend."

"I don't have a boyfriend," I said pointedly. "Let's say I'm driving down the highway with *Becky*."

I saw Becky and him exchange a look that told me they pitied me behind my back. I hardly listened after that. Basically the Layered Life theory was something about a Mack truck hitting Becky and me head on. At the moment of impact, I transcend death, move into an advanced time frame, the continuity of my life upheld, layers of existence working much the same as a roll of film passing through a sequence of exposures in a camera. In the old time frame, Becky may find me dead. Actually I've merely been shot forward into a new exposure and am waking up in the rubble of a wrecked car. I have no knowledge of my death, which really only occurred in Becky's time frame. Perhaps we're out of sync, now, the real Becky and the real me. But we've both been granted "duplicates" of each other, either alive or dead, to convince us of our separate realities. What I remember most about the Layered Life theory was that despite its crackpot, labyrinthine nonsense it was ultimately a theory of deathlessness.

I watched Randolph Lake's face as he tried to explain the theory. His eyes were milky blue behind his smudged, taped-together glasses. The rosy flush of earnestness crept up his neck and spread over his cheeks. The freckles scattered across his nose looked as sweet as brown sugar. I found myself leaning toward him, comforted in spite of my feelings of exclusion. In another time and place, another life—the life behind the book I should have been reading at the pool the day he came along, the life that awaited me after a tragic car wreck, possibly—I might have taken his face in my hands and kissed him on the mouth.

I turned fifteen and a half on August 19 and qualified for my learner's permit. It was something constructive to do. I could actually drive a car now as long as I was accompanied by a consenting, licensed adult. When I turned sixteen I would have access to my own car—the 1952 Chevrolet bequeathed to me by my grandmother before she went to live in a nursing home. The car was stored in our garage. It was finless and it had no radio, but its upholstery was in mint condition and certain gizmos, the cigarette lighter, for example, had never been used. Needless to say the car was beige.

To celebrate my obtaining the learner's permit, my parents, in a rare burst of enthusiasm, cranked the old Chevy up and let me take her for a spin. My mother even tied a festive balloon to the hood ornament. But this seemed an indignity my grandmother's car would not endure; she stalled out before we reached the corner, and my father had to fetch his jumper cables.

I was spending less and less time at the Reeces' house. There didn't seem much point in my hanging around with Randolph camped out on the doorstep, teaching Becky how to chart stars and make bottle rockets or ex-

MARIANNE GINGHER

plaining the wall theory we'd learned in science in such a way that would calm her heart. The wall theory had just about driven us crazy all year. If you drew a line near a wall and divided the distance between the line and the wall in half, then divided the distance in half again, and so on and so forth, you would never reach the wall in an eternity of division. *Never reach the wall!*

One night late in August, Becky phoned me. She sounded muffled and far away as if she was calling long-distance. I could tell she'd been crying. "You've read all those medical journals," she whispered. "You know stuff. Help me, Jennifer."

My heart fluttered. I felt a Layered Life experience about to occur. "What stuff do you need to know?"

"Like how do you get . . . oh, God, I can't say it—"

"Becky!" I cried. "Tell me."

She was sobbing. "An abortion," she said. "It's not what you're thinking. It's not me, Jenn."

"It's Rita," I said, thinking backwards to everything.

"She says she and Howard are getting married. She told the maniac tonight."

"Oh, God."

"It's like she has this death wish. You should have seen him. He ran her out of the house and chased her halfway down Dogwood Drive. When he came back inside, he started ripping her clothes out of her closet and piling them up and carting them to the Sternberger Elementary School dumpster. He yelled out the front door to whoever was listening that she was dead to him from that moment on, his daughter Rita Jane Reece was *dead*. Oh, God, Jenn."

"Oh, God," I repeated softly. "I don't think you can get a safe legal abortion in this country," I said. "You have to go some place like Puerto Rico, and it costs a fortune."

"*Jennifer Anne!*" my mother cried, peering around the doorframe, aghast. "Who on earth are you talking to?"

While my parents watched "Gunsmoke," I slipped out the back door and ran down to the Reeces'. The night felt wicked and indulgent, the sky like a twirling black skirt, lifting to show you too much. A rich, weedy fragrance thickened the air and mixed with the aroma of somebody's outdoor grill. Perfume floated out opened windows. Patios glimmered with those Japanese-lantern-lit, murmurous backyard parties that my parents were never invited to. The trees looked heavy and swashbuckling, undulating against the dark sky.

I had almost reached their yard when I saw Mr. Reece. His arms were loaded with clothes, and he hurried toward the open trunk of his car. I remember thinking with horror: that could be a body. The maniac could have done his deed, murdered Rita, murdered all of them, and me, *company*, practically an eye-witness. He slung his burden into the trunk and slammed the lid. I crouched behind some boxwoods in a neighbor's yard until he drove off.

Inside, Becky and Mrs. Reece flopped morosely across the twin beds in the room that Becky shared with Rita, the room where Mr. Reece had taken Rita's diaphragm to task. Every few minutes one of them would rally and go telephone Howard Cox. He didn't answer. They couldn't bear not knowing where she'd gone or what she was planning to do. She'd screamed that she was getting married, like it or lump it. She was twenty goddamn years old. Just try to stop her, maniac, and she'd call the police. She'd thrown a book at him, *Atlas Shrugged*, and he'd picked it up and ripped it in two.

It seemed to me, after I'd heard them describing Rita, that they were crying because she'd turned into a maniac, too. They didn't know her anymore. Mr. Reece still wasn't able to make them cry.

I couldn't stay long to comfort them. I felt awkward and inadequate, the outsider I'd always been, really, dutifully checking my watch to make certain "Gunsmoke" wasn't over yet and that I'd been missed, checking my watch almost grateful for the first time in my life that my life was so circumscribed. I could just leave all this like a bad movie and go home.

In the days that followed we learned that Howard Cox had quit his summer job at the A&P and vacated his apartment. But nobody knew where he'd gone, and nobody had seen Rita. The community college resumed fall classes and neither of their names appeared on any class rosters.

Rita's disappearance felt like a death in the family. Becky and Mrs. Reece dragged around with pathetic, tear-swollen faces. Mother and I made them a spaghetti casserole, but they wouldn't eat. Only Mr. Reece seemed content. Every day when he came home from his hosiery mill, he'd slip on old clothes and putter around his garden until dark. He hummed vigorously, tunelessly to himself. Becky and I called him Farmer McGregor behind his back. Once I saw him snip a butterfly in two, midair, with his garden shears. When he saw me staring, he made the excuse that it was only a moth, the kind that eats holes in leaves, a pest like the Japanese beetle. I didn't be-

MARIANNE GINGHER

lieve him, and I let him see that I didn't. It seemed like the most dangerous commitment I had ever made.

The last week of our summer vacation, Becky and I spent almost every night together, endlessly speculating about Rita's fate. Were they already married? Had they flown to Puerto Rico for an abortion? What was she doing for clothes? Money? Were they doing it all the time now that they were constantly together? Or had the novelty paled? Could you even do it when you were pregnant? I tried to find out from my father's medical textbooks, but the only chapters on sex I could locate were about disease.

I prayed to fall in love some day like Rita: the sort of love for which you'd hurl yourself into the night, leave family and friends, vanish without a trace. The pain of it all created its beauty, the heart's descent like a meteor, burning itself up in such an inexorable plunge. I lay in bed and thought such thoughts until I felt feverish. I moved my top sheet up and down, pretending it was Howard Cox.

I thought about sex all the time, and in some of the most unlikely places: church, Girl Scouts, taking the mail our postman, Mr. McBee, handed me, wondering when he and Mrs. McBee had last done it, trying to imagine the same businesslike hand that sorted and delivered our letters fooling around with a breast.

It was a blessing when school started after Labor Day, although high school wasn't like anything I'd expected. Ours was an enormous, consolidated high school, and I felt dwarfed rather than exhilarated by its offerings. On the first day of school I found myself looking down at my feet all the time rather than meeting people's eyes. Roaming the vast, unchartered corridors, my loafers felt as unwieldy and conspicuous as canoes. I'd put bright new dimes in their slits for good luck, and some upperclassman cheerleader, standing in the cafeteria line at lunch, had pointed and laughed. Or maybe I *thought* she did. But in high school it was only what you *thought* that mattered anyway.

When my last class let out, I headed toward the parking lot to meet Becky. I recognized Randolph Lake standing near a school bus. He was wearing a short-sleeved seersucker shirt decorated with rocket ships and planets; it looked like a little kid's pajama top. His glasses were still taped together, only the tape looked yellow and brittle. He'd crooked pencils behind each ear and was reading this cinder-block-size physics manual and chuckling to himself as if it were a book of jokes. Impulsively I headed toward him, glad to see a familiar face.

"*Pssst!*" somebody whispered. "Jennifer!" It was Becky, crouched behind a nearby trash can.

"What on earth are you doing?"

"I don't want Randolph to see me."

"Why not?"

She rolled her eyes heavenward. "Because this is *high school*, Jennifer," she said. "*Tabula rasa.*"

"Are you dumping him?" I asked. "I thought you were in love."

She shrugged sadly. "Not like Rita," she said.

We sneaked away from the parking lot and started walking home, though it's possible that we got hit by a school bus and never realized it. Maybe we were killed on our very first day of high school, collectively ignorant of our deaths, and passed, unremorseful, into the next layer of our lives.

When we arrived at Becky's house, everything looked the same, but everything felt different. Mrs. Reece greeted us at the back door, smiling broadly, doing this jivey little shuffle. I could hear Connie Francis on the radio singing "Where the Boys Are." Mrs. Reece had just gotten home from the beauty salon, where she'd had her hair newly frosted and her fingernails manicured. She wore a crackling linen dress, two-toned maroon and white like my father's Buick. It had a matching two-toned straw hat with a veil. She said she'd just clipped off the price tags. "Mother of the bride!" she exclaimed radiantly, striking a pose. "I've got big news, girls!" Then she hugged the breath out of both of us.

Rita had called. She was staying in Goldsboro, a mere hundred miles away, with Howard Cox's grandmother. The wedding would take place this Saturday afternoon, weather permitting, in old Mrs. Cox's backyard. Everything was all arranged.

My first reaction was feeling strange about knowing where Howard Cox was from, Goldsboro, and that he had a grandmother feisty enough to provide him a wedding. Howard Cox had not seemed very real to me before.

Becky was worried about logistics. "Everything's all arranged except our escape," she told her mother gloomily. "Don't forget that the maniac is supernatural. He's going to know."

"Why, he won't suspect one thing," Mrs. Reece chirped. "We'll get up Saturday morning, put on some normal-looking clothes, and tell him we're going out shopping. *Meanwhile*," she said slyly, "the car will have been loaded up with all our wedding paraphernalia, locked in the trunk for days." Mrs. Reece clasped her hands together over her heart, and her eyes

MARIANNE GINGHER

sparkled. "Oh, this is so exciting!" she cried, twirling around. It was as if she were the one eloping. She linked arms with Becky and they promenaded around the living room.

I couldn't sleep at all Friday night. I kept getting up to stare back at the round-faced Peeping Tom of a moon. It was a hot, dry September night and the trees, filled with scorched-out insects, made a sound like frying. Overhead stars wheeled and sizzled like the sparks from a bonfire.

I wished I were going with Becky and Mrs. Reece to the wedding, but I wasn't. Mrs. Figg, our next-door neighbor, had asked me to baby-sit. But also the true nature of their Goldsboro mission was top secret, and I wasn't capable of concocting the sort of elaborate lie that might have duped my parents into freeing me to accompany them. My one request was that Becky bring me a slice of wedding cake so that I could sleep with it under my pillow and dream of the man I'd marry.

When I finally fell asleep, the insects had calmed down but the birds were starting to twitter. I slept until almost noon. What finally woke me, I think, was the sensation of an empty house. My parents had already left to visit my grandmother who lived at Green Willow Nursing Home and didn't know us anymore. Normally I was expected to go with them to visit her. It took up an entire Saturday and I always left her feeling depressed. I was glad to have the baby-sitting job lined up as an excuse not to join them. My grandmother had been such a sweet, genteel woman, and now she spat her food at us and glared. She took out her dentures and worked them like a hand puppet while she talked. Once, when we'd gone to visit, we found her and her roommate, Mrs. Wiggins, dancing together in their underwear. They'd picked out a rock-and-roll station on the radio and turned it up full blast. My father shook his head sadly and diagnosed my grandmother as having gone backwards in time, reverting to adolescence. Of course I doubted that she'd ever behaved that way during her teenage years, and I wondered what was so awful about dancing around in your underwear anyway. She was in her own room, wasn't she? She had the door closed. The radio wasn't on *that* loud. It wasn't even a boy she was dancing with.

My parents wouldn't return from the nursing home until late afternoon, so I indulged myself. How pleasant to dawdle about the house in my nightgown on Saturday. I flipped on the television and watched "Mr. Wizard" for a while, then I poured myself a bowl of cereal and sliced some peaches. My baby-sitting job wasn't until three: Mr. and Mrs. Figg were going to play golf and have supper at the country club.

I turned on the radio and WCOG was playing "Teen Angel." Somebody over at the station really loved that song. It had never had much appeal for me; I thought it was sappy. Since it was not a favorite of mine, I don't know why my mother crusaded against it so, but she did. She was riveted to it with disgust, the way people driving past wrecks couldn't help staring. Whenever it came on the radio within her hearing, she'd listen intently with a down-turned mouth until the song was half over. Then she'd pounce on the volume control knob and switch it off. "Teen Angel," she'd say with derision. "That's a contradiction in terms."

I can't say that I blamed her. The lyrics were appalling. The souped-up grief going on in that song oozed over you, shamelessly seductive. But as a *love* story, as something contagiously sexy—the sort of music that got banned in those days—the song was pretty thin. It morosely documented the aftermath of one fateful night when two teenaged lovers stalled their car on a railroad track. As the train bore down upon them, the boy jumped from the car and yanked the girl to safety. Then, inexplicably, seconds before impact, the girl broke free from the boy and dove back into the doomed car while he looked on in horror. Of course a girl so mysteriously impetuous was bound to haunt the memory of the boy who loved her. At sweet sixteen she was an untimely angel. And while he beseeched her to love him beyond the grave, he puzzled over her fatal haste to return to the car. What was she searching for? She was searching for his high school ring that the authorities found clutched in her poor dead hand.

I remembered Rita listening to "Teen Angel" after Mr. Reece burned the hole in her diaphragm. She'd gazed into the night, admiring the dead girl not for her bravery or loyalty, but for her consumptive foolishness. She'd regarded the girl in the song as an ally. As I listened closely to the lyrics, I heard them as if for the first time and I felt shocked. Teen Angel had lost her life because she went back to hunt for a ring that belonged to a boy she'd obviously decided to dump. Why else wasn't the ring on her finger? And what had made her change her mind and run back for the ring? Was it love? Dying for love didn't seem nearly as tragic as dying for guilt, wasting yourself out of some spellbinding sense of obligation. Her boyfriend singing the song sounded bereft, but wasn't he ignorant not to figure things out, not to figure out that, as much for the loss of her, he should be wailing for her change of heart? His sorrow was uninformed.

I let the song run its course without switching stations, only because, with Mother gone, it was the chance of a lifetime. It depressed me, though, to strive so hard to make sense out of nonsense. It's as if I believed that was how you reached maturity: by being able to explain things. When the doorbell rang, I leapt up guiltily and raced to find my robe and slippers. I thought it was probably one of the Figg kids, but when I opened the door, there stood Becky and Mrs. Reece, panting and disheveled. Mrs. Reece had lost one earring, and runs streaked her stockings. They were dressed up as if to go shopping, only they were barefooted and didn't have their purses.

"What's happened?" I asked. "Where are your shoes?"

"Oh, Jennifer! Thank God you're here," Mrs. Reece said, leaping inside the doorway. "When we didn't see your parents' car in the drive—"

"He's locked us out of the house," Becky cried. "He's taken Mother's car and *hidden* it."

I'm certain my jaw dropped.

"I swear to you, this is *it*," Mrs. Reece said. "I can't live another day like this. He's done it now. This is the limit."

"He ought to *die*," Becky said, wild-eyed and through clenched teeth.

"But how did he find out about Goldsboro?" I asked. "Who told?"

"Because he's the goddamn Devil," Becky said. "He knew the plan before we ever thought it up."

"But it's impossible that he just found out on his own," I argued. "Somebody spilled the beans. Who knew besides the three of us?" But they didn't really seem concerned about *how* he knew; it's what he'd done about it that mattered to them now. They had no car to take them to Rita's wedding. They collapsed in each other's arms, sobbing. "Calm down, we'll think of something," I said to them. "Think backwards."

Becky looked at me like I was a lunatic. "No more *thinking*, period," she said. "*Action*," she said, and the way she said the word made it seem as dangerous as a live grenade. "You've got to help us, Jenn."

I guessed I knew what was coming: the end of my life as I'd always known it and taken it for granted. Dreamy with fright, I lay on the pavement of some uncharted highway and watched the encroachment of a Mack truck. I felt that excruciating pause before impact during which I recalled, in a flash of beige scenes, the sensible shelter of my upbringing. What was I doing out here in the middle of nowhere? I loved Becky and her mother, but was that sort of love worth dying for? Becky and Mrs. Reece were driving the Mack truck, and if I didn't leap out of the way they were going to ask me to help them murder Mr. Reece. *And I was going to do it.*

Then Becky hugged me and she said, "You've got your grandmother's car, Jenn. We want you to drive us to Goldsboro."

I will never forget our exhilaration, and I will honor and cherish my wickedness, if that was what it truly was, until death I do part: backing my grandmother's unlicensed Chevrolet down the driveway, running over my mother's chrysanthemums, waving at Mrs. Figg and all the little Figgs out watering their yard, never stopping to explain that I would not show up at three, stopping at the Bi-Lo where they all knew my father and charging a tank of gas, dragging the Boar and Castle once and even honking as we sailed past the Passion Pit.

Once on the Interstate we rolled all the windows down, and I watched Becky and Mrs. Reece light their cigarettes from my grandmother's virginal cigarette lighter and drop their ashes on the car's unblemished upholstery. I hunkered over the steering wheel, awash in wind, an opulence of sunshine, high-toned with purpose, heroic, deft, singing because we had no radio, harmonizing, making up naughty lyrics to "Louie Louie" in honor of Rita, on my way to a bad girl's wedding, on my way to life.

Mrs. Reece leaned back in her seat looking dreamy and smoked one Newport after another. She had runs in her stockings, no purse, no shoes, but God she looked happy. She sang the loudest of all, her face abloom with the satisfactions of survival. We couldn't have guessed that she would go back to him and live on Dogwood Drive as his wife for twenty more years until he finally died of emphysema, not murder. Just as we couldn't have guessed that it was she who had told Mr. Reece about the trip to Goldsboro, Friday night after they had gone to bed and she was feeling at peace with him, believing that, like his passion, his understanding and forgiveness were possible. The looming disappointments of our lives were not what we imagined when we viewed the sun-spangled horizon. We rode within that shimmering dimension between departure and arrival as if entitled to our joy, empowered by as much unhindered delusion as anyone could invent.

MARIANNE GINGHER

Friends and Oranges

MICHELLE AND I

Teen angels. We lie to our mothers. We say we have to study. Algebra, history, awful biology. But she is a year older, Mother says, not in your class. She can help, I say. It is choir practice night. On Sundays we sing like angels. Our robes have wings. We lift and float over the rolling music to the pious sea. We like being almost bad. We like being so very, very good. Old ladies with saggy crepe arms pat our smooth and shiny heads. We wear thin dresses, tiny heels, straps of nothing shoes. When we sing, we arch our white throats sweet as song sparrows.

We have to practice, we have to study. We go to the movies. *Sadie Thompson* with Rita Hayworth, José Ferrer. A cat cries in the alley. She is thin and white with clear green eyes. We hold her, stroke her, say kitty, kitty things. We have to hurry, take the cat along. Mikki buys the tickets. I hide the cat inside my sweater. It does not cry out, but kneads my skin with soft, firm paws.

In the movie the cat sleeps, takes turns on our laps. Afterwards, Mikki and I walk home, carry the cat. We name the cat "Sadie"; discuss the movie. Why was it called *Rain*? Why are men so mean? Mikki doesn't answer. Sadie, who was so light, is now all heavy legs and fur.

We sleep at Mikki's house. Her mother has changed the sheets and the four-poster bed is a summer hill. Under the window, the mock orange blooms and thorns. Its fingers scratch the screen like a peeping tom. We open the window, reach out and pick the teasing oranges. My favorite smell in the whole world, says Mikki, tossing them up. That's all they're good for. Smell. She throws me one for under my pillow. It is mapped and green, fuzzy as a baby's head. The room is all citrus and flowers. We sleep in the top of a blossom tree, Mikki profile. Her nose and chin in the light are sharply drawn and beautiful. I prop on my elbow, watch her eyelids flutter as though she watches a movie. She moans and whimpers like a child; a three-year-old with bad dreams, half-asleep, afraid in the dark. I rub her hand and arms and finally sleep in the special scent of her.

Next morning, Sadie is gone. No one let her out, but she is nowhere we can find. Mikki and I look and call all the way to school, but the cat has disappeared.

GIRL GRADUATES

I help Mikki pack. Plaids and sweaters, pajamas and socks, panties for each day of the week; Saturday embroidered in red, Sunday crude blue on shining yellow. We hug, promise to write. I do, Mikki doesn't. A year later, I pack and go away to school, meet a hundred girls, gossip and pry, pick and giggle. Mikki is a mugging photo, a silly two pages in my annual, something pressed like flowers between rough paper and leather bound.

Once, home for Christmas, someone calls. It's me, she shouts, it's Mikki. I'm at Mother's. We talk old times. Friends and boys, clothes and parents, school, books and friends. We promise to write. I do. She doesn't. In the summer I go to work for a dentist, wear a uniform crisp as paper, say Yes Doctor, Of Course Doctor, Certainly Doctor. I hand him tools, smile all the time, feel good and clean and tired, tired, tired. Mikki goes out West with a friend. She writes a card picture of the desert. You ought to see the colors. You would not believe how brilliant. I am sending you some. Look out.

My second year I marry. An artist. He is tall and thin and full of dreams. He smokes a lot, waves his hands when he talks, lives in museums and galleries. He paints, goes to school at night. I work in a department store. Lingerie. You would not believe the styles and patterns. Old ladies gasp. Teens giggle. I cook and clean and scrub his paints off furniture, shirts, the bathroom sink. Titian, Umber, Cadmium, Venetian. The words ring in my head. He is so full of Eakins, Homer, Whistler, Wyeth, and Wyeth. I am a study for a still life without apples.

He graduates, goes to work for an agency where the heads snap and roll. He is regarded as eccentric, a genius, highly creative, an exceptional individual. I am regarded as the artist's wife who makes babies and marvelous pies. I am a commercial for all the well-known brands. I know which are best and fast and better priced. I recite them like an alphabet, a spelling bee, and win. How clever. All my friends are into Tupperware and Sara Coventry. I listen well, learn that language. What you can store where, in what and for how long. Miracles of Tutankhamen's tomb. What you wear with jade and pearls.

.

ANOTHER CHRISTMAS

Michelle marries. Mother sends me a clipping from the paper, *Central News and Views.* An announcement and paragraph of a shower her mother gave. Finger sandwiches, pastel mints, assorted nuts. There is nothing I can send Mikki but good wishes and a pot for tears. Who is Barton Francis Roberts III? Mikki's western friend? A few days after New Year's mother sends another clipping. Mikki on the front page of the *News and Views.* New Mother and Baby of the Year. Five hundred dollars in prizes. Mikki has a ribbon in her hair, a smile like Mona Lisa's sister. Her picture tells me nothing a stranger wouldn't know.

A year later, her mother sees my mother in the beauty shop. They each have standings. Mikki and Rob have moved to Texas. They are building a lovely home. Something on the order of Tara. They have horses, a pool.

They have another child. Someone sends me a clipping. Is it Mother? There is no note. The postmark is smeared.

My husband wins awards, frames and hangs them in the den. Soon he has the whole wall. He works nights, holidays, weekends. He is brilliant in design, grows a mustache, sings country/western in the shower.

What do you do, people ask at parties. I tell them I am an astronomer, a conchologist, a doctor, a lawyer, a princess, a tax collector and thief. They say how wonderfully talented you are. I do so many things well. My, we are a wonderful team. They haven't heard a word I said.

My husband plays the guitar, sings "The Wreck of the Edmund Fitzgerald." Everyone applauds. He hands me the case to carry. I bow. Thank you very much, I play better, but only at home.

In a class at the Y, I find a wheel, learn to spin. It takes me a year to center. I throw and throw, develop glazes, show my work. The rest of the time, I am my husband's wife, president of the PTA, carpool queen and Bear Cubs mother. Isn't this what you wanted, he says. All hours, wheels in my head turn the clay into forms.

One day Mikki calls. I'm here, she says. I'm in town. I'm coming to see you. I give her directions. Past the Golden Arches, the Kentucky Fried, the Innerbelt, the cemetery, the brick breezeway and lighted lanterns and third box on the left. We laugh and laugh. She sounds the same. I'm into clay, I tell her. She screams, I'm into fibers. You ought to see my work. It's good.

It's different. I think it will sell. I wait with the coffeepot and hot brownies, clean hands and house. Mikki never comes. Did I dream her voice? Fibers? I told you, my husband says. She's always been like that. Unpredictable. Unstable. What did you ever see in her? What kind of friend is she?

DOWN ON THE FARM

We buy some land, with house and barn, pastures, fences, sheep, cows, chickens and two large dogs. My husband wants to paint his greatest thing. He needs quiet. I take the children to school fifteen miles away, become the long-distance carpool queen, shop the six stores in town, buy little, have sodas in a bitter-smelling, marble-cool drugstore. I see myself in the mirror behind the counter. My face above the oranges, limes, bananas waiting to be used, my dark eyes. I ask if anyone is in there. One eye waters and cries.

The sheep die, cows break fences, eat corn, wander away. Pigs get big and hard to discipline. The barn falls, fences sprawl, drag their wire bellies. There is a drought and our crops burn, savings melt. We have great green thunderstorms with lightning that zips open the sky, rains hard balls of hail. The roof leaks and we sleep in ruin until a panel truck ruts up the rocky drive. The roofer is a naked man in boots. He has an even tan, only works in good weather. I like his voice, his wide shoulders, his quick and fun hands. He whistles down the chimney, adjusts the gutters, smooths the hearth.

My husband paints. He paints an apple, a chicken, and finally a nude. Our neighbor poses. Her hair is long and blond and thin. It brushes her buttocks like a hand. She stands on a crop of far rocks in the pasture. My husband gets excited. Did you ever see such skin? The way the light reflects? He sits by the pond for water. I braid cattails by the creek, wade, pick wildflowers and watch. The work gets in a show and everyone asks did you pose? Of course, I answer. See my long blond hair, my lovely skin. He never asked. The artist's wife is always last. I am plain and brown, dusty as a wren. A mother mouse with her tail snapped in a trap.

Clay is all I know. I make flat things into something that holds and waits empty to hold again.

I TAKE A SATURDAY OFF

The kiln is emptied and cool. My wheel wiped clean as an after-dinner platter. The pots sit in rows on shelves of hope. All day Catherine and I lie in a field of red clover. The air is all lavender and thick honey. I could eat it and fly. We count birds, began the count that morning with a pair of pileated woodpeckers. We write them down. Bluebirds, flickers, red-eyed vireos, kingbirds, doves. A red-tailed hawk. This is a dangerous sport, she says. Her binoculars are black and heavy against my chest. Field larks. She points, holds my eyes with her hand. Nine, she whispers. Last year we counted an even dozen in this spot. I watch the brown arrows dart and fan in the blue. I have never felt so happy. Alive in every humming cell. The top of my head feels electric. If I reached out my hand, touched Cath, we'd both be illuminated. She stands, reaches down for me. We have to go now, she says. We have hungry husbands and children waiting. I never want to go but take her cool hand that still smells of fresh water where we swam in the creek, of willow and wet fern.

Did you have fun, my husband asks? Tweet, tweet. He has built a rock wall, piled stone upon stone upon stone. All the ones I liked best where they were. I knew them there. Now there are pock marks in the pasture, gaps in my daily walk. How dare he? How could he?

Someone had to stop the erosion, he shrugs. What is one wall against a mile? He is the Dutch boy with his finger in the dike. The whole damn wall.

MICHELLE AGAIN

It's me, she calls, I'm coming out. This time she does. All in black, like a widow, mourning. She wears a sheer black dress with sweeping balloon sleeves; long black gloves, a large black braided hat. Her hair is up and hidden. Her face opaque as a cloud, and her eyes are gray and full of hurt. She is all silver and black and sad. I got the children, she says. That's all. Would you believe? His boss's wife. I believe. She hooks her arm around my husband's waist. Tell me, she coos, are all artists sexy? She bats her eyes, pale lashes and transparent lids. Would you want to paint me nude she asks? Want a mortgage, I seethe. I know where there's a big one. It goes with him.

After she leaves, he says she is not his type. Too clingy, too much heavy perfume. Magnolia, I say, tons of magnolia. Oh, Mikki, how could you?

In my potting shed, I turn and turn. The clay is me. Raku and sawdust, fire and water. I glaze and etch, sand and salt and fire. The kids complain. You never cook. I burn and bake with life. Sometimes when I tuck them in, my hands are dry and rough. There is mud under my nails. They don't like the smell. It is all I have. I am the clay.

She is different this time. She is copper and red. Her nose is tipped, her smile recapped, she has diamonds in her eyes, on her hands, at her throat. William is in stocks. She met William at a Parents Without Partners meeting. Only William isn't a parent. Don't tell anyone, she cautions. He came to meet people and guess who he found? Tra-la . . . little ole me, she sings. Across the smoky room. William is so rich. He buys me everything. A condo, a car . . . a white MG. We're learning to fly, she says. Now he wants a plane.

What about your weaving, I ask. Who has time? She blows smoke at the ceiling. It is so dusty and full of lint and lonely. She wants a farm like ours. All the joys and charm of country life. But William won't live on a farm she says. Not in a thousand years, he only needs the write-off. You got the bright idea, my husband says.

The farm they buy is in the next county. Mikki says it has sixty cows, but not the milking kind. How do you know? William asks. He looks deep into her eyes. Mikki can't believe him. Isn't he cute? She says he is a prince. A man in his prime. He writes poetry. Brings her a poem a day with a vitamin like a rose. She can't believe he is real. He is everything she always wanted. Everything. She does not look at me when she says this. After she leaves, I look around. The poor farm, my husband with his paints, my filled potting shed . . . and God knows the kids. Who is kidding whom?

I GO ON THE ROAD WITH A GREEN CHAIR

The beanbag chair wears my husband's hat. Dumb, he says. But I am afraid to travel three hundred miles alone. I need a male companion. The green chair beside me has a thick neck, wears a pulled-down black felt hat. Little old man. Quiet fellow. I leave at 5:00 a.m. in the dark. A van chases me fifty miles through dense forest. All my doors are locked, the gas tank full, no one else on the road. I speed, hope for a ticket, listen for sirens, finally lose the van. The beanbag chair slumps to the dash. I stop in a city for breakfast, cut my hand on a map, leave bloody prints, a trail for whoever has to look when I am kidnapped, raped, and killed. All day I sell my work. I can't price and wrap pots fast enough. That night I stay with friends. You work too hard, they say. Come have fun with us. I call home. Are you painting, I ask? It's too quiet, he says, come home. At the end of the week, I limp ragged home, rip off my ERA for Everyone sticker, and fall in the door. He wants to have fun, go out to eat and dance, drink wine, make love. I want to sleep and sleep and sleep. At least a hundred years. At least until the true prince wakes me up and someone has cleaned out the kingdom. The Augean world of the house.

My husband has learned to cook. He can read packages, measure, time, and taste. He can wash and dry, but not fold or find homes for the mingled crowd of clothes that hovers in the laundry room door. He has watered my plants and each one greets me like a favorite child.

The children have gone to live with friends. They never plan to return. They are sixteen and mature. Who needs adults? They have jobs, cars, school, friends. They have tennis and music, disco and pinball.

In my pottery shed, I throw mud against the world that never stops. It turns like time, a spinning clock that wears my face.

My husband's work does not sell. He says no one knows what great art really is. He refuses to paint birds or flowers, wildlife or friends. He hates buckets and wagons, old barns, wants to paint his message to the world, repent at leisure.

A piece of my pottery is accepted in a museum show. Porcelain pears in a lattice basket. They display it under glass. My husband asks, are you proud of that? That? Yes. It's an original. It's beautiful and I made it. He walks away. Ha. A museum guard stares. Are you the artist? Yes, I answer. The word seeks my husband, finds and taps him on the shoulder. He turns around. Come on, he says, let's get out of here.

He paints a weathered board with rusty nails and insect writing. It looks real, I tell him, really nice, really good. Behind the wood and through a hole, he paints his eye. A blue vision. Do you realize that is your eye? It is your self-portrait. Call it *Self-Portrait of the Artist as an I*. He makes an ugly noise in his nose. I make a pot with the same name and nose, mustache and glasses. It sells to a collector and I pay the current bills. My husband never asks when the money comes, where it goes. Bills come to stay like aged relatives, grow cantankerous and ill, but never die.

He has another show. I help him pack and price and hang. I play good hostess with the cups of punch and good cheer. I circulate at the opening event. Isn't he great, people ask and reach for another glass. I know you are so proud. They say all the right things, but don't buy his work. One day he takes his books, mustache cup, guitar, and leaves. At first I hear strange noises. The house seems large and I am Alice who drank the wrong bottle. Then I learn to play the radio loud, dance by myself in all the places I never knew before.

Mikki calls. I'm here, she yells. It's me. It's Mikki. I'll be out to see you. She drives a small red car, the dogs wag and lick the sweet air around her. She is slender gold and silver. She brings mock oranges in a basket. Aren't they marvelous? She holds one to her nose, juggles others in her arms. There's nothing like them in the world. She heaps them high in my largest blue pottery bowl. The room is alive with citrus smell.

Remember the cat? Mikki says. Sadie the cat? I thought you died. I hug Mikki. Her bones are sharp as saws and she feels light as knitting. I did, she laughs, O God, I did. I died. She says she has been through hell and home. William left. His secretary,—she rolls her green eyes. That old cliché. I should have known. The least suspected. Five psychiatrists pulled me through.

Why didn't you call? I ask. I couldn't talk, she says. All I did was cry. Not Mikki. I'm glad she didn't call. I wouldn't want to know, to see, to hear. Not Mikki.

But I won, she says. I won. You should have seen me on the stand. I was the perfect little wounded wife. The cast-aside waif. The judge held my hand, cheered me up. O that judge was great. And I got the condo, the car, five thou a month for the rest of my life . . . and—she screams—I got the farm. All that grass and crazy cows and house and barn are mine. He fought like a fish, a big, big fish, but I won.

I pour red wine into new goblets still warm from the kiln. Their glaze is smooth as Mikki's skin. We finish the bottle and another, talk silly, then serious. We compare battle scars, wounds from war. Mikki lost her breasts, I my uterus. The crocheted scar is pink from my crotch to my waist. What a waste, we lament and laugh. Then march like veterans in a no day parade. Mikki, I open my arms, welcome home. Her eyes are the same. Sadie the cat. O Sadie the cat.

RUTH MOOSE

Umbrella

The dripping faucet was the beginning of the end for me and Robert. It was loud, like a heartbeat, falling right over the one brown rusty stain that Robert claimed to have given up scrubbing after deciding it was not dirt but age, and therefore "classic" in some way. Classic, like Keats or eggshell white tea saucers.

I thought the stain looked kind of like Mickey Mouse. Whenever I asked Robert what he thought, as I stood flossing and he was in the shower meticulously scrubbing, there would be a long pause before he asked if he could PLEASE have some privacy. Robert is the kind of person who talks in capital letters.

It's not something you can explain: You just hear it. Once I was outside, I'd always hear him turn off the water and get out and dry before starting to scrub that stain again, muttering to himself in lowercase. It was this neatness that drew me to him in the first place. It was somehow sexy, the way ankles can be sexy. Some part of me craved a man who folded the toothpaste from the bottom and scrubbed the blinds one by one on alternate Sundays.

I myself come from a long line of slobs. My mother was the type to walk through a room with a dustcloth, slapping it around halfheartedly as if she could just scare the dirt into retreating. Our living room consisted of not so much furniture as piles: books, magazines, firewood, odds and ends to be fixed or used someday. Everything we owned was secondhand and barely working, kind of like my father, who had not been granted tenure and taught Shakespeare in night school. On weekends, he and my mother took us to the flea market, and we'd bring home more treasures to be stepped over the next time we passed through the living room.

The first time I brought Robert home to meet my parents, I wondered if I should sedate him. The first thing we saw when we pulled up were the numerous old fans piled on the front porch: standing fans, ceiling fans, box fans. Inside, it was incredibly hot. The air didn't move as my father asked Robert about his work and my mother smoked and kept trying to catch my eye to wink at me. I could see Robert was sweating, the collar of his blue oxford turning darker and darker as he kept shifting his arms, worried, I knew, about pit stains. And thinking, all along, what about all those fans. What about those fans.

"None of them work," I explained on the way home, with the air conditioner blasting. "Nothing works. Nothing."

To him, it was madness. And from then on, I could only see my parents and my old life through Robert's eyes. But one day, I just didn't recognize myself anymore.

It wasn't just the faucet. It was the way my magazines were fanned out with a neat half-inch between them on my glass coffee table, which was an exact parallel to my couch, which was a perfect two feet from the wall, which was precisely seven paces from the bathroom door, which was two strides from the dripping faucet, which seemed to get louder and more insistent every day I did these calculations, listening: plink, plink, plink.

Then, one day on my way home, I saw the flea market. I recognized it at first glance: the rows of tables, vendors sitting in lawn chairs, the light glittering off stacks of chipped glass plates and ceramic ashtrays from Mexico City and Niagara Falls. Minutes later I found myself walking across the blacktop to a woman selling teapots and old 45s. I picked up an umbrella, the folding kind with a button you push to spring it open, turning it in my hands.

"Does this work?" I asked her.

She smiled. "Sure," she said, as if we were striking a bargain. "Sure it does."

I bought it. And I went back each day, somehow pulled there, my heart beating faster as if I were sneaking off to meet a lover in a hotel on the bad side of town. I wore my sunglasses and looked at no one as I picked through old Frank Sinatra eight-tracks and dimpled green glass tumblers. I'd take my purchases home and put them around the house, daring Robert to find them.

"What is this?" he said one day, referring to a laughing cow ceramic creamer I'd gotten for 50 cents.

"It's a creamer," I told him. Then, I'd felt like a surly adolescent, daring him to catch me. Now I was surprised at how nervous I was. "You put cream in it."

"I KNOW that," he said. He was looking at the cow as if it had insulted his mother. "What is it DOING here?"

"I bought it," I said. "I liked it."

"We have a creamer," he said. "I bought it at Pottery Barn."

I knew that. It was blue porcelain and matched the coffee pot and the butter dish. It was CLASSIC. "I liked it," I said again. He took it back in the kitchen, burying it behind the wok and the ice cream maker. At night, when I couldn't sleep, I'd imagine it back there in the dark. Smiling.

I think I knew he would leave then. I knew it even before I upped my trips to the flea market, coming home with something new every day: a snow globe of New York, a toy metal double-decker bus that rattled when Robert kicked it across the floor. But I was happy. For once, I could look around the house and see something of myself in all the right angles and dustless corners.

The music box was the last straw. It was old and dirty, with a tiny ballerina that spun when you lifted the lid. Someone, probably a previous owner's older brother, had snipped her tutu very short and painted her head with magic marker. But I could see she had once been beautiful.

Robert didn't say anything at first. He just lifted the lid and watched her wobble around in a circle as "Thank Heaven for Little Girls" played off-key.

"Emily," he said, letting the lid drop, mid-twirl, "what are you DOING to us?"

I didn't know what to tell him. The truth was I had let Robert come in and make hospital corners of my life, but now I wanted to kick the covers back and let my feet dangle loose. And as I realized this, the faucet kept dripping down on that classic stain, plink plink plink, ignored by both of us, like the beating of my heart.

When Robert moved out he took everything, but I didn't care. I put my smiling cow in the empty cupboard, right up front, and left the door open so I could see it.

A few days later it was raining, and as I reached into the hall closet I found the one folding umbrella I'd bought at the flea market my first day. By the time I got out on the street it was pouring, people rushing by with newspapers over their heads, trying to shake off the water. The wind was blowing hard as I undid the tie of my umbrella, shook out the folds and put my finger on the button.

It started to open, sliding up the handle, but then something else happened: It kept going, past the point it should have, opening wide and shooting through the air like some strange bird, flapping and rising as it caught a gust of breeze. People all along the block stopped, lifting their chins and staring with me as it drifted upward, spinning, flying above us to move over the street and into the sky.

PETER TURCHI

The Night Sky

Rodney shifted the heavy wooden console a few inches each night, hoping the hotel manager wouldn't notice the newly revealed depression in the commercial-grade carpet. By the end of the week he could comfortably stand at the far left-hand side of the desk—actually a long laminated counter—and see the entire picture without distortion. He stood there now, watching the final minutes of a National Basketball Association playoff game.

Having decided to drop out of college at least until the fall, he had taken the night clerk job with the expectation that he would witness clandestine, even exotic behavior. At first he imagined every lone late-night arrival to be a criminal one step ahead of the law, every couple to be engaging in strenuous, costumed intercourse. Occasionally a couple checked in whom he was sure were having an affair—local address, no bags, more excited than weary—but the unresolved mysteries of the hotel's guests soon gave way to the tedium of long, quiet hours. On a typical night he watched television until 12:30, then read a paperback until the sun beamed over the forested mountains beyond the opthamologist's office across the street.

Rodney had briefly considered the circumstances of a woman who had been staying on the second floor for nearly two weeks. She gave a local address, and one of the maids said her room was empty except for toiletries, a few clothes, and some papers, but there was no sign of a man—or, for that matter, another woman. Rodney saw her blue sedan enter the parking lot every night between midnight and one, always from the west, not from the highway exit. She appeared to be in her sixties, and her body was heavily rounded in a way that made it difficult for Rodney to stay interested in her secret, whatever it was. From the way she walked, it seemed she meant to climb the stairs, unlock the door, and collapse onto the bed.

Elizabeth did not collapse but sat on the edge of her bed, ignoring two upholstered chairs flanking the small circular table centered under a hanging lamp. In two weeks the bed had become hers, the way this room had become hers; while she hadn't moved the furniture, or taken down the undistinguished landscape print of the surrounding mountains, she felt as intensely identified by this room as by any room she had ever lived in. Her feet ached, but she did not remove her shoes. Instead she took off her glasses, setting them on the bed beside her, and cupped her face in her hands. Even this room, lit by a single fixture just outside the bathroom door, was too bright, and too large; only by pressing her hands over her forehead and eyes could she contain the world long enough to concentrate.

Though the effect was lessening, every night the opening of the hotel room door filled her with as much guilt as any illicit lover ever felt; she thought of Terry's affair, his childish, stereotypical midlife boyhood—though she wasn't convinced he had felt any guilt before she confronted him. They hadn't talked about when he had felt guilty. She knew enough, and Terry said enough. Only recently had she wondered if it would have been better to have talked it all through. In the years since, there had been a terrible vulnerability in their marriage, as if someone had let a poisonous snake loose in the house. For months you might forget about it, but one day, in the laundry room, you would catch a glimpse of mottled coils, or you would remember how, when you first moved here, there had been mice.

Given any opportunity, Terry would have discussed it. He believed in talking through every problem, every disagreement. Silence frustrated him. She knew how badly he wanted to explain it all, to tell her why he had gotten involved with his other woman, why he would never do it again—and, since telling her everything would relieve him, she would not let him talk. Take it with you to your grave, she remembered thinking. The memory made her shoulders knot, her forehead tighten. She had been embarrassed and ashamed, having fallen for his lies and excuses, refusing to believe that all the situational clichés of movies and television were coming true.

What she was doing now was no cliché. She had never heard of anyone doing it before. She imagined she knew how it felt to be a bad soldier: one who believed in the cause, but who nevertheless ran from battle. To add to

PETER TURCHI

her shame, her guilt and cowardice, Terry was quick to tell everyone that he had asked her to stay here. To lie was his idea.

They had known he was sick; two years ago the doctors hadn't been able to remove all of the cancer. Last month, when the dogwoods and tulips were blooming, they learned the inevitable had grown closer. "The situation," Dr. Foote told her, was worse. They could try the chemotherapy again, but at best it would slow the disease's progress. Rachel, who missed two classes to be there, had put one strong arm around her. Anticipating the worst, Elizabeth thought she might slump heavily, but when the news came she felt strangely buoyant; it was as if someone had just told her that the earth was inside out. As if she had stepped into a marsh and found herself peacefully suspended. Then discovered she was not quite able to walk, not able to swim.

Terry refused the chemotherapy. "I want to go out hairy," he said, trying to cheer them up. "I want apple pie and cheesecake—I want a goddamned prime rib." They talked of travel: Hawaii, Southern France, Australia, or back to Scotland, where they had spent the summer over a decade ago. "Antarctica," he proposed. "Just to see a circle of those male emperor penguins holding eggs on their feet." In a serious moment, he admitted he didn't want to be far from home.

"I could take incompletes," Rachel told him. She was in her junior year at the state university in the city, majoring in education and theater, playing varsity volleyball. "No need," Terry said. "But if you'd like to come around for dinner more often, I think we could find an extra plate."

So that's how he's going to be, Elizabeth thought. Stoic. He had succumbed to weakness the first time; the radiation and chemo had made him miserable. He was embarrassed about having been such a bad—scared, needy—patient. Bob Martin, one of her colleagues in the math department, had given her a quotation about "the kingdom of the sick." It ended: "Sooner or later each of us is obliged, at least for a spell, to identify ourselves as citizens of that other place."

Those first nights after Dr. Foote quietly estimated two months, six at the outside, they stayed awake together to consider and reject traveling plans, meals he would enjoy while he was still hungry, movies he wanted to see, friends and family who should visit. Then Terry began to return to routine. He watched the day's sports summary at eleven, attended to his teeth—first flossing, then brushing, then massaging his gums with a special small-bristled brush the dentist had prescribed—then read around in a magazine or a book until it fell on his chest. She would prod him awake; he would set the book on the floor, turn off his bedside light, and roll onto his side. He offered a single kiss, scented with the faint remains of aftershave or, more often now that the weather was warmer, sour perspiration.

Elizabeth could not sleep. After dinner she busied herself with the dishes and cleaning, then they would take a walk. She taught trigonometry and geometry at one of the county high schools, and there was grading to do. Her department was one of four statewide participating in a three-year study of the effective teaching of national standards, so two or three times a week she was obliged to log on to a computer bulletin board and correspond with other participants in the study. When she couldn't concentrate on that, she went back down to the living room. Some nights they played backgammon; others they watched television, or a movie. When the sports came on, she got ready for bed, and when Terry came to the bedroom, she pretended to read, or to sleep.

A woman at the hospital had given her information on counseling for family members of patients with terminal illnesses. This is what they would talk about, she thought: gathering important papers, evaluating your financial situation, learning how to take on new responsibilities. Elizabeth paid their bills and balanced the checkbook, and they made decisions about investments together. When Rachel was born, Terry insisted on buying what Elizabeth argued was far too much life insurance; when the policy arrived, he pretended to read from the envelope: "You May Have Won a Million Dollars." She wasn't scared about money. She worried about being alone, and her worry surfaced in absurd details. He did things to the cars and lawn mower, things she had never bothered to ask about, and now it was unthinkable. In the yard, he pruned what needed to be pruned, thinned what needed to be thinned, watered and fertilized with results such that friends were always asking him for advice. He knew how the Christmas decorations were most efficiently packed in the storage space under the stairwell, he knew what colors of stain they had used on the house and trim three years ago, he knew how to program the VCR. All things she could learn. Things she dreaded having to learn.

What haunted her most was his physical presence: his thin, graying hair, his crooked teeth, the mole on his neck. Even the faded paisley pajama bottoms seemed a part of his body. He breathed through his mouth, but when his allergies were bad or he slept on his back, he snored loudly. He had an office worker's paunch, a flabby belly with an appendectomy scar. At one time or another she had had nearly every inch of his skin in her hands,

PETER TURCHI

on her tongue. The memory of those moments of intimacy most terrified her now as he lay beside her, large as life. There was something the boys at school were saying this spring, one of those momentarily popular all-occasion expressions: Dead meat. It could be used as a threat (You touch me again and you're dead meat) or an expression of resignation (As soon as I saw the first problem, I was dead meat). Like a bee at a picnic, the phrase buzzed behind and beside and around every thought. She hated the way Terry looked when he slept.

In the middle of honors geometry one morning, she paused, exhaustion passed over her, and she suddenly had no idea what she had been saying. Angela, one of the eager front-row girls, offered politely, "You were reminding us about the theorems."

What theorems? Elizabeth thought. What class is this? The moment, horrifying, stretched on. She thought she would have to leave the room.

"I'm very sorry," she said. "I seem to have lost my train of thought." Aaron, an exemplary student, suggested with great diplomacy that she had been referring to their work with triangles and cones in the fall to demonstrate the relationship of analytic geometry to demonstrative geometry. "Thank you" she said, genuinely grateful, and went on.

The next day she sat in her room during her free period meaning to write comments for the awards ceremony, only to be awakened by her fourth-period class.

That weekend she told Terry, "I have something horrible to confess." He had been describing his plan to kill all the grass on the slope down to the driveway and create a new flower bed. He looked up from his drawing.

"I don't think," she began, then realized what she had been about to say. I don't think I can sleep beside you again. "I haven't been sleeping well," she said.

"I know this is ungentlemanly," he told her, "but you've looked absolutely exhausted. I thought it was end-of-the-year overload." He must have known, but he wouldn't say it.

She didn't want to cry. She was so tired. "Maybe it is," she allowed.

Terry suggested, "Why don't I sleep in Rachel's room tonight?"

"No." She spoke more loudly than she intended. She wanted to tell him, Stop being so generous.

She said, "You should have the big bed. I thought I'd try Rachel's, just until I catch up on my rest. I don't think I told you, but Friday I actually dozed off at my desk." She hadn't meant to tell him now.

"Have I been snoring?"

"No more than usual. I really think it's me."

Terry smiled at her across the dining room table. "I'll miss you. But whatever, sure. Get a good night's rest." He picked up a catalogue. "I'm thinking about making this border heaths and heathers, and they're not going to have a chance in the clay we've got here. With the retaining wall, we'll essentially create a huge planter. The summer heat might be too much for them, but they shouldn't get any afternoon sun if this works out . . ."

Rachel's room offered no comfort. The past accumulated on Elizabeth's chest the way she imagined it would if she were the one dying. Meeting Terry at school, that first awful date, the wonderful Indian dinner, seeing Casablanca in that horrible-smelling theater, his clumsy proposal, her mistake with the wedding invitations, first jobs, trying not to get pregnant, then trying to, losing the first two, finally getting all the way through with Rachel . . . why was she the one feeling this way, as if the door to the past was about to be shut tight, locked, sealed off? Why was she the one who felt she was suffocating, being drawn toward an unavoidable horror? Laying in her daughter's bed tortured her; she was the child, the one who couldn't understand, couldn't accept the simple fact. Was Rachel thinking these things? Rachel had forgiven Terry the affair; did that somehow make it easier for her to accept this? Elizabeth pictured the three of them as an isosceles triangle, then realized the sides should be uneven. Were Rachel and Terry closer to each other than she was to either of them, or was Terry the distant point? She pictured triangles turning like images on her computer monitor, turning in space but also distorted by time. She imagined three triangles, one to represent the way each of them saw their family—or was it that she saw it three different ways? She saw the triangles overlaid, imagined her parents, Terry's, the other woman, Rachel's roommate and boyfriend, the two children she had lost—all points on a star, then distinct stars, some bright, some faint. She tried to count them all.

She awoke without having slept. Her head ached, her body was sore. Sunlight pierced the curtains, glaring over Rachel's high school memorabilia. She smelled coffee, which Terry no longer drank, so must have brewed for her. Lying in her daughter's bed, she thought, I want someone to take care of me. Repulsed by her selfishness, she rose to shower.

"I've been feeling guilty," Terry announced. Sitting on the edge of the jetted tub, he handed her a warm cup when she finished drying off. With the word guilty, the snake dropped into view. He continued, "I'm guessing these new beds, hardscaping, plants, mulch, the whole nine yards, will run two thousand dollars."

PETER TURCHI

In this room, the trees in front of the house filtered the sunlight. Despite the coffee, Elizabeth felt a chill. "Beds plural?"

"Still that one area, but I'm thinking it needs some steps." Squinting, she saw he was cleaning her glasses for her. He held them out. "I could be talked out of that. Anyway, my argument is that it's still a lot cheaper than the chemo. Or a trip to the Loire Valley. However you want to think of it."

Vision corrected, she glanced into the mirror expecting to see bags under her eyes. Craving sleep, she drank coffee.

"You know," she told Terry, "it's fine with me. Whatever you want to do." She headed toward the closet, leaving him on the side of the tub.

"If you're serious" he called after her, "I'm going to call some people, get some estimates on the labor."

The walk-in closet allowed just one person to stand between the lines of clothes, shoes regimented below, sweaters stacked on the head-high shelf. She put her hand out, comforted by the cloth all around. She should put a pillow down in here.

When she came out he was sitting on the end of the bed. Their room, like Rachel's, got the morning sun. The light angled across Terry so that his outline, particularly his head, seemed to glow. He was already gone.

"Sleep any better?"

"It helped." She pulled on a sweatshirt, fighting off the chill.

"You," he said, "are a rotten liar."

But you've always been such a good one, she thought.

When that night was no different—she last checked Rachel's clock, a wall-mounted Elvis Presley whose hips shifted with each tick and tock, at 3:45, but doubted she drifted off before 4:30—she nearly wept from exhaustion. Now the phrase that repeated itself was a throbbing I'm so tired, so tired. It reminded her of a Beatles song, but she couldn't recall the rest of the lyric. The thought of going to school the next morning was nearly unbearable.

"Maybe I should try a hotel," she suggested at lunch, trying to sound facetious. She made chicken salad sandwiches. She was starving; she had no appetite. Her body didn't know what it wanted. Sleep.

"You don't feel sick?" Terry asked. "You aren't being a martyr?"

"I feel all right," she said, carrying the sandwiches through the sliding glass door to the patio. "I'm just—"

She couldn't stop; tears pooled in her eyes. "I'm so tired!" She sat heavily on one of the comfortless wrought-iron chairs, one of Terry's choices. They looked like something in one of the fine homes magazines, but she had never liked them. Now she thought, I shouldn't have to sit in this hard chair.

That night, after the awkwardness of checking in, certain even the desk clerk knew what she was avoiding, she turned on the television for distraction, lay down, and woke with the alarm she almost hadn't bothered to set.

Rachel moved back home. There was only a week left in the semester, followed by final exams. She was glad for the excuse to have more time near her father, but worried about her mother. Even when she was rested, Elizabeth carried a hint of desperation around the edges, a woman on the verge. She devoted herself to her work at school, staying late as extracurricular projects met their end, had the members of the math team over for their annual dinner. They finished third in the state this year.

Rachel had a lifeguarding job for the summer, her ongoing gig at the country club pool. The pay was good—lifeguards were in high demand these days, she had turned down a dozen jobs—but she wondered if she shouldn't be doing something more career-oriented by now. She thought about applying for a position as summer school tutor, but the idea of staying indoors all day was too dreary. Maybe next year.

She immediately understood her father's plans for the hillside.

"We can put the heathers in this fall," he said, handing her the plant list, "but most of the perennials should wait until spring. Not the daylilies, or the peonies. But the butterfly weed and echinacea and liatris. I'd rather let the beds settle over the winter." He had bought a planning kit which included a large green cardboard grid, the surface treated so it could be written on with a wax pencil. The kit also included dozens of stickers, green branches on smaller and larger circles meant to represent plants. Terry, who had been a design engineer for a tool company, had carefully measured off the length and curve of the hillside and transcribed it here, to scale.

"What are these big ones?" she asked, pointing to the largest circles, each penciled with a number 7.

"Dogwoods. I was thinking two white, one pink." He had gone back and forth over the steps. In the current plan, they didn't appear.

"I'll have to label all these," he admitted. "I've got names and numbers there on the list, but it's a mess. I'll mark which come from which catalogues. Most of them you should be able to get around here."

He wasn't deceiving himself; he knew he wouldn't see the work finished. That's why Rachel decided she would spend the summer helping. It was impossible for her to think of preparing the ground without picturing his grave being dug, but she liked the idea that, instead of a tombstone, he would have this: not just the yard, with the footbridge he had built over the creek that rarely ran, and the hemlocks and sugar maples he had planted when he and her mother built the house, but this last creation, his attempt not at immortality—plants had their cycles, in a dozen or fifteen years the heathers would be spent—but at life transferred.

As Terry had feared, the best landscapers were booked at least until August. Rachel suggested that he hire strong arms and backs; as long as he supervised, they didn't need experienced help. Reynolds, a biology major she had been seeing, and his friend Christian had intended to spend the summer traveling, but those plans were stalled by lack of funds. Soon she found herself impatient sitting high in the lifeguard chair, oiling herself hourly to ward off skin cancer, watching the swimmers all around her: children hoping she wouldn't see them running on wet cement, some pretending to drown, some straining to dunk each other, one or two people floating, and a few calmly treading water, making slow progress against the length of the pool. At six o'clock she could put shorts on over her suit; at home she would find Terry measuring, adjusting the strings tied to pegs across the slope, as Reynolds and Christian dug.

"The bottom course of timbers is the slowest," he reassured them as the young men sat, shirtless, drinking beer from bottles. "Once they go in level, we'll get the rest up in two days, three at the most."

"I need calluses," Reynolds told Rachel, showing her his hands. Blisters had formed and torn open.

"Doesn't that hurt?"

He held up the bottle. "I take one of these every hour."

They were all inspired by Terry's refusal to complain. Occasionally he would stop in the middle of leveling a spot, walk a few steps away, and slowly sit. Sometimes he looked down; sometimes he rested his forehead on his knees, so that the brim of his baseball cap tilted high, revealing arches of hair. Reynolds and Christian responded by continuing their work; when Rachel was there, if her father looked particularly drawn, she would walk over and sit behind him, put one leg on either side, and lean her chest against his back. Not today, she thought. Not yet.

On one of these occasions he must have read her mind. So softly she could barely hear, he said, "I'm not going anywhere."

She couldn't tell whether he was optimistic or resigned.

A moment later he raised his head. She stared at the back of his neck, the soft creases of flesh, the mole on his left side. He said, "I worry about your mother."

She nodded. Then said, "She's scared."

He didn't respond. At times like this, she believed her father had secrets. Other times she knew there was nothing as simple as a mystery, no dramatic revelation. She wanted him to tell her about his parents; his life, beginning with his earliest memory; everything he had aspired to, every possibility he had decided against. But that was too much; and there was no single thing she most wanted to know. She wanted what only he could tell her, the way he would tell it. She wanted him.

With his left hand, Terry covered her knee. Squeezed.

Elizabeth came home for dinner. From then until bedtime their schedule was the same as ever, except that she stayed dressed while he read, and when he finally dozed off, instead of prodding him, she sneaked away. That's how it felt.

"You don't have to wait," he told her one night. "Unless, of course, you want to see the baseball highlights."

Elizabeth said, "I want to be with you."

Come watch the dying man, Terry thought. His anger rose closer to the surface each day.

He said, "Maybe we should do something." True, his time felt precious. Even so, he liked baseball, had always liked baseball, the game without a clock, and reading the box scores didn't replace seeing the day's home runs and final outs.

"Let's sit outside," Elizabeth suggested. "It's beautiful out tonight."

He watched the Orioles' centerfielder disappoint Boston fans with a ninth-inning homer, then tapped the remote control. "Sure."

On the patio, Rachel had been about to turn on the floodlights when Elizabeth said, "Let's just look for a minute."

He looked at the worksite, where the first layers of timbers were finally straight and level. The boys were strong, but they didn't appreciate what dirt could do to a wall. If the rebar didn't extend deep into the ground, if the timbers weren't stepped slightly back, in a few years the pressure of the earth would push them forward. The boys had been impatient, but now the hardest work was finished.

Eyes adjusting to the dark, he looked at the curve of hemlocks around back, the rhododendron silhouette that concealed a mahogany bench. He had intended to sink a pond there, with lilies and cattails and fish. He looked up at the maples and oaks, the tulip poplar with its tall, crooked trunk. He had meant to cut that down. Poplars were fast-growing, weak, and this one was close to the house. But there had been a poplar in their yard when he was young, and so this one lived, protected by sentiment. Was that foolish? Was he being foolish again, dragging them all through this construction? How should he be spending this time? He intended to make lists for Elizabeth, reminding her what to do, explaining things he had done. Was this an act of ego? The world would go on without him.

A bat flitted by.

Elizabeth said, "There's the Big Dipper."

"Where?" Rachel asked.

Elizabeth pointed out the arced handle, the angled bowl. "Isn't there a way, once you've got the Dipper, to see the North Star?"

That jogged a memory. "Follow the handle?" he asked.

"Just two of them," Elizabeth corrected. The longer they looked, the more stars appeared, as if their very looking created dots of light. "But which ones?"

"Look north," Rachel said logically. But now there were countless stars visible, with no telling which was the benchmark of their sky.

They all slouched in their chairs, faces tilted back as if to receive the light of the sun, or a dentist's drill. Rachel asked, "How many constellations do you know?"

The sparks above them revealed no design. Terry turned his head, wondered if that reddish one was Mars.

"Well, the Little Dipper," Elizabeth said. "And Orion."

How many nights had he done this? How many times had he looked up without ever bothering to locate himself among the stars? He remembered the childhood diversion of sitting on a sofa or bed, tilting his head backwards over the edge, and imagining the world where he would walk on ceilings, step up to pass through doors, duck under tall furniture. He remembered the sound of his mother's old canister vacuum drawing closer, its yellow light shining as she threatened to suck up his hair. What could he have been? Five?

"Here's what we'll do," he told his wife and daughter. "We'll get a good book, and maybe a star chart, and we'll learn the constellations together."

The next evening, after Reynolds and Christian had finished their beers and the coals had grayed in the grill, Rachel arrived.

"Hey," she said from the bottom of the hill. "It's a wall."

The retaining wall, now two feet high and forty feet long, with angled ends anchoring it in the hill, was nearly finished. After laying the top row they would give all of the timbers a final coat of stain with the sprayer. He had bought locust, which wouldn't rot, but he wanted the extra protection.

"Do lifeguards eat tuna?" he called as she brought two plastic bags from the car.

"We aren't picky," she told him. "Around four o'clock I nearly ate a toddler."

He watched the boys watch his daughter follow the brick walkway to the patio. In cutoff shorts over her close-fitting swimsuit, strong legs leading to worn sneakers, her long brown hair pulled through the gap in back of a baseball cap, she looked like an advertisement for summer.

"I went hog wild." Rachel set her bags on the iron garden table and began pulling things out. "I found two computer programs on the solar system, a neat-looking old book by the guy who wrote Curious George—remember, about the monkey?—a glow-in-the-dark star chart, and another little book that tells you the names of everything."

Terry looked and read the title, A Guide to the Night Sky. "Everything but a telescope."

Reynolds said, "You know that camera shop in the mall? They sell binoculars and lenses. I bet they'd have them."

Rachel put her purchases back into their bags. "More beers?" she asked the boys.

Terry felt it coming, and when Rachel came back with three bottles, having already twisted off the caps, and sat casually, knees spread the way girls never spread their knees when he was young, the wave fell onto him. She would get married, have a house, children, job, a life so long that this day, if she could remember it, would be a faint moment in the distant past. He would be memories to her; to her children he would be photographs and occasional boring stories. Standing on the patio beside the stone wall he had built, surrounded by greenery he had planted, outside of the house he designed, he felt like a ghost. He would be forgotten the way fire forgets coal.

"I'll be back," he told them, both to remind them that he was there and to reassure himself. Sitting on the living room sofa, he gathered his strength, as he had to more and more often. He would not think this way. He would not yield to self-pity. As much as he wanted to talk about it all— the fatigue, the irrational hope, the betrayal of being eaten from the inside, the crush of regret—he would not. He would not ask Elizabeth for forgiveness, because now she had no choice but to forgive him. He would not pray, because his entire adult life he had been a non-believer. He would not ask why no one asked him what he was thinking. He had been genuinely relieved when Elizabeth suggested spending a night in Rachel's room; it was at night, after he worked to read himself to sleep, that his fate confronted him. Now he could curl on his side without worrying that Elizabeth would stop pretending to be asleep. She pretended during the day as well: she never mentioned that he stood less and less, moving from one seat to another, that he no longer reached for or held anything over his head, that his stride was shorter. He wanted to make love with her, but he refused to ask, because she could not refuse. And I heard a voice from heaven saying unto me, seal up those things which the seven thunders uttered, and write them not. This was his gift to them.

Terry had been right: Mars.

"Without a telescope," Rachel reported, "we should eventually be able to see all of the planets except Neptune, Uranus, and Pluto."

The three of them sat on the patio in the dark. Elizabeth had brought one of the captain's chairs from the den.

"As for constellations," Rachel continued, glancing at the dimly glowing star chart in her hand, "there's the Big Dipper. The pointers, on the outside, go up to Polaris. The handle and top of the Dipper are half of the spine of Ursa Major—the end of the handle would be the tail. And Polaris is the end of the handle of the Little Dipper."

"Slow down," Elizabeth said.

"Little Richard," Terry told her. "Right next to the Big Bopper."

"You see Polaris?" Rachel asked.

Elizabeth said, "I think so. That one?"

Rachel pointed. "That one."

"What's that other bright star, on the left?"

Terry told her, "That's the sun."

"Kochap," Rachel corrected. "The end of the Dipper. Now you should be able to connect them with those one, two . . ."

"I see it," Terry said. "Three stars in between, and another brightish on the far corner, for the bottom of the basket."

"Dipper," Elizabeth corrected. "Going that way." She drew a line in the air with her finger. "As if someone is pouring something out of the Little Dipper into the big one."

After installing the computer programs, Elizabeth had poked around in them. You could visit the planets, click so they slid into cutaway views, click them into orbit, animate Saturn's rings, learn the years Neptune was more distant from the sun than Pluto, and, disturbingly, see how the sun would eventually devour Venus, Mercury, and perhaps even Earth five billion or so years from now. With one click, the screen filled with the theoretical view from their longitude and latitude on this very day at this very moment. In a box in the lower right-hand corner, seconds ticked into minutes, minutes into hours. Time could be sped up, reversed, or stopped altogether. The sky could be viewed from Athens or Sydney, the globe could shift to put, say, Saturn front and center. With one click, stars were labeled; with another, the lines of the constellations were drawn; with yet another, elaborate drawings of mythological figures appeared. Three more clicks left the stars, dots of light on a monitor, alone.

"And that," Elizabeth said now, wishing the real sky were as bordered and orderly, "must be Cancer's southern claw." It was out before she thought.

"Where?" Terry asked.

She pointed it out.

Terry stared at the specks of light. Then said, "Well. No hard feelings."

The next night was overcast. H. A. Rey claimed, in his book, that coping with an obscured view was part of the challenge of learning the stars, but without the Big Dipper they were lost. Turning on one of the outside lights, Rachel read to them from A Guide to the Night Sky. "Listen to this: 'Many of the most recently recognized constellations have no stories attached to them. These include Antila, the air pump; Fornax, the furnace; Horologium, the clock; and Norma, the carpenter's square.' Did you guys know about these?" She continued, " 'However, the vast majority of the constellations, particularly those most easily perceived by the unaided eye, carry with them tales which reveal little about the heavens, but much about those fascinated by wondrous objects afar.' "

Listening to her daughter's voice, Elizabeth found unexpected comfort. She was rested now. Each night the hotel bed welcomed her, its sheets pulled tight, the room vacuumed, a fresh bar of soap recently released from its wrapper resting by the sink. She was almost ready. At first she had only wanted to tell someone how angry she was. One night, searching for relevant discussions on the Internet, she came across a group of people talking about friends and relatives who had died horribly: drunken driving, Russian roulette, a brain hemorrhage. She had thought that on the computer, anonymous, she would be able to talk openly, but instead she simply lurked. It was the right word for how she felt. She recognized expressions of grief and loss familiar from bad books and television; they struck her as unoriginal, insufficient, and true. As her daughter's voice continued like a song she wanted to hear again, Elizabeth reached out in the direction of her husband.

Rachel remembered some of these stories. Reading this book's condensed versions of myths was similar, she thought, to looking at the stars; each chapter seemed unnaturally abrupt, but if you knew the context, there was sense to it all. Tomorrow she would buy a telescope, a strong one, so they could see everything. Early this morning, before the pool opened, she and Reynolds had made love in the clubhouse. "He's so brave," she had told him, thinking of her father even then. Every day that summer, the title of her job mocked her. What could she do? The wall was finished, the planting diagram complete. Terry explained that few people grew heathers this far south, but at their elevation, if the drainage was improved, and the bed had plenty of peat moss, they should thrive. The red and orange perennials would draw hummingbirds, and butterflies. She asked questions, wanting to be able to finish what he had planned. What she couldn't ask him was, if her mother wouldn't sleep in the house now, what would she do once he was dead? Were they patronizing him, pretending they would keep this house, that they could keep what was his, without him to possess it?

Terry vaguely recognized a few of the stories of the constellations. What eluded him was the physics of the stars. Rachel had read them an article from the paper about an astronomer who claimed to have found another sun, a sun one million times brighter than Earth's, but so far away that it had never before been seen. How could that be? A million times brighter than the sun, and impossible to see.

He had always meant to read more of the classics. For half his life he had been aware of all the pursuits that would, in all likelihood, remain unpursued. And now, when he should feel free to take risks — go hang gliding, what's to lose? — he had dedicated his strength to self-control. He had thought at least he could stop the damned flossing every night, even brushing; but when he did, the next morning his teeth felt dirty. In some way he was grateful for the small irritation, the distraction.

Aaron, Elizabeth's best honors geometry student, was a textbook overachiever, preparing for tests by creating his own. In three years he would be accepted by both Harvard and Yale; in fifteen he would be a successful cardiovascular surgeon. Tonight he sat up in bed, eating orange slices, re-

reading Sir Thomas More's Utopia, occasionally pausing to make notes. He had amused himself by removing the orange's peel whole, then flattening it, which made him think map, and then Gerardus Mercator, the cartographer whose collection of maps was the first to be called Atlas.

Above their heads, beyond the trees, constant in a boundless night, the stars stood fixed by shapes they yearned to know. Cetus. Cepheus. Andromeda.

Slippered Feet

We tried to learn the language, Eva and I. We bought a book and tapes and three or four days a week a couple of months before the trip we listened and read and asked each other questions. We worked on increasing our vocabulary.

In the morning, for instance, at breakfast, Eva would say "Pass the milk, please," or rather simply "Milk," and then she would point to it and I would say "Here is the milk, Eva." And she would say "Thank you, Robert," and I would say "Think nothing of it."

Learning a new language at our age was a challenge, but it was also fun. It made us feel like kids again, studying together for the final exam. That's where we met, Eva and I, at college, back east, reading Chaucer on the steps in front of the library. But that was some time ago, more like history than any kind of real memory. We were both retired: Eva from teaching grammar school, me from management. I mean we had the time now, and so we tried to learn a new word every day.

At night after dinner we'd listen to the voice on tape and repeat after it. It was the same man, the same voice, night after night. We would drag our slippered feet into the living room, and with the tape player on the coffee table before us we would say what he said in just the way he said it. Or tried to: he gave us very little time to respond. There was only so much blank space before he went on to the next question or Useful Expression ("How much is this?" "How long before the next train arrives?") and only rarely was there a sufficient pause allowed, a *reasonable* pause allowed in which we could speak without stumbling. The tapes irritated me a little bit, but we did the best we could. We tried to learn one Useful Expression every evening.

There was progress, a notable progress with both of us. But women, I've heard, are naturals with this kind of thing, and Eva was no exception. She was always a few vocabulary words ahead of me. She had the better accent. She was a bit more keen on learning. Still, it surprised me, one night not long after we'd begun with these sessions, when Eva claimed to have actually dreamed the language. Said she dreamed in the words of the language.

I've never seen her so excited, telling me about it.

She was at breakfast in the dream, she told me, she was at breakfast downstairs in the morning room which was no different in the dream, she said, than it was in real life: there was the same small round maplewood table we sit at every morning, the same wicker chairs; the window framed a view of the same old patch of pine. Even the same squirrels were there, in her dream, the same squirrels I've threatened to maim and kill and eat with my hands on more occasions than I can remember. All this was the same, and Eva was speaking the language. She said "Pass the milk, please" and "Butter, please," and "Is there a way out of here?" —straight from the book, all of it, nothing special.

But the man she was speaking to wasn't me. I wasn't the man in her dream. The person she was speaking to, the person facing her on the other side of the table, was the man on the tape. Rather, it was to the voice of the man on the tape that was there; she couldn't actually see him, she said. All her questions were answered—the milk was passed, the butter, too—but by no one she could see in the dream. It was just his voice, the sound of his voice in her dream.

I didn't believe her, of course. Though I'd heard of this kind of thing happening before, I knew that there was no way she could have attained this level of—what? *linguistic intimacy*, I think they call it—in such a short time; I hadn't, at any rate, and we were both shooting par on this language thing. She wasn't that much better than me. What I thought was this, and I told her: I said she probably hadn't had the dream she thought she'd had. I said that she hadn't been studying the language long enough for her to have such a dream. What I did say is that it was quite possible that she had *dreamed* she dreamed the dream in the language—which is quite some difference.

Eva listened patiently, nodding when I made my main points, smiling. Then she kind of laughed.

"I think it's funny," she said, "that anyone would try to tell anyone else what they did and didn't dream. Granted, you sleep beside me, and we

DANIEL WALLACE

do spend almost every minute of our waking lives together, since you retired. And though you seem to have a knowledge superior to mine on most things, especially on those things you know nothing about, I must tell you, you cannot, and never will tell me what I did and what I did not dream. It's absurd."

Well, this surprised me, coming from Eva. Usually she dreams about flying through shopping malls on her father's back, or being outside in the front yard without any clothes on—harmless, meaningless dreams. I had never said anything about them before. But now I had, and I saw that she had a point: I should stay out of her mind while she was sleeping.

"You're absolutely correct, Eva," I said. "I had no right, I was out of line and I'm sorry."

But I still don't believe you, I thought.

If the inside of her head was private, so mine could be too.

" 'A garden spot,' " I read to Eva the next evening, " 'one of the very last on earth.' " This was from one of the many books we had purchased about the place. There was a picture of a group of black-haired children lapping up water from a stream. Behind them, in the distance, were the famous Kotomanzi forests, near the eastern ridge of the island country. I showed the picture to Eva, and she nodded, smiled.

"Nice," she said.

We never had or wanted children, but we have always enjoyed looking at pictures which have children in them.

" 'It is a country of hills, bridges and streams,' " I read, " 'where the past becomes present, and where the present remains fixed in the past.' What now?" I said. "What do you think *that* means?" I asked her. " 'Where the present remains fixed in the past?' That's impossible. That's impossible, isn't it? The present is *now*, the past is *then*. How can it be now and then at the same time?"

"It's a guide book, Robert."

"I know what it is," I said. "I know it's a guide book."

"Sometimes they exaggerate," she said.

"And lie," I said. "Sometimes they just flat-out lie. And it doesn't mention anything about the future. But I suppose the future is past as well. Or maybe it just never happens."

But Eva wasn't listening to me. This was after dinner, and she was fooling with the tape. Even though it was hardly past eight, she had changed into her nightgown and slippers—a habit of hers. I looked at her, trying to remember how beautiful she had been as a young woman—which was quite an exercise, I must say, for those days were a part of history now as well. She had been beautiful, of course, a great beauty, finely wrought, a porcelain, elegant beauty. But she had not aged as gracefully as I might have hoped, or, I'm sure, as she would have liked to. She had become old, painfully, obviously old. She had reached that age where every bit of her that wasn't made of bone began to fall away from her body, as if gravity were exerting a special pressure on it. Eva wasn't built to take such pressure: she was slender, and when she moved pieces of her shook, her arms and legs, and when she slept she looked dead—dead! In the middle of the night I've opened my eyes and thought, Here I am, sleeping with a dead woman! But it is just what the pillow has done to her soft face, and the way her mouth hangs open, and the general lifelessness of everything in the middle of the night.

She isn't dead, I think. She's my wife. We've been married for thirty-five years, and I love her.

Still, I wished she had turned out to look different.

I wish she had stayed pretty.

"Ready?" she said. "Tonight's lesson is on what to do in case of an emergency."

"Ready," I said, and she hit the Play button, and the man's voice filled the room.

Tonight, as he did every night, the man said the sentences much too fast. It was almost impossible to say "My wallet was stolen, can you help me?" before he proceeded with "I think I'm bleeding, call an ambulance." Eva didn't seem to be having as much trouble with him as I was: she was poised like a swimmer on a platform, ready to dive, except she was on the edge of the sofa, intent, listening, almost trembling she was so stiff.

Looking at her like this I completely forgot to listen to the next Useful Expression.

"Play that back," I said. "I didn't quite get that."

She glanced at me, I thought, with an expression of both amusement and irritation.

"With pleasure," she said.

So she rewound the tape, and the man said, "I have been wandering this road for three days. I need a glass of water."

I stared at the translation in our books.

"Stop the tape," I said.

"What?"

"Stop the tape, please, Eva. Now."

She sighed, and somewhat reluctantly hit the Off button.

"What is it Robert?" she said. "We only have a little more to go for tonight."

"Did you hear what he just said?" I asked her. "Did you hear what he wants us to learn? 'I have been wandering this road for three days. I need a glass of water.' Now, why in the world would we need to learn that? What kind of Useful Expression is that? 'Wandering this road for three days . . .' Who's going to be wandering a road? We're going to get a guide, for heaven's sakes."

"It's a primitive country in many ways," she said. "You can never tell what might happen. Their priests still perform magic. You read that, didn't you? The Prime Minister himself is a priest, Robert. What happens if our guide gets mixed up in some voodoo-like ritual and dies on a day trip? What happens if we have to fend for ourselves after that? Under the circumstances," she said, "I think it might be wise to memorize everything he says."

"Okay," I said, sort of throwing up my hands. "Hit Play."

"*May I sleep with your wife?*" came the voice.

"This is ridiculous!" I said, standing.

"It's a custom, Robert!" she said, calling after me. But I had had enough for the night. I went upstairs to read, and to sleep, listening to the sound of their voices below.

Learning the language had been Eva's idea—a good one, I thought at the time. When we decided we wanted to see a part of the world, neither of us wanted to become your typical American tourist—especially of the old, oceanliner kind—and so I suppose that was why I agreed so readily to the tapes and books. It would distinguish us. It would make us, in some way, new—I mean young, or like the young, open-minded. You hear so much about old age all your life that by the time you get to it the only thing that's a surprise is the truth of all you've heard, all the infirmities and strange failures, all the bones in your body becoming tight and dry. Old age is an old story. It is, more than anything, ugly, plain and simple, and the work comes from trying to see past these things. But it's like being deprived of most of your vocabulary.

We were trying to escape the cliché.

I mean we were trying to learn the language.

"How late did you stay up last night?" I asked Eva the next morning in the breakfast room. She was frying an egg, humming a strange tune. I had never heard it before. Then I recognized it: it was the music which introduced the Useful Expression section of the tapes.

"Oh, I don't know," she said. "I didn't notice. Not too late."

"I guess you got pretty far ahead of me," I said.

"Not really," she said. "I went back. I just listened to his voice."

"What?"

"I reviewed," she said, smiling at me over her shoulder.

She brought me my egg, humming her little tune. She hummed with the quivering voice of an older woman. It sounded as if she was in pain and it irked me.

"Eva," I said. "Please stop humming."

"As you wish, dear."

She stopped humming, but she still seemed to be in a good humor: I could tell she was humming inside. Even her arm, as she reached for the butter, did so with a sing-songy kind of grace, as if it were dancing. Her flesh shook. In that moment I pitied in a profound way all women who lived to be old: so few of them stayed together. So few of them were easy to look at. Most of them, I thought at that moment, are like junky antiques, attic-bound. But even my pity, which I felt radiating from me, did not affect her mood.

"You seem cheerful today," I said.

"I had another dream," she said. "Would you like to hear about it?"

"Not particularly," I said.

I wouldn't give her the satisfaction.

"What about the dream I dreamed I dreamed?" she said and laughed.

I set my fork and knife down on the plate.

"What's so funny, Eva?"

"Oh," she said. "Things. This and that. You know."

Then she picked up her eggs with her fingers, and stuffed them in her mouth.

"For God's sake Eva, what—"

"Like they do in the islands," she said.

"I see," I said.

But I didn't. I didn't see anything at all but my old, tired wife, eating breakfast with her hands.

Over the next few days a change took place in Eva, a change I would at the time ascribe to fragility, to the brain of an aging woman losing balance and making a fall. She smiled a great deal, and hummed, and time and again I would find her in the living room, sitting in a chair, staring at nothing. "Eva," I would say, and she would blush, stammer, and rush into the kitchen, as if I had embarrassed her. Through the kitchen door, if I pressed my ear close enough to it, I could hear her giggling like a little girl.

Our trip was only a few weeks away now; everything had been arranged. Our itinerary, along with our plane tickets, had arrived, and I kept them in a dresser drawer beneath a pair of black socks. We were all set, and I for one was looking forward to the land that lay ahead.

But as Eva's sickness—and it was a sickness—progressed, I felt uncertain about the voyage. Was it wise to leave home now, I wondered, to go so far away, into strange and perhaps dangerous country, as Eva was falling apart?

She gave me odd looks.

Every night before bed she said, "Bostandurasi-silamingo," which is the island word for "Sweet dreams."

"Good night, Eva," I would say.

The odd thing was, she seemed happy. She seemed so happy, and acted so absurdly girlish, it was sad. It was very, very sad.

And yet we continued our evening sessions. After dinner she would rush into the living room, set up the tape player, and call for me to join her.

"Sahashi is ready," she said. "Come on!"

"Sahashi?" I asked her, and laughed. "Who in God's name is Sahashi?"

I felt a little cruel for laughing, and touched her on the shoulder to make up for it. I felt so sorry for her.

"Sahashi," she said, "is the voice. I was looking through the manual and came upon his name. Isn't it a pretty name, Robert: Sahashi?"

"It's probably something like Frank or Elmer in their language," I said. "But yes, it has a ring to it."

"He's thirty-seven years old!" she said. "Doesn't he sound older?"

"They give his age?" I said.

"Let's start," she said.

And so we did. His voice began. We listened. My heart, however, wasn't in it, and as Sahashi spoke and Eva spoke back to him—she had such a knack for languages—all I could do was watch her old eyes sparkle and shine. She was looking forward to this trip even more than I. For the last week she had been reading all she could about the islands, their history and culture, and from time to time would catch her breath, and if I were in the room would read to me, ". . . At night in the country the darkness is as deep as velvet, and a low fog, a thick mist covers all roads. It is the mist that reminds one of heat rising from the jungle floor, of history and pre-history, of the ancient animals who once roamed these volcanic islands, some of which are said to still exist." The words made her eyes grow wide, and some nights, long after I'd gone to sleep, she would be up reading, licking her fingers, turning another dry page.

Suddenly Eva hit the machine with the palm of her hand, shutting it off.

"You're not listening!" she said. "You're not listening, Robert. Why aren't you listening to Sahashi?"

"I . . . my mind was elsewhere, Eva."

"Why," she said, stuttering in a queer rage, "that's the most inconsiderate thing I've ever heard! I can't believe you! Sahashi has gone out of his way to help us with this language, and you—your mind is elsewhere! You're such an oaf, Robert! I don't know what to say, I—don't want to talk about it anymore. So please leave us. Please leave us alone."

"What?"

"Please leave the room. Now, Robert."

I did. I did as Eva told me to.

But as of that moment, the trip was off.

There have been times, a number of them over the years, when I wished that Eva and I had gone to the trouble of having children. If we'd had children when we'd thought about it, thirty-five years ago, they would be grown now, and I could call one of them up and say, Your mother isn't well. For some time now she has been acting strangely. What do you think I should do?

I needed advice then—I still do—and I wished I had a son or a daughter who could give it to me.

Because Eva took a plunge. I'd seen it coming, of course. I knew she wasn't right for a long time, but when she finally took the plunge and was lost to me, I had nowhere to go, no one to turn to.

The night she asked me to leave the room I went upstairs and prepared

DANIEL WALLACE

for bed. I opened my sock drawer and stared at the plane tickets we'd never use, read the names of the places we'd never see. The forests of the Kotomanzi, the bridges, the little black-haired chicken drinking water from the streams. I'd been looking forward to taking a few pictures, maybe even turning it into a slide show, and was wondering what Eva would do when I broke the news to her—when I heard laughter coming from the living room downstairs. It wasn't just Eve, either. There was a man laughing, too.

"Eva?" I said, coming to the bottom of the stairs. "Is everything okay?"

I peered around the corner and saw her wiping a tear from her eye, and breathing deeply after her last fit of laughter.

"Oh, Robert," she said. "Did we disturb you? It's just that Sahashi was telling me some jokes. Tape Six," she said, "is all about the native sense of humor. You have to listen to this. Sit down. I'll play it back."

"Now listen," she said, after she had found the right place.

And I listened. But not a word of what I heard coming from the little black box made any sense to me. Oh, I did pick out some sounds I thought I recognized—"banana," he went at one point—but I was lost as far as any real meaning went.

When the "joke" was over Eva collapsed into another frenzy of laughter, while I stood there, uncomprehending.

"Eva," I said, walking toward her. "I think we need to talk."

"I know what you're going to say," she said.

"You do?"

If she knew I supposed she wasn't as sick as I thought she was. Maybe, I thought, there was some hope.

"You don't get it, do you?"

"No," I said. "I don't understand why you've—"

"It's in the way he tells it, really isn't it? I mean, you can't talk about a joke, can you? You either get it or you don't. I'm sorry, Robert."

"Come to bed, Eva."

"In a minute," she said. "He's got one about a traveling salesman he says I have to hear before bed."

"A traveling salesman?" I said. "In the islands?"

"Some things," she said, "are universal." She stood and kissed me on the cheek. "Bostandurasi-silamingo," she said. "Taskedashi. Mabarareta! Good night!"

Though I have hoped for one, there is no happy ending for Eva and me. There is not even an ending. We simply go on.

When I told Eva, the morning after her scene in the living room, that we would not be going on our trip, she took it much worse than even I had imagined she would. I was ready for another scene, for a tantrum, but she didn't say a word. She didn't even ask why. She just looked at me for a moment, excused herself from the table and went upstairs, where she stayed for most of the day. I didn't bother her, of course. I wanted to give her time to accept the disappointment, and when she came downstairs later that day, almost six hours later, I thought she had. The small, sad smile she gave me seemed to say that she was resigned to my decision.

"Eva," I said. "I don't mean to say that we'll never go. Just not for a while. Not until we get our own lives in order."

She smiled again, and went about preparing dinner.

"Eva," I said. "I know how badly you wanted to go. But I did too. I really did. I'm not happy about what's happened either. I just wish you would say something."

"Tastandi," she said. "Sta kustandi rina-sta."

"What's that mean?" I said hopefully. " 'All's well?' "

"Tastandi!" she screamed. "Sta kustandi rina-sta!"

Then she broke down crying and ran into the living room, and though I followed her she was too fast, and by the time I reached her she already had the tape deck out and on.

"Taskete," Sahashi said. "Las nastashi. Las nastashi."

"Las nastashi," she said. "Las nastashi . . ."

And so on.

Spring came, then summer. No matter what happens, the world keeps turning. Seasons change.

It's January now, and the streets are covered with snow. It's too cold to do anything but sit inside and study, to listen to these tapes. Sahashi still irritates me—he doesn't work with me the way he works with Eva—but I am trying to keep up with her, it's important to me, now that she seems to have forgotten English completely. I don't think she's forgotten it, though. I think she just refuses to speak it anymore.

As hard as I work, though, as much as I study, Eva seems to be just that far ahead, and I can only understand about ten per cent of everything she says to me. And I can't bring myself to eat with my hands, as she does, and Eva laughs at me because of it.

What happened? How is it things turn out the way they do? Eva is old and ugly. We are, both of us, closer to the end of our lives than to the beginning. Sometimes I wish I had never met her. But now she is all I have. I have to learn how to talk all over again. Every night she calls to me, and I drag my slippered feet into the living room, and we sit there, the two of us, listening to that man. And though I wish I was better at this sort of thing, and that one day, soon, I might be able to speak with her, I wonder: When I finally do learn, what will I say? What words will I strike her with in this new language? How, dear Eva, will we begin?

P. B. PARRIS

Carmen Miranda's Navel

Inside the front door of F. W. Woolworth's, a machine automatically made doughnuts. Biddy watched as one after the other, behind the glass, rings of batter, squeezed out of a container at the top, plopped into a well of hot shortening. A carousel of metal spokes slowly pushed the rings in a lazy circle. Halfway round, a mechanical arm flipped each one over so the pale side fried dark brown, too. Almost back to where it started, another arm turned the doughnut out onto the counter where a fat lady in a starched white uniform frosted it and arranged a dozen at a time on trays in the showcase.

The mesmerizing machine cranking out doughnuts, the sweet, heavy smell of frying, the big bowls of chocolate and vanilla frosting, these were only a few of the attractions in this garden of earthly delights. Back home, they had a five-and-ten, but nothing like this.

Eleven years old, a skinny girl with a light summer tan and long brown braids hanging down her back, Biddy wore sandals and a yellow cotton sundress with a pocket like a butterfly sewn on the skirt. She was visiting Grandma and Grandpa Greenwald, whose apartment was a few blocks away. She supposed they were rich because they lived in such a big building, half a city block of Victorian bay windows and stone porches. Biddy thought their three high-ceilinged rooms and narrow kitchen and bath with its claw-footed tub were grand. She liked all the dark woodwork and the fancy fireplace in the front room, even though its opening was bricked up now and most of the apartment was shadowy with reflected light.

Grandpa in his gray suit went to an office every morning, and Grandma sat at a card table in the front room, doing imaginary roses in watercolor in a sketch book or playing complicated versions of solitaire. During her visit, Biddy slept on a daybed in the dining room, and whenever she had some money, collected a penny at a time for drying the dishes or taking the trash down to the incinerator or helping with the dusting, she went off on her own to wander through Woolworth's wonderland.

The store waited at a busy corner. Even though there was a war on—her daddy was in a khaki uniform someplace over in Europe—Woolworth's didn't seem to have any shortage of shiny, brightly colored things for sale inside. Biddy never had more than a few cents at a time, so she considered any purchase endlessly. She came there mostly to look. It was her museum of arts and sciences. She always stopped first at the doughnut machine and watched, debating with herself over whether, if she ever did buy a doughnut, it should be chocolate or vanilla. But she never bought a doughnut. Too many other things competed for her attention.

Another miraculous machine stood on the other side of the entrance to the store. Twice the size of an electric refrigerator, it was an automatic photo booth, four poses for a quarter. On the outside, a mirror for primping and rows and rows of little gray and white faces staring and grinning and clowning for the camera. Sometimes, Biddy watched people get ready to have their pictures taken. Couples and bunches of friends kidded and laughed a lot before they crowded in together. By themselves, women patted and plumped their hair and put on fresh lipstick before they pulled back the blue curtain and stepped inside. One time, Biddy peeked into the empty booth at the padded seat and the lights and the little slot to put the money in, but she never had twenty-five cents all at one time. Besides, she thought it smelled funny in there, like sweat and Mercurochrome.

On most of her visits to Woolworth's, Biddy strolled up and down the aisles with her hand fisted around the money in her pocket, weighing the merits of pincushions shaped like strawberries and pencils that could be imprinted with her name, in real gold. Biddy especially admired the costume jewelry of pot metal and rhinestones and the celluloid Scotty dog pins.

When she did buy something, it was always a substitute for something else too expensive or otherwise beyond her that she really wanted. At the cosmetics counter, she looked every time at the little bottles of Blue Waltz perfume and the tubes of Tangee lipstick. Once, she ended up spending a penny for a pair of red wax lips at the candy counter instead, which she saw didn't make her look grown-up and glamorous at all in the photo booth mirror, but clownish and ugly. The lips smelled sweet, tasted sweet at first as she bit into them, but lost their flavor the longer she chewed. And, finally, after she swallowed the waxy lump, she got a stomachache.

The soda fountain with strawberry and hot fudge sundaes in tulip-shaped glasses, the stationery section with Big Chief tablets and rainbow boxes of Crayolas, the glass bins of butterscotch balls and cinnamon red hots: the street floor was filled with tempting ways to spend her money, but the basement — "Lower Level" the sign said — was where the real treasures lay.

Down the buff terrazzo steps, holding on to the stainless steel railing, Biddy would go, catching sight of more and more wonders through the metal fretwork of the balustrade. At the bottom of the stairs stood a baby grand piano where a woman with red hair piled up in stiff curls on top of her head played from sheet music to help customers decide whether or not to buy a copy.

The piano music followed Biddy into the pet department, which made plenty of music of its own. The aerator in the goldfish tanks bubbled, the canaries in their wire cages twittered, and a big green and red parrot flapped its wings and squawked when she came by. It sidled back and forth along its perch, its leg tethered with a length of leather thong to its wooden stand, and tossed sunflower seeds out of its dish and onto the floor. In glass cases, chameleons froze and disappeared against the sand, and little turtles with flower decals on their painted shells crawled over plaster rocks and each other to pile up in the corners and sleep. It was as good as a trip to a zoo, she thought, although she'd never actually been to one.

Biddy always ended up in the toy department among the rubber balls and the board games, the jigsaw puzzles and the Old Maid cards, the dominoes and the jacks. On high shelves behind the counter, the dolls were displayed, each protected by cellophane wrap. Biddy wanted to hold them all, one at a time, and look at them up close, but the one she wanted for her very own was the bride doll. She was dressed in white satin and tulle and displayed like Mary Queen of Heaven: all the baby dolls lined up on either side turned to face her. Even from where she stood, Biddy could see that the doll had real eyelashes and tiny pearl earrings. She wanted that doll, that beautiful bride, but she knew there was no way she would ever have enough money. So she always stopped to look up at it in worshipful longing for a few moments and then moved on when the saleslady with the blue-gray hair showed up, eyes like black marbles behind her glasses.

"You want something, little girl?" It was more an accusation than a question.

Biddy held out her hands to show she hadn't taken anything, hadn't done anything wrong. "No, thank you."

While the saleslady watched, Biddy walked, a choir girl in a Sunday processional, to the end of the counter and the books of paper dolls in the rack that stood there. In the past, she'd gone through each one and looked at the families of people to cut out and all the clothes with little tabs on the shoulders to dress them in. She knew them all by heart.

One day, a new group of books filled a pocket in the rack. Biddy pulled out a copy and looked at the cover: a color illustration of Carmen Miranda in an elaborate headdress, her trademark, piled high with birds and orchids and bananas. Biddy had seen her once in a Saturday matinee movie musical and thought she was the strangest, the most exotic, the most glamorous woman in the world. Carmen Miranda smiled at Biddy, was always smiling, with shiny red lips, a smile so broad it almost squeezed shut her dark eyes ringed in spidery black lashes. She was called the Brazilian Bombshell and spoke with an accent that made her rapid-fire wisecracks in the movie almost unintelligible. Biddy loved her.

She turned the pages of the paper doll book, savoring every one. They were printed with carnival-colored costumes from Carmen Miranda's movies. All of the two-piece outfits were variations of a short top with full sleeves and a long skirt, split partway up the front to show her legs. Even though all of the costumes featured a bare midriff, the skirts were discreetly fitted from just above the waist over the hipline, then flared and flounced into a short train behind. Included on each page was a fancy matching headdress with big, loopy earrings.

On the back cover, Biddy found a full-length perforated-to-be-punched-out paper doll of Carmen Miranda herself, wearing a surprisingly restrained pink turban, demure two-piece bathing suit, and thick platform high heels. Even uncostumed, she was the embodiment of female glamor.

Biddy reached into the pocket of her sundress. Under a crumpled Kleenex, she could feel six pennies. She turned the paper doll book over and looked at the price: 10¢. It had taken her two days to collect six cents. Biddy calculated that if she didn't spend the money on anything else and saved whatever she might get from Grandma over the next couple days, she could buy Carmen Miranda. She just had to resist temptation and get out of the store with her six cents and stay away until she had the full amount she needed.

"You want something, little girl?" The blue-haired glasses leaned over the book rack.

Biddy put the paper doll book back. "Not today, thank you."

When Biddy let herself into the apartment, she saw right away that Grandma had been crying. Biddy had never seen a grown-up in her family cry before. She was afraid she'd stumbled into something she wasn't supposed to know about, at least not until she was grown up herself. Biddy stood by the door and watched Grandma at the card table, looking down at a letter in her hand. The light through the lace curtains in the bay window behind her made the waves and pin curls in Grandma's hair shine like silver. Biddy wanted to go over and put a hand on her shoulder, to touch her in some way to make her feel better, but people in her family didn't do that. Then, with a spasm of panic, it occurred to Biddy that the letter might be about her mama or daddy.

"Grandma, what's the matter?" Biddy crossed the room to the table.

Grandma took off her glasses and dabbed her eyes with a hankie, the kind she always had in her pocket or tucked under the belt of the flowered housedresses she wore. She put her glasses back on. "It's all right, Biddy. Just a letter from your Aunt Louise in San Diego. Mac's getting shipped overseas, and she's coming home to stay with your grandpa and me for a while."

"Aren't you glad?" Biddy couldn't understand the tears.

"Oh, yes, yes. We haven't seen Louise since she and Mac got married."

No one ever seemed to tell Biddy anything directly, so she'd learned to be quiet, listen carefully, and put the puzzle pieces together for herself as best she could. She'd overheard enough at home to know that Louise and Mac had run off together after he enlisted in the Navy. Biddy was just relieved to find out nobody was sick or dead.

Grandma looked down at the letter again. "She's coming in on the train late tomorrow night. That means we'll have to send you home on the bus tomorrow afternoon. I'm sorry, Biddy, but there just isn't room for both of you here at the same time."

Biddy hadn't thought of that. Her stomach began to hurt the way it had when she ate the wax lips. She felt like crying, too, but she didn't. She sat down at the card table opposite Grandma and looked hard out the window to hold back the tears. Beyond the lace pattern of the curtain, the afternoon sun lit the top floor of the apartment building across the way.

"She's going to have a baby. I don't know what your grandpa's going to say about that." Grandma started to sniff back tears again. Biddy got

P. B. PARRIS

up and went through the dining room into the kitchen. She took a slice of bread out of the metal box on the counter, folded it in half, and took a dry, tasteless bite as she went out the back door. She wanted to think.

In back of the apartments was a service yard. Biddy tore up the rest of her bread and tossed it to the sparrows pecking the ground in front of the incinerator. She watched the birds scatter in a dusty flutter of wings. Leading off the service yard were narrow, window-lined corridors that let a little brick-reflected light and air into the apartments. Biddy went deep into the recess outside her grandparents' rooms and sat down and leaned back against the stone wall. Velvety green moss grew between the paving bricks. If she looked straight up, she could see a strip of bright azure sky. Otherwise, it was cool and shadowy and quiet.

She pulled her legs up against her chest and rested her chin on her knees. Because she'd never actually been around anyone who had one, she'd always thought babies were wonderful, something everybody was pleased about. Biddy couldn't understand why Grandpa would be so upset at Aunt Louise. But worse was the news that she was going home on such short notice. Biddy had looked forward to a whole summer's visit, and now, after only a little more than a week, it was over, just like that. Worst of all, she wouldn't have enough time to collect money to buy the Carmen Miranda paper doll. At that moment, it was the most desirable thing in the world. The more she thought about it, the sadder she felt, until she was crying, too, just like Grandma. Afraid somebody in the apartments above might hear her, she pressed her forehead against her knees and wept into her skirt.

When she raised her head again, the sky had grown darker and the shadows were deep blue around her. She wiped her eyes with the back of her hand and got up slowly, stiff from sitting cramped up for so long. She climbed the back stairs and went into the kitchen where Grandma was stirring something for supper on the stove.

"I'm sorry, Biddy. But you can come visit again someday." She kept on stirring. She reached for the salt and shook it over the pot. "Your grandpa's been home already and gone to the bus station," she added without looking up, "to see about your ticket." Because of the war and gas rationing, the buses were crowded, and the only way to be sure of getting a ticket was to buy it as far ahead as possible. "I'll tell you what," Grandma said, turning around and wiping her hands on her polka-dot apron, "why don't you go in the bedroom and get my jewelry box. I'd like you to straighten it up for me before you leave, all right?"

Playing with Grandma's costume jewelry, sorting it into little piles of glass beads and rhinestone earrings and celluloid brooches, trying each piece on, admiring how it looked in the mirrored lid, rearranging the jewelry in the velveteen-lined box, had been, next to strolling Woolworth's, Biddy's favorite pastime during her visit. Even though she wasn't enthusiastic about it now, it did seem like a way to pass the time until dinner.

Biddy opened the door to her grandparents' bedroom. The shades were drawn. It was warm and still there and smelled faintly of "Evening in Paris," Grandma's cologne. A colored print of the Sacred Heart hung above the chest of drawers, and Grandma's rosary was looped over the post on the far side of the bed. Biddy went over to the triple-mirrored dresser. As she reached to pick up the pink leatherette jewelry box, she saw something shiny where Grandpa emptied his pants pockets every night before going to bed. Caught in the ruffle of one of Grandma's crocheted doilies was a dime.

Biddy stood there, hypnotized by the coin, until she heard the front door open and Grandpa come into the apartment. She snatched up the money, shoved it deep into her pocket, and carried the jewelry box out to the card table in the front room.

The next morning, she was awake early, but she lay with her face turned to the wall and studied the faded pattern in the paper, bouquets of tea-colored roses connected by swags of twisted ribbons. She thought about the evening before. Without any conversation, they'd eaten their supper at the dining room table, Biddy feeling too guilty and fearful even to look up from her plate of macaroni and cheese. Later, while Grandpa read behind his newspaper in his overstuffed chair and Grandma, pulled up close to the floor lamp, embroidered on a pillowcase, Biddy mechanically arranged the pieces of jewelry into meaningless piles on the card table. Long before anything was said about bedtime, she'd given the box to Grandma and said good-night. Now, in the morning light, Biddy's fear had lessened and her desire grown stronger.

About eight-thirty, Grandpa got ready to leave for the office. Still turned toward the wall and pretending to be asleep, she heard him tell Grandma that he'd be home before lunch, in time to walk Biddy to the bus station. When the front door closed, she jumped out of bed and ran to the bathroom. At midmorning, when she couldn't stand it any longer, Biddy told Grandma she had something she had to do. "I'll be right back," she promised, and before anything more could be said, she was out the front door and down the stone steps. Biddy knew she was wicked. Nevertheless, she skipped all the way to Woolworth's.

Past the doughnut machine and the photo booth she went, down the steps to where the redheaded lady was picking out "Sentimental Journey" on the baby grand. There were hardly any customers in the store that early in the day. Biddy ignored the squawk of the parrot and gave the bride doll one last, quick glance as she went by. At the end of the counter, she pulled the paper doll book out of the rack and smiled at Carmen Miranda. When the saleslady came over to her, Biddy handed her the book in one hand and the dime in the other. Clearly surprised, she took them to the cash register, rang up the sale, put the purchase into a paper sack, and gave it to Biddy. "Thank you," the saleslady said automatically.

Biddy said, "You're welcome," and turned and skipped away.

When she opened the front door to the apartment, she could hear Grandpa's voice coming from the dining room. It was hard to understand what he was talking about even when she got inside, although it was clear he was angry. He sounded exasperated, and practiced, like he'd been over and over the same ground before. "Jesus, Mary and Joseph, us crowded in here like sardines. How could she do such a thing?"

Biddy watched him from the front room. He was a slightly stooped, balding man with puffy eyes that turned down at the corners and made him look tired and unhappy. "Running off like a criminal was bad enough, but this. . . ." He walked around the end of the dining room table toward Grandma. "I know what this means. I can count. And she'll get off that train looking like she swallowed a watermelon. . . ."

Biddy wanted to run away, but it was too late. He saw her and motioned for her to come in to where he and Grandma stood by the table.

"And you, Missy, where've you been? It's almost time to go. What've you got there?" He held out his hand. Biddy gave him the paper sack. He pulled out the book and leafed through it. "What kind of thing is this for a young girl to have?"

Biddy looked down at her toes curled tightly in her sandals.

"Those are her paper dolls, Harold," Grandma said softly, but with a firmness that surprised Biddy.

"Dolls? This tarted-up tramp with her bare stomach sticking out?"

"Now, Harry, let me see." Grandma took the book and turned to the back cover. "Look here, she's respectable enough for any little girl. She doesn't even have a navel."

"Not in front of the child, Edna. She already knows more than any decent girl ought to." With that he turned and went into the kitchen. Biddy could hear him run himself a drink of water. Grandma handed the paper doll book back to Biddy. As he came back into the room, Grandpa sighed, "Let's go." He sounded defeated, as if he'd been fighting a battle for years and had only just realized he'd lost. And Biddy, clasping Carmen Miranda to her flat chest, tried to figure out what it was that she had won.

Basse Ville

It was sunshiny but cold out on the river in the wind on the open deck of the ferry returning to Québec from Lévis one afternoon seven or eight years ago, going on four o'clock, September. The customs house where the ferry would dock looked derelict and the sight of it made the wind sweeping down the river feel even colder. Toward the middle of the crossing, passengers who had strolled on the outer deck retreated to the glassed-in promenades. But one passenger stayed out in the wind through the whole crossing—an old, squat red-nosed man in a tatterdemalion greatcoat, me, name of Alex Van Frank, not minding the wind one bit (too tough) on my way back from seeing my daughter Ida and son-in-law Sammy.

I was half Sammy's age with twice his I.Q. and more experience of the world than he'll ever get when I first set foot in this damn country. I started oil painting at the age of eighty-one and in eighteen months and a few days I've painted more than a hundred pictures. Those paintings will be worth a lot of money when I kick the bucket. I've given only two or three away—the rest are home, some framed in our dining room and the others wrapped in waxed paper under the bed. Anne'll be rich—they're better than any life insurance I could afford. I'm leaving everything to her even though I probably should set a few paintings aside for Ida and Sammy because who knows, Anne might lose her mind or leave everything to charity. But what the hell. It's only money, let her do what she wants.

In 1932 Alex sailed from Ostend to Québec with high hopes for the new world. From childhood he had been destined for the priesthood but scarcely had he begun to read Descartes and then other subversives, especially Spinoza, when he underwent a change of heart. "The pope has to take a shit just like everybody else does," is how he summarized his new sentiments to fellow students in coffeehouses. When he left the university, his father disowned him. He found work as a cobbler's assistant and lived frugally for two years in Louvain. An acquaintance who had emigrated to Québec wrote that socialism was on the doorstep of the Americas, and people were saying the same thing in Louvain newspapers and coffeehouses. Alex believed them enough to decline buying a pension when he came to Québec.

Socialism dragged its feet but Alex liked Québec anyway. He signed on with a shipping firm and traveled up and down the St. Lawrence, up and down the Atlantic seaboard, to the Orient, off and on thirty-five years for the company. Through the war he served as ship's engineer dodging U-boats in the North Atlantic to provision the Allies. He was no wild-eyed revolutionary, but he continued to believe that economic inequality was an evil and a shame. During the late thirties, when once again socialism seemed to have a chance in the New World, he attended various rallies and at one of them in Québec he met Anne, a native Québecoise twenty years younger than he. They married.

Anne was a schoolteacher. She had left her parents' farm in the north and come to the city to make her own living. Now she abandoned her profession for full-time housekeeping and motherhood. She and Alex bought two adjoining houses in the lower town, all their savings going for the down payment. In three decades the houses were paid for. Alex and Anne stayed in the smaller—after Ida was born they talked of changing and it might have been sensible, but by then they knew how each square meter of the floor sloped. They rented the adjoining house to a series of tenants over the years.

Thooo-oog. Thoog. The ferry slowed until without any perceptible moment of contact it had berthed and gangplanks were being lowered.

Over the years Alex made good use of his knowledge of cobbling. His work was coarse, not for Anne's shoes but okay for his own, like these in which he descended the gangplank among the last passengers in a splay-footed sashay step by step through the shelter where others waited to board, out into the open space with dogs and pedestrians and a few parked cars. There was less wind. Over the dark customs house stood the evening star.

It was the same celestial object as the morning star and not a star at all, but Venus. In a thrift shop Alex had found a book about the universe with many pictures and diagrams. He had read the entire book ostensibly browsing in the course of several visits to the shop, and then he had bought and reread it. Some stars are so dense that gravity holds back their very light, he informed Anne, even though such a fact rolled off her like water off a duck. What the hell, wonders of the universe probably only matter to you if you're about to kick off, so maybe it's all to the good for your wife not to bat an eye at them.

Alex could walk a long distance but he went slowly and often had to stop to rest on a low wall or a bench. It was in these rests that this apparently genial little man who looked like the father of his favorite painter Rembrandt would be seized by anger he could barely contain. There was no knowing what he might find himself remembering. It could as easily be something he hadn't thought of in decades—gathering eggs winter mornings in his boyhood—as it could a frequently recalled event like his and Anne's wedding night. The recollection had a life of its own, and it seemed the most natural thing in the world while it lasted. During these rests also Alex was prone to hallucinate as he sat with his hands on his knees, the sun in his face. He might smell rope or jasmine, a long vista might open in the shrubbery or a face move back and forth there to say no. Or so it seemed: half an hour later he couldn't be sure whether it had happened or not and by evening he would have forgotten it.

Alex proceeded along one of the narrow streets of the lower town and turned right into Cleroux Street, the cul-de-sac where he and Anne and their new tenants the Schumanns lived. Alex tipped his hat to his young neighbor Laure Poujade, who sketched tourists in the upper town. She was okay, not like those wild teenagers on their motorbikes who tried to run you over in the upper town, and lately had once even roared up and down Cleroux. Alex had given them what for, and stepped off the curb so they had to veer around him, and the one in black leather had nicely scuffed the elbow of his jacket when his machine skidded out from under him. But what if they ever tried it again? Alex scowled, and scowled more at the flower boxes in Mr. Catanese's windows, which practically blocked the sidewalk. Well before that obstruction Alex crossed to his house.

He shut the door behind him. If those ungoverned youths continued to appear on their motorbikes, wouldn't it be necessary to lock doors? Might as well move south of the border and get murdered right away. He hung up his coat and blew his nose. "Anne?" The air was cool and still. "Anne?"

"*Cogito!*" came a cry from the dining room. "*Cogito! Ergo sum!*" The bright insistent voice was not Anne's but that of Alex's parrot, Sinbad. "Shut up," Alex muttered. Anne should be home at this hour. Alex frowned.

Sinbad moved sideways on the bar he spent most of his hours on, to have a better view of the doorway Alex was coming through. Alex had bought him when he was less than a year old, almost thirty years before in what is now the Malagasy Republic. The sea voyage to Canada had been like the movement of a branch in the wind repeated ad nauseam. Since then he had lived here in Cleroux Street. Sinbad was large, strong, and beautiful. Though he had not flown since '47, he kept his wings and tail preened. He would outlive Alex by many years, and possibly when that little man, who had shortened and thickened over the years as his schnoz reddened and swelled and lumped up, when he was in the ground there might be reason to have one's flying feathers in trim.

The insistence with which Sinbad proclaimed that he thought and therefore was had nothing to do with the expressed claim. He used the same tone for everything Alex had made him learn: it was the tone Alex had used to insist that he con the phrase.

Alex was starting to glower. Where was Anne who should be home at this hour? Sinbad turned a cool eye on him, muttered, "What the hell," and blinked.

Alex half-suspected that Anne was keeping a rendezvous with the dapper young instructor of the social dances held Saturday afternoons at the senior citizens' center and attended assiduously by Anne in the face of Alex's scoffs. In fact she was clip-clopping down the Breakneck Steps to the lower town in her sensible black shoes, on her way back from the post office, and minutes later she was in the house slipping off her flowered scarf and telling Alex how she had given the postal worker a piece of her mind. "I asked him why we should paste the queen's face on our letters. I think it was educational for them to hear somebody speak up." Anne smoothed her white blouse and khaki skirt, the clothes she wore in Alex's portrait of her.

Anne was birdlike (though not much like Sinbad), fine-boned and discreet. In the twenty-by-thirty-centimeter painting, which hung with fifteen others the same size above the sideboard in the dining room, she was taking an afternoon nap, hands under her cheek. Her blouse had become pink and the twill skirt a robin's-egg blue, and her shoes sat side by side on the floor. You could see that her eyes were closed and that her hair was short and gray, but little more than that in the tiny face. This was the only

JOE ASHBY PORTER

painting Alex had yet attempted from life. And, while it might not enable you to distinguish Anne among other petite gray-haired women, it was one of Alex's best works. Inspiration would be the simplest explanation for his having chosen to show Anne asleep. She did take the occasional afternoon nap, but when she was awake you only needed observe her a short time to know how hard it was to imagine her asleep, and so appreciate how Alex's imagination had zeroed in.

René Catanese had no idea his window boxes occasioned grumbling. He didn't suppose his neighbors might think anything at all about his window boxes or, for that matter, about him. His legal residence was in the upper town and, though he had come to spend nearly all his time down in the narrow building with geraniums, still in his mind it remained an office where he managed the Québec Orient Company.

At one time the company had swayed the governments of Canada and of some Chinese provinces, but the Chinese revolution had accelerated a decline already in progress. From the beginning René had managed the moribund company as a diversion, looking in from time to time before returning to what he called his work or, for a brief time later, to his wife. His work was amateur botany, "amateur" not because desultory but because he did it out of a disinterested love.

René let this work he loved direct him and when it pointed straight at succulents he followed without cadging. For Québec it was about as ill-chosen as could be but the point was that René hadn't chosen it, he had followed it, around the world in tropical deserts to find new species. He named them for people who had helped him, and then for his wife. When he married her he was in his midthirties and could not imagine being happier. They had the house off the Grande Allée and a cottage on Prince Edward Island, she accompanied him into the desert or he went alone and came back to her. The beatitude was deepening and widening and promising a long future when near their third wedding anniversary she died.

She was in no pain and there had been a lightness in the last weeks, her cues for the tone, champagne in the morning, and for a while after she was gone forever René held the wondering lightness she had found, in which the truth that she was dying and then that she had died could be seen so clearly that there was no cause to dwell on it. Then the lightness had broken. He tried to think his way back, but there was no shelter from the desolation that used him brutally for a long time with no relief in sight.

But eventually that too had come to be over and done with. He was not old yet and it was time to recommence his work. He went down to the Yucatan for samples but back in Québec he realized that his heart hadn't quite been in the expedition. He stopped by the Québec Orient and chatted with the secretary. René was mounting the steps to the upper town when it occurred to him that a window box of geraniums would be good for the office. From then on he took an increasing interest in the company, its history, the rare current business and the comfortable office. He let the succulent work slide some but he didn't abandon it. He built a small greenhouse behind the office. In the upper town he would have used a builder but down here it seemed right to give the work to neighbors or their people, so he had hired Patrick Clusel from up the street to build the structure for him in a corner where it would get afternoon sun. In the upper town if a new floorboard had given way he would have asked the builder for explanation and repair, but down here it seemed better to move something over the hole when he thought about it and say nothing. Some of the boards had developed dry rot anyway, so next summer Patrick could install a whole new floor. René fitted out a bedroom on the second floor of the company building and slept there more often than in the upper town.

He was a large man with coal-black hair that had receded from his high brow. His face was like a Roman senator's, heavy and distinguished, with flat vertical cheeks and pendulous earlobes. He sat patiently at his rolltop desk in the dim office. There was a shaded lamp and beside it a humidor, an ivory puzzle, and a letter opener. Behind glass in bookcases along two walls stood company records, botanical journals, histories, dictionaries, grammars, dog-eared catalogues of porcelain, jade, and other goods the company had traded in, marine atlases bound in green morocco embossed with the company's initials, and desert notebooks of laid vellum covered with René's blunt, even script and graceful line drawings of plants.

You get old and your mind feels like a garbage bag. Sometimes more and more of what Alex Van Frank had stuffed in over eighty-two years was turning out to be garbage—not to mention the crap that had found its way in without ever looking like anything different. It makes thinking harder when it feels that way. It isn't senility—what it is is that there doesn't seem room to turn around in, never mind make noble strides. So be it, what the hell.

Indian summer ended toward early October. It might get down to freezing some nights. When a temperate day came along Alex went out into it

JOE ASHBY PORTER

for a walk. Anne was over in Lévis keeping an eye on the grandchildren. Sammy and Ida had gone to Montréal to look for a new television set with color. Anne would give Sammy the interesting article on the universe Alex had found in a *National Geographic*. Sammy could read it and then give it back. Maybe he'd have something to say about it. It might make him think, the blankety-blank overgrown boy. He might read it.

Woolen trousers, two moth-eaten cardigans over a shirt and Sammy's old canvas golf hat were all Alex needed to defy the worst a tame air like today's could do, and his horny wide splay feet were shod in his own creations. He lit up a black stogie.

Alex suspected that Julien Schumann was a backstairs Lothario not to be trusted alone with Anne. Alex guessed just from the way the guy looked that his own wife wasn't enough for him. He ran a bookstore in the upper town. He looked about as bookish as a monkey. Hate literature is what Alex guessed Schumann was selling under the counter in his store, or he might be forming a religious sect for loonies.

Otherwise though Alex thought Julien was okay, and he saluted him with good cheer when he saw him in the street. "How'd you like the kick in the pants they gave the pope in Italy?"

"Birth control no less. I wouldn't have expected it," said Julien.

"Ha! I'd like to have seen the look on his face when he opened the paper the next morning. I wonder if he forgot who he was and said goddamn. They probably bring him the paper on a silver platter. Ha, ha, I'd like to have been there."

Julien smiled. "Did you ever see a pope in the flesh?"

Alex said, "I wouldn't sully my eyes," and took a puff of his stogie. "Any trouble with the house? If your rent's not in on time I'll call the police and have you evicted."

Julien smiled. "I'll remember."

Alex chuckled and bade him good day. He could forget his designs on Anne. He seemed brighter than Sammy—Alex enjoyed talking with him whatever his so-called bookstore was a front for. Anne's out of his league though. A Lothario worth his salt ought to be able to see that, no matter how tall he was.

Alex turned and shaded his eyes to look up at the cliff. There it was, the "American Gibraltar." Tourists gaped, inhabitants hardly looked at it. To Alex, gaping seemed the more absurd of the two though he knew that he must have gaped when he saw the rock for the first time as a boy fresh over from Ostend. It was a big rock for a city, and big compared to Alex, but pretty small potatoes compared to the universe. Alex shrugged. He looked from the top down the face of the precipice, and he had a fleeting hallucination of a smile on the rock as his gaze descended.

Then he saw Sinbad his parrot on the front of the second house from the corner hobbling along the cornice at the level of the upper floor, clear as anything. "Malarky," muttered Alex. He looked away at something else. When he looked back—he couldn't resist—Sinbad was gone and a pigeon was alighting where he had been. Puffing his stogie, Alex watched until the pigeon had made its landing. Then he resumed his promenade.

He splurged a quarter on the escalator up to the Place d'Armes. In the upper town people went about their business in larger numbers and with more of a bustle on some of the streets. Others were as quiet as Cleroux Street. Alex stopped in at an Indian shop to peruse some watercolors a Cree inspired by tribal legends had painted. They were selling at forty dollars apiece. After a judicious appraisal Alex decided they weren't bad even though they were nothing like Rembrandt. Anyway what mattered was that people buy them. Like the rich dame who came in fiddling with her purse as Alex left. She disregarded his appearance with gracious tolerance. "Your shit stinks as much as mine," thought Alex as he tipped his hat. "Shabby creature," she must've been thinking. So be it.

Alex spent the noon hour on a park bench with a hardboiled egg he'd brought in his pocket and a soft drink he'd picked up on the way. It was a sunny park where Alex had first ventured to hold Anne's hand years and years before, and that wasn't the only good idea he'd had here, taking his rest in different seasons. This noon no especially good idea came to him. It had to be that way sometimes too.

The November vandalism in René Catanese's greenhouse occurred during the night or early morning. Around noon when he went out to pot some cuttings an ugly sight awaited him. The shattered pots in the southeast corner could be replaced, and succulents survive root exposure, but plants had been butchered, large ones it had taken years to raise hacked and gouged. One of these wouldn't survive as it stood and the only thing for it was to finish the butchery, divide it into pieces and start again. Nausea and something like panic washed over René. In the hot dry air he broke into a cold sweat looking at this destruction, and he wiped his brow with the back of a hand. He spent the day dressing the green and gray wounds. Absurd as it was, from time to time as he worked he thought he heard a movement behind him and his skin prickled. The next day he had the Clusel boy install a lock on the greenhouse door.

On the surface the incident looked like the kind of random violence cities seemed to be fostering more and more as the century wore on. Outbreaks of it were less common in Canada than south of the border, rarer in Québec than in most other Canadian cities, far rarer in the old town than in the suburbs, and rarest of all in the quiet streets of the lower town. If it was that sort of violence it would be nearly unprecedented, and alarming. If on the other hand it was some malice directed specifically at René, so far as he knew it was entirely unprecedented. Yet in some ways it did seem personal. Nothing else on the premises had been attacked nor apparently anything else in the street. How likely was it that someone destroying randomly would choose something so dear to René as the succulents?

If personal malice did figure, it would seem to follow that the culprit was a fellow botanist or, failing that, one of his neighbors. The first hypothesis seemed ludicrous but the second was worse because of the suspicion it could infect his daily life with. As when old Pascale Mackenzie next door sweeping her stoop bade him good morning and he listened for a hint of mischief or craziness in her voice. Or when, watching the Clusel boy install the lock, it occurred to him that, motives aside, no one in the street looked as capable of the vandalism as Patrick. Who, if he was the culprit, must be enjoying the irony of being paid to install the lock. Which he alone besides René knew how to operate, so he would give himself away should he be mad enough to return for another bout of destruction. Such were the disquieting trains of thought René found himself giving way to.

After the Van Franks had their roof repaired, Anne moved the clothes hamper away from the door where it had stood as a nuisance ever since the roof started to leak in the spring, back to its place in the far corner. The next day while she was out Alex moved it back near the door. Anne reminded him that it had stood in the corner ten years at least, and that in any case she should be able to have it where she pleased since she did the laundry. Alex scowled and reminded her that his earnings had enabled them to buy this and the other house, and said sarcastically that if washing clothes was crippling her he could assume the responsibility. Anne was tempted to accept his offer, her nerves were so frazzled by his new arbitrariness. He gave the hamper a kick that sent it back toward its corner and then stalked in his shambling way out of the room. Anne couldn't ignore the possibility that she was seeing him go senile. After a moment she pushed the hamper the rest of the way into its corner.

Alex was surly and querulous by turns, resentful, forgetful, arbitrary and, as if that weren't enough, suspicious. That was the most grievous part of it for Anne, his seeming to suspect even her of impossible motives and deeds. With a start she guessed that he thought her responsible for Sinbad's disappearance. She had been over in Lévis with Ida and Sammy's children when the parrot vanished, but facts seemed to count for nothing in Alex's present mood and in any case trotting them out was too saddening. Nor, until such a time as she might know he suspected her, did she want to risk implanting suspicion by a denial. She recalled how she had found him sitting under his reading light that evening. She had supposed that something in the Spinoza open in his lap had moved him to tears. She had hung up her coat and hat, noticed the empty cage and asked where Sinbad was. "Ahhh the sonofabitch is gone," Alex had said with a snuffling laugh and a shake of his head. Anne did fear he thought she'd done it herself or arranged it.

Some groups of a few hundred snowflakes had fallen from nowhere all by themselves like lint shook out a casement above, but the first snow you'd call a snow started after midnight on December eleventh, the day Alex took a painting to the museum. Sinbad was gone all right, a fortnight already. There were no clues Alex could find. Not a soul answered his ad in the newspaper's lost-and-found though he offered a reward. At one time or another Alex suspected everyone in the street including his own wife Anne—why not? somebody had to have done it. He intended to be magnanimous, forget the whole thing as soon as the culprit came forward and made a clean breast. But there wasn't a peep out of the culprit.

Maybe Alex did cry when he first found the bird gone. Maybe blubbering made him feel unworthy to expect help from Spinoza, too. All the same, life goes on. So what: Sinbad was never anything but a parrot. He could've been a human being and life would still go on. Bigwigs think they're indispensable, and con little wigs into half-believing it. But the pope could choke on frog's legs tonight and even if a dozen presidents, sheiks, and the like met their appropriate ends tomorrow dawn we could still enjoy our breakfasts. We could boot out any or all their highnesses like the Shah of Iran. Close their Swiss bank accounts and put them on an island where they could spend the rest of their lives trying to impress one another. They could institute solemnity contests, award a coconut hat to the highness who made other highnesses clam up and quake best. We could bug the island with TV

JOE ASHBY PORTER

cameras and tune in for a laugh when we didn't have something better to watch.

Alex grinned. He was in bed under three quilts, in his flannel nightshirt. Anne was downstairs reading. Alex turned off his bedside lamp and looked through the window to see if snow had started.

It had been a busy day, up and down the Breakneck Steps twice. In the morning he'd gone up to the art supply store for some turp and a few more canvas boards. As always, he browsed awhile examining supplies in a kind of trance. He was deciding as he nearly always did to resist the temptation to buy this or that luscious tube of a hue he should after all be able to make out of primaries when young Laure Poujade greeted him. "I didn't know you painted, Mr. Van Frank."

"Thought you was the only artist in the street, eh?" Game for ribbing she was and not at all hard on the eyes in her bloom.

Laure had heard about Sinbad's disappearance. When Alex told her he'd given up hope of finding any leads, she suggested buying another parrot.

Alex had already thought of doing that and rejected it as beneath his dignity. But Laure made it sound so right that now upon leaving her he reconsidered. He went so far as to maneuver himself into a phone booth for the first time ever—and the last, he vowed—to consult yellow pages under "Parrots," "Birds," "Animals," and finally "Pets." Odd a designation for a parrot as that was, the store listed there seemed the best bet, and it was just around the corner. Before extricating himself from the booth, Alex rang up the rescue league he'd found under "Animal." A brisk helpful voice answered.

"Good morning," said Alex. "You take care of lost animals?"

"Yes, if they're found and brought in. Have you found an animal?"

"Me? No. Me, I lost one."

"Oh dear, too bad. We may have it though. Could you describe the animal?"

"A big parrot," Alex began. "He . . ."

"Sinbad?" interrupted the voice.

This was downright startling. "You mean you have him?"

"If we did, you'd be the first to know. Sorry. Good-bye."

"Hold the show!" roared Alex. "How the hell do you know my parrot's goddamn name?"

In the street patient automobiles moved, slowed to a stop, began moving. A couple of hippies were slipping off their backpacks beside the phone booth.

"I'm a citizen," Alex said.

The traffic advanced like an accordion, closing as it slowed to a pause, fanning out again when it moved.

"A taxpayer."

The voice at the other end said, "You must not be the party who's made such a . . . who's inquired so repeatedly about this Sinbad. One moment."

The hippies were sitting on the curb smiling at Alex to let him know they wanted the phone. A new voice came on to say that Alex must be the Mr. Van Frank whose wife he ought to thank for her concern over his pet's loss inasmuch as she had been calling the league more often than was necessary. "Okay," said Alex. He worked his way out of the booth—the smiling couple was welcome to it.

The pet store was like a miniature zoo. Had Alex known of it, he'd already have been dropping in from time to time. They had two parrots, neither nearly so handsome as Sinbad. Still, it wouldn't hurt to ask the price, off-handedly so as not to get rooked. The answer sounded like a joke: either of those mediocre birds was selling for almost a thousand times what Sinbad had cost.

Anne was out when Alex came home. He thought about her as he ate lunch at the kitchen table—soup, bread, cider, half a pear. So she'd been making a nuisance of herself in his behalf. He thought about what he had learned at the pet store too. It made sense for somebody to have swiped Sinbad if he was worth such a bundle after all. So.

Then, when Alex was upstairs unwrapping his canvas boards, a plan jelled out of the morning. Laure Poujade was right, he should have a new parrot. More important, he was ashamed about Anne's having borne the brunt of his recent bad moods—Anne of all people—and he should make it up to her with an apology and a gift like an electric typewriter to replace her old manual one. Wherewithal for typewriter and parrot was the crux of the matter. Which he could get by selling one of his paintings. One wouldn't hurt—there'd be plenty for Anne to get rich on after he kicked off.

Selecting the painting was like choosing one of your children to sell into slavery. On the other hand, since Alex didn't know who Québec's richest art patrons might be, he had decided to let the university museum make the purchase and he would be able to step in for a look whenever he wanted. He chose a view of "the most perfect of the northern medieval towns of Europe," Bruges. He had copied it mostly from a black-and-white magazine illustration, replacing the grays with bright pastels, and he had added a vegetable vendor with carrots, leeks, and radishes. Alex wrapped the painting in waxed paper and went up to the museum.

The director couldn't have been over forty. He was standing at a window looking out at something in the courtyard below and he must've thought Alex was his secretary because Alex had come all the way across the room to the big empty desk before the man turned and took in Alex and doubtless the secretary signaling from the doorway. "Yes?"

Alex chuckled. He laid the package on the desk, opened it and stepped back. "Don't be scared, have a look."

With a puzzled smile the man came to his desk and looked at the painting. The smile drained away.

Alex laughed. "Don't worry if you think you can't afford it. We'll say five hundred—call it my charity to Québec."

The museum director inhaled. "Where did you learn to paint, sir?"

Alex beamed. "Self-taught!"

The museum director started to say one thing and then thought better of it. "No . . ." he began, "I'm sorry to disappoint you but no, we won't buy this piece. Whatever the price. So now good day."

Alex shook his head.

"Miss Philippe," said the director, "is there a guard nearby?"

"Okay," Alex said. "Okay then." He folded the paper over the bright panel, tucked the package under his arm, tipped his hat and strolled past Miss Philippe, out into the wintry afternoon, and home.

But the joke was on the museum director. Because Alex would have to have been born yesterday to have really believed they'd buy his painting— wait till you're pushing up daisies, the guy might as well have said. Alex had known it then as well as he knew it now under his quilts. He could see out his window that snow should start soon. He wondered if it might be possible to raise Schumann's rent long enough to supply the money he needed without Anne's getting wind of it.

The parrot Sinbad had been released by a mischief-maker, while Alex was outside talking of the pope with Julien Schumann, and Anne was in Lévis. The person slipped into the house from the back and, when he saw the birdcage, was inspired to undo the latch Sinbad himself had pecked at on occasion over the years.

What was up? Blamed if Sinbad could say. Many another bird's heart would have quailed. Sinbad clambered into his cage's doorway. Perched there, head cocked to one side, he regarded the stranger in its scuffed motorcycle jacket. Sinbad wasn't frightened: although the person radiated no affection like Alex's, it didn't seem to mean him harm. It was in a hurry for him to do something, though. Could it be that old short Alex's time had come? Like a good bird, Sinbad jumped out the cage doorway. He barely had time to half-open his wings before he landed on the rug.

The stranger closed the cage door and then with small movements made it clear that Sinbad wasn't to walk anywhere but across the clean rugs and wood into the hallway and up the stairs. Sinbad took them one at a time. Midway in the climb when he rested a minute, with a glance over his shoulder he saw that the stranger was not far behind, insistent and wordless, with a bluish aura around it. Couldn't have been less like Alex.

Sinbad had never been upstairs. It all looked interesting and, but for the stranger, he could have explored every room. As it was, not knowing how much time there was, he made a U-turn at the banister and went straight to the far end of the corridor, observing as much as he could along the way. At the end he climbed up a bentwood chair and stepped from atop it through a bright hole in the wall onto a ledge. He could see the entire street. Wasn't that old Alex at the bottom shambling past the street sign there? It was bright and chilly. Sinbad turned to reenter the house and found the window closing behind him. A pretty kettle of fish this was.

He was meant to fly, then.

He appraised the scene. A windy blue sky, jumbles of rooftops, pigeons. To his left the terrain rose vertically in stone higher than trees. That was the obvious place to take bearings. Sinbad ruffled his feathers and leapt into the breeze.

He had forgotten that in his youth certain muscles in his wings had been severed as a precaution against such escapades as this. Because the surgery was imperfect or because his vigor had tended to cancel its effects, Sinbad didn't stoop to his death, but flight would hardly be the word for his topsy-turvy gyrations. Too astonished to utter cries of alarm, he tumbled through the air across the street until more by chance than design he alighted on an ornamental ledge on the front of a house. He shut his eyes and then opened them. At the bottom of the street stood old Alex (yes, that was his unforgettable profile with vile stogie) gaping up at the very crest of rock Sinbad had meant to fly to. Otherwise no sign of life in the street. It could hardly have been less like a jungle, and it was cold. "Tsk, tsk," said Sinbad. He made for where the ledge turned into the crevice between its house and the adjacent one. Alex saw him and looked away. When he looked back, Sinbad had turned the corner.

Monday after five Julien Schumann tended his bookstore in the upper town by himself. When the last customer had gone he locked up and drove home. Many stores in the upper town were still open for Christmas shoppers but streets were empty in the lower town. Julien parked and walked toward his house on crackling new ice. At the corner, a voice clear as crystal laughed and said in Corneille's French, "Oh rage! Oh despair! Inimical old age!" Julien listened. Vivid silence. Then in a voice not quite a scream, whose gender he couldn't determine, "Have I lived so long for this infamy?"

Julien approached old Pascale Mackenzie's house where the voice seemed to originate. He watched and listened in the dark freezing air. Julien was no more than two meters away when Pascale flung open her shutters. Each watched to see what the other would do next until the voice shrilled again, "Rage!" Pascale held up a hand—"Wait!"—and beckoned Julien through her house and out the back where a third time they heard the wild Corneille coming over the low wall from Catanese's dark greenhouse. Julien had to break the lock young Clusel had installed. Inside, Julien and Pascale found Alex Van Frank's missing parrot. Pascale went to telephone Alex. He and Anne arrived within minutes. Meanwhile Catanese reading in his bedroom had heard the commotion and come down expecting to find more vandalism in progress.

Sinbad hadn't known if he and Alex would ever be reunited. He was so glad to see the old geezer he flew straight at him, landed on his shoulder and held on for dear life, so tight his claws pierced the wool and cotton and went into Alex's flesh. Alex felt like clouting the dumb bird in the kisser but he kept gritting his teeth and grinning, and holding Anne close beside him while the flashbulbs went off.

Sinbad had lost 150 grams and he had bronchitis and fungal infections between his toes. Life in the crawl space under the greenhouse had been no honeymoon. The cold was the worst of it. Sinbad would have frozen solid without the radiator pipes under the floor, or had their insulation been better—whenever he could feel warmth coming through he pecked at it and a little more came through. He slept huddled against those places. There was a grated opening in the foundation wall that Catanese ought to have boarded up for the winter. Light and mice entered the crawl space there, but so did cold. Near the grate the ground froze and stayed frozen. Sometimes the most terrible wind came in and whistled around the pilings. Day after night after day after night, it got colder and colder until one night it grew acute because the radiator pipes were freezing. Huddled against the torn insulation Sinbad felt the temperature fall. He pressed closer for the warmth. There was less and less. Sinbad grew frantic and with the strength of desperation tore his way up through a weak place in the floor into the greenhouse. It was warm and he rested, but he soon realized that the temperature was falling here too. It was nightmarish. Beyond the glass walls and ceilings it was colder still. It was a horror show and Sinbad protested in the cries that brought Julien Schumann and Pascale Mackenzie to his rescue.

Sinbad ate mice in the crawl space, insects, spiders, vegetable matter off the pilings, bits of insulation. Mostly though he went hungry, especially earlier. Had he foreseen a tenth of the tribulation in store for him under the greenhouse he would have turned tail at first sight of it. The ledge he had half-flown, half-blown to from the Van Frank window took him around the corner back between houses. From the ledge he climbed a downspout to the rooftops and proceeded over them to the one with a view of the greenhouse.

In the beginning there was access to the crawl space from inside, and the door of the greenhouse had been ajar. Sinbad slipped in because it looked as if it contained a jungle. Inside was warm but dry, and the vegetation looked like a patch of jungle that had lost its flexibility and most of its color from swelling. Sinbad was exploring and had noticed a small opening in the floor and walked over for a closer look when he heard the door open wider and close. He thought perhaps it was the stranger who had evicted him — perhaps he hadn't yet done what it wanted. He hopped down through the opening onto cold earth. He listened to the tread he was to hear again and again. Catanese came into view above, an unhappy figure in black with slow movements that frightened Sinbad. It darkened the opening and then passed. Sinbad heard ominous little noises from time to time and then with a rumble the opening above closed. Then the footsteps, the greenhouse door opening and closing.

Several days passed during which Sinbad did everything he could to stave off terror. That was before he discovered the heat leaks in the insulation, nor had he yet learned what he could eat in the crawl space. He hadn't gone hungry a day in his life before and he was starving. For an eternity there were occasional noises above, unhurried footsteps, creaks.

JOE ASHBY PORTER

Sinbad couldn't have stood it another second when with a rumble the way into the greenhouse opened like an hallucination. Sinbad heard Catanese walk across overhead. He heard the greenhouse door open and close. He thought he heard Catanese walk away on snow, and a more distant door. He stuck his head through the hole. Nothing moved, least of all the succulents. Outside it was snowing. Sinbad scrambled up into the greenhouse. It was warm.

So it was that, to slake his delirious hunger and thirst, Sinbad proceeded to wreak the carnage that had disquieted Catanese. And as the man absorbed the shock and set about the salvage, there beneath his feet lay the culprit with diarrhea and toes insulted by sharp leaves, who saw his escape hatch close for the second and last time. Parrots are judgment-proof but were there a question of reparations Catanese's benefit would tell against his loss, for the cries that saved Sinbad also saved the plants. Neighbors helped restore the heat and celebrated the reunion of man and bird, recording it in photos, one of which appeared in the newspaper. Patrick Clusel, who took the photo, gave Alex an enlarged color print, which Alex framed and hung on his dining room wall. Sammy over in Lévis asked why he didn't make a painting of it. What the hell, Alex said, photography is an art now. I read it in a magazine.

In the close-up Anne's face is tightened. She almost smiles, her eyes already scouting for the next disaster. Alex looks ready to take even the pope under his free arm. He grins for Spinoza and Venus, he beams with exoneration. Between them you see blue, green, and yellow Sinbad. A wing touches Alex's cheek. The bird has turned his head at right angles to his breast, to bill the crown of Alex's head. His black eye is the brightest in the picture.

Soon the mystery of how Sinbad came to be in the greenhouse ceased to concern anyone. Alex and Anne supposed that one of them had left the cage unlocked, and that the parrot had somehow found his way out of the house and to the greenhouse on his own, as could perfectly well have happened.

It seemed likely that Alex would die before Anne and Sinbad, probably during the next decade, and his body be reduced to ash. The separatist sentiment in Québec would subside, and Anne be grateful it hadn't happened earlier. And old Sinbad would take food from her hand and speak in her voice, and Catanese sell the house in the upper town he by then never used, and the ferry ply the river as before.

JOHN KESSEL
Buffalo

In April 1934 H. G. Wells made a trip to the United States, where he visited Washington, D.C., and met with President Franklin Delano Roosevelt. Wells, sixty-eighty years old, hoped the New Deal might herald a revolutionary change in the U.S. economy, a step forward in an "Open Conspiracy" of rational thinkers that would culminate in a world socialist state. For forty years he'd subordinated every scrap of his artistic ambition to promoting this vision. But by 1934 Wells's optimism, along with his energy for saving the world, was waning.

While in Washington he requested to see something of the new social welfare agencies, and Harold Ickes, Roosevelt's Interior Secretary, arranged for Wells to visit a Civilian Conservation Corps camp at Fort Hunt, Virginia.

It happens that at that time my father was a CCC member at that camp. From his boyhood he had been a reader of adventure stories; he was a big fan of Edgar Rice Burroughs, and of H. G. Wells. This is the story of their encounter, which never took place.

In Buffalo it's cold, but here the trees are in bloom, the mockingbirds sing in the mornings, and the sweat the men work up clearing brush, planting dogwoods, and cutting roads is wafted away by warm breezes. Two hundred of them live in the Fort Hunt barracks high on the bluff above the Virginia side of the Potomac. They wear surplus army uniforms. In the morning, after a breakfast of grits, Sergeant Sauter musters them up in the parade yard, they climb onto trucks and are driven by Forest Service men out to wherever they're to work that day.

For several weeks Kessel's squad has been working along the river road, clearing rest stops and turnarounds. The tall pines have shallow root systems, and spring rain has softened the earth to the point where wind is forever knocking trees across the road. While most of the men work on the ground, a couple are sent up to cut off the tops of the pines adjoining the road, so if they do fall, they won't block it. Most of the men claim to be afraid of heights. Kessel isn't. A year or two ago back in Michigan he worked in a logging camp. It's hard work, but he is used to hard work. And at least he's out of Buffalo.

The truck rumbles and jounces out the river road, which is going to be the George Washington Memorial Parkway in our time, once the WPA project that will build it gets started. The humid air is cool now, but it will be hot again today, in the eighties. A couple of the guys get into a debate about whether the feds will ever catch Dillinger. Some others talk women. They're planning to go into Washington on the weekend and check out the dance halls. Kessel likes to dance; he's a good dancer. The fox-trot, the lindy hop. When he gets drunk he likes to sing, and has a ready wit. He talks a lot more, kids the girls.

When they get to the site the foreman sets most of the men to work clearing the roadside for a scenic overlook. Kessel straps on a climbing belt, takes an ax, and climbs his first tree. The first twenty feet are limbless, then climbing gets trickier. He looks down only enough to estimate when he's gotten high enough. He sets himself, cleats biting into the shoulder of a lower limb, and chops away at the road side of the trunk. There's a trick to cutting the top so that it falls the right way. When he's got it ready to go he calls down to warn the men below. Then a few quick bites of the ax on the opposite side of the cut, a shove, a crack, and the top starts to go. He braces his legs, ducks his head, and grips the trunk. The treetop skids off, and the bole of the pine waves ponderously back and forth, with Kessel swinging at its end like an ant on a metronome. After the pine stops swinging he shinnies down and climbs the next tree.

He's good at this work, efficient, careful. He's not a particularly strong man—slender, not burly—but even in his youth he shows the attention to detail that, as a boy, I remember seeing when he built our house.

The squad works through the morning, then breaks for lunch from the mess truck. The men are always complaining about the food, and how there isn't enough of it, but until recently a lot of them were living in Hoovervilles—shack cities—and eating nothing at all. As they're eating, a couple of the guys rag Kessel for working too fast. "What do you expect from a Yankee?" one of the southern boys says.

"He ain't a Yankee. He's a Polack."

Kessel tries to ignore them.

"Whyn't you lay off him, Turkel?" says Cole, one of Kessel's buddies.

Turkel is a big blond guy from Chicago. Some say he joined the CCC to duck an armed robbery rap. "He works too hard," Turkel says. "He makes us look bad."

"Don't have to work much to make you look bad, Lou," Cole says. The others laugh, and Kessel appreciates it. "Give Jack some credit. At least he had enough sense to come down out of Buffalo." More laughter.

"There's nothing wrong with Buffalo," Kessel says.

"Except fifty thousand out-of-work Polacks," Turkel says.

"I guess you got no out-of-work people in Chicago," Kessel says. "You just joined for the exercise."

"Except he's not getting any exercise, if he can help it!" Cole says.

The foreman comes by and tells them to get back to work. Kessel climbs another tree, stung by Turkel's charge. What kind of man complains if someone else works hard? It only shows how even decent guys have to put up with assholes dragging them down. But it's nothing new. He's seen it before, back in Buffalo.

Buffalo, New York, is the symbolic home of this story. In the years preceding the First World War it grew into one of the great industrial metropolises of the United States. Located where Lake Erie flows into the Niagara River, strategically close to cheap electricity from Niagara Falls and cheap transportation by lake boat from the Midwest, it was a center of steel, automobiles, chemicals, grain milling, and brewing. Its major employers—Bethlehem Steel, Ford, Pierce-Arrow, Gold Medal Flour, the National Biscuit Company, Ralston Purina, Quaker Oats, National Aniline—drew thousands of immigrants like Kessel's family. Along Delaware Avenue stood the imperious and stylized mansions of the city's old-money, ersatz-Renaissance homes designed by Stanford White, huge Protestant churches, and a Byzantine synagogue. The city boasted the first modern skyscraper, designed by Louis Sullivan in the 1890s. From its productive factories to its polyglot workforce to its class system and its boosterism, Buffalo was a monument to modern industrial capitalism. It is the place Kessel has come from—almost an expression of his personality itself— and the place he, at times, fears he can never escape. A cold, grimy city dominated by church and family, blinkered and cramped, forever playing second fiddle to Chicago, New York, and Boston. It offers the immigrant the opportunity to find steady work in some factory or mill, but, though Kessel could not have put it into these words, it also puts a lid on his opportunities. It stands for all disappointed expectations, human limitations, tawdry compromises, for the inevitable choice of the expedient over the beautiful, for an American economic system that turns all things into commodities and measures men by their bank accounts. It is the home of the industrial proletariat.

It's not unique. It could be Youngstown, Akron, Detroit. It's the place my father, and I, grew up.

The afternoon turns hot and still; during a work break Kessel strips to the waist. About two o'clock a big black De Soto comes up the road and pulls off onto the shoulder. A couple of men in suits get out of the back, and one of them talks to the Forest Service foreman, who nods deferentially. The foreman calls over to the men.

"Boys, this here's Mr. Pike from the Interior Department. He's got a guest here to see how we work, a writer, Mr. H. G. Wells from England."

Most of the men couldn't care less, but the name strikes a spark in Kessel. He looks over at the little potbellied man in the dark suit. The man is sweating; he brushes his mustache.

The foreman sends Kessel up to show them how they're topping the trees. He points out to the visitors where the others with rakes and shovels are leveling the ground for the overlook. Several other men are building a log-rail fence from the treetops. From way above, Kessel can hear their voices between the thunks of his ax. H. G. Wells. He remembers reading "The War of the Worlds" in *Amazing Stories*. He's read *The Outline of History*, too. The stories, the history, are so large, it seems impossible that the man who wrote them could be standing not thirty feet below him. He tries to concentrate on the ax, the tree.

Time for this one to go. He calls down. The men below look up. Wells takes off his hat and shields his eyes with his hand. He's balding, and looks even smaller from up here. Strange that such big ideas could come from such a small man. It's kind of disappointing. Wells leans over to Pike and says something. The treetop falls away. The pine sways like a bucking bronco, and Kessel holds on for dear life.

He comes down with the intention of saying something to Wells, telling him how much he admires him, but when he gets down the sight of the two men in suits and his awareness of his own sweaty chest make him timid. He heads down to the next tree. After another ten minutes the men get back in the car, drive away. Kessel curses himself for the opportunity lost.

That evening at the New Willard Hotel, Wells dines with his old friends Clarence Darrow and Charles Russell. Darrow and Russell are in Washington to testify before a congressional committee on a report they have just submitted to the administration concerning the monopolistic effects of the National Recovery Act. The right wing is trying to eviscerate Roosevelt's program for large-scale industrial management, and the Darrow Report is playing right into their hands. Wells tries, with little success, to convince Darrow of the shortsightedness of his position.

"Roosevelt is willing to sacrifice the small man to the huge corporations," Darrow insists, his eyes bright.

"The small man? Your small man is a romantic fantasy," Wells says. "It's not the New Deal that's doing him in—it's the process of industrial progress. It's the twentieth century. You can't legislate yourself back into 1870."

"What about the individual?" Russell asks.

Wells snorts. "Walk out into the street. The individual is out on the street corner selling apples. The only thing that's going to save him is some co-ordinated effort, by intelligent, selfless men. Not your free market."

Darrow puffs on his cigar, exhales, smiles. "Don't get exasperated, H. G. We're not working for Standard Oil. But if I have to choose between the bureaucrat and the man pumping gas at the filling station, I'll take the pump jockey."

Wells sees he's got no chance against the American mythology of the common man. "Your pump jockey works for Standard Oil. And the last I checked, the free market hasn't expended much energy looking out for his interests."

"Have some more wine," Russell says.

Russell refills their glasses with the excellent Bordeaux. It's been a first-rate meal. Wells finds the debate stimulating even when he can't prevail; at one time that would have been enough, but as the years go on the need to prevail grows stronger in him. The times are out of joint, and when he looks around he sees desperation growing. A new world order is necessary— it's so clear that even a fool ought to see it—but if he can't even convince radicals like Darrow, what hope is there of gaining the acquiescence of the shareholders in the utility trusts?

The answer is that the changes will have to be made over their objections. As Roosevelt seems prepared to do. Wells's dinner with the president has heartened him in a way that his debate cannot negate.

Wells brings up an item he read in *The Washington Post*. A lecturer for the Communist party—a young Negro—was barred from speaking at the University of Virginia. Wells's question is, was the man barred because he was a Communist or because he was Negro?

"Either condition," Darrow says sardonically, "is fatal in Virginia."

"But students point out the university has allowed Communists to speak on campus before, and has allowed Negroes to perform music there."

"They can perform, but they can't speak," Russell says. "This isn't unusual. Go down to the Paradise Ballroom, not a mile from here. There's a Negro orchestra playing there, but no Negroes are allowed inside to listen."

"You should go to hear them anyway," Darrow says. "It's Duke Ellington. Have you heard of him?"

"I don't get on with the titled nobility," Wells quips.

"Oh, this Ellington's a noble fellow, all right, but I don't think you'll find him in the peerage," Russell says.

"He plays jazz, doesn't he?"

"Not like any jazz you've heard," Darrow says. "It's something totally new. You should find a place for it in one of your utopias."

All three of them are for helping the colored peoples. Darrow has defended Negroes accused of capital crimes. Wells, on his first visit to America almost thirty years ago, met with Booker T. Washington and came away impressed, although he still considers the peaceable coexistence of the white and colored races problematical.

"What are you working on now, Wells?" Russell says. "What new improbability are you preparing to assault us with? Racial equality? Sexual liberation?"

"I'm writing a screen treatment based on *The Shape of Things to Come*," Wells says. He tells them about his screenplay, sketching out for them the future he has in his mind. An apocalyptic war, a war of unsurpassed brutality that will begin, in his film, in 1939. In this war, the creations of science will be put to the services of destruction in ways that will make the horrors of the Great War pale in comparison. Whole populations will be exterminated. But then, out of the ruins will arise the new world. The orgy of violence will purge the human race of the last vestiges of tribal thinking. Then will come the organization of the directionless and weak by the intelligent and purposeful. The new man. Cleaner, stronger, more rational.

Wells can see it. He talks on, supplely, surely, late into the night. His mind is fertile with invention, still. He can see that Darrow and Russell, despite their Yankee individualism, are caught up by his vision. The future may be threatened, but it is not entirely closed.

Friday night, back in the barracks at Fort Hunt, Kessel lies on his bunk reading a secondhand *Wonder Stories*. He's halfway through the tale of a scientist who invents an evolution chamber that progresses him through fifty thousand years of evolution in an hour, turning him into a big-brained telepathic monster. The evolved scientist is totally without emotions and wants to control the world. But his body's atrophied. Will the hero, a young engineer, be able to stop him?

At a plank table in the aisle a bunch of men are playing poker for cigarettes. They're talking about women and dogs. Cole throws in his hand and comes over to sit on the next bunk. "Still reading that stuff, Jack?"

"Don't knock it until you've tried it."

"Are you coming into D.C. with us tomorrow? Sergeant Sauter says we can catch a ride in on one of the trucks."

Kessel thinks about it. Cole probably wants to borrow some money. Two days after he gets his monthly pay he's broke. He's always looking for a good time. Kessel spends his leave more quietly; he usually walks into Alexandria—about six miles—and sees a movie or just strolls around town. Still, he would like to see more of Washington. "Okay."

Cole looks at the sketchbook poking out from beneath Kessel's pillow. "Any more hot pictures?"

Immediately Kessel regrets trusting Cole. Yet there's not much he can say—the book is full of pictures of movie stars he's drawn. "I'm learning to draw. And at least I don't waste my time like the rest of you guys."

Cole looks serious. "You know, you're not any better than the rest of us," he says, not angrily. "You're just another Polack. Don't get so high-and-mighty."

"Just because I want to improve myself doesn't mean I'm high-and-mighty."

"Hey, Cole, are you in or out?" Turkel yells from the table.

"Dream on, Jack," Cole says, and returns to the game.

Kessel tries to go back to the story, but he isn't interested anymore. He can figure out that the hero is going to defeat the hyperevolved scientist in the end. He folds his arms behind his head and stares at the knots in the rafters.

JOHN KESSEL

It's true, Kessel does spend a lot of time dreaming. But he has things he wants to do, and he's not going to waste his life drinking and whoring like the rest of them.

Kessel's always been different. Quieter, smarter. He was always going to do something better than the rest of them; he's well spoken, he likes to read. Even though he didn't finish high school he reads everything: *Amazing, Astounding, Wonder Stories.* He believes in the future. He doesn't want to end up trapped in some factory his whole life.

Kessel's parents emigrated from Poland in 1911. Their name was Kisiel, but his got Germanized in Catholic school. For ten years the family moved from one to another middle-sized industrial town, as Joe Kisiel bounced from job to job. Springfield. Utica. Syracuse. Rochester. Kessel remembers them loading up a wagon in the middle of night with all their belongings in order to jump the rent on the run-down house in Syracuse. He remembers pulling a cart down to the Utica Club brewery, a nickel in his hand, to buy his father a keg of beer. He remembers them finally settling in the First Ward of Buffalo. The First Ward, at the foot of the Erie Canal, was an Irish neighborhood as far back as anybody could remember, and the Kisiels were the only Poles there. That's where he developed his chameleon ability to fit in, despite the fact he wanted nothing more than to get out. But he had to protect his mother, sister, and little brothers from their father's drunken rages. When Joe Kisiel died in 1924 it was a relief, despite the fact that his son ended up supporting the family.

For ten years Kessel has strained against the tug of that responsibility. He's sought the free and easy feeling of the road, of places different from where he grew up, romantic places where the sun shines and he can make something entirely American of himself.

Despite his ambitions, he's never accomplished much. He's been essentially a drifter, moving from job to job. Starting as a pinsetter in a bowling alley, he moved on to a flour mill. He would have stayed in the mill only he developed an allergy to the flour dust, so he became an electrician. He would have stayed an electrician except he had a fight with a boss and got blacklisted. He left Buffalo because of his father; he kept coming back because of his mother. When the Depression hit he tried to get a job in Detroit at the auto factories, but that was plain stupid in the face of the universal collapse, and he ended up working up in the peninsula as a farmhand, then as a logger. It was seasonal work, and when the season was over he was out of a job. In the winter of 1933, rather than freeze his ass off in northern Michigan, he joined the CCC. Now he sends twenty-five of his thirty dollars a month back to his mother and sister in Buffalo. And imagines the future.

When he thinks about it, there are two futures. The first is the one from the magazines and books. Bright, slick, easy. We, looking back on it, can see it to be the fifteen-cent utopianism of Hugo Gernsback's *Science and Mechanics*, which flourished in the midst of the Depression. A degradation of the marvelous inventions that made Wells his early reputation, minus the social theorizing that drove Wells's technological speculations. The common man's boosterism. There's money to be made telling people like Jack Kessel about the wonderful world of the future.

The second future is Kessel's own. That one's a lot harder to see. It contains work. A good job, doing something he likes, using his skills. Not working for another man, but making something that would be useful for others. Building something for the future. And a woman, a gentle woman, for his wife. Not some cheap dance-hall queen.

So when Kessel saw H. G. Wells in person, that meant something to him. He's had his doubts. He's twenty-nine years old, not a kid anymore. If he's ever going to get anywhere, it's going to have to start happening soon. He has the feeling that something significant is going to happen to him. Wells is a man who sees the future. He moves in that bright world where things make sense. He represents something that Kessel wants.

But the last thing Kessel wants is to end up back in Buffalo.

He pulls the sketchbook, the sketchbook he was to show me twenty years later, from under his pillow. He turns past drawings of movie stars: Jean Harlow, Mae West, Carole Lombard—the beautiful, unreachable faces of his longing—and of natural scenes: rivers, forests, birds—to a blank page. The page is as empty as the future, waiting for him to write upon it. He lets his imagination soar. He envisions an eagle, gliding high above the mountains of the West that he has never seen, but that he knows he will visit someday. The eagle is America; it is his own dreams. He begins to draw.

Kessel does not know that Wells's life has not worked out as well as he planned. At that moment Wells is pining after the Russian émigrée Moura Budberg, once Maxim Gorky's secretary, with whom Wells has been carrying on an off-and-on affair since 1920. His wife of thirty years, Amy Catherine "Jane" Wells, died in 1927. Since that time Wells has been adrift, alternating spells of furious pamphleteering with listless periods of suicidal depression. Meanwhile, all London is gossiping about the recent attack

JOHN KESSEL

published in *Time and Tide* by his vengeful ex-lover Odette Keun. Have his mistakes followed him across the Atlantic to undermine his purpose? Does Darrow think him a jumped-up cockney? A moment of doubt overwhelms him. In the end, the future depends as much on the open-mindedness of men like Darrow as it does on a reorganization of society. What good is a guild of samurai if no one arises to take the job?

Wells doesn't like the trend of these thoughts. If human nature lets him down, then his whole life has been a waste.

But he's seen the president. He's seen those workers on the road. Those men climbing the trees risk their lives without complaining, for minimal pay. It's easy to think of them as stupid or desperate or simply young, but it's also possible to give them credit for dedication to their work. They don't seem to be ridden by the desire to grub and clutch that capitalism rewards; if you look at it properly that may be the explanation for their ending up wards of the state. And is Wells any better? If he hadn't got an education he would have ended up a miserable draper's assistant.

Wells is due to leave for New York Sunday. Saturday night finds him sitting in his room, trying to write, after a solitary dinner in the New Willard. Another bottle of wine, or his age, has stirred something in Wells, and despite his rationalizations he finds himself near despair. Moura has rejected him. He needs the soft, supportive embrace of a lover, but instead he has this stuffy hotel room in a heat wave.

He remembers writing *The Time Machine*, he and Jane living in rented rooms in Sevenoaks with her ailing mother, worried about money, about whether the landlady would put them out. In the drawer of the dresser was a writ from the court that refused to grant him a divorce from his wife Isabel. He remembers a warm night, late in August—much like this one—sitting up after Jane and her mother went to bed, writing at the round table before the open window, under the light of a paraffin lamp. One part of his mind was caught up in the rush of creation, burning, following the Time Traveler back to the Sphinx, pursued by the Morlocks, only to discover that his machine is gone and he is trapped without escape from his desperate circumstance. At the same moment he could hear the landlady, out in the garden, fully aware that he could hear her, complaining to the neighbor about his and Jane's scandalous habits. On the one side, the petty conventions of a crabbed world; on the other, in his mind—the future, their peril and hope. Moths fluttering through the window beat themselves against the lamp-shade and fell onto the manuscript; he brushed them away unconsciously and continued, furiously, in a white heat. The Time Traveler, battered and hungry, returning from the future with a warning, and a flower.

He opens the hotel windows all the way, but the curtains aren't stirred by a breath of air. Below, in the street, he hears the sound of traffic, and music. He decides to send a telegram to Moura, but after several false starts he finds he has nothing to say. Why has she refused to marry him? Maybe he is finally too old, and the magnetism of sex or power or intellect that has drawn women to him for forty years has finally all been squandered. The prospect of spending the last years remaining to him alone fills him with dread.

He turns on the radio, gets successive band shows: Morton Downey, Fats Waller. Jazz. Paging through the newspaper, he comes across an advertisement for the Ellington orchestra Darrow mentioned: it's at the ballroom just down the block. But the thought of a smoky room doesn't appeal to him. He considers the cinema. He has never been much for the "movies." Though he thinks them an unrivaled opportunity to educate, that promise has never been properly seized—something he hopes to do in *Things to Come*. The newspaper reveals an uninspiring selection: *Twenty Million Sweethearts*, a musical at the Earle, *The Black Cat*, with Boris Karloff and Bela Lugosi at the Rialto, and *Tarzan and His Mate* at the Palace. To these Americans he is the equivalent of this hack, Edgar Rice Burroughs. The books I read as a child, that fired my father's imagination and my own, Wells considers his frivolous apprentice work. His serious work is discounted. His ideas mean nothing.

Wells decides to try the Tarzan movie. He dresses for the sultry weather —Washington in spring is like high summer in London—and goes down to the lobby. He checks his street guide and takes the streetcar to the Palace Theater, where he buys an orchestra seat, for twenty-five cents, to see *Tarzan and His Mate*.

It is a perfectly wretched movie, comprised wholly of romantic fantasy, melodrama, and sexual innuendo. The dramatic leads perform with wooden idiocy surpassed only by the idiocy of the screenplay. Wells is attracted by the undeniable charms of the young heroine, Maureen O'Sullivan, but the film is devoid of intellectual content. Thinking of the audience at which such a farrago must be aimed depresses him. This is art as fodder. Yet the theater is filled, and the people are held in rapt attention. This only depresses Wells more. If these citizens are the future of America, then the future of America is dim.

An hour into the film the antics of an anthropomorphized chimpanzee, a scene of transcendent stupidity that nevertheless sends the audience into gales of laughter, drives Wells from the theater. It is still midevening. He wanders down the avenue of theaters, restaurants, and clubs. On the sidewalk are beggars, ignored by the passersby. In an alley behind a hotel Wells spots a woman and child picking through the ashcans beside the restaurant kitchen.

Unexpectedly, he comes upon the marquee announcing DUKE ELLINGTON AND HIS ORCHESTRA. From within the open doors of the ballroom wafts the sound of jazz. Impulsively, Wells buys a ticket and goes in.

Kessel and his cronies have spent the day walking around the mall, which the WPA is relandscaping. They've seen the Lincoln Memorial, the Capitol, the Washington Monument, the Smithsonian, the White House. Kessel has his picture taken in front of a statue of a soldier—a photo I have sitting on my desk. I've studied it many times. He looks forthrightly into the camera, faintly smiling. His face is confident, unlined.

When night comes they hit the bars. Prohibition was lifted only last year, and the novelty has not yet worn off. The younger men get plastered, but Kessel finds himself uninterested in getting drunk. A couple of them set their minds on women and head for the Gayety Burlesque; Cole, Kessel, and Turkel end up in the Paradise Ballroom listening to Duke Ellington.

They have a couple of drinks, ask some girls to dance. Kessel dances with a short girl with a southern accent who refuses to look him in the eyes. After thanking her he returns to the others at the bar. He sips his beer. "Not so lucky, Jack?" Cole says.

"She doesn't like a tall man," Turkel says.

Kessel wonders why Turkel came along. Turkel is always complaining about "niggers," and his only comment on the Ellington band so far has been to complain about how a bunch of jigs can make a living playing jungle music while white men sleep in barracks and eat grits three times a day. Kessel's got nothing against the colored, and he likes the music, though it's not exactly the kind of jazz he's used to. It doesn't sound much like Dixieland. It's darker, bigger, more dangerous. Ellington, resplendent in tie and tails, looks like he's enjoying himself up there at his piano, knocking out minimal solos while the orchestra plays cool and low.

Turning from them to look across the tables, Kessel sees a little man sitting alone beside the dance floor, watching the young couples sway in the music. To his astonishment he recognizes Wells. He's been given another chance. Hesitating only a moment, Kessel abandons his friends, goes over to the table and introduces himself.

"Excuse me, Mr. Wells. You might not remember me, but I was one of the men you saw yesterday in Virginia working along the road. The CCC?"

Wells looks up at a gangling young man wearing a khaki uniform, his olive tie neatly knotted and tucked between the second and third buttons of his shirt. His hair is slicked down, parted in the middle. Wells doesn't remember anything of him. "Yes?"

"I—I been reading your stories and books a lot of years. I admire your work."

Something in the man's earnestness affects Wells. "Please sit down," he says.

Kessel takes a seat. "Thank you." He pronounces "th" as "t" so that "thank" comes out "tank." He sits tentatively, as if the chair is mortgaged, and seems at a loss for words.

"What's your name?"

"John Kessel. My friends call me Jack."

The orchestra finishes a song and the dancers stop in their places, applauding. Up on the bandstand, Ellington leans into the microphone. "Mood Indigo," he says, and instantly they swing into it: the clarinet moans in low register, in unison with the muted trumpet and trombone, paced by the steady rhythm guitar, the brushed drums. The song's melancholy suits Wells's mood.

"Are you from Virginia?"

"My family lives in Buffalo. That's in New York."

"Ah—yes. Many years ago I visited Niagara Falls, and took the train through Buffalo." Wells remembers riding along a lakefront of factories spewing waste water into the lake, past heaps of coal, clouds of orange and black smoke from blast furnaces. In front of dingy row houses, ragged hedges struggled through the smoky air. The landscape of laissez-faire. "I imagine the Depression has hit Buffalo severely."

"Yes sir."

"What work did you do there?"

Kessel feels nervous, but he opens up a little. "A lot of things. I used to be an electrician until I got blacklisted."

"Blacklisted?"

"I was working on this job where the super told me to set the wiring wrong. I argued with him, but he just told me to do it his way. So I waited until he went away, then I sneaked into the construction shack and checked the blueprints. He didn't think I could read blueprints, but I could. I found out I was right and he was wrong. So I went back and did it right. The next day when he found out, he fired me. Then the so-and-so went and got me blacklisted."

Though he doesn't know how much credence to put in this story, Wells finds that his sympathies are aroused. It's the kind of thing that must happen all the time. He recognizes in Kessel the immigrant stock that, when Wells visited the U.S. in 1906, made him skeptical about the future of America. He'd theorized that these Italians and Slavs, coming from lands with no democratic tradition, unable to speak English, would degrade the already corrupt political process. They could not be made into good citizens; they would not work well when they could work poorly, and given the way the economic deal was stacked against them would seldom rise high enough to do better.

But Kessel is clean, well spoken despite his accent, and deferential. Wells realizes that this is one of the men who was topping trees along the river road.

Meanwhile, Kessel detects a sadness in Wells's manner. He had not imagined that Wells might be sad, and he feels sympathy for him. It occurs to him, to his own surprise, that he might be able to make *Wells* feel better. "So—what do you think of our country?" he asks.

"Good things seem to be happening here. I'm impressed with your President Roosevelt."

"Roosevelt's the best friend the workingman ever had." Kessel pronounces the name "Roozvelt." "He's a man that . . ." he struggles for the words, ". . . that's not for the past. He's for the future."

It begins to dawn on Wells that Kessel is not an example of a class, or a sociological study, but a man like himself with an intellect, opinions, dreams. He thinks of his own youth, struggling to rise in a class-bound society. He leans forward across the table. "You believe in the future? You think things can be different?"

"I think they have to be, Mr. Wells."

Wells sits back. "Good. So do I."

Kessel is stunned by this intimacy. It is more than he had hoped for, yet it leaves him with little to say. He wants to tell Wells about his dreams, and at the same time ask him a thousand questions. He wants to tell Wells everything he has seen in the world, and to hear Wells tell him the same. He casts about for something to say.

"I always liked your writing. I like to read scientifiction."

"Scientifiction?"

Kessel shifts his long legs. "You know—stories about the future. Monsters from outer space. The Martians. *The Time Machine.* You're the best scientifiction writer I ever read, next to Edgar Rice Burroughs." Kessel pronounces "Edgar" as "Eedgar."

"Edgar Rice Burroughs?"

"Yes."

"You *like* Burroughs?"

Kessel hears the disapproval in Wells's voice. "Well—maybe not as much as, as *The Time Machine*," he stutters. "Burroughs never wrote about monsters as good as your Morlocks."

Wells is nonplussed. "Monsters."

"Yes." Kessel feels something's going wrong, but he sees no way out. "But he does put more romance in his stories. That princess—Dejah Thoris?"

All Wells can think of is Tarzan in his loincloth on the movie screen, and the moronic audience. After a lifetime of struggling, a hundred books written to change the world, in the service of men like this, is this all his work has come to? To be compared to the writer of pulp trash? To "Eedgar" Rice Burroughs? He laughs aloud.

At Wells's laugh, Kessel stops. He knows he's done something wrong, but he doesn't know what.

Wells's weariness has dropped down onto his shoulders again like an iron cloak. "Young man—go away," he says. "You don't know what you're saying. Go back to Buffalo."

Kessel's face burns. He stumbles from the table. The room is full of noise and laughter. He's run up against that wall again. He's just an ignorant Polack after all; it's his stupid accent, his clothes. He should have talked about something else—*The Outline of History*, politics. But what made him think he could talk like an equal with a man like Wells in the first place? Wells lives in a different world. The future is for men like him. Kessel feels himself the prey of fantasies. It's a bitter joke.

He clutches the bar, orders another beer. His reflection in the mirror behind the ranked bottles is small and ugly.

"Whatsa matter, Jack?" Turkel asks him. "Didn't he want to dance neither?"

And that's the story, essentially, that never happened.

Not long after this, Kessel did go back to Buffalo. During the Second

World War he worked as a crane operator in the forty-inch rolling mill of Bethlehem Steel. He met his wife, Angela Giorlandino, during the war, and they married in June 1945. After the war he quit the plant and became a carpenter. Their first child, a girl, died in infancy. Their second, a boy, was born in 1950. At that time Kessel began building the house that, like so many things in his life, he was never entirely to complete. He worked hard, had two more children. There were good years and bad ones. He held a lot of jobs. The recession of 1958 just about flattened him; our family had to go on welfare. Things got better, but they never got good. After the 1950s, the economy of Buffalo, like that of all U.S. industrial cities caught in the transition to a postindustrial age, declined steadily. Kessel never did work for himself, and as an old man was little more prosperous than he had been as a young one.

In the years preceding his death in 1946 Wells was to go on to further disillusionment. His efforts to create a sane world met with increasing frustration. He became bitter, enraged. Moura Budberg never agreed to marry him, and he lived alone. The war came, and it was, in some ways, even worse than he had predicted. He continued to propagandize for the socialist world state throughout, but with increasing irrelevance. The new leftists like Orwell considered him a dinosaur, fatally out of touch with the realities of world politics, a simpleminded technocrat with no under-standing of the darkness of the human heart. Wells's last book, *Mind at the End of Its Tether*, proposed that the human race faced an evolutionary crisis that would lead to its extinction unless humanity leapt to a higher state of consciousness; a leap about which Wells speculated with little hope or conviction.

Sitting there in the Washington ballroom in 1934, Wells might well have understood that for all his thinking and preaching about the future, the future had irrevocably passed him by.

But the story isn't quite over yet. Back in the Washington ballroom Wells sits humiliated, a little guilty for sending Kessel away so harshly. Kessel, his back to the dance floor, stares humiliated into his glass of beer. Gradually, both of them are pulled back from dark thoughts of their own inadequacies by the sound of Ellington's orchestra.

Ellington stands in front of the big grand piano, behind him the band: three saxes, two clarinets, two trumpets, trombones, a drummer, guitarist, bass. "Creole Love Call," Ellington whispers into the microphone, then sits again at the piano. He waves his hand once, twice, and the clarinets slide into a low wavering theme. The trumpet, muted, echoes it. The bass player and guitarist strum ahead at a deliberate pace, rhythmic, erotic, bluesy. Kessel and Wells, separate across the room, each unaware of the other, are alike drawn in. The trumpet growls eight bars of raucous solo. The clarinet follows, wailing. The music is full of pain and longing—but pain controlled, ordered, mastered. Longing unfulfilled, but not overpowering.

As I write this, it plays on my stereo. If anyone has a right to bitterness at thwarted dreams, a black man in 1934 has that right. That such men can, in such conditions, make this music opens a world of possibilities.

Through the music speaks a truth about art that Wells does not understand, but that I hope to: that art doesn't have to deliver a message in order to say something important. That art isn't always a means to an end but sometimes an end in itself. That art may not be able to change the world, but it can still change the moment.

Through the music speaks a truth about life that Kessel, sixteen years before my birth, doesn't understand, but that I hope to: that life constrained is not life wasted. That despite unfulfilled dreams, peace is possible.

Listening, Wells feels that peace steal over his soul. Kessel feels it too.

And so they wait, poised, calm, before they move on into their respective futures, into our own present. Into the world of limitation and loss. Into Buffalo.

for my father

TOM HAWKINS
Wedding Night

I have worked at the bus-station magazine stand since 1953, waiting for the right girl to come along. When I took this job, the paint on that wall over there was new; it was a light green color then. The servicemen from the Korean War would stop and buy cigarettes, and I learned the insignia from the Army, Coast Guard, Navy, and Marines.

Once I was held up by a stocky white man in a brown jacket. Showed me the two teeth he had left in his head and the barrel of a little tape-wrapped automatic pointed at my heart. I gave him all the dough but never felt scared. Way I saw it, he was just like me, and I could die behind that counter and just walk away inside his skin, with a few dollars to spend. We were all one thing. So I handed him the money, feeling richer right away— three-hundred-twenty-three dollars, and let him get away before I called the cops.

I heard they never caught him, then I heard they caught him in another state—Utah I think—and then I heard they found him dead in an airport parking lot in Kansas. I don't know. He may be out there yet. He may be back. May hold me up tonight, or just shoot me dead, or both.

Anything can happen in the bus station. In the 1960s, we had what we called the hippies, young people in ragged get-ups. They used to sleep all over the furniture in sleeping bags, with packs and rolled-up tents.

That's when I began to think that the right girl might come along after all, some girl who'd grown tired of the long-haired boys, and tired of the road, and walk home with me and hold my hand, and curl up with me in my bed and on my squeaky springs. I kept an eye out. One day I saw a young lady. She looked so long-tired and in need of a friend. I bought her a sandwich and coffee, and a peanut-butter cup. I bought her some aspirin and a pint of milk, fingernail clippers and a souvenir shirt.

I told her I had a place where she could come to rest and stay, as long as she might want. I told her it wasn't fancy and wasn't but one room, but what was mine was hers. I knew it was clean. I'd cleaned it up the day before when I saw this girl hanging around.

She stroked my hair and said my heart was full of love. She said she had to sleep about twelve hours and then she'd go away. I took her home. She slumped down on the bed and cried—told me I was "so very kind." And then she slept like the dead. I lay down on the floor beside her, where I said I'd stay. In the middle of the night I woke up on fire, and the room was turning. I couldn't think. The air turned furry, where I crept up and slid in bed beside her, that girl still completely dressed. She breathed like the sea. I touched her skin, just her skin inside her clothes. She really never woke, just sighed and turned. In the morning when I woke up in the bed, she was gone.

I've worked here since 1953, waiting for the right girl to come along. I guess she did. Some good marriages don't last long.

TOM HAWKINS

PHILIP GERARD
Death by Reputation

Thursday morning Paul Sartorius awoke to the certainty that something would happen today to change his life. In the steam of the shower he recalled having the same feeling on the morning of the day he met his wife, Connie, and on the morning of the day she died in traffic, five years ago now, when he'd first taken the archaeology appointment at State University. And that feeling had overtaken him like a virus on the morning of the day his draft notice arrived in the mail.

But the feeling had been present on an equal number of mornings of days on which nothing happened. He shut the water off as suddenly as changing the subject and toweled vigorously, raising blood to the surface of his skin.

Paul walked briskly the three blocks to campus clutching a hard-used leather bookbag. He gave more attention than usual to his Introduction to Archaeology class this morning. He was a good teacher and a popular one, at ease behind a lectern or stalking the dais in restless pursuit of archaeological truth.

Nothing happened at lunch, except that Dean Willis came by to congratulate him on his book, *The Speaking Creature*, which would assure tenure. In it he argued that, since the australopithecines developed modern locomotive apparatus and articulate fingers long before their brain case increased in size, the evolution of the brain was directly caused by social developments, especially language, an offshoot of specialized sign language and play. After *A. Africanus* disappeared a million years ago, the human brain mushroomed to three times its previous size.

"Much obliged," he said to Dean Willis, shaking his dog-eared hand, wondering if this was all his premonition would amount to.

After a review session in his Methods course, he held his office hours, argued range of variation among individuals of the same species with three graduate students, and walked home to an ordinary supper of baked fish, chowder, and beer, and went to sleep early over William Longacre's article in his theory textbook after several glasses of scotch, which he had discovered while mourning his wife. (A forgotten Christmas present stashed away in a bottom cupboard, suddenly come in useful.) It was a quiet night, and he decided, as he often had since Connie's death, to sleep in his overstuffed chair by the fireplace among the insulating walls of books and artifacts of days in sere, rock-hard places like Africa, New Mexico, and Arizona: potsherds, human jawbones, fossilized maize, shreds of ancient fabric dyed with blood and plant juice, a petrified wooden club some plains Paleo-Indian had once used to stun buffalo and wolves. Or that was his theory, since it was an oddity among other easily categorized artifacts found in the same complex, a kill site in Colorado. The club was found in association with parts of a human skeleton and the bones of an extinct kind of bison, and the supposition was that this particular individual had come to a bad end in pursuit of red meat. Hunting was a dicey business in those days.

He let the fire burn down, snapped off his reading light, and dreamed of nothing.

Shortly after three a.m. Paul Sartorius killed a burglar who startled him awake and stood in the doorway to his study glazed by moonlight. The draught from the open window woke him, he decided later. The man poised on the balls of his feet, his back to Paul, a heavy spanner wrench in his left hand. When he turned his head, Paul struck him with the petrified club. Once, in the head, dead on the spot.

The police arrived so immediately Paul wondered if someone else had called them first, and they escorted him to the station while their men and the coroner did all the official things that have to be done when one man kills another. "It's only a formality, Professor," the detective said. He didn't look like a detective to Paul: tall and loose, his face unlined by care, his blue eyes bright behind sporty wire-rimmed glasses, comfortably well-dressed in a sweater, slacks, and corduroy jacket. More like a writer or a professional man. Still, he was a man acquainted with murder. "He's one we've been after for a long time for a dozen different things. Robbery, assault, the violent stuff. And he had a weapon, correct?"

Paul nodded. The housebreaking tool had already been collected, labeled, and sent to the police lab for verification of fingerprints.

"There won't be any trouble. This is merely to protect you, in case anybody makes any accusations later."

It made sense. Paul said, "I don't mind." He remembered his premonition and wanted to tell the detective about it, but he knew better than to tell people more than they wanted to know.

The squad car dropped him back at home a little before six and the study was full of light. He had bought the house mainly because of all the windows, but now he felt they had exposed him, let in things that were better kept out, and he felt a rush of fear now the danger was past. The place on the shelf formerly occupied by the club was empty—it was evidence, after all. For just a second Paul imagined a circle of wolves and other menacing creatures accumulating outside the pale of a campfire, around which squatting bearded men gestured seriously and plotted how to consolidate their tenuous hold on a hostile world.

The window through which the burglar had entered was still open. Paul shivered in the draught and closed it, took a steaming shower, and walked to campus early. He wanted to be walking. He balked at being alone in the house with the enormity of what had happened. He felt no guilt, just that nagging belated fear. He wished he'd had time to mull over his choices and reach a proper, reasoned decision in a matter so grave, but that was not how it happened. He could not say, in fact, what had caused him to act in such an instinctive, violent fashion, and this troubled him. It seemed to him, in retrospect, that he had not even been fully awake when he laid the club over the man's head. He could not remember reaching for the club, could only recall the rough fact of it dangling in his hand after the man was down, the moonlight lying across him like a sudden illumination of conscience. He realized he hadn't even seen the man's face, then or afterward, so he didn't have that cliché of memory to haunt him. What, then? He had the unshakable sense of having been plunged into the heart of a mystery as fundamental as religion, and yet the whole thing was a *fait accompli*, nothing to ponder, nothing to solve.

At his office he left the door ajar and handled a model skull like a baseball, fingering the eye sockets, imagining the impudent hump of *medulla oblongata*, running a finger along the blade of brow ridge, feeling the smooth globe of the cap where more primitive ancestors had a spikey sagittal crest to anchor the *temporalis*, a massive chewing muscle attached to the jaw. Larry Thompson, the chairman of the department, slipped in.

"God, you're here. I called the house. It's on the radio, Paul. Lord. Can I do anything?"

"That was fast." Paul continued turning the skull in his fingertips, searching it like a globe, probing each recess and orifice like a doubting Thomas.

"You don't have to meet your classes today. What have you got? I'll take care of it." His enormous horn rims made him look like a man wearing a mask.

"There's just the one. I'll be all right, Larry." Today was Physical Anthropology. They were considering the brain case, the *calvaria*, the armored hollow in the skull where thought and reason resided, often at odds. It had shrunk since Neanderthal, and no one could say just why. Paul had always found the irony reassuring.

"If you need me, stop by. I'll be around all day. We can have a drink later. How about two o'clock?"

"Righto. Thanks." He had the urge for a drink right now. Instead, he scanned the skull with his magnifying lens and watched the imperfections come up: the faults in joining the parts, indentations, bumps, discolorations, the minute violations of the artistic form as the sculptor would have wrought it. Then he gently hammered his fist into the plastic temple and imagined the brain case erupting under the pressure of the club, thought and reason scattering in an instant like cartoon stars.

In Physical Anthropology, Paul stressed stereoscopic vision, a flattening of the nose, and the enlargement of the brain case as primary adaptations of the savannah-dwelling *Australophithecus Africanus*, an upstart lately descended from the trees, and his larger cousin, *Robustus*.

"Stereoscopic vision? Like binoculars?" queried a game student in the back row.

"Exactly. It allows perspective, especially over distance, and particularly in an environment where depth perception is essential to survival."

"Like in trees?"

"Like in trees. With bad vision, they'd be falling out like so many ripe apples. Olfaction wasn't so important anymore, but good vision was. Vision was all they had, and color, naturally, was a part of it." He thought momentarily of the man he'd killed, silver on black, two-dimensional, the outlines fogged by sleepiness, and later, the study clarified by the morning sun through the windows like a movie finally focused.

"But these jaspers were walking, not swinging from trees." A titter from the back.

"Certainly. But they developed from the most advanced arboreal primates, or so we believe on good evidence. Once on the savannah, *Australo-*

pithecus probably discovered that his highly specialized eyesight was also his best defense against predators. He was virtually helpless, except for his ability to think and see. His olfactory sense had receded, you see, and was far inferior to that of the other savannah dwellers."

"Why?"

"His brain needed the room formerly occupied by the apparatus of a muzzle, or his head would be dangerously large and heavy."

All at once, he realized the class had stopped taking notes, as if it were a decision reached by jury. Paul was baffled, stopped stalking the platform in mid-stride. A girl in the front row, a favorite of his, looked up at him and said, all at once, "Professor, are you going to tell us about it?"

He was stunned. How could he tell them about something he himself felt he had witnessed only secondhand, of which he knew less and less with each passing hour? He shook his head, sheathed his papers, and walked out, feeling somehow accountable to them and having no idea at all of what to do about it.

Paul ate lunch in a sandwich shop off campus, but Harrison, the social anthropologist, found him anyway.

"You've broken a taboo, old buddy. But not to worry. The only thing for it is to go get drunk together."

It sounded reasonable to Paul, whose eyes were burning from concentration and lack of rest. His mouth was dry and his tongue tasted like a foreign object, never mind that he couldn't eat a bite of his club sandwich, assembled there on his plate like artifacts.

At Murphy's, over their second scotch, Harrison said, "I'm sorry as hell it happened. But don't let it, you know, get to you." Paul watched his eyes, noticed a certain restless excitement there. Harrison leaned in confidentially. "Listen. You may not believe this, but everybody's killed somebody." He swigged the rest of his drink to make the point.

Paul was stunned. "How's that?"

"You heard me, Paul. Everybody. Even me. I shot a Chinese in Korea. I did that."

"Just one?"

"Yeah."

"It's not the same."

"Don't you believe it."

"It was my house. My house."

"You know what I mean."

Paul had nothing to say.

"You need a place to stay till it blows over?"

Paul drank. "No, really. I'm fine." He was beginning to feel the liquor. His headache was gone, his mouth full of saliva, his heart beating normally. "I never knew about Korea," Paul said, for lack of anything better. He resented Harrison for bringing it up, though he was not sorry for the company. Man has always been a social creature, he reflected, organized against the lovers of the primitive night who would digest him as an offhand imperative.

"Hell, it's not the kind of thing you advertise, especially in my line. People expect a certain objectivity, some tolerance."

"Yeah."

"I never even think about it now, except when I eat Chinese."

Paul had no answer for that. Harrison had to get going. Paul opted for another drink. Harrison left a twenty on the table. "Have one on me. Meditate on some Zuni ruins."

Paul didn't watch him leave. His only meditation was Connie, and his grief was that he had loved her more each year since her passing, something he could neither explain nor accept. It had to do with need, he thought, basic things. Without her his life had skewed far out of balance, for she had been his truing agent, and lately more and more he had immersed himself in his work with all the grim efficiency of a ghoul, a graverobber. But so are all men, he thought: picking through the sacred grave goods of their forebears like dogs, worrying the clean bones with the gnaw of curiosity. Two drinks later one of his students walked in. She was one of his brightest. Paul thought it unusual for her to be coming to this bar alone.

"Hello, Professor Sartorius."

"Hello, Miss Dubus."

"Oh, call me Andy, please. We're not in class."

"Okay." He did not say, "Call me Paul," and he didn't know why.

"Should I sit here and pretend like I don't know?"

He shook his head. "I could buy you a drink, though."

"Okay, that's nice."

Paul ordered and got an Irish coffee for her.

"I don't mean to take liberties, but you handled yourself very well in class today, considering all you've been through."

"Thanks. It's kind of you to tell me." He drank, unsure what to say. What *had* he been through?

"What will happen now?"

"Oh, I don't know. Some kind of a hearing, I guess."

PHILIP GERARD

"You're not in any trouble?"

"The detective said don't worry about it."

"That's a relief."

But it wasn't a relief to him. Somehow it should be more trouble to fix. They were all being too easy on him. He looked at her face in a manner he himself would have considered rude, had he been one of the dozen early patrons drinking furtively in the dim, filtered light. Outside it had begun to snow, and this helped his mood. He felt that somehow this long moment in his life must be frozen, last long enough to be analyzed to some conclusion. The girl was not a beauty, but her gesture touched him, and her chubby, unformed face held something essentially good. The oversized designer glasses she wore only exaggerated her look of innocence, for they belonged on someone much older. He did not want to sleep with her, except in the way one wants to cuddle a child, a son or daughter, chastely and without words, only nonsensical sounds of love and reassurance.

"I can't really believe what I did."

"You can talk about it if you want, or you can just drink. I know you don't have anyone. This isn't the time to not have anyone."

She was right, Paul knew, only it wasn't the sympathy of an ingenue he needed, but the love of years. "I think I'll just drink, but I don't mind the company."

She smoothed her blonde hair over her temples and adjusted herself in her seat. "Look, here's a story. I met a boy in high school, and we used to make love at the drive-in."

"That's an old story."

"That's not it." She was blushing so that he could hardly stand it. "He never amounted to much. Last I heard, he's still pumping gas back home. But he told me something once, the only thing he ever said that I remember. He said, 'We're the only creature on earth that's ever surprised by what we do.' That's what he said." She drank confidently, as though she had somehow laid the whole matter to rest.

"I don't know if surprised is the right word."

"You know what I mean."

Paul nodded as he finished the drink and almost before it was drained ordered another with a wave of the hand.

"You're going to have an awful head tomorrow."

"Tomorrow isn't the problem, dear."

After three more, she said, "One more and then I'm walking you home." It was a small town, everybody walked. "The snow will clear your head."

"Not that." He was getting drunk. He liked the feeling. It somehow relieved him of responsibility, decision, and floated him along as he knew most men floated along all the time. He deserved this one time. He hadn't been stinking drunk since Connie's accident. That time he had fallen and broken his arm and been grateful and ashamed of the cast he wore for six weeks while he continued to belt the scotch and eat his dinner out of cans blackened on the gas flame of his stove.

The drink came. He faced it with sudden disgust, as if it were medicine, drained it in one swallow, and rose to leave, staggering. Andy held him by the arm, like a little girl guiding her drunken old man home. He almost fell down the steps going out, but she hoisted him with a sturdy grip.

"Surprise," she said.

The sudden cold did clear his head somewhat. It was only a few blocks to his house, and he let Andrea handle the complex matter of getting the key into the keyhole. Such a maneuver was beyond him for the moment. Inside, she sat him nervously on the couch and loosened his tie. He closed his eyes.

"I can't stay. You realize that. But I only live up the street. My address is here, if you need me." He heard a pen scratching and a paper folded and weighted with a coffee mug on the end table. "Good night, Professor."

Some time after the door had clicked shut, he opened his eyes and realized he had forgotten to meet Larry, hours ago. He put the girl's address in his overcoat pocket, then went outside and urinated in the snow without a second thought, catching the sudden tang of it in his nostrils. Halfway through the act, he realized what he was doing and was mortified. What if the neighbors had seen? But no one was out and about. He watched his breath float for a moment in the snowy light and then walked for hours through brittle cold along snow-slicked streets, careful to watch straight ahead and avoid looking in windows, afraid of what he might see in them.

At the doorway to a tavern he passed a hot cider vendor and breathed in the aroma of spiced apples. He passed a restaurant venting the odor of hot grease and broiling meat, and the alley nearby exuded the unmistakable smell of bile and human juices. The wind freshened and scoured his face. He felt all the bones in his face and imagined that he must look changed, skin tight and slick and primitive, eyes hard and cold as marbles. He felt several lifetimes removed from the fresh, soft, fleshy youngster who had guided him home with such care and gentleness.

At six a.m. he was still walking. Despite a cold so intense it had frozen brittle the hairs of his nostrils and glazed the water of his eyes like a skin of

PHILIP GERARD

ice, his head still felt feverish. He remembered little of the night, but was alert enough to realize the snow had stopped. He would go and see her. If an answer was to be found that would let him go on as he had before, she must have it.

"Have you got a telephone?" he asked her.

She stood before him in the doorway holding a flannel nightgown closed with one pink hand, smelling of sleep. "I thought you might come over. Come in, I'll put some coffee on."

He dialed Larry Thompson's number and got Larry after a dozen rings. "What's wrong, guy? You in trouble or something?"

"Listen, Larry. You still have that cabin upstate, the one we all stayed at year before last?" It had been a hunting trip, a chance for men to get away from their wives and their towns and drink without glasses and urinate out of doors.

"Why? You want to go up there?"

"I've got the weekend. I thought it might help."

"You know how to get there? You know the turnoff?"

"I can remember all right."

"Key's in the woodbox."

"Can you let the detectives know where I am? I don't want them to get the wrong idea."

"Righto. Have a ball. Call me if you have to—there's a phone at the lodge store. You going alone?"

Paul cradled the phone without answering and blinked his eyes twice to clear them. The sudden warmth of her house was almost more than he could stand. He still could not feel his toes.

She was at his elbow with a cup of coffee in a handmade ceramic mug. "I'll just get dressed," she said.

"You don't mind?"

"I said it's not the time to not have anyone."

They walked back to Paul's house. With a courage born of company and light, he entered the place and rifled through his drawers for a change of clothes, a raggwool sweater and a Greek fisherman's cap he had not worn in years. Connie had given them to him. He changed his shoes for boots, found gloves, and they were out of town before he had spoken another word to her, his old Volvo taking the turns nicely, the tricky road an exercise in focus.

It was an hour and a half to the cutoff and twenty minutes more up a steep muddy track to the cabin. The mud thawed in the sun and the wheels spun vigorously for purchase in each patch of sunlight, but they made it. In a fit of pragmatism, he had stopped at the lodge store and provisioned them with bacon and eggs, coffee, steaks, beer, and scotch.

"What are we going to do here?" she said, stepping out of the car into the muddy snow and flexing her back, arms akimbo.

"How should I know?"

He found the key and they entered the cabin like spelunkers, testing the light, listening for sounds of habitation, stepping as though each floorboard were a trap. It smelled of sweet pinesap, woodsmoke, and damp animal fur. He lit a kerosene lamp and the room was illumined like a stage: double bunks along the far wall, wood stove for cooking in the center, fireplace in the corner, table, chairs, cupboards, a threadbare rug. Above the mantel the mounted head and cape of a black bear.

"Cozy."

"Don't get the wrong idea. I don't even know why I brought you. Nothing in my life seems to be following a plot anymore."

In a gesture he did not anticipate, she hugged him hard, tucking her head in so close to his chin that for the first time he was aware of her smell. He liked it, but in this context he was repelled by it, for it was the smell of sugar and milk, a nursery smell.

"Make love to me, Paul. Maybe you'll feel better. Maybe I will, too."

He broke off clumsily and staggered like a man reeling from a blow. "Let's unpack," he said.

"That wasn't the right thing to say, was it?"

"Look, Andy, you're a good girl." He paused. The last thing he wished to do was to hurt this girl, who wanted only the best for him. The words he had, though, were only the vaguest shadow of what he wanted to say. "It just wouldn't be right, you know? Maybe it was unfair to bring you up here like this, to lead you on. That's not what I meant at all."

Andrea had not moved. "I don't mind. I just wasn't sure what you wanted."

"I just wanted . . . company."

"Shall I make a fire?"

"Yes," he said. "By all means." Paul shed his parka and gathered the raggwool sweater around his shivering body in bunches.

Hours later, they sat before the fire with a single blanket draped across their shoulders and a good meal heavy on their stomachs and sipped scotch from the bottle. Outside the snow had resumed, tentatively at first, then with real, bewildering force. The winds swept over the roof like surf and broke with the same thunder, wailed around the chimney top like restive spirits and occasionally blew up a starburst of cinders from the fire.

Paul held the poker in his hand. The end of it glowed from the heat. His hand trembled with the weight of it, and he allowed the hooked brass tip to rest in the embers. It seemed after a few minutes so heavy he could not lift it again in this lifetime. Outside he imagined animals snowbound in their dens or prowling for prey, badgers and weasels stalking the night killing ground among the black posts of pine and spruce, moose and deer and bear safely bedded down in windless places snug enough to hold and husband their own warmth, all they had of life. In his mind's eye, the steep forest was a negative, the air silvered with snow, all else only shadows, owning no weight or substance. By midnight he knew they were cut off, the precarious road up from the highway a long warp of drifted snow, and he breathed easier. The blizzard descended upon them like a living thing, capricious, vengeful, and blind, weighting the air with primal spasms of sound rent from an ungodly silence, pounding at the walls of the world and threatening to break through at any moment. In the old days, Paul knew, such a storm would have made men pray.

He thought again of those bearded forms crouching at the edge of light and arguing, as men and only men will do. He imagined their passionate voices rising with the wind in shrill dissonance as the argument heightened and the danger moved in furtively from the hills, the woods, the shrouded mountains where other deadly creatures lurked, their progress steady as rain, their brains blunt as cobbles, their collective will inevitable as weather, waiting their turn.

Paul longed for Connie the way a tortured man longs for death, and he had only this girl, this amiable child, who was not his mate. The snow continued. He listened. He rocked her in his arms. He watched the fire and waited. The light of the flames betrayed his vision, and the heat pressed the bones of his face like fingers until he could no longer feel his skin, only the hot rings of his eye sockets and the dumb gape of his mouth. For hours, he listened to it gathering outside.

He ought to be hanged, he knew now. He was a murderer. He understood at last why the club had been so anomalous, what had been the fate of the Indian hunter whose disarticulated bones had been catalogued with it. The thesis was so simple, so naturally elegant, that Paul could not quite believe he had missed it all these years. It was not play, not even language, that had bloated the brain of Homo sapiens like a tumor. They had all been too easy on the beast. Docile, uncompetitive man would never have needed to rise so high, to be so smart, to achieve such social complexity, including tact, gentleness, the ability for fierce love and loyalty. Nothing like a social imperative had selected for cleverness, cunning, ambition. For the hunger to invent words and tools, tribes and religions. For will.

He conjured again the ring of men around the open hearth, watched them waggle their frail flinted spears, listened to their yabbering voices: they were bickering over meat. In an instant of inspired prescience that would assure the survival of his kind world without end, the shrewdest of them discovered murder.

So that was it. Paul knew his book was a fraud, his future an exile from the world of light, this fire the only real thing he could ever count on again.

When at last she had fallen sleep in front of the hearth, he banked the fire, tucked the blanket around her pliant shoulders, and stood shirtless at her back. Then he slipped into the thick raggwool sweater like a second skin, put on his hat, and stepped outdoors. The air was thick with nightsmells: the bite of woodsmoke, the tang of pine boughs, the sting of snow. The wind had slacked, and the snow sifted down through the barren branches gently, like dust, layer upon layer, lens upon lens, like the amber seal of history. It drifted high around the foundations with a soft rattle, settled ever deeper on the lost road, powdered the brim of Paul's cap like a residue of fallen light.

He stared up into the black trees, blind, in his quickening man's heart the rapture of fear, the thrill of recognition, the blessed weight of choice.

PETER MAKUCK
Piecework

Where I live now, the only real snow is remembered, so it wasn't until the patterns of farmland below the jet pod began to turn white that the purpose of my trip came back. The last time home, at a summer reunion picnic, I became unaccountably irritated with a younger cousin who complained that his mother still asked in phone conversations when he was coming "home." He wasn't a kid anymore, and his home, he said with annoyance, was southern California, not New England.

At LaGuardia I switched planes, and was almost glad for the heavy weather that buffeted the small twin-engine DeHavilland. Thoughts of my mother disappeared as we bounced and made sickening turns. The cockpit curtain was open; I could see a red flashing light, hear the kind of beep a smoke alarm makes. The engines suddenly changed pitch. Outside the window nothing but blackness. The sailor beside me hadn't spoken once since boarding. Finally he groaned, "Oh mama," then laughed. Beads of sweat had collected like tiny pearls along his dark hairline. Suddenly a torrent of personal history poured out of him: the Sixth Fleet, Beirut, Libya, long watches, alerts, shore leave, the lure of Italian quiff—the last not for him: disease. Besides, he was a Christian. He couldn't wait to see his wife and parents. His mother-in-law, though, was a mutant, an alien, but after almost a year, he'd be happy to see even her—well, for the first few minutes anyway.

The plane plunged and my stomach rose. The sailor looked at the book I was squeezing to death. "They made a movie of that," he laughed, but nothing was funny. The wings of the aircraft creaked loudly and a great knock came from the hull. Then the smile died from his lips. After a lifetime, the nose of the plane dipped and you could see between the pilot and co-pilot's shoulders—a runway lined with white lights. My seatmate said nothing further. As we taxied, the pilot cautioned continuing passengers not to deplane: "Our stay on the ground will be brief."

Through a tattered curtain of snow, and the morbid smell of jet fuel, I walked a few paces behind the sailor. In the terminal, Bill Dumfy was waiting. "You look a wreck," he said. "Rough flight?"

I said it was. His handshake was clean and hard. Bill was good-looking, had clear blue eyes that were always on guard, and a jaw shaped like a trowel.

"Bags?"

"This is it," I said, holding up my carry-on. "I've got to be back day after tomorrow."

"Your father's got some plumbing problem at the house," he said, as we left the parking lot. "He asked me to pick you up."

Bill and I hung around together in high school, worked on our cars at my father's Flying A station, and were in college together until Bill flunked out. After that, he worked at my father's place until he could find something better. If you were friends in high school, you were supposed to be friends forever—that was my mother's sentimental idea, to a lesser extent my father's. People were very important to my mother. She collected them, or they gravitated to her easy humor, told her their stories, like Herb the furnace man who, when I was very small, bet my mother a shot and a beer that he could put three golf balls into his mouth at the same time. To head off the attempt, she quickly put the shot and beer on the oak table in our kitchen, and told him to forget it, but he wedged them anyway into his mouth until his eyes goggled and cheeks got bigger than Dizzy Gillespie's at full blow. All, no doubt, to entertain a kid kept home during a blizzard.

"Hey, how about my new wheels?"

"Very nice," I said, not able to sound enthusiastic.

"Look, why don't you call your old man, tell him you got in okay."

I said there was no point in stopping—we would be home in twenty minutes.

"Hey, we don't have to stop." And he presented me with a cellular phone. "Neat, huh? Saves me lots of time and mileage."

"You're doing all right," I said.

"Not bad for a kid who didn't finish college."

PETER MAKUCK

What Dumfy did for a living was hard to nail down. He worked for a jeweler named Fenster who not only had three stores but was silent partner in the cable TV company, owned two new condos, and was a heavy gambler. Though Dumfy would neither confirm nor deny, Fenster was into other things as well, things that required a karate psycho like Dumfy for a driver. A teenage destroyer of bricks, boards, bones and faces, Dumfy had been lethal, way ahead of his time. I wondered if my father knew of his doings.

"You still working for Fenster?"

"I might be," he said.

On the radio, too loud as usual, was an oldie by the Byrds, "Turn, Turn, Turn." I asked him to lower the volume so I could hear the phone, which rang and rang. I began to worry, but my father finally answered. His voice was a husk. Was I okay? I said yes. Then there was no sense talking now. He'd see me soon.

Dumfy recradled the phone. "Killer, huh?"

I said it was, then, for something to say, I asked about our buddy Fagan.

"You'll see him later. You coming to Hooter's tonight, aren't you?"

I said I didn't know: this trip wasn't business as usual.

"Well, bring your father down. Take his mind off things. Your old man's a great piece of work. Remember the time . . ."

Time and memory—a heaven and a hell, I thought, but this was not something I could say to Dumfy. He played his cards close. The personal or reflective was best kept private. On the radio, the Byrds were singing about seasons, a time to get and a time to lose.

From the crest of the new bridge I could see the pink sodium lights of the hospital parking lot where my mother lay in a coma. I asked him to take me there.

"Your father told the nurse not to let anybody in."

I asked why.

"That friend of your mother's—the one who used to buy ground sirloin and feed stray dogs in front of the A & P—"

"Mrs. Penland."

"Right. What a piece of work, huh?" He laughed, a great lover of new slang, amusing himself.

"Well, what about her?"

"She, ah, was taking Polaroid pictures."

I told him I didn't get it.

"You know, of your mother, in that . . . state. Your father went ape, told the head nurse not to let anyone in."

Dumfy's taillights got small and disappeared at the curve. With no streetlights on our road, it was very dark and the basement windows of my father's house were warm squares of yellow. A small plane droned overhead. Glad to be on the ground, I crunched through the snow and peered in. They were laughing. Stan, as usual, needed a shave. Bulky and bearish, he held a beer in his big paw. A recent widower and one of my father's old buddies from the gas station, he wore only a T-shirt, tufts of brillo-like hair escaping from the frayed collar. My father illustrated something funny with his hands, and they laughed again. I threw up the overhead door.

"Christ, it's cold," said Stan, "get that door down."

We shook hands. The gust of cold air and my presence made them solemn. I set my bag on the floor and blew on my frozen knuckles. My father asked how the flight was. Stan asked if the weather was any better in the South. We said things about our new President who, during the campaign, claimed he was a Southerner. "He claimed three states as his home," said my father. "Like the devil, he's from everywhere."

They shook their heads. A reminder to mourn, I had shattered their good mood, but finally Stan said, "Politicians would say they was from Mars to get elected. Then they tell you to go hump a sandbag."

It was a relief to laugh. We avoided any talk about my mother, talking instead about college and pro basketball. Stan popped a propane torch, heated a joint, and Dad muscled an overhead pipe with a Stillson until the joint gave and a braid of red water bled into a white plastic pail. I asked about the plumbing problem. Stan handed me the length of old pipe he had just hauled down, explaining there was mineral build-up. I held it to the light like a telescope and squinted; the inside diameter was reduced to the size of a pencil.

"Makes the water pump work twice as hard," said Stan.

"Pressure really builds up inside the system," said Dad. "Then something's got to give."

Every move Stan made was an effort. His breath came heavily. I wondered how he could stand it with just a T-shirt. Though the pipes wouldn't freeze, the basement was fairly cold. A drinking man, he reminded me of Herb, our old furnace fixer. "This pvc is great stuff, huh Ace?" He had always called my father Ace—something that annoyed my mother, who disliked nicknames.

"Great stuff," said my father. "What an improvement over that old cop-per."

Stan carefully poured himself a hooker from the jug of Seagrams on top of the furnace. "PVC," he said, looking at me over the rim of the jelly glass, "won't narrow down with mineral build-up." He winked then knocked it back. "This stuff'll outlast the house."

I looked up at the ceiling where bright white lengths of it ran ahead and disappeared in the dim light.

"We'll have plenty of water pressure now," said my father, almost apolo-getically, for our shower ran weakly, something my mother had long com-plained about.

"We're going to put in a new water pump too," said Stan.

My father looked at me. "No sense taking any chances," he said. "Might as well do it all. Won't take too much longer."

Fine, but why now, especially given the circumstances? I wanted to talk, but I couldn't, not in front of Stan.

"How's Dumfy doing?" my father asked.

I told them about his cellular phone.

Stan finished sawing a pipe and grunted himself up from a kneeling position. His face was red and shiny with sweat. When he finally caught his breath, he said, "Car phones! What'll they think of next, huh Ace?"

I asked them if I could help.

"We're knocking off," said Dad.

I headed for the stairs.

"Oh, by the way," said Dad, "we don't have water. If you have to, you know, take a leak, go out back. Otherwise, drive down to Mr. Donut on the Post Road."

I couldn't believe it. Climbing the basement stairs, I heard Stan telling my father how easy life was now, what with indoor plumbing, and conve-niences they never had as kids.

Restless, I walked from room to room. My trips home were usually in the summertime, so I had never seen the heavy thermal curtain hung in the doorway to the front room. Conservation. Oil's expensive, my father was fond of saying, though he never hung this black curtain with white lilies until I left home. Your father's a riot, my mother would say, and joke about his Depression mentality. My mother grew up in the city, my father on a farm, and at first she resented living in the country, in "the sticks" as she put it. But she learned to make every stick matter, grew to love birds and could name every one that came to the three or four feeders she put up near the living room and kitchen windows. She was proud of her self-reliance, the way she managed while my father was off working two jobs. Foxes, pheasants, raccoons, deer, and even ducks from the pond across the street would make their way into our yard for handouts. My mother described them and talked about them to her telephone friends. "What else have I got to do out here in the sticks?" she used to ask, exhaling a noxious cloud of cigarette smoke in mock exasperation. We also had a dog, two cats, two parakeets. My father was indifferent to animals. "You and your mother wouldn't be so crazy about animals if you had to take care of them like I did as a kid, get out of a warm bed at four in the morning to milk the cows," he said.

Then I remembered Molly, the black and white cat, wondered where she was, and opened the door to my mother's room. There was a bleak odor of cigarettes. The room had always been a private sanctum and I was almost afraid to enter. Her bureau mirror held an empty wall. Suddenly it hit me that this would be the first night I had ever spent in the house with my mother not here. Looking at the empty mirror, I imagined what she saw years ago when I finally left home, for I had been her only career.

The hollow strokes of a hammer boomed from below.

TV greased the walls with its narcotic blue flicker and made it easier somehow for us to talk while watching the screen. Dad said he hadn't been able to go to the hospital for the last two days.

"Do you want to go tonight?" I asked.

He shook his head. He had been there for ten straight days, staying all day. He could do nothing but hold her hand, and that didn't help either of them. He couldn't take it—he needed to skip a few days. Besides, he wanted to be here to help Stan, who was saving him the arm and leg that a real plumber would take. I told him I'd pay for a real plumber but he laughed. "Big spender."

"Really," I said.

"If I threw away money like you and your mother, you'd never have gone to college."

"Lighten up," I said. "We can afford it now."

"What about when the hospital gets finished with us? Now don't get upset with me, but somebody's got to think about these things."

"I'm not upset with you," I said, and tried to peer past my reflection in the window. Then I told him that a few days before her stroke, my mother and I had argued on the phone; she got angry and hung up on me.

PETER MAKUCK

He shook his head. "She never told me, so it must not have amounted to anything. Forget about it."

"I was trying to get her to stop smoking again."

"But *why*?" he asked. "You *know* how she is."

"But those damned cigarettes," I said. "They don't call the fucking things coffin nails for nothing."

He shook his head and looked away, then suddenly assumed my mother's role, fixing me with a disgusted look for "that kind of language." I must have expected him, a lifelong nonsmoker, to side with me, but there was no such betrayal. Finally he said, "You don't know what it was like for your mother."

"I just wanted her to live," I said, probably implying that he didn't, and should have long ago taken measures to put a stop to that chronic, ratchety cough of hers that was never long silent.

"She really worked at it a couple of times, you know?"

I knew, and didn't want to know. Cigarettes were merely a symptom, one term of the complicated equation of which I was a part. After a while, I said, "I'm going to the hospital."

"There's no point," he said.

I explained that I needed to say a few things. There was an outside chance she could still hear.

"Suit yourself," he said, eyes glazing, "but Dr. Farrington told me there's too much damage for her to hear anything."

The refrigerator was frighteningly empty. Shelves that were usually laden with nicely wrapped leftovers, cheeses, crackers, juices, fruits and fresh vegetables were now almost bare. There was a jar with one pickle afloat, black bananas, cold cuts, and two six-packs of beer. I made us sandwiches, and we sat at the kitchen table where I had eaten thousands of my mother's good meals, the grainy oak table where old Herb had long ago performed for a shot and a beer.

After we had eaten, Dad told me that there were things we had to do in the morning. "We've got to be ready," he said.

"Sure," I said, "I'll help you." I vaguely knew what he meant, but didn't want to think about it.

"I've already done a few things," he said. "Made some arrangements myself." *Myself* meant alone, utterly alone. I should have come sooner, but he told me not to, there was nothing I could do. She might stay in this coma for months. "Tomorrow I want you to help me with something else."

"Sure."

We cleaned up and went back to the TV room. On the screen, Mickey Rooney, in a comical green top hat, was flying a helicopter to rescue a downed jet pilot played by William Holden, who was in a muddy ditch and being shot at by North Korean soldiers. The sound was down low as it usually was after my mother went to bed, for our house was small. The radiators pinged and sighed to each other from different rooms. I hadn't been tired but suddenly found myself exhausted. I drained the last of my beer and went out the back door to take a leak before turning in. Woodsmoke, that most nostalgic of scents, and the feel of snow underfoot worked a cruel magic, and I had the feeling I had never left home. Snowflakes were softly falling, touching my cheek and melting. An airplane made its blind way toward the northeast. *Our stay on the ground will be brief.*

Stan's first poundings in the basement woke me. Then it was quiet. He and my father were talking. My old room, small, with the faded fleurs-de-lys wallpaper, college pennant, the same crack in the ceiling plaster that suggested the outlines of Italy, the bedside table and doily—nothing had changed except for the presence of a big cobweb on the bedside lampshade.

A few more inches of snow had accumulated during the night, and the sun made everything dazzle. The radiators sighed in their sad, familiar way. The kitchen smelled of coffee and for a little while, home seemed more than just a word. Warm cup in hand, I wandered from room to room, looking at objects I knew so well, wedding pictures, pictures of my grandparents, an embarrassing one of me in an altar boy's cassock and surplice, my mother's huge collection of books. I was looking for something new or never before seen, something that would answer all questions and make happily-ever-after a possibility. Then I sat in her chair by the window. Puffs of snow drifted from the pine boughs. My mother, at this hour, would be enjoying the birds, except that the feeders were all empty, and there were few birds in sight. On the back porch I found the various kinds of seed and filled the feeders. Scarcely had I finished when juncos, chickadees, titmice, and a few jays arrived. Not to mention squirrels. The pines gave a moaning sound to the wind and made the cold seem colder. I was glad for the movement, something to do. I noticed cat tracks at the back door but Molly, the big black-and-white, was nowhere to be seen. Then my father came upstairs.

"I don't know," he said. "I haven't seen her since the rescue squad took your mother."

"I see her dish on the back porch."

He looked puzzled, as if the cat were something from another life. He scratched his head. "Look, could you go to the hardware store for us?"

"Sure."

"We've run out of U brackets to hold up the pipe."

"Tell me about Mrs. Penland."

He bit his lip and shook his head. "Since Sam's gone, she's not all there. Never was, but she's worse now. Did Dumfy tell you? She was taking Polaroid pictures of your mother, right there in the hospital. Can you imagine!"

Pieces of family history that had somehow escaped my attention now seemed very important. "How did you and Mom ever get to know the Penlands anyway?"

"Tim, we need those brackets, hunh? I'll tell you later."

My father's Ford, always garaged, was spotless, perfectly tuned, and had, as he put it, lots of "pep." You had to have power, had to be ready for difficult situations. After my first teenage accident, and the few other accidents I'd had over the years, I'd always get the lecture about defensive driving and hear about his perfect record; but the lecture was never cruel and, in fact, became a joke, my mother playing an imaginary violin every time he started. Nonetheless, he was quite serious when he said you had to be alert, ready to react—it was a personal philosophy more than just a way to drive. My mother was too preoccupied to drive, he said. Too much of a dreamer behind the wheel. Of an old college friend of mine, a guy who was stupendously absent-minded, and about whose impracticality Mom loved to hear stories, my father would always shake his head in genuine dismay: "When's that guy going to snap out of it, wake up? You know what happens to lambs, don't you?"

I drove to the True Value by way of Immaculate Heart and the hospital. I stopped for a minute next to the parochial school and watched an old nun gingerly pick her way over a patch of ice on the sidewalk. I thought of going into the church to say a prayer. At the hospital, I looked up at the windows, trying to accomplish . . . I didn't know what. There too I thought of going in, but didn't. Instead, I just stared at a huge wall of windows, as if my mother might suddenly appear and bless me with a wave.

At a light on Boston Post Road, a Jaguar pulled up beside us in the next lane. The guy had a phone to his ear. My father spotted him and said it must be the kind Dumfy had.

"Cellular," I said.

"Right. I read they have fake ones people can impress each other with. TV ads for the real ones say you need 'em to beat the competition."

The guy had a grave look on his face. He exhaled deeply, shook his head solemnly. I hoped he wasn't simply beating the competition. I hoped he was saying just the right thing to the right person, hoped the expensive phone, in this case, was a matter of personal salvation.

We pulled under the portico. The building was of brown brick, new, with cloister walks joining both wings, two white birch trees in the atrium where that special taped music of all funeral homes meets you either before or just after the unctuous man in a formal dark suit. My father gave his name and said "The director, Mr. Sullivan, is expecting me."

"Oh yes, right this way, Mr. Maloney."

The heavy high-pile carpet silenced footfalls and gave me an unreal sense of floating. And there was that grim flowery odor, always too strong, as if to conceal.

But Mr. Sullivan was a good man; we had known him for years. An old classmate of my mother's from Immaculate Heart, he always had his cars serviced at Dad's Flying A. "A terrible thing," he said softly to Dad, coming from behind his walnut desk. "Laura was too young for this." He shook his head. "I'll never forget her wonderful humor." Tall, dark-haired, and stoop-shouldered, he ushered us into a room with row upon row of coffins on display: metal and wood. Bronze, silver, and gold; oak, pine, and mahogany. Glossy. Hidden hinges. Brass and stainless-steel handles. Sectioned lids, the top half of each open for inspection, printed cards on the pillows, each describing the materials. A wall phone discreetly chimed three times. "Excuse me," said Mr. Sullivan.

The coffins had supports curtained off so that each seemed to be fixed in permanent levitation, the magician gone. Unwanted, an image from a sci-fi movie came to me: brain-dead humans in a special environment, vitally tethered, were suspended from ceilings, warehoused for their organs. Suddenly I felt the shame of what the nuns at Immaculate, in a different context, used to call "impure thoughts." I felt even less pure when Mr. Sullivan returned and we had to ask prices, decide how much my mother was worth. Finally we simply chose oak with a lovely rivering grain that was much like our kitchen table.

When we got outside, an icy wind lashed at us. The broomlike tops of trees rocked back and forth. Streamers of slate cloud were moving quickly

PETER MAKUCK

across the sky. My father shivered as he got into the car. "Now we're ready," he said.

I wasn't so sure, and neither was he, but I knew what he meant.

"I've got to get back to help Stan, but there's just one more thing I want you to see."

I stood in the curtained-off, cold front room, and looked out at the snow-field and swamp across the street. The late light was pale and cold. Night seemed to lurk in two or three of the big swamp cedars, ready to spread. An owl, chased by three or four other birds, swooped and swerved out of sight around the corner of the house. Stan was gone when we returned. Without him, my father seemed lost. "I wonder where he's gotten to?"

"He'll be along," I said. "He probably needed something else at the hardware store."

"Or the liquor store," said Dad. "He's a good soul though."

Soul—my mother used the word exactly that way too, a word from another time. I wondered about the soul, the spirit, where it went, if anywhere. Was it like smoke that curled from a bottle and dissolved once the cork was pulled? An obsolete poetic idea?

Dad looked out the window at the woods beyond the swamp. "They're going to build a new mall over there," he said from a distance, from some gray place in the future, from a time without my mother or maybe anyone else to share his time. Old people, you saw them often in malls. I was angry that my mother had left him.

"Ah, here he comes," said my father, hustling off.

I watched the red Chevy pickup plunge up the drive, and Stan, carrying a large bag in one hand, a toolbox in the other, lumber toward the house. My father met him halfway and took the toolbox.

A doer, my father wasted no time. After the funeral home, he had taken me to the cemetery. We stood at the southernmost end of the stones under the extended left hand of a bronze Blessed Mother twenty feet high where steady wind had blown away the snow and exposed the earth. At our feet was a new marker stone, flush with the ground. At first, I was confused; it said:

Leo J. Maloney
August 20, 1924–

"I bought two plots," he said. "Your mother's marker will go right beside mine. The Benetti Monument people have it ready and are just waiting. . . ." His breath caught. He sighed and turned quickly away. I followed him. I wanted to put my arm around him, but my father wasn't physical that way, and I knew he wouldn't want it.

Heavy clouds scudded out of the northeast. The sunshine was spotty. Dad was looking east, out toward the bay below us and several miles away. "Beautiful, isn't it?"

I said it was. The cemetery was on a narrow strip of high ground confined on three sides; over the years since my grandparents died, gravestones had migrated almost a quarter mile eastward. I could see the end—a stone wall some hundred yards down the snowy slope, then the twiggy crowns of winter maples, then the distant water. "Your grandparents are way up the other end," said my father, as if reading my thoughts. I watched the cloud of his breath dissolve. Skin was tight on his face; it was ruddy, weathered from years of outside work, and now all the little lines were showing deep and sharp, like cuts, as if made by a sculptor's knife. His eyes watered.

I said, "Every year Mom and I pulled weeds, trimmed around their headstone."

After a while, he said, "Cemetery's come a long way. That's progress, huh?"

I tried to smile.

"You know why they have these high walls?" he pointed.

I said no.

"People are dying to get in."

Just when I got the joke, he sobbed. It was like a soft retch. "O Christ, let's go."

Far out on the wrinkled silver plane of the bay, a tiny black boat was pushing out to sea.

I walked around the house, looking at my mother's objects of affection (knickknacks that belonged to her mother), then her books, finding the Hardy Boys, *Treasure Island*, *Robinson Crusoe*—things she started me off with in grammar school. I stood by the rocker where she liked to read, the one where she once sat, a book splayed in her lap, and wanted to talk. A teenager just home from school, I was in a rush to get somewhere; but, to make matters worse, she lit a cigarette, and the smoke, like deadly angel hair, curled toward me with its odor of defeat. She talked about a blue parrot she had as a little girl; the bird was given to her by her adoptive parents and was killed when a drunken friend of her father's staggered into the cage. The parrot fluttered to the floor, and the heavy cage fell on top of it,

PETER MAKUCK

breaking its back. That blue Brazilian with a gold breast had brightened her girlhood. The loss was terrible, like the early loss of parents. Her nostalgic mood would have produced other pieces of the same story had I not said, in an unthinking adolescent way, that the tale was a rerun. Her look was stricken. Saying nothing further, she simply picked up her book and continued to read. I apologized immediately, but it did no good, and over the years she reminded me how deeply she had been cut.

Once, on a rare visit to our home, Mrs. Penland said, "The more I realize how cruel human beings are, the more I love animals." My mother, newly angered by some empty argument we'd had, looked at me and said, "Amen," driving me toward the door with her black eyes.

The phone rang. It was Mary Dryer. I didn't recognize the name. School. She had gone to Immaculate Heart with my mother and was a friend in high school too. It was a real shame, my mother was so young, such a good soul. Becky Penland had run into this Mary Dryer and given her the news. Had my mother's condition changed? Was there any hope? How was my father taking it? She felt bad that she had lost touch with my mother; as a matter of fact, she had just recently been thinking of calling her, renewing their friendship. I felt like saying she was a bit late but knew she needed to talk, needed to tell me that life was sometimes hard but God was good, that after a certain point people start to fall like autumn leaves. Then she began to list the fallen leaves, describe for me how hard it was for her after Jake, Tillie, and Wendell went. Finally, though, having no idea who she was or who any of these people were, I interrupted, describing things I needed to help my father with. Of course, of course, she knew how much I must have on my mind. God bless me, my mother was so lucky. And how was I doing? In my life? Where was I now? I told her where I was living, but her voice was full of doubt; she was positive I was living in Nebraska. That was what Becky Penland told her, and she was always right about things like that. I was fairly certain, I said, that I was living in North Carolina. In fact, I'd never even been to Nebraska. Well, she said, your mother would have wanted it that way.

All the new one-way streets and redevelopment made the once-familiar somewhat strange, but the steeple of Immaculate Heart, Star of the Sea, always told you where you were, and Hooter's was in sight of it. Though I wasn't any longer a kid, a bedside visit to my mother was nonetheless daunting, as difficult in its own way as remaining home above the whine of

Stan's power tools and pounding. I stood in the icy street of this working-class neighborhood and looked up at the steeple, remembering the door behind the organ in the choir loft, the climb up to the forbidden bell tower with Fagan one recess, and paying bitterly at the hands of Sister Paulita for that shining view of the town that threw itself together at our feet, a vivid geography of origins.

Peering through the sweaty plate glass of Hooter's, I could see Fagan at the bar sitting under the sign that read "Blarney Spoken Here." It was crowded, smoky. Dumfy, in shirt and tie, circled the pool table, cue in hand. Fagan's eyes were already at half mast, and he was back on cigarettes again, his face fogged in by smoke. Eddie, the bartender, brought me a beer. Fagan told him I was bad news, there would definitely be trouble.

Eddie said he was sorry to hear about my mother. Bald down the center of the skull, with bushy eyebrows and thin lips, Eddie reminded me of the actor Peter Boyle. Younger than my father, he looked older. In between customers, prompted perhaps by my situation, he told us about his mother's final illness, how he was still paying bills. She wanted to die at home, and he saw to it. She wanted visits from the priest, and he tried to see to that too. "But those priests," he said, "are like doctors nowadays—they don't like to make house calls. I phone the rectory at Immaculate and get Father O'Brien. Ya 'member him?"

Keat, hunched next to Fagan, laughed. "He must have beaten the shit out of all of us."

"At least once," said Fagan.

"Whatta piece of work," said Dumfy.

"So he asks all these questions," said Eddie. "How bad is she? What parish do we belong to, Immaculate or Saint Joe's? Did she make her Easter Duty? What color's an orange? All this shit. Finally he says he'll come, right? 'Meet me at the door with a lighted candle,' he says. Fine. So he comes with the holy water, oil, and all that shit, and hears my mother's confession. What can she tell him? She's an old lady, a saint, right? Anyway, he gives her the Last Rites. And I give him a contribution. Nothing for nothing, right? But guess what? My mother perks up, fools everybody. Seeing the priest made her feel good. A week or so goes by, and she wants the priest again. I call, beg him to come. Another priest, this time a young guy, different generation. I get all these excuses. He's going on a retreat, needs to get in touch with himself, he's got a cold, can't get his ass in gear, what have you. Not lazy, right? Just resting before he gets tired. So a week goes by, and I call again. This time they're short-handed, etc. The bottom line is: We *gave* your mother Last Rites. One per customer. As far as we're concerned, she's already dead! End of story."

Everyone laughed. When Eddie was off on refills, Fagan said, "He's in heaven, loves an audience."

Dumfy said, "Is he a piece of work, or what?"

Keat said, "He got kicked out of Immaculate in the eighth grade, and he's never forgiven them. End of story."

"Eddie's an act," said Fagan.

Keat shook his head. "Wrong. The Church has got him bent out of shape. If you're against, he's for. If you're for, he mocks the clergy."

Eddie came back and drew beers from the tap in front of us. "Watch out," he said, "here comes another Immaculate wacko."

It was Mike Murray, dragging in fresh cold air that reddened his large face. Snow on his black overcoat quickly lost its white and glittered.

"It's the bullshitter," said Keat.

"Look who's talking," said Murray.

Keat laughed and began taunting Murray, who was already well into his Friday night tour of duty. Drinking, Keat could be quickly mean.

"The Church," sighed Eddie. Then he wondered why the most screwed up people he knew all graduated from Immaculate, why we had swallowed all the crap the nuns dished out. Dumfy objected—he never believed any of it. Eddie laughed. "What are you talking about? You're all contradictions. You wouldn't say *fuck* or *Jesus Hairy Christ* if your life depended on it, but if Fenster told you to put one of his bad loans in the hospital, you wouldn't think twice."

"I just don't like profanity," said Dumfy.

Everyone laughed.

"What a piece of work," said Keat.

Eddie, Keat, and Dumfy began to argue about lying, what was wrong with it, why it was sinful, wondered why Murray was such a bullshit artist.

"Great theologians," said Fagan. He told me I brought out the worst in people. Normally these guys talked about sports.

I asked Fagan how his parents were. "Christ, I haven't seen my parents since—well, I didn't even see them at Christmas. You know, I've been reading this essay in *Psychology Today* about how you're never free until your parents are dead." He dragged on his cigarette. "I believe it." He looked at me and laughed. "You're too sentimental, man. I mix cement all day, I'm a realist."

Man. He used that word all the time, as if he had been born on the Black side of town and his father wasn't president of Valley Tool and Die. But tonight that didn't bother me. I liked Fagan, his openness. Tall, he often stood one-footed, if there was something to lean against, and put you in mind of a heron with a salt-and-pepper cowlick. He had left college only a few credits shy of graduation, probably to spite his parents, and dramatically say no to what he called "all the brie and chablis people of Glen Cove." He read a fair amount and saw himself as a kind of Eric Hoffer.

Eddie delivered two more beers. "So how long you home for?"

Home—that word again. I explained I had to leave tomorrow afternoon. How did I like it down there? I coughed up the usual clichés about mild winters, how nice it was not to have to scrape my windshield, a slower way of life, etc.

"Lotus land," sneered Fagan.

I didn't say anything.

"Hey, just kidding," he said. "Maybe your mother'll pull through. Doctors might be wrong—it wouldn't be a first."

Keat and Murray were heating up. "You wouldn't know truth," said Keat, "if it pissed in your eye."

"The fuck I wouldn't."

"The fuck you would."

Fagan informed me that this was a continuation of an argument about Murray now claiming he was a college graduate. Over the years, Murray had claimed lots of things, like being in a bar in Tijuana when the margarita was invented, sometimes saying that salt around the rim was his contribution. Sometimes he claimed to have met and talked with various celebrities. Though Murray verged on small, and we all went to the same high school, he once claimed he and Keat played football on the same team. That was too much. Keat had warned him about insulting other people's intelligence. For some, Murray's stories were a harmless, if not pathetic, way of keeping the hounds of insignificance at bay, but Keat was pathological about truth telling. And now this story about the college degree. The pressure, I suppose, was too great.

I looked into the mirror just at the moment he hit Murray square in the face. Murray dropped below the bar. Fagan, jumping back, clipped my ear with his elbow. I saw things as if the sound were suddenly turned down. The fighting was far away for a moment. Murray came up with blood on his face, his mouth a black O. Dumfy jumped in to break it up. Somebody held Murray. Dumfy cocked a warning finger, but Keat swung. Dumfy blocked the punch and executed one of those short karate thrusts with the fingertips. Keat doubled and held his stomach.

Then the sound was back, far too loud, and the air seemed thicker than ever with cigarette smoke. Leaving, I heard Eddie asking what the hell was the matter with them. "You known each other for years, you supposed to be friends, for Christ's sake!"

I drove around in the lightly falling snow, rolling slowly through familiar streets, but the closer to the hospital I came, the more detours I made. I felt like a criminal rehearsing some horrible deed, worse for having stopped at Hooter's. Nothing had the right feel, the needed ritual touches. I was flying blind.

The hospital was an old rupture that popped out here and there, all annex and bulge. As instructed at the desk, I went left and right, up and down ramps, through tunnels, past glassy labs and supply rooms. The place was a labyrinth of secretive twists that led me past green-garbed workers and a woman shuffling along with a walker. Finally I took an elevator to the indicated floor and asked further directions at the nurses' station. The nurse at the desk had reddish hair and pale freckly skin, large green eyes that seemed to brim. Because of my father's orders, I had to identify myself. Then she told me she was sorry and pointed to a door a few feet away.

My mother lay peacefully on her side. Freshly washed by someone who had taken pains, her hair was fluffy and had more luster than I had seen in years, had very little gray. Not knowing what to expect, I was surprised. She breathed heavily and made slight snoring noises, the kind I always heard at home when passing her room, sneaking in late at night. There were not, as in movies, a lot of wires or hoses. Just an oxygen clip under her nose, and a wire to monitor her vital signs. And a mouthpiece, taped in place, to keep her from swallowing or biting her tongue.

I sat down and took her hand; it was warm and dry. I told her it was me, that I had flown home to see her. I sat close enough to see the pores of her nose. Her fingers, astonishingly, were not yellow from years of cigarettes (I wondered if they had been cleaned with some kind of solvent). And the nails were nicely manicured, not bitten. Her hand, though warm and alive in mine, did not clasp, did not respond to the pressure of my grip. These were the hands that had held me, cooked and washed, played the piano, and written to me—when I was in college and abroad—hundreds of mentor-like letters full of the titles of books I should read, the names of museums and places I should see. Was it simply this body I needed to be free of, or was it this kind of sentimental thought, the kind that had my breath coming hard? I cleared my throat, hoping I'd find the right thing to say; but before I could speak, one of her eyes opened. Her breath altered, paused, then the eye that burned a hole through me finally closed. Was this simply reflex, or was she giving me a sign?

She had lost weight and her face was almost youthful. The expression was dreamy, almost smiling, as I'd often seen it when she was especially enthralled by a good book. Instead of saying I was sorry about anything, about what was unchangeable and beyond us in the past, I told her things I thought would amuse her. I told her about my blurting seatmate on the commuter flight, I told her about Stan, about my father's bathroom arrangements, and about Mrs. Penland taking photos. Once started, like the sailor, I couldn't stop, and remembered aloud our one dinner at the Penlands' years ago when their high-strung Lakeland terrier growled under the table. "He won't bite, he won't bite," her husband kept saying, but the dog finally latched onto my father's trousers and tore them up. My mother thought the incident was wildly funny; she enjoyed the Penlands' eccentricities, their house filthy but full of artwork, and teased my father that he had no sense of humor. "Sure," said my father, "laugh, but pet that dog, and you'll be wearing a three-fingered glove next winter." It was a story she liked to tell, and when the red-haired nurse looked in, she found me, to her astonishment, laughing and talking excitedly. Her look said I was unhinged, as bad as the other nut-case with the Polaroid, and when she left, I laughed again, but quickly sobered. What if my mother died just then? Would they accuse me of mercy killing? What was wrong with me? The impure thoughts were back.

But I had little time for thought, for her eyes snapped open, her throat rattled, and her body stiffened under the sheet. Maybe she was not hearing what she wanted to hear and was telling me so. I felt myself pinned by her stare until the eyes again closed. I had only one more thing to say, but after I whispered my apology, I still could not leave. Her rattling breath measured the minutes. Several times I was vaguely aware of a figure in the doorway, then the rustle of clothing faded away. There is no telling how long I sat without words. I knew I was seeing my mother alive for the last time; to let go of her hand and rise from her bedside was to take leave of her forever. There was nothing further to be said or done, yet I needed permission. Then it came to me that this was a body and not my mother; my mother had been absolved by her body, quickly, and was likely already gone; the way of my own absolution would be longer and less certain. Permission would have to come from within. I put the left hand on the right where it rested on the chest. Then, to avoid being turned to stone once again by that terrible look, I kissed the cheek and hurried from the room.

Under a cold starry sky, I took a deep breath and felt the sharp air slide in and bite; it hurt, and that's what I needed.

At home, my father and I were watching a Celtics game. I asked him about the Penlands, how he and my mother ever came to know them.

"I answered a newspaper ad," he said. "She wanted a driver to take her and a few of her friends to the operas in Boston."

"You did that often?" I asked.

"Maybe once a month. They paid me good money, bought me dinner, then a ticket so's I wouldn't have to wait in the cold."

I didn't realize he had ever been to operas, and asked if he liked them.

"Sure. I didn't much follow the stories, but the music was nice. To tell the truth though, I sometimes slept all the way through. I was working, don't forget, two other jobs at the time."

"Did Mom ever go?"

"Once, that's how she met Mrs. Penland, Becky."

"Were they really good friends?"

"I guess. Your mother got a kick out of her."

"Why?"

"She was different. Listen, she was way ahead of her time with this, ah, Animal Rights business. She carried a protest sign against vivisection right at the university where her husband taught. She didn't care what people thought. And that was back in the fifties."

"So Mom just saw her as an amusing crank?"

"I wouldn't say that. They talked to each other on the phone two or three times a week. Women things, you know. They talked about books too. Remember the time you and me poured concrete and repaired their driveway?"

I said I did.

"Becky Penland is more eccentric now than ever. Maybe even crazy. Taking pictures of your mother!" He sipped his beer and shook his head. "Generous people though. Dr. Penland wrote you that recommendation for college. On the other hand, though, your mother listened to Becky Penland's troubles by the hour. Mostly neurotic, imaginary stuff."

I had to say that the imaginary was real too, but he wasn't really listening; he was going on about my mother's virtues in a way that made me worry. What he said was true, but I had never heard him talk this way. It was a question of control. "Your mother," he said, "is a very generous and sympathetic person. Another thing I've never denied—she's a lot smarter than me. She did the books for the station, taxes and all, and, I'll tell you, she didn't need a calculator to do it either."

A fight had broken out between Kevin McHale and one of the Lakers. Benches emptied and things escalated. It was ugly, and I saw Murray's face like a bloody moon rising above the bar. I stood up, said I was going to bed, but my father asked me to have another beer with him. I said I had to go to the bathroom first. "Wait, we still don't have water," he said.

"I thought—"

"Stan miscalculated a little bit," he said. Then he explained that two lengths of PVC had been cut too short.

"Dad, the guy drinks too much. You ought to hire a real plumber."

"Yeah, well," he said. "I've got my reasons."

I went out the back door. Everything was powdery, the snow squeaky underfoot. A thin crust of a moon was embedded in the sky with a filigree overlay of winter branches. Lots of stars. I watched the red lights of a faraway plane disappear. Urinating in the backyard—it was absurd. I could imagine my mother, ever tolerant of my father's foolish economies, finding the situation amusing, telling my aunt or one of her phone friends the story.

When I sat down again, he said, "Your mother thinks Stan's life is almost funny, but it's not. He got arrested down on Bank Street, the gin-mill section Dumfy calls Dodge City."

"Drunken driving?"

"Solicitation I think they call it. He was caught in a parking lot in some prostitute's car. Well, I laughed too, but it's sad. It was in the newspaper, a bigger story than usual because the new police chief is cracking down on pimps, drug dealers, and hookers. Johns too. But imagine how Stan's kids must have felt. You know? How would you feel if that happened to me?"

"It wouldn't," I said.

"Listen, like your mother always says, 'You never know.'"

His use of the present tense was beginning to bother me because I knew a widow who still could not bring herself to use the past when speaking of a husband long dead, and her life was a fragile dream.

"Since his case is coming up next week," Dad continued, "I asked him

PETER MAKUCK

this afternoon if he had a good lawyer. I said I knew the cops probably set him up. But he says, 'Hell, what good's a lawyer going to do? Christ, I didn't have any pants on. Like the saying, you know, caught with my pants down!' "

I asked why he didn't take her to a motel.

"He was probably drunk, not thinking." He laughed, then his eyes misted. Finally he said, "I feel sorry for him."

After a story like that, or when someone in the family died, my mother would sigh deeply and say, "What can anybody do?"

Sometime during the night I was awakened. A choking sound or the muffled sound of a child crying. Maybe the cat, I thought. I rushed into the hallway. The sound seemed to be coming from my father's room, but when I moved to his door, ajar as always, I could hear nothing but our old house creaking in its bones, the radiators plinking and sighing in their familiar way. I eased open his door. He was turned to the wall. He always slept with the shades up and moonlight blazed on the snowfield beyond his window. I stood there staring at the snow until the room came back.

In bed again, I had trouble sleeping and lay awake thinking about home. Maybe it was just the place where you slept, or especially where you dreamed. Stan, my father said, often passed out and slept in his truck. Stan, as Dumfy liked to say, was a piece of work. And my father too. Everyone was a piece of work. There were many things to tell my mother. Fagan and his essay were wrong. It wasn't over yet and wouldn't be even when it was over. The story would go on, like our exchange of letters over the years. Overhead the drone of a light plane. The radiators sighed. *Our stay on the ground will be brief.*

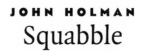

JOHN HOLMAN
Squabble

Aaron thought about retrenchment. That was what the dean had termed it, peppering his letter with other such phrases — "financial cutbacks" and "organizational shifts." If the dean had simply written "Last hired, first fired," Aaron would not have needed an extra few seconds to catch the drift.

Anyway, he was back in his hometown, living with his aunt — no hope of teaching in the fall and no desire to move again, either. He had watched the late-night Employment Security Commission report on TV and heard of an opening for an electrical engineer with twenty years' experience. He had a Ph.D. in geography. His morning mail included a job list bearing a yellow sticker with his change of address and listing nothing he was qualified for.

As he sat in his pajamas on the porch, the late May sun across his lap, a Skylark pulled into the driveway, the exhaust clean and guttural. Aaron had watched the sparkling old white convertible roar up and down the street several times that morning, its red roof puffed with wind. Dennis, his buddy from high school, whom he had seen maybe twice in seven years of grad school and teaching, leaped out of the car, wearing cutoff khakis and black-and-red high-top basketball shoes. His sweatshirt was inside out and the sleeves were cut away. He carried a Wilson basketball and a yellow thermos.

"I'm a foreman at the factory, I still play a little ball, and I frequent a dive," Dennis said when Aaron asked what he had been up to.

"The car, those shoes," Aaron said.

"Gotta keep up with the jitterbugs, since I can't keep up with the Joneses," Dennis said, and he slapped Aaron's knee with the palmed ball.

"I need a job."

"So get one."

They drank Dennis's Kickapoo juice, a mild mix of orange juice and gin, from clear plastic cups Aaron brought out.

"There's a guy at this dive you gotta see," Dennis said. "He's Clara's nephew. It's Clara's new place. He's got half a face from prison surgery."

"What does he do?"

"He's the life of the party."

Aaron thought a place that prized a half-a-face ex-con would be a good place to work. He could tend bar, just pour shots and open beers. Maybe not even open them. "I want to work at the dive," he said.

"Well, clean up. We'll talk to Clara. You seen her yet?"

"Not yet. You talk to her first. I haven't kept contact."

"I know."

After Dennis left, Aaron took a shower and put on fresh clothes—white deep-pleated cuffed pants and a checked blue shirt. He slipped on last summer's espadrilles, got the car keys his aunt had left before she flew away on vacation, and drove into town in her new blue Topaz.

The skyline was changing. Places were sprouting all over. Streets were barricaded, sidewalks torn up. He parked on a side street and walked inside the new Tower Plaza. He decided the Tower must be a city project. An entrepreneur would have piped in some music. It was pristinely quiet, not many people. Otherwise, things looked nice. A wide circular stairway went up a few levels. On the entrance level there were mostly cafés—China Falls, Indian Cuisine, Mexican Pleasure, Victoria's Jubilee.

He went inside Mexican Pleasure and sat at the bar. The motif was Art Deco Mexican—shiny surfaces and large sharp angles. There was low-volume Trini Lopez music from some unseen speakers. The woman behind the bar looked bored. She didn't look Mexican. Doughy and young, in a white off-the-shoulder blouse and colorful striped skirt, she seemed embarrassed to be wearing a costume.

"Where is everybody?" Aaron asked.

"This time of day is dead," she said. "Our special today is gin and tonic."

Aaron asked for a beer and lit a cigarette. "Is that music your choice or the management's?"

"I could change it. Pay up first."

He did, and she went out through a swinging door behind the bar. When she returned, some piano jazz started playing. Then another woman came through the door with a glass of iced tea. Aaron smiled at her. She was wearing the same getup as the bartender, and her hair was bright blond, pulled tight into a ponytail. She came around the bar and sat two stools away.

"I got some lousy tips," she said to the bartender, spreading bills and coins on the bar top. "Ten dollars and a Canadian nigger."

Aaron looked over at her, and at the first woman. Neither looked at him. Maybe he had heard wrong.

A tall black woman peeped in the entrance, lingered a little to look at Aaron, and went away. The woman with the tips started talking about Mr. T. She was talking about his haircut.

"What do you think?" She was speaking to Aaron. "I could do with a style, am I right?"

He smiled again. He still had his beer to finish, which was dark, imported, and good. He drank it rather fast anyway. He left the bartender a hefty tip.

He saw the tall black woman browsing in a jewelry store where an Oriental man sat behind a low glass counter stringing gold-bead necklaces. The woman's feet were spread ducklike. He walked up beside her and stood on the plum carpet. Fluorescent lights were overhead and in all the counters. The jeweler had a glass to his eye, and his face was tinged blue from the long piece of blue felt cushioning the gold.

"This stuff is all broken," Aaron said to the woman. She was young, maybe twenty-one at most. "You don't want this stuff."

"Jeepers, you're right. I don't want this stuff."

She looked at him. Her eyes were as brown as bottles and seemed the same color as her skin. He unrolled his shirt sleeve, buttoned the cuff, and started on the other one.

"I don't want anything," she said, as if just that moment realizing it.

"Then you don't mind if I stay?"

"Why should I?" She walked out.

Aaron caught up with her at China Falls. It was a takeout place with orange neon trimming the order window. She stood talking through the window. Her hair was long, loose, and dry-looking. Her jeans were tight, and she wore a big white T-shirt.

"That was a nasty trick," Aaron said. "I'm devastated."

"That reminds me of a song."

"You're not supposed to find fault."

"O.K. I feel sorry for you. What's your name?"

"Aaron. You can be Caroline."

"I'll stick with Wanda," she said. "You be Taiwo."

"No. I be Aaron."

Her egg-drop soup came to the window in a clear plastic bowl with a beige plastic spoon. Wanda took it to an iron table, and Aaron brought over a few napkins.

"This is delicious," she said.

"It looks nutritious."

She swirled the soup with a spoon. "Want some?"

He shook his head. "Is this a good place? I was just insulted back there in the Mexican place. Racial stuff."

"Really? Never happened to me. I don't have time for it."

"I guess I do."

"It's the town. Neo-hick."

"I was born here. Where are you from?"

"Nowhere. Notice an accent? I go to school. Sing and dance and say the words. I'm decultured by culture. I'm an actress."

"That's nice. How do I look?"

"Spiffy."

"Thanks. That's what I was shooting for. It's important when you're between jobs."

"I guess." She dabbed her mouth with a napkin. "What jobs are you between?"

"Geography teacher and bartender. My interview is tonight. I'd invite you if you wanted."

"Invite me anyway." She tilted the bowl and poured the last of the soup onto the spoon.

That night, Aaron stood at the end of the driveway waiting for Wanda, not wanting her to miss the house. It was set back from the road behind eighty-year-old trees. He had been waiting twenty minutes, since dusk. Fireflies were out. He wore black—silk shirt, pleated pants, shiny loafers. Neo-hick, he thought. She pulled into the driveway in an orange Chevette. He had made a pitcher of grape Kool-Aid and placed it and two glasses on a TV tray on the porch. He had lit a low flame in a hurricane lamp. Wanda wore a denim miniskirt and a beaded African bracelet, perfume, a purple T-shirt, a matador's jacket, and purple sandals. Her hair was combed a little wilder.

"You always look so city," Aaron said.

"You live in the sticks, man. Took me forever."

"We call it the country."

"Sure you do." She looked him over. "Wyatt Earp?"

"I'm still real. What about you?"

"Don't I act like it?"

He led her up the steps to a lawn chair and poured the Kool-Aid. He took a chair on the other side of the tray.

"Mind if I smoke?" he said. "I ask because you look so healthy." He lit the cigarette and fanned periodically to keep the smoke from lingering too long between them. "Do you think I'll get the job?"

"There's probably no doubt about it. What's this bar like?"

"It's called the Bellaire. I've never been. Started up while I was away. It's sort of illegal."

"Don't get me arrested," she said. "Who's the clientele?"

"People with no time for racial stuff. You ought to fit in."

"Gee whiz, man. Don't be so cute."

"Gee whiz? What language are we speaking?"

"Squabble. We're squabbling."

"You can get along, can't you?"

"I'm here. Squabbling's good now and then."

"Kiss me."

"You kiss me."

They stared at each other.

"Why don't I just take these things inside."

He stood the tray by the kitchen sink. He ran water over the cigarette and put it in the garbage. He came back, pulled the door, and blew out the lamp. Wanda stood with her back to him, looking out toward the fireflies, hips and shoulders as sturdy as a statue's.

"I'll drive," she said. "You're nervous."

"Fine," he said, glad she wanted to drive. The interview was half a joke anyway. He wasn't sure what Wanda thought he was nervous about.

Clara had told him that afternoon he could work anytime he wanted. It was after meeting Wanda at the Tower that he'd driven out June Street, a pitted rock road shaped like a *b*, sided by dusty woods that gave way to small frame houses like his, separated by wide yards. Dennis's Skylark was in Clara's driveway, and Dennis and a fat man were sitting in the yard by Clara's tan brick house, on metal and wood auditorium chairs. The yard was landscaped with winter-killed shrubs and blue ceramic chickens. The fat man was dark and shirtless, with the legs of his pants rolled to the knees and one foot submerged in a tin pail of water. He fanned himself with a large elephant-ear leaf from a weed that grew unchecked and fuzzy against the side of the house. He looked extremely hot and agitated.

Dennis introduced Aaron as Dr. Stets. "This is Duke," he said of the fat man. "Clara's boyfriend."

Duke shook hands weakly. "Take a look at these feet, Doc," he said. "They're killing me."

The foot resting on the short brown grass was so swollen that the yellowed nails were nearly buried in flesh.

"I'm not that kind of doctor," Aaron said. "But you ought to see one."

Duke looked disgusted and waved the fuzzy leaf at him.

"Let's go inside," Dennis said. "Clara would love to see you."

Clara's screen door was decorated with aluminum birds. Dennis led the way into a darkened living room with low fifties furniture covered in puckered plastic. It was years since Aaron had been here. They went through a doorless entrance to the kitchen, where Clara stood at the sink drying dishes.

"Look who's back," Dennis said.

Clara turned around, smiled broadly, and said, "Well, if it ain't the good doctor. I'm not too well today. Can you get me a private room?"

"I'm not that kind of doctor, Clara."

"Oh? What kind are you?"

"Just a different kind."

She walked over, sliding her feet in scuffed men's leather slippers, and hugged him. She was wide and soft, and her cheek was wet. She smelled of baby powder. She moved to an oscillating fan on the counter, put her face down to the grille, and then turned around to let it blow on her back. "Air conditioner's broke. Over there is Claude, my nephew you never met."

Claude, hard-looking and lean, sat in a breakfast nook. Aaron had to step farther into the kitchen to see him, sitting at a Formica table eating a bowl of navy beans.

"Dog," he said. "Call me Dog."

Dennis snickered and made a face of mock fright. Dog's right cheekbone was gone and replaced with a long slick scar.

"I'm as drunk as a skunk," Dog said. "Beans?" he offered, without looking up or altering his hunched posture over the bowl.

Squeezed into Wanda's Chevette, smelling her light perfume, Aaron considered that bringing her to the Bellaire was not a good idea. June Street was bumpy and dark, with only lights in back windows to mark the houses. Seeing it as she must, he thought it looked like another planet. He had told Dennis, using the language of high school, that Wanda was a first-round draft choice, no tryout necessary, so he had to back it up. But he didn't want to scare her.

The Bellaire was at the bottom of the *b*. A few cars were pulled into the yard. Dennis's Skylark was on the roadside, and Aaron pointed for Wanda to park by it. Three gray plank steps led to a small gray deck where Duke, dressed in a burgundy short-sleeved shirt, dark pants, and black socks on his swollen feet, leaned over the rail. He'd had his hair done up in tight, oily curls.

"Evening, Duke," Aaron said.

Duke straightened up and said to Wanda, "Ma'am, you have to leave your purse outside unless you want me to search it. You can leave your some-kind-of-doctor out, too, unless you want me to search him."

Wanda went back to the car. When she opened the trunk, a light came on and Aaron could see the taut muscles of her thigh as she bent to place the purse under something. The gold of her jacket glittered. Then Duke's hands started moving over Aaron's ribs and down his legs. "Anything in the socks?"

Aaron lifted his pants to show he wasn't wearing any. "What's this about?"

"Trouble. Don't want none." He snorted.

Wanda came back and flashed a game smile. "She's clean," Aaron said, gangster-style, and Duke let them through.

Inside was a living room with card tables and straight-backed chairs instead of regular living room furniture, arranged on a scuffed hardwood floor. The room was long, and maybe some walls had been knocked down to make the bedrooms part of the action. A raised plywood dance floor was at the rear, with a jukebox booming out funk tunes. A bar was just to the left, where Dennis and Dog sat drinking from Dixie cups. When Dennis saw them, he stood and waved his hand at some empty stools. They sat, and Aaron introduced Wanda.

"Nice," she said, and looked up to scan the walls. Signs, hand-painted in red, were everywhere—house codes of behavior: "NO CURSING," "NO DRINKING OR SMOKING ON THE DANCE FLOOR," "CASH ONLY," "IF YOU ARE JEALOUS OF YOUR MAN OR WOMAN GO HOME." Another sign, propped against the wall behind a cardboard box, read:

"So chic," Dog said.

Aaron nudged Wanda, who had shifted her gaze to the people around the room. There weren't many. It was early. Dog repeated the compliment.

"Holy moly," Wanda said. "What happened to your face?"

"So brave, too. I'm attracted to temerity. Dance with me and I'll tell you."

They left, linking fingers, for the dance floor. Clara was sitting behind the bar near the computerized cash register, and Aaron asked her for two beers. She rolled back the stainless steel top of a gas station cooler and took out two tall Millers. She wore a black-and-gold cycling cap and a lime green cardigan over a white diner uniform. The air conditioning worked here. In the smoky light from a lectern lamp mounted on the register, her face pocketed shadows, like dented metal.

Aaron turned toward her on his stool. "Are you sure you ought to be here? You don't look well."

"That line's not too popular," she said, and then let out a loud, long laugh.

"She's on medication," Dennis said. "Now, Wanda, I can tell, is drug-free. Never had an aspirin. Look at her slam-dunking Dog."

Aaron slid around. Wanda and Dog had cleared out a space for themselves. The other dancers had about lost their rhythm as they watched Dog doing a silly knee dance and Wanda showing off her art school energy. She was all movement, muscles and hair, circles and angles, reaching down low and pulling something unseen from the red-and-blue air, reaching up and pulling something else, spinning and shaking something to death with her teeth. Dog was nearly applauding, splashing his Dixie cup empty.

"He's as happy as a sissy at the Y," Clara said, letting loose that laugh again.

On her way back to the bar, Wanda turned down two drunks who met her crouched in knee-bent dance postures, snapping their fingers. Dog sat again beside Dennis, Wanda beside Aaron.

Dog pulled his shirt cuffs so they showed out the sleeves of his shiny blue jacket. "She's perfect," he said.

Aaron thought Dog didn't look too bad all dressed up. His suit was impossibly blue. His face was playful, with a friendly smile that might have been infectious if it could spread to more right cheek. Wanda gave Dog a seated bow and sipped from her can of beer. Clara moved off her chair behind the cash register and brought Wanda a cup.

"Thanks," Wanda said.

"You want a job? I'd pay you to come in and dance like that, keep my customers coming in and thirsty."

"That's my job," Dog said.

Wanda waved her hands. "No, thanks. This guy's the one who needs work."

"He's overqualified and can't do nothing no way," Clara said. "But his momma and daddy were friends of mine. His daddy died in Korea, you know. And she bled to death when he was a baby. His aunt don't like me, though. She raised him after his folks died. Moved all the way from Jersey to raise him. He tell you that? I don't want no trouble with her. I'm his momma, too, but he don't act like it. Hell, I don't act like it."

Wanda had one leg crossed over the other, and one finger, just one long glossed fingernail, between her teeth. She had been frowning since his parents were mentioned.

"I just met the guy," she said. They both looked at Aaron.

"I guess he can open some beers and pour straight," Clara said.

Aaron went around to where part of the bar top lifted up, and got behind. He rolled up his sleeves and the cooler top, flexed his fingers, and started opening cans and bottles really fast. When he finished, his silk sleeves hung loose and beers were lined up, some foaming over. His fingers hurt. Dennis and Wanda applauded him slowly.

"Not bad," Clara said. "All you need now is some customers and some sleeve garters."

Aaron shouted, "Anybody want a beer?"

A few people at nearby tables looked but didn't get up. One man kept his head down on his folded arms. Those dancing kept dancing. Wanda raised her hand, and Aaron gave her one. He pushed the rest toward Dennis and Dog.

"Watch out," Dog said. "My dates are here." Two young women were standing by the door. "They drink like Maseratis."

The women were unsmiling. They approximated Wanda's style—short skirts, T-shirts—but with high heels and lacy anklets. Their skirts were leather, one black and one red, and they were heavily into makeup and frosted hair.

Dog introduced them with a flourish: "Ebony Angel and Pinky." He gave each a beer. Aaron took the money from the bills on the bar in front of Dog.

"Let's get a table," Dog said. "Take a break," he said to Aaron.

Dennis pulled two card tables together and Aaron joined them, bringing the rest of the opened beers.

"What's with the search?" Ebony Angel asked. She was gold-skinned, with buzzed temples and a yellow fringe of hair at the top. She looked to Aaron like Woodstock the bird, except her eye shadow was rainbows.

"We had a fellow get shotgunned last week," Dog said.

"Googly moogly," Wanda said.

"You believe that?" Pinky, heavier and darker than Ebony Angel, looked at Wanda incredulously. "I don't believe *you*."

"Right over there," Dog said, pointing at the door. "Maybe it was last month. Two fellows sitting on those stools started fussing at the bar. Somebody's mother was mentioned. Another fellow, tired of hearing it, said he had a shotgun in his car. He threw his keys on the bar and one of them picked them up, got the gun, came back, and shot. The poor fellow was on his way out."

Dog sat back looking smug, as if no one could challenge him. They all looked at him and kept quiet for a while.

"Guess how old I am," Dog said. "Fifty-five. You believe that?"

"Why not?" Pinky said. She had pink metallic lips. She pressed them together and relaxed them full again, like an instant azalea blossom.

"Are you always so beautiful?" Wanda said.

"Every day. We both are."

"They're sex muffins," Dog said.

"No, we are not. We are women," Pinky said.

Dog put his nose to Ebony Angel's neck. She laughed and pushed him away with her hand on his forehead.

"You smell like muffins."

"We don't even like sex," Ebony Angel said.

Dennis, looking at Aaron, mouthed the words, "You believe that?"

Aaron shrugged.

"I don't care," Dog said. "I am glad to be alive. Glad to be out. I went to prison innocent, right? Fifteen years. All I did was give a fellow a ride. Said he wanted bubble gum and robbed the damn store. So they said I had cancer and they whittled my face. Really, I look better. Kept me out of trouble, that's a fact. Now I'm back among family and the free. When I was in the joint, I read *Time* magazine the whole time. Y'all don't surprise me a bit."

"Say something in *Time*," Dennis said.

"I only know a few words."

"I know *Time*," Wanda said. "Salubrious, dolorous, specious."

"You don't know squat," Pinky said.

"I know your daddy."

"I've got a shotgun in the car," Dennis said.

"So do I," Pinky said.

"Great," Wanda said. "Let's get dangerous."

"Let's dance," Dennis said to Pinky.

Dog and Ebony Angel got up, too.

"That was cute," Aaron said.

"That was squabble." Wanda winked.

Another couple came in and took seats at the bar. They wore matching yellow suits and caps.

"Shouldn't you be helping?" Wanda asked.

"Possibly."

"I might dance some more. Get to know your friends."

"They're not my friends, except Dennis."

"They're friendly, though."

"Somewhat."

"You should see me perform. I'm slow in real life. Not like Dog's dates."

"I don't know. I can't keep up with you."

"Good. That means I'm winning."

"Winning what?"

"You know. The game, the race, the war." She took off her jacket and draped it on the back of the chair. "You really do need a new name," she said. "From now on you are Nick. You're a tough guy. Get yourself a hat, too."

"You're sweet," he said.

"Sure I am. I'm molasses." She smacked her lips.

"You know what I'm thinking?" Aaron said. "I'm thinking I've got to fall in love with you. I'm thinking it's urgent. Otherwise Pinky or Ebony Angel is gonna make me marry her and take out her future on me. But this is a struggle, because quite frankly I'm losing the will to get to know you."

She held out her hands, palms up. "No problem, Nick," she said, and laughed. "Know what I mean?"

"Right," he said. "Give me a clue. Are we squabbling?"

She clasped her hands behind her head. "I don't squabble with Nick."

He gave her the O.K. sign. He got up and went behind the bar. Clara tied a butcher's apron around him, and he nodded to the couple in yellow. Each smoked an extra-long cigarette, and they seemed to be sharing a wine cooler. Duke hobbled in, jiggling flesh, and eased his weight onto a stool. He lifted a foot over the opposite knee and pulled at the elastic sock. Aaron asked what he could get him, but he said he didn't drink. "Real doctor's orders."

So Aaron looked at Wanda, who was watching him, moving her head to the music. She was beautiful, having the time of her life, he supposed. He thought he should go back over there and kiss her. He figured it needed doing. But first he would check out the stock behind the bar, just to get his bearings, before the all-night crowd rushed in.

Dancing with Father

Even after an absence of three seasons we are recognized as we return to The Homestead, that welcoming resort in the Virginia mountains. "We" meaning my father and me; my husband is making his first trip here. Rusty opens the trunk while Daddy and I alight to proffered hands. My father moves with alacrity, wanting, I'm sure, to appear as he always has: quick, vital, embracing, never daunted by the trials of this existence.

"Welcome back to The Homestead, Miz Vannoppen, Mistah Vannoppen, sir," the doorman says. I recognize his ancient yet unlined black face but cannot recall his name. My father can.

"It's good to be here, Guilford." My father smiles his careful smile. He is hoping, I suspect, that Guilford will not ask him about Mrs. Vannoppen. I know Guilford won't.

Guilford does not have superhuman powers, only a good memory for an unusual last name, and he probably checks the list of expected arrivals every day. Still, until my mother's death, three years ago, we came to The Homestead the first weekend in June for nineteen years, ever since I was four and my sisters, Judith and Louise, were three and one. We probably deserve to be recognized.

We've had a subdued drive up from North Carolina. Although there's been plenty of conversation, the gaiety that always accompanied our trips has been absent. We've talked about our golf games, about the Upper Cascades course, which for the first time my father doesn't want to play ("Too hilly," he comments), about the Lower Cascades course ("Too easy and too buggy"), and about the Homestead course, which we will probably play every day. We did not, as we always had, ooh and ahh over the castlelike

Hotel Roanoke when we passed it, an hour back; nor did we become quiet over the poverty in Clifton Forge, or even gag over the paper-mill smell in Covington, as, when Mother was here, we had done ritualistically. We didn't want to talk about anything we used to talk about.

"This is a one-time experiment," my father had cautioned, when he called to say he wanted to take the family—minus grandchildren—back to The Homestead. "Not to relive old times," he continued. "Not that. I want to go there as if we've never been there before."

I thought of suggesting another place, perhaps the nearby Greenbrier, where we would not be weighed down by nineteen years of memories, but I did not.

Father has not dated anyone since Mother died, which has not bothered Judith and me though it has Louise. We want him to remarry if he wants to, but in the past year our youngest sister has become passionate about Father's finding a companion. She says he'll suffer less. She says a man like him should not be alone. I have told her that loneliness is sometimes preferable to empty togetherness, but she doesn't believe me. I'm not even sure I'm right. A few months ago I agreed to speak to him about his social life. Louise believes that because I became a lawyer, like Father, I have his ear more than she does.

"We want you to know that if you would like to go out with anyone, it's okay with us," I said to him. We were sitting across from each other in the study where all the conferences I'd ever had with him had taken place. This was the first time he had been the subject. "We want you to be happy." He listened with the glimmer of amusement I've seen in the eyes of someone who will listen to you, who will even consider what you're saying, but who believes you don't know what you're talking about.

His answer was quiet but impassioned. "Your mother and I had something extraordinary," he said, his eyes focusing on his folded hands. "You probably know that." I nodded, even though he wasn't watching. "She was a rare, magnificent woman. I could never find her equal. I would never even want to try." Then his tone lightened. "The three of you are enough women for me."

I had always known that my parents were lovers, because of a lifetime of locked doors, but I knew it more, I think, because of how they fought: so passionately, so fearlessly, so frighteningly. You can fight like that only if you are certain of your hold on the other person, if you are unafraid of the consequences of fury.

Father raised his eyes; an unexpected pleasure flooded his face. "You remind me a great deal of her," he said.

I blushed, but because my complexion is olive, he couldn't tell. He had probably said the same thing to Judith and Louise. Even though I couldn't imagine a compliment more exhilarating, I knew I was not the most like Mother. Judith was. Or maybe the truth was this: if the three of us—Judith with Mother's flair, Louise with her irony, and I with her passion—could be one person, we would probably approximate her.

Seven of us will be at The Homestead, since this year all three sisters are married. Judith and Louise live in the D.C. area and are expected to arrive with their husbands late this afternoon. Daddy, Rusty, and I will probably hike the north trail first and then have saunas or massages. Golf begins tomorrow morning, followed by lunch in the garden, mineral baths, salt glows ("Don't shave your legs beforehand," we've reminded each other since we were teenagers), and Scotch hose, the high-pressure massage that washes the salt away. One day we will take a carriage ride—Mother's least favorite activity, because it took us away from the center of things. Even naps are scheduled, from four to five, just as when Mother was in charge. Only now I know that that's when everyone makes love.

Of the entire Homestead experience, though, what we all most look forward to is dancing with Daddy. Will he dance with us? Judith asked me on the telephone last week. I said I could not imagine him not dancing.

"But won't it make him think of Mother?" she said.

"Why shouldn't he think about her?"

"Maybe he'll finally have a chance to eat his dinner."

"Maybe so."

Daddy tips Guilford and walks through the immense screen door that is held graciously for him by a green-coated bellhop. The grand hall glows yellow. The decor is familiar, no wearing of the upholstery and carpeting, but the room has the look of something aged, something comfortable, even though the paint is fresh. Fires blaze in the fireplaces, although by now the sun has finally knocked the chill off the day. We are greeted by older employees who aren't so clever as Guilford yet remember our faces.

Daddy turns from the front desk, holding up our keys as if he has achieved a sort of victory. Perhaps it is a victory for him to walk into this grand hall and not simply turn around and walk out. Perhaps it should be a victory for all of us. But I don't feel sad. I am happy thinking about my mother and all that she taught me.

Daddy stops the car and puts the top down just moments before we arrive at The Homestead. And Mommie turns the heat on high, because everybody in the back seat is so cold. It's June, school's out, but this is the mountains. It's so cold, Daddy says, because we are at a higher elevation. At higher elevations the air is colder because it's thinner. "Why is thin air cold?" I ask, when he leans over me to unzip the plastic window, but he doesn't know the answer.

Daddy says, "This is silly," but Mommie says, "No, it isn't. This is fun. Do you want to look like everyone else?"

Around her neck Mommie wraps a thin white scarf, which trickles behind her in the wind. She tells us to sit up like ladies. We are all huddled on the floor because the wind is so cold. "It's summer," she commands. She cranes her neck over the seat to see us. Her tone suddenly becomes conciliatory, the only tone that we are honor-bound to obey. "If I ask you to do something for me," she has told all three of us hundreds of times, "you are required to obey me. If I scream at you in anger, you are entitled to resist. Sit up," she says kindly. "For five minutes. Do it for me."

We sit almost eagerly. At times we each, even the baby, would do anything in our limited power to please her.

We are dressed in dotted swiss. Just before we left home, our shoulder-length hair was barretted back and twisted by Mommie into long curls, her curling iron held the way a teacher holds a ruler. We wear ruffled socks, ruffled panties, and black patent-leather shoes. As a special treat for me, the oldest, Mommie has applied a touch of her rouge to my cheeks. When Judith asked for rouge too, Mommie said rouge was allowed only after you were six. Then, to make Judith feel better, she said: "Katherine's complexion is olive. It needs rouge. You already have rosy cheeks." Judith was not satisfied, and I went to the mirror to look at my olive skin, with which from that moment on, I knew, I would never be happy. Fortunately, though, now I was old enough to color it.

So that we won't miss lunch, Daddy sends our bags up to our adjoining rooms, and we hurry to the garden. Mommie selects a table and sits with Louise in her lap while Daddy takes us to the buffet. Judith heads for the great round dessert table, where a smiling, pudgy woman stands ready to help us build our own chocolate sundaes. In a stern voice Daddy calls Judith back to the vast array of hot and cold foods. She starts down the line without making any selections.

"Judith," I call, angrily. Since I am the oldest, I try to help Daddy. He leans down and whispers in my ear that he will handle her. Mommie would have pinched me. Daddy's sharp fragrance lingers in my head even after he has walked down the line and drawn Judith and her tray back to the beginning.

With guidance we both select a meager amount of food and join Mommie and Louise. We have been away from them for what seems hours, but Mommie shows no sign of irritation. She stands grandly at our arrival, stationing Louise in the grass, helping Judith and me deposit our plates. Daddy returns to the line to fill his own plate, and Mommie instructs us to think carefully about our manners as we eat. "Decide on one particular bad manner that for this meal you won't commit," she says. "If you commit others, that's all right. Just don't commit that one bad one." She smiles an arch, encompassing smile that always seems to take in the world; it is caring and yet removed from us, as if to say to anyone who might be watching that she is more than a mother. Of course, we know this, Judith and I. We know that our mother is different from every other mother. But we don't quite know in what way.

"Enjoy yourselves, little darlings," she says, softly but with resonance. This means we may start eating. My father walks up behind her with his plate and leans so that his cheek is within an inch of her own.

"You know you're beautiful, don't you?" he whispers. He often tells us that we are beautiful too, not in front of everybody, the way he tells Mommie, but privately, as if it's a secret. I keep my secret but Judith doesn't. She always reports to me, "Daddy told me I'm beautiful," as if only one of us could be. I think of my olive complexion and how grateful I am that there is such a thing as rouge. And that Mommie will let me wear it even though I am only six.

"Do I look smug?" Mommie asks, her face turning dark.

"I was only kidding," he says, taking his chair, which is close to hers. Her petulance settles over the table. "It was a new way of saying how beautiful I think you are."

"It sounds like a new way to hurt my feelings," she says.

The three of us chew, looking at our plates, waiting for the moment to either pass or erupt. It passes.

We are not having "supper," Mommie tells Louise; we are dining in the main ballroom of one of the loveliest resorts in the world. "Can you say that?"

Louise, long acquainted with mimicry, says, "We are dining in the main ballroom of one of the loveliest resorts in the world." Since we have been bickering this afternoon about who is going to sleep on the rollaway, Mommie makes us draw straws. Judith loses and throws herself onto the rollaway. Mommie commands her to get up before she wrinkles her dress. We are wearing our blue velvet party dresses tonight. Mommie has put my rouge on carefully, more carefully than she did for the trip here. The closet doors are faced with mirrors, and she lines us up before them, telling us to hold back our shoulders, which each of us does to the extreme. "Never mind that," she says. "But do hold up your chins. Just a little higher than level. That's the prim look a young lady wants at night."

Mommie winds her hair on top of her head, securing it with so many bobby pins that finally Louise begins to complain she's hungry, although we had tea and cookies in the parlor only an hour ago. She is tired of waiting. Mommie pats her hair "finished" and summons Daddy by his name, Max, instead of the usual "darling." His whole name is Maximilian, but I don't think anyone except me thinks of him that way. She gathers us around her like puppies, and we smile even before the approval shows in his eyes. He has on his white dinner jacket, with buttons that glitter like jewels. His black hair is as shiny as the ribbons down the legs of his trousers. He is handsome, handsome. And we are beautiful, though this time he has used the word exquisite.

We will learn poise by leading rather than by following, so the three of us are urged down the stairs ahead of our parents. My patent-leather shoes are slick on the carpet, and I take hold of the banister. In single file Judith and Louise do the same. Louise keeps looking to see if Mommie and Daddy are coming, and Mommie keeps admonishing her to look where she is going and to hold up her chin. At the foot of the stairs Mommie gently directs me, "To your left, darling." I remember which is my left hand and move in that direction. Judith moves abreast of me, either unwilling for me to have all the glory or unwilling to walk with the baby.

My father greets the maitre d' and says that he would like the same table we have had in years past—at the center edge of the dance floor.

"Oh, yes," the khaki-skinned man says. Later my father explains to me that there are ways of making people remember you. One of them is to be accompanied by an exquisite wife and three exquisite daughters. But he also tells me about the other way.

After we eat our dinner, Mommie arranges us in a corner of the dance floor, where we sidestep as a threesome while she and Daddy dance. When it is our turn to dance with him, she sits at the table with two of us while Daddy takes the third out on the floor. We watch while she describes how one dances. We are to be supple, not limp in Daddy's arms. "Like spaghetti that's not done," she says. We are to let him lead. "Step toward him if you feel his hand pulling you forward. Step back if he nudges you that way. To the right or to the left according to the way his palm rocks in the center of your back." But the best part of dancing was something that Mommie never got to do. It was when Daddy picked me up and swung me around so that my legs had no choice but to go limp. And when I said Ouch, Daddy, because his rough whiskers scraped my cheek. It was the kind of hurt that I found myself wanting again.

1967

"What a show-off," I say to Mother and Louise, as we watch Judith throw back her head in a sort of wild gaiety, revealing the soap-white skin of her long, graceful neck. She is dancing with Father, who has nearly stopped moving in order to applaud her exaggerated rhumba. Of the three of us she most resembles Mother, with her self-aware beauty, her long, perfect legs, her willingness to display herself in those spontaneous poses men seem so to appreciate. Before my comment Mother's eyes were lit with vicarious pleasure, as if she were watching herself in a mirror. She does not keep it a secret that Judith is the one of us whom physically she most enjoys. But she enjoys talking most with me, and she enjoys laughing with Louise.

I would not want to have to follow Judith's act, something Mother has instinctively realized, so she has rearranged the order of the dancing partners. As the oldest, I now dance with Father first, followed by Louise, then Judith, and finally Mother. But perhaps after this year's visit to The Homestead, Mother will dance with Daddy ahead of Judith. By now they have danced so many years together that no room is left for the unexpected. They move as intricately as the cogs of a fine watch: seeing them provides us with pleasure but no thrill.

An entire table of silver-headed pediatricians and pediatricians' wives from Chattanooga, whom we met earlier, turn as Judith leads Daddy off the floor. The wives offer askance looks, as if being wholehearted were somehow wrong, but the doctors smile in appreciation. At various tables around the room sit young men who are also watching us. None of us was asked to dance last night, our first of the holiday, but Daddy has predicted we will hardly have time to eat tonight. Already one of the doctors has danced with our mother. The same man, I notice, has pushed back his chair and will evidently approach our table again. It's time for Mother and Father to dance, I think protectively, trying to send the doctor that message by telepathy. Mother smiles in welcome, always appreciative of the attention of attractive men. This doctor has eyebrows so black that they might be dyed. I wonder if he knows why some of his hair has changed color and some has not. Or even why hair changes color.

The doctor has come not for Mother but for Judith. Daddy fills the awkward moment—Mother has begun to rise—standing so quickly that he is on his feet before she is.

"My beautiful daughter," Mother says graciously, as if Judith were a sort of gift. She is not as embarrassed as Father thought she might be.

"Our beautiful daughters," Daddy says. The remark succeeds in encouraging the man to dance eventually with each of us. Judith smiles coolly. She has been noticing a pink-cheeked young man in a not entirely appropriate sports jacket and hopes he will summon the courage to invite her to dance. She does not look at the pediatrician as they step onto the floor, but suddenly, as the band strikes up a fast tune, she comes alive. She has realized, as I could have told her, that she has another perfect opportunity to show off.

When the doctor finally dances with me, I ask him about his eyebrows. Judith made dancing with him look easy, but, unlike Daddy, the doctor has a rather ineffectual lead that keeps me continually off-balance.

"Do you dye your eyebrows?" I say.

"Of course not." He seems insulted by my brashness, although our family brashness is what attracted him in the first place. He proceeds to ask me proper questions about what I am going to do with my life. "Something meaningful, but I'm not sure what" is my answer.

When the doctor finishes dancing with me, he dances one more time with Mother—out of a sense of honor, I suppose. It occurs to me to ask him about age and stamina, because by this time I have finished the glass of wine Mother allows me and I am feeling resentful that he danced with both my sisters before he danced with me.

Now that we are apparently available, the young men descend, and each of us dances until the band packs up its instruments. We know we will not be allowed to remain behind and talk to the young men we have met, although if we were dating at home, we would have been allowed to remain in our den until midnight. Mother believes that the unknown offers more temptation than the known, and what she means by that is the temptation of hotel rooms.

1977

Ironically, we have all married men who do not like to dance. They would like it if they tried, Judith, Louise, and I are all certain, but our husbands are self-made men who were not exposed, as we were, to such things as ballroom dancing. My husband, Rusty, comes closest to being a dancer, because he will at least venture out on the floor, but it is not exactly exhilarating to two-step through a waltz.

"Must all three of us count entirely on Father?" Judith asks, her eyes rolling in what is a teasing mockery of the three husbands, who seem glued to their seats. The band has played two numbers, and none of the men has suggested dancing, although Judith, with her swaying body and her tapping fingers, has certainly announced her inclination. None of us is too timid to suggest a dance, but we would much prefer to be asked. Privately, to me, Judith has promised to ask men at surrounding tables if Jimmy refuses to dance with her. I have asked her, for Father's sake, not to cause a scene. Of the three husbands, Jimmy is the least likely to tolerate having his wife dance with another man. Dancing, we grew up believing, is recreational, not sexual, but none of our husbands views it that way.

Father has not gotten to his feet either, although I believe that it's because he prefers not to overshadow our husbands. Our mother never exhibited such generosity. Each of the men we are married to is attractive in his own way — Rusty, whose large, athletic build and glad face seem so solid; Jimmy, whose face offers a cultivated yet interesting detachment; and Rod, whose baby-blue eyes and boyish face so perfectly match our baby, Louise. But none approaches that unusual combination of sensuality and civility, male beauty and style, that has always made Father such an overwhelming presence for all of us, Judith and me in particular. Perhaps our husbands are simply too young. We are not yet our mother either.

"Dance, Daddy?" Judith says.

Before Louise and Judith and their husbands arrived, Father and I hiked the north trail this afternoon, leaving Rusty on the putting green. We talked about my work and his, and about the beauty and staying power of The

Homestead. Finally, when he allowed a pause, I asked him if being here made him sad. He said, "Sad and happy."

Although Father does not rise immediately at Judith's invitation—he is actually eating his smoked-salmon hors d'oeuvre—I notice a positive change in his expression. Life goes on, I think, but the idea gives me an unexpectedly dismal feeling. Are any losses insurmountable? Is life always the greatest thing?

"I'll dance with Judith," Rusty says. I have confided my fears about Judith's causing a scene and asked him to try to sidetrack her in any way he can think of. I am a more thorough orchestrator than my mother was. She liked to initiate a scene and let the participants resolve it themselves, while I prefer to control, as much as I can, from beginning to end.

"I really should dance with Katherine," Father says. "She's always first."

I remember the year that the order of dancing with him changed, but how Mother always danced last with Father, never giving Judith that slot even the year I thought she might.

We learned the year of the pediatricians not to rise at an invitation until we were sure who was being asked to dance. Father comes to me now and takes my hand, and I rise like the first princess. I am in love with him in the fierce, pure way one can be in love with something that one can never have. I love my husband, of course, but in a steady, patient way.

We finish the fast dance that the band is playing, and Father signals for a waltz. I am wearing my beautiful tea-length gown—royal blue, to match my eyes. I feel the bristle of his cheek, unusually heavy, I think, against my skin. Father normally shaves twice a day, but perhaps he has given up the extra effort since Mother died. I know that Judith is dancing with Rusty and that perhaps I should find her in order to exchange looks—we are, after all, happily dancing. Father is dancing. We thought he might not even want to, but he is leading me now with such gentle power that I know his heart is in it. Maybe he will grow melancholy only after he dances with Judith, when Mother does not await. Other couples have moved to the edge of the dance floor, allowing Father and me the full circumference we need. When I rise on my tiptoes, my heart rises too. I feel perfect, graceful, exquisite. I feel that all the world is watching and approving. For the first time in my life I know how much like my mother I am. Daddy does not even have to say so.

When he returns me to my seat and takes Louise's arm, I feel such an amazing sense of loss that I have to excuse myself from the table. I am not my mother in love with him. I am not even the last woman with whom he will dance. By the time I return from the ladies' room, my makeup repaired, Daddy has finished dancing with Louise and is leading Judith to the floor. I must admit that they move beautifully together, though never quite as perfectly as he and Mother did. I sit watching with Rusty, Jimmy, Rod, and Louise. I try to remind myself how unimportant dancing actually is in the larger scheme of things, but I yearn to be out there too.

Close by my ear Rusty says, "May I have this dance?" The band has picked up its tempo, playing music that he can shag to. My husband leads me to the floor. Over Judith's sequined shoulder strap my father smiles at me, a vague, wistful, unseeing smile. I am one of his three daughters.

Shell Island

Eban's wife, who had left him, would eat anything but reds. Stayman, Jonathan . . . occasionally a Golden Delicious. Most apple people felt that way. After Alex was born they had moved from Washington to Smithsburg, Maryland, because Lila's brother had died and she wanted to take over his job in her father's orchard. Autumn weekends she stood on the loading docks selling bushels of reds to people who drove up from the city. "They think you can use them for pies and sauce, but you can't. Reds get an ugly taste if you heat them," she'd say. Not Red Delicious, just reds, the way communists were reds in the '50s.

Eban knew nothing of the apple business. He taught some classes in town and drove into D.C. two days a week for his research. Alex had just turned ten when Lila announced she was moving in with her father's foreman, Larry. "I don't know why, Eban, I can't give you a clear explanation," she said when he demanded one. "Maybe it's because he can tell a red from a Macintosh and you can't. Honest to goodness, maybe that's why."

So it was that at the age of forty-seven Eban came to take a job on the coast of southeastern North Carolina, where there were no mountains and no apple trees and—except in the fall, brought to the grocery stores from great distance and at great expense per pound—no reds.

He took Alex with him. "When you're young, it's good to have all the different experiences you can," he explained to the boy. "We've never lived by the sea." Alex shrugged his shoulders. He had fallen into a state of lethargy and could register only indifference. Indifference to Eban, indifference to his mother, indifference to leaving the school he'd attended since kindergarten. They went at the end of August, before the new term, driving the eight-hour stretch south with only two brief stops for gas and lunch.

The land was flat along the coast, and sandy, with squat houses and scrubby trees. A real estate agent greeted them. Alex had always lived in a house and Eban did not wish to make a drastic change. The agent drove them around under a bright sky she described as Tar Heel Blue, blasting her air-conditioning against 93-degree heat. Tall stands of pines lined the roadways, shedding needles onto exhausted Southern grass. She showed them tiny ranch houses on flat lots, dwarfed by the pines. Eban found them depressing. Alex did not react. The humidity was overpowering.

"Or you could rent at the beach until May," the agent finally said. "People let the houses by the week in summer, but they like long-term tenants after that. September and October are really the nicest months."

She drove them across the drawbridge toward Johnnie Mercer's Fishing Pier, where the evening before they had sat on the beach after swimming. She showed them an apartment jammed between graying frame houses, then a claustrophobic condominium overlooking the marsh. Finally she brought them to an oceanfront house at the uncrowded north end of the beach, which looked like a shack on stilts from outside, but inside was spacious, well furnished, and clean.

"Of course out here you'll have all the little problems of living on a barrier island," she said as they stood on the deck looking out at the water. "They'll evacuate you every time there's a hurricane warning." Alex perked up at the mention of hurricanes. The woman had anticipated that. "Don't worry, these places have been here for a while. They've withstood a few storms, they don't blow down that easily." Alex glowed. Eban himself was beginning to like the idea of living on a barrier island.

To the north and south were other, similar dwellings, facing the dunes and the sea. In town, the sad little houses had been landscaped with pampas grass and myrtles, but here even grass did not grow on the lots, only weeds and burrs. There was not a single tree. It suited him. Alex was watching the ocean curl toward them in the late-afternoon light.

"We'll take it," Eban said.

The section of beach on which they lived was called Shell Island. The streets were named for shells — Sand Dollar, Conch, Cowrie, and Scotch Bonnet. Scotch Bonnet? Eban bought shell books at the souvenir store on Johnnie Mercer's pier, and was surprised to find shells he'd never heard of occupying so much space in his illustrated paperbacks — 160 species of cowries alone, commoner than he would have thought.

Except for Eban's job at the university, and Alex's school — a private

ELLYN BACHE

school Eban had chosen because of the small classes and Alex's emotional state—they had nothing to do but explore the island. Each morning they drove over the drawbridge into the town of Wilmington, where Eban arranged his schedule to coincide with Alex's, picking him up at three each afternoon. They bought styrofoam belly boards to float on in the ocean—Alex at ten, Eban at 47—learning to catch the breakers just so. Alex—lighter, braver, more indifferent—repeatedly skinned his belly on the drifts of shells which washed onto the shore with each tide. He didn't complain. The sun remained intense through September, the weather stayed hot; and all around them was water—ocean to the east; to the west, the Sound.

Alex spent hours fashioning sailboats out of cardboard milk cartons, using straws for masts and Kleenex for sails. Holding the boats delicately in his hands, he crossed the narrow road that ran the length of the island and set his creations afloat in the Sound. Eban's passion was not boats but the sea itself. He stood on the deck, putting off housework and laundry, making note of the colors as the ocean changed from green to deep blue in the late afternoon light. He watched the gulls circle and dip in the breakers. He searched for the dolphins that sometimes came leaping by, breaking water with their fins. Peering through the set of good binoculars Lila had given him early in their marriage, he charted the ships that floated against the horizon. Finally weary of staring, he hiked up a new road that had been built to the northern tip of the island, where construction had already begun on rows of condominiums and a hotel, but where for now there was still an unobstructed view of long-legged water birds in the marsh to the west, and pink-and-gold sunsets over the reeds. Many days, after work, Eban spoke to no one but Alex.

In the evenings fishermen lined the shore as the tide came in, casting out in the areas where the gulls were feeding. At first Eban and Alex only watched, peering into buckets filled with ice and bait and the day's catch. Finally Eban, whose fishing experience consisted of a day on a bass boat in Western Maryland, bought surf fishing gear at the marine store across the drawbridge. "All right, I'm going out to catch our dinner," he said—and by luck or stubbornness he did.

It didn't happen again. He tried different baits—shrimp, which slipped off the hook, bloodworms, which bit, and cut mullet. "You could try for spots off the pier," Alex suggested, knowing his father had a weakness for small panfish. But Eban, thinking use of the pier was somehow cheating, refused. He gave up fishing and returned to his study of shore life, identifying birds in the marsh and shells on the beach. He watched the boats.

He bought their seafood at the strong-smelling fish market just across the drawbridge, where mako shark and swordfish steaks were placed on ice and the cheaper fish dumped unceremoniously into bushel baskets. At night, glutted by sight of brown pelicans and sand sharks, by talk of spots and whiting and blues—at night he often slept.

Mornings, he woke from dreams of Larry and Lila together, touching, or of his inlaws having the two of them over for dinner. He had liked his inlaws, before. Country people, they had deferred to his better education, his maturity (compared to Lila's), his lack of impulsiveness. He in turn admired their pulling the orchards through four years of recession. Only their speech, dotted with colloquialisms and bad grammar, embarrassed him. When Lila left, they claimed to be bewildered by her behavior, but they never fired Larry. A long-time foreman, they said, the only one familiar with the work. It had never occurred to Eban that he—the scholar—would become the embarrassment. Waking from dreams of that, he looked out to ocean sunrises rather than blue mountains—red sky, white breakers, hungry gulls. The scenery struck him as exotic, and eased his pain.

They were often stopped by the drawbridge on their way into town. The bridge opened every hour on the hour to let the boat traffic through. Bearing down on the Intracoastal Waterway at 45 miles an hour, they became accustomed to seeing red lights flashing in the distance and wooden barriers coming down, telling them without question that they were going to be late.

Neither of them minded much. Stopped in traffic, waiting for the steel girders to rise, Alex got out of the car and ran up for a closer look. Eban was pleased to see him taking an interest in the boats heading south on the Intracoastal for the winter. For himself, the appeal was being locked on the island seven or ten minutes longer, caught in view of the reedy growth from the bright water, fishing rigs unloading at the market, unfamiliar island life. He rather liked the bridge blocking passage so effectively—making the island a barrier from the mainland as well as the sea: impermeable: safe.

Alex often returned to the car disconsolate—for what reason, Eban could not decide. Perhaps the southbound boats unsettled the boy, traveling so freely while he was due at school. Later Eban realized Alex was not watching the boats at all, but rather the shore itself—shelves of sand rising from the shallows, long stretches of marsh grass, clusters of reeds. Alex had been seeking something there and was disappointed not to find it. But as to the object of the search, which disturbed his son so, Eban had no clue.

ELLYN BACHE

Then one evening as Alex walked toward the Sound with the day's newly completed sailboat, Eban understood with sudden insight that *his boat* was what his son expected to see, morning after morning. Alex thought somehow that the sea would carry it from Banks Channel into the Intracoastal, and give it back to him the following day. Perhaps he believed that the same law would also bring back his mother.

Eban, helpless, began to buy milk in large plastic gallons, unsuitable (he hoped) for fitting out with sails.

They had been there less than a month when a hurricane warning came. For days there were reports of a storm moving northwest from this coordinate to that coordinate, packing winds of 120 miles an hour, but so far away. A momentary bleep of excitement in Alex's eyes, followed by indifference.

Then one day they woke to a metal-gray sea, churning. All the schools had been closed. If the storm continued on its present course, it would make landfall at Wrightsville Beach sometime the following night. Its power, coupled with the evening's high tide, could make for untold damage. The beach communities were to be evacuated. "All right," Alex sang, dancing. Eban pulled the porch furniture inside from the deck and tacked boards (left by the landlord) over the sliding glass doors facing the sea. Alex helped him, having abandoned altogether his previous indifference.

Inside, the phone was ringing. *Lila*, Eban thought. She had called once before at an awkward moment, to check on Alex when classes began. Hearing that the boy was in private school, she'd said bitterly, "Trying to get around that bussing order for racial balance, aren't you, Eban? Don't tell me it never entered your mind." (In fact, it hadn't.) "I never thought you had it in you to be a bigot."

Since she'd left, she'd made a point of lacing their conversations with whatever wounding comments she could. Eban wondered if she was trying to insulate herself against the accusations he might make otherwise, or if the insults had been stored up all the time they'd lived together—directed, in those years, against the reds instead of Eban. He believed that now, secure with Larry, she might have managed to be kind.

"Well, I never thought you had it in you to be an adulteress," he'd replied.

A shriek of wind, shearing over the deck. Eban envisioned Lila wrenched from her distant bliss by a momentary pang of conscience at abandoning her son to storms. The phone rang a fifth time, a sixth. He was annoyed that she'd choose just then to call, when Alex seemed to have recovered a measure of normality.

"Eban?" The woman's voice startled him because it wasn't Lila's, surely: but reedier, and more Southern, a Carolina voice.

"Dennie Mattson," she said. It was a moment before he placed her: the middle-aged departmental secretary whose car sometimes occupied the parking spot next to his, adorned with a bumper sticker that read: "If God isn't a Tar Heel, why did He make the sky Carolina blue?"

She was always inquiring about his adjustment, suggesting sightseeing trips, offering to help. She might have annoyed him except that she seemed so sincere. Once, to make conversation, he'd mentioned the salt-spray glaze that stuck to his windows—a housewifely detail—and she'd said: "We had a place out there once with the same problem, and the only thing we could ever get to cut that stuff was Softscrub"—looking almost triumphant at being able to offer a solution. Now she wanted to know how they had taken the news of the evacuation, what he was going to do.

"We're getting ready to go over to the high school, I guess," he said. "They say it's the evacuation center for this area."

"I was calling to invite you here instead," she told him. "Last year the centers were just misery. Babies crying, and you couldn't get into the bathrooms." Hurricane Diana had hit Wilmington the previous fall, sweeping through the center of town, spawning tornadoes which uprooted masses of trees. "I've got some other people coming, too. We'll have a hurricane party."

"We couldn't really," he said.

"Bring some sleeping bags, and flashlights if you have any. Last year the electricity was off a couple days." She gave directions to one of the flat, pine-woods developments where a month before Eban had refused to rent a house. She sounded—in her Southern way—as if she expected them.

To the east, the sky had grown darker, and the wind had begun to rise. The sea, whitecapped, came almost to the dunes. *Hurricane.* Alex was watching with glittering eyes. On the drawbridge, police in slickers stood in the rain, allowing people off the island but not on. Eban felt suddenly displaced, as he had in the days preceeding his move from Maryland. What if the beach house should be ruined? A vision rose before him of the evacuation center some days hence, in the sticky aftermath of storm: a high school gym dim from lack of electricity, filled with the anxious sweat of unbathed families, crowded bathrooms smelling of urine. And Alex, indifferent. Eban headed not to the school, but to the woman's house.

"I'm so pleased you decided to come," Dennie Mattson said, opening the door to a small beige living room full of people. Introductions all around:

an elderly aunt and uncle who lived out on the beach; their son; a fat X-ray technician and her daughter from the house next door.

They all behaved as if his joining them were normal. The adults watched the weather reports on TV, drank beer from cans, ate Cheese Nips out of a box. At some point hamburgers and chips were served for dinner. Alex perched himself by the window to chart the storm, which so far wasn't much. No danger, the broadcasters said, until night. The others talked of the eye of the terrible hurricane last year, a perfectly calm and yellow eye. "There were ten people staying with us, and I'll tell you, that's something you don't forget," the X-ray technician said. Eban had nothing to offer on the subject except the fogs that haunted the Maryland mountains. Driving up from town in the rain, he came to know exactly at what altitude the zone would change, above which the clouds would close in, leaving him to cling to the white line at the side of the winding road. He'd been more wary of fog than Lila had—she had grown up with it, after all—and she had held him (he realized now) in contempt. Her own terror had been of lightning on the mountain, which did its damage, he supposed, but was, after all—in contrast to the fog—light.

He didn't speak of Lila aloud. He drank yet another beer, waited for them to ask. No one did. He realized that, from their perspective, he was merely a man alone, with a school-aged child . . . he might have been divorced for years.

The announcer said the storm had begun to turn north. Perhaps it would hit Morehead City, or even Cape Hatteras farther up the coast. The Wilmington area would see only heavy gales. In the dark, with rain slashing and wind whipping, the X-ray technician announced that she'd better go home and feed her cats. Her daughter went with her. Eban heard himself saying (he was a little drunk by then), "And all the rest of us can go out for a walk."

Dennie clapped her hands—a blond, middle-aged cheerleader. "Oh, wonderful!" The elderly aunt and uncle declined, but Dennie and the cousin and Alex went, wrapped in slickers, into the night. The wind buffeted them, less (they all noted) than it would have during a typical afternoon thunderstorm. Even so, Alex's color was high. The hurricane might yet hit. Last year it had changed course several times before making landfall. A few blocks from Dennie's house, a man, watching the storm from his porch, asked as they passed: "Do you need shelter?"

"No, we're just walking." But they were pleased.

Back in the house Dennie and Eban and the cousin watched the news and had a final beer after Alex went to bed. The storm was definitely heading north. Loose and slightly dizzy, Eban realized that he had not tasted alcohol since Lila's departure. In the aftershock of her going, he had stopped drinking altogether—had disciplined himself, rather, to prepare regular meals for Alex, to go to bed (though not always to sleep) at normal hours, marshalling his forces, as it were, to survive the hardship. He had no sense that his difficulties were over. But for the moment, sitting in a stranger's living room in a circle of light, talking of innocuous matters like winds and tides, with the buzz of alcohol between his ears, he felt, mind and body, like a tense muscle that had suddenly unclenched—one of those absolutely still moments he had not known for some time, when life breaks and pauses before it goes rushing on.

By morning the wind was calm; the evacuation order on the beach had been lifted. Dennie wanted everyone to stay for pancakes, but Eban was anxious to get back. The newspaper reported that the ocean had overreached the dunes during the night on parts of the beach. The speed limit was an absurd twenty-five miles per hour, but he observed it. Arriving home, he found everything intact. They removed the wooden boards from over the sliding glass doors just as the clouds blew off and the sun came out, giving them a clear blue holiday, because in anticipation of damage, most schools and businesses had been closed. He and Alex wandered the beach in the dry sunny air. Alex gathered the large, conical shells the high stormtides had washed in. Eban looked them up in his book. "Whelks," he said. Normally whelk shells did not reach shore, he supposed, because they were too large for the ordinary tides to propel them in. The specimens Alex had gathered were mostly broken and worn down to gray, but he lined them up on the picnic table on the deck. So: the hurricane had brought whelks, but no damage. Eban walked the house, testing faucets and outlets. All of them worked.

That was Friday. By Monday the heat had returned and Alex was tired of the whelk shells. "Some hurricane. This is what they give two days off of school for. Big whoop. I'd like to show them a big snow on the mountain."

After that Alex's mood stayed grim. "It's too hot for fall," he whined, as they slid into October and it was. He wanted crisp mornings, gold and auburn hills. He made no more sailboats. Eban could not, or did not, try to offer a defense. He had no wife, no dignity, no mountains and no apple harvest. He watched the sea.

Three days a week he had early classes, so he tended to his students and then brought his research materials back to the beach house. Positioning

ELLYN BACHE

his desk to face the ocean, he worked until it was time to get Alex, his binoculars by his side. He allowed himself a session of bird-watching instead of a coffee break, gazing at brown pelicans flying in straight lines close to the shore, casing the surf for fish. He lunched to the sight of dolphins, noticing that they almost always traveled south. Perhaps they liked the warmer waters. He did not investigate further. The dolphins cheered him, and he preferred they keep their mystery. He was beginning the draft of his first new paper since the move. The heat was no longer stifling, though Alex thought it was. He turned the air-conditioning off and opened the sliders to the breeze.

Dennie, by virtue of their spending the hurricane together, now considered herself his friend. Days he lunched at the university, she wandered into his office with her own brown bag, filled with sensible egg-on-pumpernickel sandwiches and carrot sticks, much like the lunches he packed for Alex and himself. Had she reminded him in any way of Lila, he might have minded, but Lila was only 35, dark and flirtatious, while Dennie was as old as Eban — a pale, straightforward woman with spindly limbs and a cumbersome bust. Eating her nutritious lunches, she seemed not a woman at all — in the sense that Lila, who lunched on Diet Pepsi, had been — but simply a companion, which Eban could accept.

She read his horoscopes from the newspaper and told him about astrology. "Once we got audited by the IRS and ever after that we mailed the tax when the moon was void of course, and we never got audited again," she asserted.

"And what does that mean exactly — void of course?"

"All I know is, it happens every other day. And any project you start then, you'll never hear anything more of it."

Eban raised his eyebrows. "You have that superior look on your face," she said. "But I bet right now you're making a note to yourself to mail your tax next year when the moon is void of course." And, in fact, Eban was.

She told him the departmental gossip and enthused about Wilmington's building boom. Later, she told Eban about herself. Her son was at college in Chapel Hill; her husband, Edward (she pronounced it Ed-wood) had worked for Corning glass when he wasn't fishing, and died of a heart attack at the age of 53. She spoke of him cheerfully enough. He'd had a boat which she'd finally sold, and had entered the King Mackerel contest every year. "Ever taste King Mackerel?" She made an unpleasant face.

"I've seen the steaks in the fish store. Look kind of dark."

"Terrible, if you ask me." He liked her frankness, coupled with her soft

North Carolina drawl. Much better, he thought, than the country quality Lila's speech had. With Lila it was: "Don't wear that, it needs washed," always dropping the infinitive, and once, when Alex was small, "It's new, but I wore it on him once," which annoyed him disproportionately.

"I suppose out there at the beach you do some fishing yourself," Dennie said, biting into a pickle.

"I gave it up," he said, looking at the pickle. "I felt too sorry for the fish."

"Fish don't have feelings."

"How do you know?"

"You eat them, don't you?" That seemed to settle it for her. "I even feel a little sorry for the worm," he said.

She broke off a piece of the pickle and handed it to him, having noticed how he was staring it down.

It was the middle of October and the temperature had not gone below seventy degrees for a week, even at night. There were occasional cool spells, but the tendency of the air was always to heat up. "It's not normal," Alex said.

"We have no way of knowing what's normal. We've never been here before in fall." Eban rather liked the idea of a climate without autumn. At any rate, they had nothing by which to judge it; normal didn't exist.

"Well, I hate it," Alex said.

In the increasingly angled light, the sea was blue-green, fading to darker blue in the depths. "It doesn't look like itself," Alex asserted. But the ocean *was* itself, Eban argued; what else could it be? What did they know of North Carolina waters in the seasons? Yet when he looked at the aqua shallows, he was reminded less of the Atlantic than of the Caribbean, where he and Lila had been on the company trip that ended his marriage. His inlaws had hosted an early December vacation—after the harvest—on which most of the employees had come with their wives. Larry had been alone.

It was then that Lila's affair had begun. She had bought three new bathing suits, one of them a bright turquoise which set off the darkness of her skin. He thought three suits was excessive for a five-day trip. He said she would always have the figure of a young boy, regardless. That was a joke, but Lila glared at him. She looked good in clothes and knew it—everyone said so. There was something lyrical about her appearance. She spent hours preparing for the trip in a tanning salon. She didn't want to burn, she said. She never burned.

The group rented a boat and went out to the reefs to snorkel. Under the water, plants waved tendrils at him and colorful angelfish wiggled by. In the distance, just visible from where he swam, a barracuda lurked with all its shadowy menace. Surfacing, he was so absorbed by the experience that he barely noticed Larry staring at Lila's turquoise bathing suit and approving, and Lila looking back. He'd always felt his failure to observe them just then had left him, later, responsible.

"The boy is bored," Dennie said, "Living there on the beach. That and the adjustment." Most of the houses on Shell Island were empty now, not having been rented for the winter. Their little lane housed a group of college students next door and a retired couple across the way, but Alex was the only child. The bathers and surfers and fishermen that had given the beach its festive quality had deserted. Alex's one friend from school lived twenty minutes away in town. "At least shoot a few baskets," Eban urged, pointing to a basketball goal at one of the abandoned houses nearby. "That's something you can do by yourself."

But Alex would not. "I miss grass," he said, looking at the lot below: weeds and sand. He spent hours watching "You Can't Do That on Television." It was a pastiche of one-liners and throwup jokes: Mother, I think you love Tommy better than you love me. —Oh Alistair, I never loved you. Sometimes Alex laughed out loud.

"Just the adjustment," Dennie said. On weekends she invented outings for them, inviting herself along. "Remember, he's been through a lot," she admonished, though Eban had not once offered up the details of his broken marriage. They took Alex to a surfing competition and a chowder tasting at Greenfield Park. "Are you going to marry her?" the boy asked. "Of course not. We're just friends. I don't even find her attractive." "Me neither," Alex agreed. But Dennie had adopted them, swept them up, was out of their control.

She insisted they go to the aquarium at Fort Fisher, where there were slide shows, nature walks, and a shark in a huge tank. A sign announced that it was a nurse shark, one of the species known to attack man. Alex stared at the beast swimming around in circles, its huge skin like pinkish sandpaper, its small blue eyes lashless and mean. "So that's it," he said flatly. "Big whoop."

In the newspaper, the fishing columns lamented the lack of autumn fish because of the warm waters. The speckled trout hadn't come in and only a few mullet were being caught at night. The ocean was ten or fifteen degrees warmer than usual. "God, do you believe this?" Alex said. Eban reminded him of the bare bones of trees on winter mountains, the cold, the death. Alex said he'd never minded. The week before Thanksgiving, the paper ran pictures of azalea bushes beginning to show bloom.

Then there was a spell of dark, rainy weather, spawned by a late hurricane in the Gulf. The first day was cool, like the sober end of the apple harvest, and they thought the season would change. It didn't. Trying to write in the rainy, humid heat, Eban felt distracted. He spent hours sitting on the dunes with his binoculars, watching the frothy gray-green sea, the pelicans dive-bombing after fish. When the hard rains came, he slept. He dreamed of the mountains. From their house he and Lila had had a clear view of the valley—neat rectangular fields, other orchards, other houses—and then more mountains on the other side, a perfect oval around the perspective. He woke to a rainy flatland: of the beach, the sea, his soul.

A terrible dank fishy smell sometimes rolled in from the ocean, the odor of decayed seaweed and rotting fish. Eban slept his afternoons away. He stopped dreaming of Lila and dreamed instead of Todd, Lila's dead brother, whom he hadn't thought about for years. In his dreams, Todd walked beside him on the beach. They walked for miles, for hours, and Eban woke exhausted, as if they really had.

Todd was a dark, rangy man who worked in the orchards but whose first love was flying. He was a student pilot at first, then licensed, and finally instrument-rated. He flew in winter when there was no work to do, and in the growing season when there was. One day when a fog rolled in, Todd flew his rented Cessna into the mountain. He was 27 at the time. Lila, pregnant with Alex, wanted to name the baby after him.

Eban refused. They'd be saddened every time they looked at a son named Todd, he said. But he begrudged Todd his dying and Lila her orgy of mourning; he begrudged the waste of a life for sport. A few months later, when Lila's father suggested she take over Todd's job, she reacted with surprising emotion. She hated the city; orcharding was the only work she knew. Eban could have his career anywhere. Having refused her on the matter of the name, he was reluctant to say no again. They moved from Washington, where Eban had been happy, to Smithsburg, where he was not. In a way, Eban had blamed Todd for that, too.

But now, ten years later, dreaming, he and Todd walked the beach with no resentment between them. Together they looked out at the sea, at fish and plants which seemed to be visible under the water—the same plants he had seen in the Caribbean—and at gulls and pelicans above. "It wasn't just for sport, you see," Todd told him. "I was in search of another element." Eban nodded, understanding. Todd had no more expected to conquer the air than Eban did the ocean; it was too unfathomable—but just, somehow, reaching, to cope.

Dennie had invited them for Thanksgiving dinner. Her son would be home from Chapel Hill. "Billy will love it," she insisted. "The thing he always hated when he was younger was if we didn't have a lot of people for the holidays. It'll be good for Alex, too." Eban tried to refuse but in the end they went, just as they had gone during the hurricane, because the other alternatives were even less attractive.

The day was hot and sunny—eighty-three degrees by noon—abnormal, as Alex pointed out. Billy turned out to be blond and nondescript and just as cordial as his mother. Seeing Alex lose interest in Dennie's shell collection, he brought out an obviously new and complicated camera, which he taught Alex to use. At one o'clock they ate turkey and gravy and potatoes in the stifling dining room, getting up from the table overstuffed and irritable. Alex might have sulked except that Billy suggested they drive out to the beach, to Eban's house, to try the camera.

"We should shoot you swimming in the ocean," Dennie said when they got there. She'd changed into shorts which showed the fine varicose veins in her legs, under the bright sun. "You can take the pictures up north to your friends." She often spoke of people going "up north," whether they came from Virginia or Maine. It was as if all places north of Wilmington were cold and gray and identical, and could not be distinguished from one other.

"It's not really up north," Alex said quickly. "Maryland is south of the Mason-Dixon line. You can see some of the stones that mark the Mason-Dixon line not far from our house."

Our house.

"I'm getting dressed," Alex told them. "I hate this sand."

Inside, the phone was ringing. Eban had no time to reflect that it might be Lila before Alex grabbed it. Eban heard him saying, "Yeah, grandma—turkey and stuffing and the works. Then we went swimming, believe it or not." His mother-in-law. Eban imagined for an instant that she'd called to apologize for not firing Larry; perhaps even to say Lila had left Larry and wanted Eban back. A lightness bloomed in his chest, where before had been a dark weight. Then Alex handed Eban the phone and his mother-in-law said: "Eban, I know how awkward this is, but I'm calling to ask if you'll let Alex come up here for the Christmas holidays. I know it's not in the agreement." She paused. "It isn't for Lila I'm asking," she said. "It's for me."

Dennie and Billy were in the living room, pretending not to listen. "I'll ask Alex." And Alex danced, shaking sand off his bare legs onto the rug, waving a fist in the air: "All right."

The drawbridge schedule had changed. Instead of opening at hourly intervals, it went up on demand, whenever a boat needed to go through. In the warm, sunny weather, boat traffic was heavy all through early December. Sometimes, running an errand into town and coming back, Eban was stopped by the bridge on both legs of the trip. One afternoon, late on his way to get Alex, he found the bridge closed, with an interminable succession of boats passing underneath. Alex hated him not to be waiting when the bell rang. Lila had left him too long at a birthday party once, and he had feared ever since being the last one to be fetched. Minutes passed, the car was hot. Eban had to pull the collar of his shirt away from his neck and wipe his sweating palms on his trousers. Boat after boat: sailboats, fishing rigs, cabin cruisers. Eban's heart beat rapidly, an uneven rhythm. His breath came short and fast. (Lila had hyperventilated during labor, and swore the labor would be her one and only.) Chest aching. Breathe slowly, he told himself. The bridge began to open. His hands were trembling. Wooden barriers rising. Foot on the accelerator. Moving now. But it was as if he had been cut off forever: from the mainland, the town, his son.

A gray sky, cooler weather, coming back from a shopping trip for Alex's winter clothes. He would need them for his trip up north. "Don't call it up north, Dad. It sounds like you're from here." Dusk was falling, night coming earlier. A line of brown pelicans swooped by them, eerie against the darkening sky. "They're creepy," Alex said. "They look like pterodactyls."

Looking at the ocean, Alex said: "I hate the way the land ends right there, and the water closes you in." Eban thought of mountains ringed by other mountains, deceptive, as if at the end of those hills, everything stopped.

The morning Alex left was blinding-bright with sun, but really cold, for once. Alex was tense with excitement, anxious to get on the plane. Eban hugged him goodbye, but the boy pulled away, embarrassed to be embraced in public. Then he had gone, down the little chute that led to the plane. Eban was sure he'd refuse to come back and had said as much to

Dennie over the past weeks. But she'd replied: "Maybe not. Maybe the trip north will get it out of his system."

Driving back through town from the airport, Eban saw there'd been a hard freeze. The first? He didn't know. On the beach the landscape was always the same: sand and weeds; no green, no bushes, no trees. In town the grass was crusty from ice and the tender plants had wilted. It looked surprisingly normal. He was visited by a vision of his Smithsburg house against a muted sky: bare orchards, violet and gray winter, masses of birds. Returning to the beach, he noted that the reedy dune grass was now brown and beaten down by salt spray. The sand was interminable. Except for the ocean, he might have been living on a desert. That had been Alex's view of it all along. He imagined his mother-in-law phoning, pleading Alex's case, begging him to leave the boy in Maryland. He'd been imagining such an outcome for three weeks, and now that he was finally alone, after all that high emotion, he couldn't sustain it. He felt drained, empty. If Alex came back, they would move into town.

Dennie insisted he come for dinner, because otherwise he would brood. She cooked an elaborate meal, wore a silky dress. "Lila wanted to name Alex for her brother," he said. "I wouldn't let her." He had not spoken of such things before and now could not make himself stop. Perhaps insisting on Alex's name had been a mistake; perhaps it had something to do, all these years, with Lila's working so hard in the orchard and Eban's raising their son. Dennie nodded, not disagreeing. "I still think after Christmas he'll be ready to come back," she said.

Sitting in the living room after the meal, she smiled at Eban in what he recognized as a come-hither way. He was vaguely surprised. He saw that she expected him to make love to her, and supposed he would. There was no hurry. In the meantime they gazed at the shells that filled her knicknack shelf, gathered during her husband's fishing days. Among the conchs and the olive shells and the cowries was a long strand of flattish beige disks, almost like segments of a sand-colored lei. He could not identify them at first, and then recognized them from a drawing in his shell book. "Whelk egg casings," he said.

"Yes. Though sometimes I have trouble imagining whelks laying eggs."

She raised her eyebrows and he tried to picture whelks mating; he couldn't, of course.

"These things wash up onto the beach in the summer," she said. "Here, let me show you."

He picked up the papery necklace and handed it to her where she sat. With a long fingernail she slit open one of the compartments and emptied it onto the coffee table. Hundreds of tiny, whitish whelk shells fell out, perfectly conical, perfectly detailed miniatures even to the spiky nobs near their tops.

"You can imagine how many eggs there must be altogether," she said. "I mean, rows and rows of these casings washing up onto the beach. And each one has—what? Maybe a hundred of these little compartments?"

He touched his index finger to his tongue and then to the table, so that several of the little whelk shells adhered to it. He raised them to his eyes. They were small and white, each one capable of a new life, and they struck him as distinctly hopeful.

Ellyn Bache has been part of the thriving writers' scene in Wilmington since 1985. She was born in Washington, D.C., in 1942, and received degrees from UNC–Chapel Hill and the University of Maryland. Her books include three novels—*Safe Passage* (1988), which was made into a movie starring Susan Sarandon and Sam Shepard, *Festival in Fire Season* (1992), and *The Activist's Daughter* (1997)—as well as two volumes of nonfiction and a collection of short stories, *The Value of Kindness* (1993), which won the Willa Cather Fiction Prize.

Sarah Dessen was born in Evanston, Illinois, in 1970, but her family moved to Chapel Hill when she was two and she has been there ever since. She graduated with highest honors in creative writing from UNC–Chapel Hill, where she now teaches fiction-writing. Her first novel, *That Summer* (1996), was named a Best Book for Young Adults by the American Library Association and a Best Book for the Teen Age by the New York Public Library. Her other novels are *Someone Like You* (1998) and *Keeping the Moon* (1999).

Tony Earley, named one of the *New Yorker's* "Twenty Best Young Fiction Writers in America" in 1999, was born in San Antonio, Texas, in 1961 but raised in the North Carolina foothills town of Rutherfordton. He received a B.A. from Warren Wilson College and worked at several mountain newspapers before taking an M.F.A. at the University of Alabama. His books are *Here We Are in Paradise: Stories* (1994) and the novel *Jim the Boy* (2000). His work appears regularly in such magazines as *Esquire*, *Harper's*, *Granta*, and the *Oxford American*. He teaches at Vanderbilt.

Candace Flynt—born in Greensboro in 1947, a graduate of Greensboro College and the celebrated M.F.A. program at UNC-Greensboro, and still a resident of her hometown—is among a number of writers who have kept Greensboro a center of literary accomplishment for many decades. She has published her work in the *Atlantic Monthly*, *Redbook*, and such North Carolina journals as the *Carolina Quarterly* and the *Greensboro Review*. Her novels are *Chasing Dad* (1980), *Sins of Omission* (1984), and *Mother Love* (1989).

Philip Gerard has been energizing UNC-Wilmington's creative writing program for many years. He was born in Wilmington, Delaware, in 1955, and educated at the Universities of Delaware and Arizona. He has published three novels—*Hatteras Light* (1986), *Cape Fear Rising* (1994), and *Desert Kill* (1994)—and three books of nonfiction, including *Writing the Big Book* (2000). He has also written a number of scripts for television and radio, and published widely in literary journals and magazines, including the *New England Review*, *Puerto del Sol*, and the *Crescent Review*.

Marianne Gingher is a native of Guam, where she was born in 1947, but she was raised in Greensboro and still lives there. She received her B.A. at Salem College and her M.F.A. at UNC-Greensboro. Her books are the novel *Bobby Rex's Greatest Hit* (1986) and the collection *Teen Angel and Other Stories of Young Love* (1988), both of which were reprinted in 1998, the latter with its titular love modified as "wayward." Her stories and essays have appeared in the *Southern Review*, *McCall's*, *Seventeen*, and the *North American Review*. She is director of the undergraduate creative writing program at UNC-Chapel Hill.

Tom Hawkins, who works as the news director for a biomedical research institute, writes and publishes both poetry and fiction. His collection of short short stories, *Paper Crown*, appeared in 1989, and one of those stories has been reprinted in *Flash Fiction* (1992) and recent editions of the *Norton Anthology of Short Fiction*. He was born in Park Ridge, Illinois, in 1946, and educated at the University of Missouri School of Journalism and the graduate creative writing program at UNC-Greensboro. He has lived in Raleigh since 1975.

John Holman has published two books of fiction, *Squabble and Other Stories* (1990) and *Luminous Mysteries* (1998), a novel-in-stories. He was born in Durham in 1951, and went on to earn degrees at UNC-Chapel Hill, North Carolina Central University, and the University of Southern Mississippi. His work has appeared in the *New Yorker*, *Fiction*, the *Mississippi Review*, and other magazines. He has taught at a number of schools, including St. Augustine's College, Winston-Salem State University, the University of South Florida in Tampa, and—currently—Georgia State University in Atlanta, where he directed the M.F.A. program for several years.

John Kessel is one of the leading authors of speculative fiction in the country and a winner of the prestigious Nebula Award. A native of Buffalo, where he was born in 1951, he has taught English at North Carolina State University in Raleigh for many years. He earned his B.A. in physics and English at the University of Rochester, and his M.A. and Ph.D. in English at the University of Kansas. Among his books are the novels *Good News from Outer Space* (1989) and *Corrupting Dr. Nice* (1997), as well as the story collections *Meeting in Infinity* (1992) and *The Pure Product* (1997).

Peter Makuck has been a literary force at East Carolina University in Greenville since 1976: as a teacher of writing (currently Distinguished Professor of Arts and Sciences), as an editor (founder of *Tar River Poetry*), and as a prolific writer of poetry and fiction. His work has appeared in dozens of leading journals — including the *Hudson* and *Sewanee Reviews* — and six prizewinning volumes of poetry and one collection of stories, *Breaking and Entering* (1981). Born in New London, Connecticut, in 1940, he received his degrees from St. Francis College, Niagara University, and Kent State University, where his dissertation was on Faulkner.

Melissa Malouf, a Southern California native, was born in Riverside in 1951 and educated at the University of California at Irvine, where she received her Ph.D. She moved to North Carolina in 1984 and now teaches literature and creative writing at Duke University in Durham. Her two books are *No Guarantees*, a collection of stories (1990), and *It Had to Be You: The Joan and Ernest Story* (1997), a novel. She has written one-act plays and libretti as well as fiction, and her work has appeared in *Antaeus*, the *Kenyon Review*, the *Mid-American Review*, and *Fiction International*.

Heather Ross Miller is perhaps the most accomplished writer from a well-known family of writers, the Rosses — father Fred, uncle James, aunt Eleanor. She was born in Albemarle, North Carolina, in 1939, raised in nearby Badin, and educated at UNC-Greensboro, where she studied with Randall Jarrell and earned B.A. and M.F.A. degrees. Her published books include six novels, six volumes of poetry, a memoir, and three collections of stories, most recently *In the Funny Papers* (1995). She has taught at Pfeiffer College and the University of Arkansas and now teaches at Washington and Lee University. Among her many honors is the North Carolina Award for Literature, which she received in 1983.

Ruth Moose lived for decades in the Uwharrie Mountains of central North Carolina and worked as a poet-in-the-schools, freelance writer, and librarian. In recent years, she has lived in Pittsboro and taught at UNC-Chapel Hill. Her poetry and fiction have appeared in a wide range of magazines; her two books of short stories are *The Wreath Ribbon Quilt and Other Stories* (1987) and *Dreaming in Color* (1989). In 1997 she edited *Twelve Christmas Stories by North Carolina Writers*. She was born in Albemarle, North Carolina, in 1938 and received her B.A. from Pfeiffer College and her M.L.S. from UNC-Greensboro.

Lawrence Naumoff has published five novels: *The Night of the Weeping Women* (1988), *Rootie Kazootie* (1990), *Taller Women* (1992), *Silk Hope, NC* (1994), and *A Plan for Women* (1997). He was born in Charlotte in 1946 and graduated from UNC-Chapel Hill in 1969. While an undergraduate, he won a number of writing prizes, including the Thomas Wolfe Memorial Award; then he stopped writing for a decade or so, supporting himself by building houses. He has lived in Silk Hope since 1971.

Jennifer Offill has lived in many parts of the country — in Greenfield, Massachusetts, where she was born in 1968; in California and Indiana; in Charlotte, where she attended high school, and Chapel Hill, where she graduated from UNC in 1990; in New Orleans and San Francisco, where she was a Stegner Fellow at Stanford; and in Brooklyn, where she now lives — but says, "North Carolina still feels like home in many ways." She has published fiction in *Story*, the *Gettysburg Review*, the *Black Warrior Review*, and *Boulevard*; her first novel, *Last Things*, appeared in 1999.

Michael Parker was born in Siler City, North Carolina, in 1959 and raised down east in Clinton. He earned his B.A. at UNC-Chapel Hill and his M.F.A. at the University of Virginia. His fiction has appeared in such journals as the *Georgia Review*, *New Virginia Review*, and *Carolina Quarterly*. *Hello Down There*, his first book, a novel, was published in 1993; it was followed by *The Geographical Cure: Novellas and Stories* (1994), which won the Sir Walter Raleigh Award for Fiction. He currently lives in Greensboro and teaches in the graduate creative writing program at UNC-Greensboro.

P. B. Parris lives in Asheville, where she is professor emeritus of literature at UNC-Asheville. She was born in Hebron, Nebraska, in 1934: the daughter of a career Air Force officer, she grew up in the United States, Canada, and Europe. She received her B.F.A. in painting at the University of Nebraska and — after some time at the Iowa Writers' Workshop — her M.A. and Ph.D. in English at Drake University. Her two published novels are *Waltzing in the Attic* (1990) and *His Arms Are Full of Broken Things* (1997). In 1988, she received a PEN Syndicated Fiction Project award.

Dale Ray Phillips was born in Alamance County, North Carolina, in 1955, and raised in Burlington. He received his B.A. from UNC–Chapel Hill (1977), his M.A. from Hollins College (1985), and his M.F.A. from the University of Arkansas (1990). His short stories have appeared in such magazines as *Harper's*, the *Atlantic Monthly*, *GQ*, *Ploughshares*, and the *Greensboro Review;* his novel-in-stories, *My People's Waltz*, was published in 1999. He has taught writing at Clemson University, the University of Arkansas, and Georgia College in Milledgeville.

Joe Ashby Porter is a scholar and a fiction-writer, who has taught both literature and creative writing at Duke University for several decades. He has published two critical volumes on Shakespeare and four books of fiction: the novels *Eelgrass* (1977) and *Resident Aliens* (2000), and the short story collections *The Kentucky Stories* (1983) and *Lithuania* (1990). Born in a small Kentucky coal-mining town in 1942, Porter received his degrees from Harvard University and the University of California–Berkeley. He has won two fellowships from the National Endowment for the Arts, and his work has appeared in *TriQuarterly*, *Antaeus*, the *Yale Review*, the *South Atlantic Review*, and many other publications.

Ron Rash has lived in North or South Carolina all his life, but always in the mountains. He was born in Chester, South Carolina, in 1953, and grew up in Boiling Springs, North Carolina; his degrees are from Gardner-Webb College and Clemson University. He has also moved back and forth between fiction and poetry, having won major prizes for both, and having published one collection of short stories (*The Night the New Jesus Fell to Earth*, 1994) and two of poems. His work has appeared in *DoubleTake*, *Shenandoah*, the *Georgia Review*, the *Southern Review*, and other journals. He now lives in Clemson.

June Spence published her first collection of short stories, *Missing Women and Others*, in 1998; it was named a *New York Times* Notable Book of the Year. The title story originally appeared in the *Southern Review* and was reprinted in the 1997 *Best American Short Stories* anthology. Spence was born in Raleigh in 1969 and received her B.A. at Southwest Missouri State University (1991) and her M.F.A. at Bowling Green State University (1994). As a visiting writer-in-residence, she has taught at Bowling Green and at Berry College in Georgia.

Peter Turchi has directed the M.F.A. Program for Writers at Warren Wilson College in Swannanoa, North Carolina, since 1994. Before that, he taught at Appalachian State University in Boone and several other universities. He was born in Baltimore in 1960 and educated at Washington College and the University of Arizona. Among his books are *The Girls Next Door* (1989), a novel, and *Magician* (1991), a collection of short stories. He has received writers' fellowships from the National Endowment for the Arts as well as the North Carolina and Illinois Arts Councils.

Daniel Wallace is a Chapel Hill illustrator whose work appears on T-shirts, refrigerator magnets, and greeting cards across the country. He is also a prolific writer of fiction, whose stories have appeared in dozens of magazines, including *Shenandoah*, *Glimmer Train*, the *Massachusetts Review*, and *Prairie Schooner*. A native of Birmingham, Alabama, where he was born in 1959, he lived there until he left to

About the Authors

study at Emory University and UNC–Chapel Hill. His novels are *Big Fish* (1998) and *Ray in Reverse* (2000).

Luke Whisnant was born in Roanoke, Virginia, in 1957, but soon thereafter his family moved to Charlotte, where he grew up. He received his B.A. from East Carolina University and his M.F.A. from Washington University in St. Louis, then returned to Greenville to teach and help edit *Tar River Poetry*. His fiction has appeared in *Frank*, *Grand Street*, and *New Stories from the South*, among other places. *Watching TV with the Red Chinese*, his first novel, was published in 1992.

Marly Youmans went to high school in Cullowhee, North Carolina, though she was born in 1953 in Aiken, South Carolina, and grew up in Louisiana, Kansas, and Delaware. She earned her B.A. at Hollins College, her M.A. at Brown, and her Ph.D. at UNC–Chapel Hill. For many years, she published stories in such magazines as the *Southern Humanities Review*, *South Carolina Review*, and *Kansas Quarterly*; then she turned to longer fiction, eventually publishing two novels—*Little Jordan* (1995) and *Catherwood* (1996)—while living in Carrboro, North Carolina. She now lives in Cooperstown, New York.

PERMISSIONS